"WHAT do you want?" Jeannie whispered, fighting panic as Kevin moved toward her. "You'd better go," she warned with shaky defiance, "or I'll scream."

"You won't scream," Kevin contradicted smugly. "Have you told your husband about us?"

"No," she admitted painfully.

"He will never know," Kevin soothed. "You have nothing to worry about. But I couldn't stand it back there on Ransome Island, thinking about you with him." He paused, his eyes glowing fanatically. "Has he come to you yet?"

"No," she whispered, shamed by this admission. She saw the glow of triumph in his eyes. "Kevin, I mean it. You touch me and I'll scream! They'll all come running!"

"Don't you dare," he taunted. He clutched her roughly by the shoulders. "Because then you'll lose this fancy life you've won for yourself."

Fawcett Crest Books
by Julie Ellis:

EDEN

THE MAGNOLIAS

THE MAGNOLIAS

A NOVEL BY

Julie Ellis

A FAWCETT CREST BOOK

Fawcett Publications, Inc., Greenwich, Connecticut

THE MAGNOLIAS

THIS BOOK CONTAINS THE COMPLETE TEXT OF THE ORIGINAL HARDCOVER EDITION.

A Fawcett Crest Book reprinted by arrangement with Simon & Schuster, Inc.

Copyright © 1976 by Julie Ellis

ISBN 0-449-23131-3

Printed in the United States of America

10 9 8 7 6 5 4 3 2 1

For Larrie and Norman

THE MAGNOLIAS

One

After a night of torrential rain, the early-December day in this year of 1848 broke weakly over the waters that surrounded Ransome Island, off the Georgia mainland. The giant, straggling cypresses that surrounded the tall, square manor house, which was an exact replica of a fifteenth-century Suffolk residence, were draped eerily with dismal gray moss that, with its wetness, appeared to be great masses of grizzled, matted hair. Jeannie Fleming loathed the moss; it was like a banner of death, a vampire sucking away the life of every tree to which it clung.

At an upstairs bedroom window Jeannie brushed her long fair hair away from her delicately featured face as she gazed in anguish at the sight below. She flinched at the sound of each nail driven into the pine box on which four slaves labored with unfamiliar vigor. In that pine box her mother would be buried.

Coldness rolled in about Jeannie as she remembered those painful, unreal moments last night when her mother had cried out suddenly over her sewing as the two of them sat in the ostentatiously furnished family parlor with Cousin Kevin, who, as on any other evening, was engrossed in the newspapers brought in to them from Savannah. Mama rose to her feet, a hand clutching at her chest.

"Jeannie," Mama gasped. "I feel so strange—I can't breathe. . . ."

"Mama!" Alarm propelled Jeannie to her feet, and at

that same moment her mother collapsed to the floor in an unconscious heap.

"Mama!" Jeannie heard in her mind the echo of her frightened outcry as she rushed to kneel beside her mother. Instantly Cousin Kevin was at her other side, reaching for her wrist.

"I'm sorry, Jeannie," her cousin said softly after a moment. "There is no pulse." So quickly death had come to Mama!

The Ransome plantation occupied the entire island of three thousand acres. There was no doctor to call. In the unrelenting rains of last night not one of the small boats that belonged to the plantation could have made it safely to the island on which a doctor resided.

Jeannie's blue eyes squinted against the glare of the still-choppy waters. She could see a boat heading north. A slave would be going to bring the minister back to Ransome Island for the burial this afternoon.

Tears blurred her view of the water. Mama was dead. How long would it be before she could think that without this awful feeling of loss? Cousin Kevin had said she was to remain here on Ransome Island as his ward. She would supervise the house, as Mama had done.

She and Mama had lived with their cousin for all but three of her seventeen years. When Papa died back in 1834 and they had no one to care for them, Kevin—a former schoolmaster who was now a widower and owner of a fine rice plantation—had agreed to take them in. Mama and Kevin were related, as they shared a great-grandmother.

Cousin Kevin himself had tutored Jeannie through the years, taking pride in giving her an astonishingly fine education. She read Latin and German, spoke fluent French. She read voraciously, because there was little else to do in the seclusion of Ransome Island. That seclusion had brought her and Mama unusually close, she thought wistfully. Now there would be just Kevin and herself in the parlor every evening. Her cousin, who was so much a part of her life, in truth still remained a cold, impersonal stranger.

Seven months after their marriage twenty-two years

ago, Cousin Kevin's wife had died in a terrible fire in Savannah that had also claimed the lives of her parents. Kevin had inherited Ransome Island, known previously as Edmunds Island, and had devoted himself to making it a model rice plantation.

This past year he had written two articles about his own methods of irrigating the rice fields that had been published in an agricultural journal. Kevin worked hard to improve each crop. Sometimes it had worried Mama that he allowed himself so few pleasures.

Jeannie started at the sound of her bedroom door opening.

"Young Missy, Ah brought yo' coffee." Small, corpulent Ninette, who was Mama's maid and hers, smiled sympathetically from the doorway of the near-monastic bedroom, with its plaster walls devoid of either paint or paper, furnished only with a simple Shaker bed and a plantation-made washstand and dresser. The two small windows were drably curtained. The upstairs bedrooms—except for the guest rooms—were in startling contrast to the lushly furnished, though forbidding, lower-floor rooms. "Yo' drink it, yo' hear?" Ninette said with mock sternness.

"Thank you, Ninette." Jeannie forced an answering smile. Ninette's huge dark eyes were red from weeping.

Jeannie sat in a chair close to the fire, obediently sipping the steaming-hot coffee while Ninette coaxed a blaze in the grate against the early-morning chill. Later, unless the rain returned, the day promised to be comfortably warm.

The cup clattered against the saucer as Jeannie set it down, her hands still unsteady with shock. Mama was so young to die! But a proper minister would lay Mama to rest, she thought gratefully. Her cousin realized that despite her deep respect for his preaching in the plantation church—because no circuit rider came to the Island—she wanted a *real* minister for Mama.

Late into the night she had heard the wailing of the slaves in their quarters to the rear of the house. They had loved Mama, for she was good to them. Cousin Kevin was a stern taskmaster. He meant well, she reassured herself guiltily; but sometimes he didn't understand.

Every Sunday she and Mama had gone with Kevin to the church that had sat for over a hundred years in the grove of pines to the east of the house. Their cousin, preaching fire and brimstone, read the services every Sabbath.

"Yo' didn' sleep much las' night," Ninette guessed compassionately.

"No," Jeannie acknowledged, wryly.

"Yo lay down an' res' awhile," Ninette coaxed. "Ah bring yo' breakfas' latuh."

"All right, Ninette." Exhausted, Jeannie fell on the bed and allowed Ninette to pull up the comforter about her.

The minister usually came to Ransome Island only for Christmas and Easter services. He had never been on the Island on any other occasion since Mrs. Ransome and her parents had died in the fire in Savannah, Cousin Kevin said. The three of them were buried in the cemetery behind the grove of live oaks to the west of the house, where Mama would be buried too.

Jeannie started to think about how she would take over for Mama in managing the house. That would not be hard, she told herself. The servants—a dozen of them—ran the house with little need for supervision. But how strange, how painful it would be to sit at the dining-room table without Mama. To sit in the family parlor in the evenings after supper without Mama. Her cousin was so stern and quiet. He hardly spoke at all, except when he tutored her. But the tutoring was over now. She would be in charge of running the household. She frowned, recoiling from the vision of the endless years ahead of her, alone on Ransome Island with Kevin.

The rain began to fall again, beating a monotonous litany against the windowpane. Grief welling afresh in her, she turned toward the wall, drew up her knees, and burrowed her face into the pillow. Mama was so young to die. Why had it had to happen this way? God's will, Cousin Kevin had said. But Jeannie was too rebellious to accept "God's will."

"Young Missy, time yo' wake up," a familiar voice said apologetically.

Jeannie stirred beneath the hand at her shoulder and frowned, reluctant to abandon the comfort of sleep. And then, quite suddenly, she was fully awake. Her eyes moved to Ninette's face, hovering sympathetically above her.

"Ninette, has the minister arrived?" Awkwardly she pulled herself into a sitting position.

"Yes'm, he's heah," Ninette said. "He wants to be leavin' 'fo' it gits da'k."

"How long have I been sleeping?" Jeannie's eyes sought the pillar and scroll-top clock that sat on the mantelpiece. "Ninette, it's past noon!"

"Ah'll bring up dinnuh when yo' dress'," Ninette soothed. "De minister, he eatin' wit' Mist' Ransome."

"I'm not hungry," Jeannie rejected. "I'll dress and go right downstairs." She paused. "I don't have a black dress. . . ."

"Yo' Mama wouldn' want yo' to weah black fo' huh," Ninette reproached. "She'd lak yo' to weah yo' pretties' dress." Her eyes filling with tears, Ninette turned about and walked determinedly to the closet to choose a garment for Jeannie. "Yo' wash, Young Missy, while de watuh wa'm."

Jeannie stood beside the four-poster bed that dated back to the founding of the country, her eyes focused on the window.

"Has the rain stopped yet?" They always had too much rain or not enough. But, of course, a lot of rain was good for the rice.

"It stop. De sun ain' comin' out, but de rain ain' fallin'," Ninette said philosophically, bringing a deep blue velvet dress from the closet. Jeannie's throat tightened as she watched Ninette lay Mama's favorite dress across the bed. "Jeannie, it's the exact blue of your eyes," she had so often said with pleasure. Yes, she would wear it.

Quickly she washed, then allowed Ninette to help her into the dress and to brush her hair until it shone like antique gold.

"Young Missy, Ah'll bring yo' dinnuh," Ninette tried again.

"No," Jeannie rejected. "I'll go downstairs to welcome Mr. King."

Kevin and the minister were already seated at the table in the dining room, furnished with massive English pieces that Jeannie loathed. Her cousin's lean, thin-mouthed, heavy-eyebrowed face showed polite interest in the elderly minister's gossip from the other island, but glints of impatience showed in his piercing dark eyes. After Mr. King expressed his condolences to Jeannie, Kevin insisted she join them for coffee.

"Mr. Ransome tells me you have a lifelong home with him," Mr. King said with a sympathetic smile. "While your loss is painful, you are not left alone in the world."

"I'm grateful to my cousin," Jeannie whispered, her eyes on the table. Must she spend the rest of her life on this near-deserted island with herself, her cousin, and the overseer the only whites living there? When Mama was alive, Jeannie had not bothered to look ahead for herself. Now she looked into the future and she was apprehensive.

While Kevin, as was his habit, lingered over a second cup of coffee, the minister surreptitiously pulled out his watch. Though the rain had ceased, a stiff wind was blowing outside. The Sound could be treacherous in rough weather for the hardly seaworthy boats that were used to travel between the islands. The days were short in December.

Finally Kevin indicated that he was ready for the unhappy task ahead of them. With her cousin towering above her on one side and the minister on the other, Jeannie walked down the hall to the front parlor—usually open only to entertain the minister when he was on the Island on Christmas and Easter mornings—where Mama lay in the pine box, waiting for burial. Ninette had dressed her beautifully, Jeannie thought with gratitude.

She fought back tears as she gazed at her mother, knowing she would never see the beloved face again.

"She is with God," the minister said gently, closing the lid of the coffin. "You must not grieve."

Kevin signaled to the four male servants who hovered, somber-faced and respectful, just outside the parlor. Silently they moved into the room and lifted the coffin.

Flanked by the two white men, Jeannie followed the coffin down the long, narrow hall and out into the bleak, chill afternoon.

Jeannie and Kevin stood before the freshly dug grave with a cluster of house servants behind them, wailing in sorrow. Water was already rising in the grave, Jeannie noticed with consternation. This land was so close to the sea.

Mr. King directed that the hymn be sung. Jeannie shivered as the first high notes welled in unison. Mama's favorite hymn, sung by the house servants she loved. When Mr. King raised his voice in prayer, the slaves and Jeannie dropped to their knees on the wet sand. Only Kevin Ransome remained standing while Mr. King read from the prayer book.

"I am the resurrection and the life," the minister intoned while lightning crackled in the sky.

When the four slaves moved forward to lift the coffin into the sodden grave, Jeannie stepped to the opening to toss a sprig of ivy onto the coffin. Mama had loved the long-leaved, graceful ivy that grew in abundance on the Island.

With a brooding storm more imminent by the moment, Mr. King took a polite but speedy departure. Jeannie, Kevin's hand protectively at her elbow, returned to the house.

"I think I'll go to my room," Jeannie said shakily. "Flora has been instructed on what to serve for supper." How unreal she sounded, talking this way! It was Mama who told Flora what to serve at each meal.

She sat in her room by the window, watching the darkening sky, the flashes of lightning, hardly hearing when Ninette slipped into the room to start up the fire in the grate again. The house—always a bit overwhelming—suddenly seemed a prison to her; yet she knew she must be grateful. Where would she be without her cousin's generosity? She had a home here. She had no one else in this world except for another distant cousin, of modest means, somewhere in Virginia.

Ninette wanted her to change into another dress for supper. But stubbornly Jeannie insisted on wearing the

15

dress she had worn when she buried her mother. She and Kevin sat in the large, ornate, candlelit dining room at supper in strained silence, broken at intervals by some impersonal observation of his.

"You're pale," he reproached firmly, his dark eyes probing hers. "You will have a glass of wine when we retire to the parlor."

Must she sit in the parlor with him tonight? Panic welled in her. To sit there in silence while he read, with Mama's empty chair? How long could she look at that chair where Mama had spent her last moments without becoming sick?

But after the meal she obediently walked with him into the darkly furnished family parlor. She sat beside the fireplace in a tapestry-covered chair, her eyes fastened to the gray-edged log that glowed with smoldering redness in the grate. The room was illuminated only by one wall sconce. Kevin was frugal.

"This is one of our finest wines," Kevin said with pride as he brought a bottle from the Chippendale cabinet that sat between the two tall, narrow, tightly draped windows. "You will enjoy it." He poured the amber liquid into a pair of stemmed Sandwich glasses, of which he was boastfully proud, and handed one glass to Jeannie.

"Thank you." She dropped her eyes before the unexpected intensity of his. Why was he gazing at her this way? Was he concerned that she would not be able to manage the household, as Mama had? She knew she could. But oh, the loneliness on the Island, with Mama gone!

Earlier than was usual, while Jeannie sat with empty wineglass in hand, staring abstractedly into the fire, Kevin rose to his feet.

"It has been an exhausting day," he said with his usual brusqueness, walking to pull the bell rope to summon Nathaniel to remove the wineglasses and close up the house for the night. "Go on up to your room, Jeannie. You must be tired."

"Good night, Cousin Kevin," she said softly, grateful to be released.

Ninette was waiting to help her prepare for the night.

"Missy, Ah'll sleep heah tonight," she offered. "Ah'll bring up a blanket an' sleep on de flo' by yo' bed." Her eyes were shining with solicitude.

"No, Ninette," Jeannie rejected firmly. "I'm all right. You go on downstairs to your own bed." Meaning, she thought with recurrent guilt, to the pallet in the kitchen where Ninette slept along with Flora. The other servants slept in a two-room cabin to the rear of the house.

"It chilly tonight. Yo' want de fire goin'?"

"I won't need it under the covers," Jeannie said reassuringly. Kevin complained they wasted too much wood in the house, though the supply, she thought wryly, seemed endless. Every bad storm brought trees crashing down in the woods.

Ninette pulled the comforter snugly about Jeannie's shoulders, turned down the lamp, and left the room. The rain had stopped. Seemingly the storm was over. Jeannie wished, wistfully, that Ninette had left the lamp lit. She could relight it, she considered, then discarded the thought. No! She was going to sleep.

The room was heavy with shadows. She stirred uneasily. The glow from the burning logs would have been a comfort. Then she frowned in self-reproach. Was she a little girl, that she was afraid of lying awake in the dark?

She closed her eyes, aware of the tiredness in every muscle. A tiredness born of tension and grief, rather than physical effort. Soon enough she would be asleep. And in minutes her eyes were closing.

She awoke with a start, instantly—terrifyingly—conscious of the lighted candle held close to her face. Her heart pounded, she drew back against the pillows, her eyes seeking to identify this intruder.

"Cousin Kevin," she gasped with relief. "Is something wrong?" Conscious that she wore only her nightdress, she pulled the comforter about her as she struggled into a semisitting position.

"You're like her!" he whispered harshly. "Like my evil wife! I've stood by, watching you grow more beautiful each day."

"I don't understand," Jeannie stammered, strangely frightened. What was her cousin doing in her room? Why was he staring at her in that hypnotic fashion? "Have I— have I done something wrong?"

"It's wicked to be so beautiful!" he said with a surge of fury. "That's why she died. My wife. Because she was too beautiful for this world. Men looked at her and they harbored evil thoughts." Suddenly he snuffed out the candle. The only sound in the total darkness was that of his labored breathing.

Had he gone mad? Jeannie thought with panic. Was he going to kill her? It was no use to scream. Ninette and Flora would not hear her all the way downstairs in the kitchen wing. She must get out of the bed, sneak to the door in the blackness, and run downstairs and out into the night!

She thrust aside the comforter and slid noiselessly from the bed, on the side away from Cousin Kevin. The floor was cold to her bare feet. She reached blindly for the bedpost, striving vainly to penetrate the blackness of the room.

"You're evil!" Cousin Kevin's voice rang out as his hands reached out and found her.

He pulled her roughly to him. The scream that welled in her throat was aborted by the bruising weight of his mouth on hers. She struggled futilely to release herself. Then his mouth drew away from hers as he swept her slight body into his arms and dropped her across the width of the mattress.

This wasn't happening. She was having a nightmare.

"No!" she cried out as his hands tore the nightdress from her shoulders. "Dear God, no!"

He slapped Jeannie hard across one side of her face, and she gasped with the shock of the impact. Again his mouth sought hers while his hands fumbled at her small, high breasts. She lay stiff with rejection while his hands moved hotly about her ice-cold body, waves of shock riding over her at each fresh indignity.

"You've sat there in the parlor every night and thought about this," he accused savagely. "You've taunted me with your beauty."

"No!" she gasped, turning her face. "No!"

But again his mouth closed in on hers, silencing the cry of outrage and pain as he threw his body on top of hers and entered her. She lay motionless, closing her ears to the stream of vile language, the passionate urgings that poured from him. Her eyes were shut, her teeth clenched beneath his hot breath as he poured his passion into her.

At last he lay spent, heavy upon her. Let me die, she thought wildly. How could she live with this shame?

"You brought me here," he accused thickly. "You're evil! You brought me to your bed!" All at once he was on his feet, leaning over her. "You harlot! You Jezebel! Put on your nightdress and kneel beside the bed with me. We'll pray, Jeannie. We'll pray for your soul."

Still feeling herself part of a nightmare, Jeannie stumbled to her feet and scrambled in the darkness for the nightdress, ripped at the shoulders by her cousin's roughness. While she pulled the nightdress over her trembling form, he fumbled for the lamp and lit it.

"Cover yourself," he ordered sternly. "In my presence you wear a dressing gown."

In a painful trance she stumbled to the closet and reached for her dressing gown. Still shaking with the insanity of this night, she drew the wrap about her.

"On your knees, girl!" A vein was distended and throbbing in his forehead. His eyes glowed strangely. "Quickly."

As she knelt beside the disarrayed bed, he lifted his arms to heaven and began to pray.

"Oh, Lord, forgive this wicked sinner, for she has erred grievously. She will walk forever in the path of repentance and remember always how she has sinned."

Two

"Young Missy. Please, Young Missy, yo' wake up. Please. Young Missy . . ."

Ninette's anxious voice intruded into Jeannie's troubled sleep. Tiredly she opened her eyes. The lamp on her dresser was lit. Ninette hovered above her with a worried expression.

"Ninette, what is it?" Instinctively she was alarmed. "What's happened?" It was still night, a swift glance toward the windows told her. "What time is it, Ninette?" But of course Ninette could not tell time. Jeannie's eyes sought the clock. It was only five! The slaves would be at their tasks already, but she never went downstairs before seven, when Flora served breakfast. "What's happened?" she reiterated fearfully.

"Nothin' happen, baby," Ninette soothed, but she was plainly troubled. "It jes' dat Mist' Ransome say tell yo' come down to de church rat away. He waitin' fo' yo' deah."

The memory of the night rolled over Jeannie, sickening her. Had it been a nightmare? She shivered with recall. Her eyes fell fleetingly to the torn shoulder of her nightdress. It truly *had* happened.

"He wishes me to come to the church at this hour?" Jeannie asked uncertainly.

"Yes'm." Ninette nodded unhappily.

How could she face him after last night? Suddenly the palms of her hands were perspiring. Her heart pounded. And in his warped mind he blamed *her*! What could she do? Where could she flee? Suddenly she remembered Mama's cousin in Virginia, her one possible chance of refuge. She must write to Mama's cousin and ask her to take her in until she could find a way to support herself.

Trembling as she rose from the bed, she allowed Ninette to help her dress in the dank chill of the morning, unalleviated by a fire starting in the grate. The lamp cast eerie shadows about the room, unnervingly reminiscent of last night, when she had knelt, terrified and bruised, by her bedside while Kevin prayed.

"Bes' take yo' cape," Ninette advised. Her eyes were apprehensive at this strange morning venture. But Ninette could not know what had happened in this blacked-out room last night. She only sensed, intuitively, that something was terribly wrong. "It nasty outdoahs."

"All right, Ninette." She forced a smile. How could he command her to come to the church to pray with him? He knew the guilt was *his*. The shame was hers.

Ninette hesitated. Her eyes were all at once defiant.

"Ah'll bring yo' coffee before yo' go to de church," she said firmly. "It ain' civilize' to go out less'n yo' has yo' coffee." That was a favorite phrase of Cousin Kevin's when he was annoyed. *It simply isn't civilized.* "Po' li'l baby," Ninette crooned, reaching to pull Jeannie into her arms. "Po' li'l muthuhless baby."

"Ninette, I'd better go to him," Jeannie said uneasily, fear reflecting in her voice. The slaves, she remembered, had always been afraid of him. The look was always in their eyes in his presence.

"Ah'll run back to de kitchen and bring a cup o' coffee to yo'. Yo' wait at de doah, yo' heah, honey?" Ninette insisted, moving out of the room with unexpected speed.

Jeannie's mind raced into action as she followed Ninette down the stairs. Cousin Kevin kept stamps in a box on his desk in the library. She would take one and a sheet of paper and some sealing wax. She would write to the cousin in Virginia. The address must be among Mama's papers, which she must bring herself to gather together. They were her inheritance.

She waited in the darkly paneled foyer. In a few

moments Ninette came waddling toward her with a small air of triumph, coffee in hand.

"Yo' drink it all down," Ninette ordered.

Obediently, Jeannie downed the coffee, grateful for its warmth, grateful to be able to postpone the encounter with her cousin, even for this brief period. Why must she come to the church at this hour of the morning? To help him wash away his guilt? Always he had seemed strange. Now she was sure he was mad.

Occasionally visitors from the other plantations came to Ransome Island. The limited conversation of these visitors constituted her meager social life. Though they did not seem afraid of their own slaves, they talked of their terror of possible uprisings at neighboring plantations. They spoke in hushed tones about the ever-present fear of their women being ravished by the slaves. But her cousin had ravished her.

Finishing her coffee, she gave the cup to Ninette, then went out into the sea-damp darkness of the early morning. The first grayness of the new day was showing in the night sky. The wet ground squooshed beneath her feet as she walked toward the grove in which the Island church was located. Greenness was on every side, even in December.

She held her skirt above her ankles to protect it from the rain-brushed greenery underfoot. Overhead, emerging from the nearby swamps, a pair of partridges winged their way toward the Sound.

A faint light glimmered in the church as she approached. Her heart pounded as she recalled yet again, with stark clarity, the horror of last night. How could she go into the church and face him, after what had happened between them?

Fearfully she opened the door of the small white pinewood church and walked inside, her face hot with shame. Cousin Kevin stood behind the pulpit, his head bowed, his mouth moving silently. At the sound of her feet down the aisle, he looked up with a thunderous glare.

"You have taken long enough to come," he rebuked sternly.

"I'm sorry," she whispered, forcing herself to move

quickly toward the pulpit. *Don't think about last night.* She was not evil. God knew.

"Kneel, Jeannie Fleming," he ordered brusquely. "Kneel and pray with me."

He called upon God in florid phrases to cleanse her of her sins, with the same fervor and frenzy he used in preaching to the slaves. Then, pausing, his voice hoarse, he dismissed her. His eyes were frightening as they dwelt on her. For an agonizing moment she feared he would take her again, right there in the church.

"Go to the house," he cried out loudly. "Go to the house and hide your shame. Each morning you will come here to pray. Do you understand, Jeannie?"

"Yes, Cousin Kevin," she whispered, her mind racing. She must get away from Ransome Island. He was a madman!

She breakfasted alone. Flora had been ordered to send Cousin Kevin's breakfast to his desk in the library. After breakfast, she knew, he would leave the house to go to the rice mill. Then she would be able to get the needed supplies to write to Mama's cousin in Virginia.

She ate without tasting the food, knowing she must go to Mama's room when she was done. At the door to her mother's room, she battled tears, resolute. She would look only for the address of the cousin in Virginia. The rest must wait until her grief was in control.

Mercifully, she found it right away, easily accessible in the top drawer of the dresser, as though Mama had known she might require it. Carefully, scrupulously polite, she wrote the cousin of her mother's death, delicately asking if there might be some way she could be useful in the Virginia household. She fought back the urge to confide in the cousin she had never seen about the brutality of their mutual cousin.

The letter folded over to reveal the address, properly sealed with wax, she went downstairs again. Earlier she had seen the schooner that took the rice from the Island pull in to shore. Ninette would take her letter to the schooner and ask that it be kindly mailed for her in Savannah.

"Ninette," she called, her voice faintly strident with anxiety. "Ninette!"

"Ah'm comin', baby." Ninette hurried into view.

"Ninette, would you please give this letter to the man at the schooner?" She tried to sound calm. "I particularly want it to go to Savannah with him. And tell him I appreciate his courtesy."

"Yes'm. Rat away." Ninette reached respectfully for the letter. "Ah won' send a boy. Ah'll take it to 'im," she said solemnly. What would Ninette think if she knew about last night? She was afraid of the Master. On occasion he was known to flog a slave himself. For minor infractions he turned the slaves out of the church. How they dreaded that!

Defiant and trembling, Jeannie mounted the stairs. Mama had kept emergency money in the tip of one of a pair of shoes she rarely wore. It had been there ever since Jeannie could remember. Not much, she guessed, but it would be enough to see her to Virginia if the cousin would have her.

In her room, she closed the door behind her and hurried to a window to watch Ninette's progress to the schooner. A sense of exhilaration, of adventure filtered through her. Oh, she hated the solitude of Ransome Island! How had Mama borne it all these years? But Mama had thought only of her, of being able to raise her to adulthood in a proper home.

She leaned out the window, following Ninette with her eyes, impatient to see the exchange at the schooner. Then all at once she stiffened with alarm. Cousin Kevin was emerging from the pine grove.

"Ninette!" he called sharply, striding toward her. "What are you doing out of the house? What have you got there?"

Pale, Jeannie watched the pantomime between the two. Ninette's frightened voice was too low to carry to her. Cousin Kevin ripped the letter from Ninette's hand and gestured for her to return to the house. While Ninette scrambled away from him, he tore open the letter, read it, then methodically tore it into shreds and dropped the pieces to the ground.

Jeannie was a prisoner on Ransome Island.

Jeannie saw nothing of her cousin until supper. At the table he was cold, reproachful, speaking hardly at all. He said nothing about the letter which he had intercepted and destroyed.

"You will go to your room and read from the Bible," he said distantly when supper was finished. "You must learn to repent."

"Good night," she whispered, outwardly submissive. But she knew that somehow, some way, she *must* escape from Ransome Island.

In her mother's room, feeling the warmth of her presence, Jeannie discovered the money in the tip of the shoe where it was always kept. She reached into a crumbling candy box for the cameo that was the single piece of jewelry Mama had left behind. Mama had been buried with her wedding ring.

At dawn, after a sleepless night of waiting, Jeannie arose, dressed quickly, and left her room with a small portmanteau which had accompanied her and her mother to Ransome Island fourteen years ago. Stealthily she made her way down the night-dark stairs. The slaves were already moving about in the kitchen. She debated a moment. Did she dare go out to say farewell to them? No! That would be too dangerous.

Clutching a coin in her hand, she hurried out into the drab grayness of the early morning. She knew that this morning, Ezra would take the small boat and go for supplies. She would bribe him to take her with him. Somehow, she must make her way to Virginia.

She walked swiftly through the chill, ever-present dampness, searching for a figure near the boats. Ezra was there, preparing to depart.

"Ezra!" she called out, fearful that he might leave without her. "Ezra, wait!"

Ezra looked up, his face alarmed. He knew what the portmanteau in her hand meant. His eyes moved past her to the big house. Was she going to have trouble with Ezra? Give him the money. He must take her with him.

"Ezra, I want you to take me to the big island," she

said breathlessly. "I—I want to do some shopping at the settlement store," she lied, clumsily. He didn't believe her.

"Young Missy, Ah dassn't," he stammered. "Mastuh kill me if Ah do dat."

"Ezra, I'm just going shopping." She tried to sound self-indulgent. "I brought along the portmanteau to carry back the yard goods I want to buy." She held out the coin enticingly.

"Ezra!" They both started at the stern, furious voice that ricocheted through the early-morning stillness. "Ezra, you tell Young Missy to get back to the house. You're *not* to take her with you."

"Young Missy, Ah cain' take yo'," Ezra said miserably, yet with compassion in his eyes. "Yo' bes' go back to de house."

Slowly, her head high, her face red with indignation, Jeannie turned around and walked back toward the house. She might be one of the slaves for all the freedom she had on Ransome Island.

Kevin waited for her in the foyer, his face etched with fury. He lifted one hand and struck her hard across the face, sending her reeling.

"You won't try to run away again," he warned brutally. "Ninette will watch you. If you try to run away again, I will have her flogged until her back is laid open."

In her room she lay across the bed, too distraught for tears. What did he want of her? Why did he insist on keeping her here? When would he come to her again in the night and have his will? If he took her again, she quietly swore, she would kill herself.

Jeannie settled into a strange, unreal existence of pushing time away. Household obligations required little of her. She sat endlessly in her room, or on warm afternoons on the gallery in the sunlight, with opened books before her, whose words she seldom read. She was too disturbed to indulge in her beloved watercoloring, no longer aware of the splendor of the birds that flitted across the sky and that she had once adored to paint.

Each morning at five Ninette came to her room to

help her prepare for the unreal minutes in the church. She would walk down the aisle each morning, with Cousin Kevin behind the pulpit waiting for her, never sure what the next few minutes would bring. Sometimes he railed in such fury she expected him to collapse in a fit. Sometimes he sobbed with anguish, blaming her for his grief. But he never touched her. Each morning, when she left the church, she thanked God that he had not touched her.

She saw nothing of him again until supper, a silent, painful meal. Afterward he closed himself up in the library. She lived an uneasy life of waiting, for she knew not what.

Christmas came with little note taken of it at the big house. Kevin Ransome was not a master to provide individual gifts for the slaves, though Jeannie found colorful scraps of cloth among her mother's remnants to make kerchiefs for the house servants, who showed—from affection, she knew—a gratitude far beyond the fabrics' worth. Because he considered it good business, an incentive to promote more work from the slaves, Kevin did give each family a bottle of whiskey for Christmas.

Christmas, the first without her mother, was particularly painful for Jeannie. She sat at Christmas dinner, tears blurring her eyes, remembering Mama sitting across the table from her. Mama, who knew how to ignore Cousin Kevin's fits of sullenness, who accepted with equanimity his scornful remarks about the waste of food that marked the holiday meal.

She tried to enjoy the succulent wild duck that Flora sent in from the kitchen. The skin was crisp the way Mama had liked it, the orange sauce pungent. Cousin Kevin ate stolidly, glowering, his eyes fastened to his plate. He said not a word until the plum pudding and mince pie arrived.

"Fearful waste," he snorted. "One or the other, not both. Tell Flora to stop this infernal parade of food. She only makes it so they can eat high on the hog out in the kitchen." But he helped himself to an excessively large wedge of mince pie.

"I'll tell Flora," Jeannie said automatically, her eyes

27

lowered lest he read the defiance in her eyes.

Then, with an air of detachment he said, "I had a letter yesterday. We'll have a visitor early next week. A young man who read my article in the agricultural journal about my new methods of irrigation." His eyes glinted with pride. "He'll be coming to consult me *personally* all the way from Charleston. It will be only polite to ask him to remain overnight. You will conduct yourself like a young lady," he cautioned ominously, and color flooded her face. How dare he talk to her that way! "Have the corner guest room prepared for him."

"Yes, Cousin Kevin." She was outwardly meek, but her mind was racing. A visitor was coming to Ransome Island! She must entreat this man to mail a letter for her. Somehow, she must impress upon him the need for secrecy. If the Virginia cousin wrote and asked her to come to live with her, would Cousin Kevin dare refuse? She would take that gamble.

The next morning Jeannie dispatched servants to prepare the ornately furnished corner guest room, in such contrast to the family bedrooms, for the gentleman from Charleston. Fresh draperies and curtains must be hung, the bed aired, the furniture polished, the rug taken up and beaten. No one had slept in this room since the engineer from New York, six years ago, who had come to advise about the new equipment Kevin had ordered for the mill. She had been only eleven then, but how exciting it had been to hear him talk about New York!

Annoyed at the clamor of the goings-on, when he was in the library working on yet another article about the cultivation of rice, Kevin climbed the stairs to upbraid the slaves. Jeannie stood in the center of the room, her color high with the excitement of imminent entertaining.

"Jeannie!"

She spun around guiltily at the sound of his voice. There was a glow about her, she realized, that he would find unseemly. He stared hard at her, hands clenched at his sides, the vein in his forehead suddenly throbbing. There was an intensity about him that unnerved her.

"Yes, Cousin Kevin?" she said uncertainly.

"Keep these heathens quiet, will you?" he said

brusquely. "I'm trying to work in the library." All at once Jeannie was trembling. He had stared at her that way the night he had come to her room. But now his face was ashen with the effort to keep himself in control. "These walls don't look fresh," he said with irritation. "Choose from the papers in the storeroom. Have them redo the walls."

"I'll take care of it," she promised, haltingly.

Kevin turned on his heel and left the room. She heard the emphatic stamp of his feet going down the carpeted stairs. Why was there no bolt on her bedroom door? she asked herself with frustration. Tonight, she promised herself, she would drag the dresser against the door after Ninette left her for the night.

The following Tuesday she sat at the window in her bedroom, thinking of nothing but the visitor due any moment at Ransome Island. Even as she thought about him, she spied the schooner pulling to shore. She leaned forward, her mouth parted expectantly.

A man was leaving the schooner, walking toward the house with the agility of youth. A handsome man, she realized as he strode toward the gallery. Tall, slender, fair-haired, with a confident bearing. A man with strength, she decided impulsively. A man who would not be afraid of Cousin Kevin.

She left her chair to cross to the dresser. Her heart pounding, she brought the brush to her hair and moved it vigorously over the silken length. She had known no young men except an occasional business associate of Cousin Kevin's who came to Ransome Island. Any overture of friendship had been swiftly scotched by her disapproving cousin.

"Jeannie, I worry about your prospects," Mama used to say. But *she* had not wanted to think, as Mama was wont to do, about the time when she would be old enough to marry. She had pretended that she could remain forever with Mama, hiding her loneliness in learning. She had not been afraid of Cousin Kevin when he tutored her. They had been almost friends.

Mama had talked about their going to Savannah for a

few days this coming spring, so that she might meet young people her own age. Had Mama guessed at the ugliness that lurked within their cousin? Did that account for her air of secret anxiety this last year? It had been more than just a normal concern for her daughter's future.

Jeannie stood in the center of the room listening to the sounds in the foyer. Someone had informed her cousin of the arrival of the ship and he was greeting the young man.

She started at the knock on the door.

"Come in," she called breathlessly.

Fourteen-year-old Celeste, grinning broadly, her eyes too wise, came into the room.

"Mist' Ransome, he say yo' please come downstaihs," she reported. "De company done arrive." Obviously she approved of their guest.

"Thank you, Celeste."

Her throat tight with excitement, Jeannie quickly changed into a fresh dress, left her room, and headed down the stairs. Would Cousin Kevin's guest mail her letter for her on his return to Charleston? Without saying anything to Cousin Kevin?

The two men, still talking in the foyer, glanced up as she moved gracefully down the stairs, her color high, an uncertain smile playing on her face as they waited for her to descend.

"Mr. Mitchell, may I present my ward, Miss Jeannie Fleming," her cousin introduced with dry formality.

"You didn't tell me she was so beautiful, Mr. Ransome," Dennis Mitchell chided, his eyes aglow with admiration, his hand clinging overly long to hers. "I'm dazzled, sir."

"I hope you enjoy your stay at Ransome Island," Jeannie stammered shyly.

"Let us go into the parlor," her cousin said peremptorily. "You must be in the mood for refreshment after your trip, Mr. Mitchell."

Dennis Mitchell shared the green velvet sofa with Kevin Ransome, Jeannie sitting in a small Queen Anne chair opposite. The two men were engrossed in a discussion about Mexico's reluctance to make peace. Jeannie was disconcerted—and exhilarated—by the frequency with which Dennis Mitchell's eyes moved to rest upon her.

"Jeannie, surely you'll want to speak to Flora about supper," Cousin Kevin said sharply, and she colored in confusion.

"Yes, of course." She rose awkwardly to her feet. "Please excuse me."

Kevin was furious that their guest was so openly admiring of her. He would try to stop any overture of friendship Dennis Mitchell might make to her. But this time, Jeannie thought with a new defiance, Cousin Kevin would find her rebellious.

Three

"Rest until you're called for supper," Kevin Ransome encouraged Dennis as they paused before the open door to the guest room. "Traveling is tiring."

"Thank you, sir," Dennis said with calculated charm. "It's most kind of you to insist that I remain overnight."

"You must stay a few days," Ransome said expansively. "It isn't often that someone comes to Ransome Island to discuss my writings in the agricultural journals."

"My father was deeply impressed," Dennis said respectfully, masking his inner contempt for this visit. "I returned from Europe only two weeks ago, but he insisted I come here to talk personally with you about your experiments."

"We'll talk at great length," Ransome promised. "I'll show you my diagrams for laying out my irrigation system."

"What an egotistical bastard," Dennis muttered to himself as Ransome went back downstairs. Dennis walked into his room, crossed to the bed, and stretched out, inspecting the room with an air of arrogance. The furniture was expensive, probably imported from France many years ago.

But damn Papa for shipping him off on this fool errand! Why hadn't Papa come himself? He was always boasting about how efficient Ron was in running the plantation. Why couldn't he leave his fine nephew in charge? A glint of cynicism showed in Dennis' eyes. Papa hadn't come to Ransome Island because the whole errand had been concocted to remove him from the house for a while.

It made Papa nervous to witness the verbal battles between Madeline and him. Only Papa sensed something passionately secretive between Ron's wife and him, Dennis thought with a flicker of sardonic amusement. It made Papa nervous to see his son battling. How had Madeline managed to rope in Ron, those months he was away? Ron was supposed to be so smart!

Dennis frowned, in his mind rerunning the overwrought battle with Papa about continuing his allowance, even though he was home. Did Papa expect him to sit around The Magnolias all the time, after seven months of high living in London and Paris?

Papa had yelled and carried on at first when he talked about going to Europe. He had given in fast enough because he was afraid their neighbors would find out about his affection for the gaming tables. That was a sensitive point to Papa. That and his way with women, Dennis thought with pride.

Papa prayed he would settle down, marry well, bring in some substantial money to The Magnolias. Papa was dying to replace some of the broken-down mill equipment. That ran into heavy money. But nobody—not even Papa —was going to tell him how to run his life.

Before he left for London, Papa had paid off the last of the mortgages on The Magnolias. The heavy debts Grandpa had incurred gambling in Charleston had devolved on Papa when Grandpa put a bullet through his head sixteen years ago.

Dennis' eyes narrowed with recall. He could remember the old man. He had been ten when Grandpa died. But his grandfather had never truly accepted him, any more than he had accepted Mama. They were two strangers who had come to live at The Magnolias.

True, Papa considered him his son. He would inherit the plantation eventually, though he wasn't blood, the way Ron was. Papa had adopted him, made him legally a Mitchell, he remembered with triumph. It didn't matter that Ron had come to live at The Magnolias when his father died when he was fourteen. He, Dennis Mitchell, would inherit The Magnolias. Why did it rankle that Ron had been *born* a Mitchell?

Fresh anger welled in him as he stared at the ceiling, visualizing his return to The Magnolias to find Madeline installed there as Ron's wife. Mama, in her vague letters, had said only that Ron had married a Charleston girl. Madeline Beauchamp, she had been. Madeline Mitchell now, playing the chatelaine of The Magnolias. Why did Mama let her get away with those airs? he asked himself with recurrent fury. But Mama lived off in a world of her own, surrounded by the newest romantic novels and choice wines imported from France.

And why had Papa allowed Madeline to bring her mother to The Magnolias, to set her up in her private rooms up there on the third floor? Like Grandpa, Mavis had an addiction for the gaming tables. And she had another for virile young men. They had best put the house out of bounds for all the black bucks under twenty.

Did Papa ever wonder what it would be like to have Madeline in his bed, or was he satisfied with the black wench he took to that small house he called his study? How long since he had slept with Mama? Probably fourteen years. After five miscarriages, Mama had refused to admit him to her room. In a rare mood Papa had confided that to him.

Papa had desperately wanted a son of his own, hadn't he? A stepson wasn't the same. Mama had done *him* a favor, Dennis thought with ironic humor, by denying Papa a child. Someday The Magnolias would belong to him, the son of a theatrical promoter who had died be-

33

cause he dallied with another man's wife.

Dennis started at the knock on his door.

"Come in," he called. A tall, slender, very young slave walked gracefully into the room. Her body beneath the homespun shift she wore was deliciously ripe, her ebony face delicately featured.

"Mist' Ransome, he say to bring yo' some wine," she said in a musical West Indian voice. "He say fo' me to unpack fo' yo'."

"Thank you." He sat up at the side of the bed, a stirring low within him. "What's your name, girl?" He reached for the wine and pointed to his portmanteau.

"Celeste." Her smile was blatantly provocative. She knew, as Dennis knew, that Kevin Ransome had sent her to him so that he might avail himself of her services.

"This wine is fine," he said with a slow smile after the initial sip. "Please bring me another glass at bedtime."

"Ah'll bring it," she promised, her eyes meeting his, a small, secretive smile crossing the doll-like face. Almost arrogant, he thought. Yet he respected that she knew her value.

Sipping the wine with obvious approval, he found his mind moving to Ransome's ward. She was beautiful in a delicate fashion that usually left him cold. He liked his women flamboyant. She was afraid of Ransome, wasn't she? Probably one of those fire-and-brimstone planters. The servants were scared of him too.

All through the splendid supper served by a bevy of servants, Dennis found his eyes moving compulsively to Jeannie. He guessed at the passion beneath that beautiful, wistful exterior. She was alarmingly well read. Madeline would loathe her, he decided complacently as he talked with eloquence about his months in London.

"Please, tell us about Paris," Jeannie urged, her eyes shining. "All I know is what I've read in novels and memoirs."

"Paris was fascinating." He leaned forward with an air of confidence, flattered by her interest. But then, his conquests were legion, he thought with pride. If he remained here one week, he could put that one on her back. Not that she was his type. Madeline was his type, he remembered truantly. "Luncheons at the Frères Provençaux," he reminisced. "The finest restaurant in all of Paris. Performances at the Théâtre National and the Opéra." His eyes glistened as he recalled the shamelessness of the *bal de l'Opéra* that arrived with the early hours of the morning, when the guests allowed themselves every liberty. The excitement was unbearable. Madeline knew these balls. She had lived in Paris with her mother for years until Mavis had decided it was time to return to their own country. "Of course, I was in Paris in the Year of the Revolutions. The Champs-Elysées was like a permanent fair with jugglers, acrobats, fortune-tellers, sellers of patent medicines. None of its usual elegance. But by the time I left, Louis Napoleon had just been elected President of the French Republic, and by now he must have brought everything back to normal. All that absurd socialist business is over—not only in France, but everywhere in Europe."

"I visited Paris for one week twenty-four years ago," Ransome said with distaste. "An evil city. I never returned." He smiled ironically. "I prefer the isolation of Ransome Island and the pleasure of working with the soil."

"We'll try to utilize your methods with the dikes," Dennis said with plotted deference. "My father was fascinated by what you've done here on the Island."

"You must stay here at least three or four days," Ransome insisted with firmness. "It will take that long to show you everything."

Ransome's eyes moved to Jeannie, who sat across from Dennis with color staining her high cheekbones, obviously enjoying the diversion of a guest at the supper table. Covertly Dennis scrutinized him. Was the old boy developing ideas about him and Jeannie? he wondered with amusement. Jeannie said she never left the Island. How often did she meet young men?

Wouldn't Madeline be furious if he brought home a bride! His wife would be the *real* mistress of The Magnolias. Madeline would sink back into the role of the nephew's new wife. Ron worked hard enough, God knew —but he had no prospects. Everything would go to *him,*

Dennis remembered with vindictive satisfaction. Ron and Madeline lived at The Magnolias on Papa's largess.

Jeannie was young, not yet wise to the ways of the world. She would be no problem for a husband who liked to spend much of his time away from the family plantation.

"We'll take our coffee and dessert in the family parlor," Ransome told the servant who hovered at the door, awaiting instructions. "And tell Flora to be quick about it."

He ran a tight household, Dennis analyzed. Strict with his ward, too. How could she bear living alone with the old man on this isolated, dull island?

Earlier than Dennis had expected, Kevin Ransome called a close to their evening. Probably because he was up early to supervise activities in the mill. But it was just as well, Dennis thought with approval. That black slave girl—Celeste—would come to his room with the glass of wine. She wouldn't forget.

Clad only in his dressing gown because he enjoyed the touch of silk against his bare body, Dennis waited in a chair with the Savannah papers his host had given him before he went to his room across his lap. His mind obsessively focused on Madeline's reactions if he came home with a bride to supplant her at The Magnolias, he did not see the papers.

A single log burned in the grate, the fire started up before he came up to his room. Back home, he thought humorously, no servant would dare be so sparing with logs. The supper had been splendid, but here was none of the abundance that was part of the dining table at The Magnolias. On Ransome Island little went back to the kitchen.

What would Kevin Ransome say if he went in pursuit of his ward? His thoughts were aborted by a light knock at the door. He stiffened in his chair, anticipating Celeste's arrival.

"Come in," he called out briskly.

Celeste opened the door and walked into the room with a glass of wine in one slender hand, her eyes inscrutable, her mouth in a faint smile. Only fourteen years old, and he'd lay odds she knew everything there was to know about men and women. Had Ransome taught her, or some young buck out in the rice fields?

He took the glass from her, allowing his eyes to rest on the thrust of her breasts beneath the limp fabric of her dress.

"Close the windows, Celeste," he ordered, his mouth going dry. "This damp night air is dangerous."

He watched, sipping the wine, while she moved to one window after another, pulling each shut. A fog was rolling in from the water, lending an air of eerie isolation to the house.

"All right, come here," he ordered with a brusqueness that startled her. He drained his wineglass and set it down on the table. "Take off that thing," he said, one hand brushing her dress.

Without a word she pulled the dress over her head with sinuous grace, then dropped it to the floor.

"How many men have taken you?" he asked carelessly.

"Jes' one," she whispered, holding her head high.

"The Master?" he drawled, but she lowered her eyes and was silent. The Master, he thought with dry humor. His prerogative to sample first. With all the Bible-spouting he had done earlier, he still had a taste for the wenches. "I'll give you a better time," he boasted, untying the belt about his dressing gown, pulling aside its silken splendor, and dropping it to the floor.

Jeannie tossed restlessly in her bed. Would she ever fall asleep tonight? The conversation at supper, and in the parlor afterward, with Dennis Mitchell filled her mind. It was so rare that they had guests. And this guest was young, and intriguingly handsome. Usually they were middle-aged planters come to arrange for the threshing of their rice.

No one had ever so entranced her as Dennis Mitchell had. He spoke so casually of living in Europe for seven months. He had walked the streets of London and Paris, had seen all the famous landmarks of which she had read so avidly. When he talked about going to the theater and the opera, she had felt almost as though she had walked beside him.

37

Cousin Kevin wanted Dennis to remain at Ransome Island for a while. He would have someone to whom he could talk about his experiments with rice growing. Dennis was not truly interested, she guessed indulgently. He was being polite, collecting data for his father.

Dennis Mitchell was quite the handsomest man she had ever seen. Celeste had been impressed with him when he had arrived this afternoon. And when Celeste had helped serve supper, her eyes had kept settling on him. Jeannie reproached herself that she was behaving like one of those silly girls in bad romantic novels.

She must write another letter to the cousin in Virginia and ask Dennis please to mail it for her when he returned to Charleston. How could she make him understand that Cousin Kevin must not know about this letter? Somehow, she must manage.

From exhaustion brought on by the excitement of the evening she eventually fell asleep, to awaken with a shattering suddenness. From habit, she now awoke each morning dreading the rendezvous with her cousin. How it sickened her to kneel there in the empty church in the dreary grayness of the morning, while Cousin Kevin read what he considered appropriate passages from the Bible, then prayed that she be forgiven for her sin. *Her sin*— she shook with recurrent exasperation. It was *he* who had violated *her*.

She shifted so that her eyes would rest upon the clock on the mantelpiece. Almost five. Where was Ninette? Guiltily she threw back the comforter, shivering in the morning chill. Lately Ninette had been coming in early to start a small fire in the grate, by which she could dress.

She turned about to face the door at the sound of a cautious movement. Ninette was coming into the room with a cup of coffee.

"Yo' git back in bed, Young Missy," Ninette said with a pleased smile, waddling toward her. "De Mastuh tell Ezra he sleepin' till close to seven dis mawnin'. Till breakfas'," she added with an air of satisfaction. "Git unduh de covuhs and have yo' coffee, baby."

Because of Dennis Mitchell's presence, Jeannie realized with relief, the agonizing session at the church would be omitted this morning—and every morning until Dennis left, she guessed.

She would go downstairs at seven, the way she used to while Mama was alive; and she would have breakfast with Cousin Kevin and Dennis Mitchell. After breakfast Cousin Kevin would take Dennis on a tour of the Island. There was nothing he enjoyed more than showing off his kingdom.

While the two men were away from the house, she would go into the library, take a sheet of paper and sealing wax, and write her letter. Her mind sought to frame words to present to Dennis. How could she explain the need for secrecy? Her face was suddenly hot. She could never tell Dennis why she felt this urgency to escape from Ransome Island.

At precisely seven Jeannie walked into the dining room. Cousin Kevin sat at his usual place at the head of the table. Nodding curtly without looking at her, he pulled out his watch with an air of annoyance. Dennis was late in arriving at breakfast.

"Ezra!" he called out sharply. "Send someone up to Mr. Mitchell's room. Tell him we're sitting down to breakfast." Even though Dennis Mitchell was a guest, Jeannie though distastefully, Cousin Kevin felt it his right to insist on promptness at mealtime.

Dennis frowned, hearing the repeated knock on the door. What the devil?

"Come in," he called with irritation.

A tall, deferential male servant came into the room, carrying a cup of steaming, fragrant coffee.

"Excuse me, suh," he apologized, "but de Mastuh say to tell yo' breakfas' bein' served now." Warily he approached the bed.

Dennis bit back the obscene retort that hovered on his lips. In Europe he had grown accustomed to staying up till dawn, then sleeping till noon. At home his family respected his ways.

"Thank you." Forcing a smile, Dennis accepted the cup of coffee.

He had forgotten. Ransome had said last night that

they would have breakfast at seven and go out about the Island immediately afterward. Why hadn't Papa come himself? he thought with a fresh surge of annoyance. All this business about dikes and canals meant nothing to him! He would not remember one-tenth of what Ransome told him. But then, Papa had sent him away to cool off. That last tense scene at the tea table between him and Madeline had upset Papa. Ron had not been there. A lot of nights Ron was in the mill, working like a laborer, struggling to repair their aging equipment.

The servant left the room. Dennis gulped down his coffee, rose, and dressed. He strode down the stairs, aware of the heavy silence on the lower floor. Ransome was a peculiar man. There was something oddly intimidating about him even when he strove to be friendly.

"Good morning." Dennis smiled with brilliant charm as he walked into the dining room. Ransome seemed preoccupied this morning, but Jeannie's face lighted at the sight of him. In her way, he thought with bitter humor, she was as beautiful as Madeline. And, unlike Madeline, she was unaware of her beauty.

"I hope you're wearing proper shoes," Ransome said abruptly to Dennis. "The earth is wet."

"I'm familiar with rice fields," he said respectfully. He hated the rice fields. The damnable swamps that surrounded the fields back home, breeding fever during the hot months. Papa was the only planter in South Carolina who insisted on staying on a rice plantation during the bad months. When he was a boy they had still had the summer house, but even then Papa couldn't bear to be away from The Magnolias more than a few weeks during the worst heat of the summer.

Deliberately Dennis allowed Jeannie to believe he was entranced by the sweetness of her smile. When Ransome fell silent, involved in some inner debate, he concentrated flatteringly on answering Jeannie's eager questions. She was uncommonly intelligent. Normally he loathed intelligent women; usually they were horse-faced, cold, and humorless.

But Jeannie Fleming had a rare combination of beauty and brains. Papa was scrupulously polite to Madeline, because she was his nephew's wife; but he would admire Jeannie Fleming. Papa had great respect for intellect and learning. How amusing it would be to see Madeline take a back seat to Jeannie Fleming! Yes, he must invite her to visit at The Magnolias. She would surely jump at the chance, provided Kevin Ransome would permit it.

While he talked with Jeannie about the magnificent theater companies in London and Paris, he became conscious of a furtive inspection by his host. Was Ransome irritated by this display of interest in his ward? But there would be nothing unseemly about an invitation to Jeannie Fleming to visit The Magnolias. He would just be returning the hospitality shown to him. Madeline, that little bitch, needed to be put in her place.

"Would you care for more coffee?" Ransome asked politely, though plainly anxious to be away from the table.

"Thank you, no." Dennis was enjoying the looks of unconscious admiration Jeannie bestowed on him at intervals. And they were not uncommon, he thought with brash recall.

Not until they were far out into the rice fields did Kevin Ransome reveal what had occupied his thoughts at the breakfast table. Walking with Dennis along a dike, he talked about Jeannie with an air of anxiety.

"I'm afraid I have been remiss in my duties to Jeannie. I should have brought young men to Ransome Island to meet her. She's seventeen. It's time she was married. A beautiful girl like Jeannie, brilliantly educated, untouched."

"She's lovely," Dennis conceded warily. The old devil was out to marry her off to him!

"I knew when I saw the way she looked at you how ready she was for marriage. I'm afraid when you leave us she'll dream wistfully about your time at the Island. Of course," he added smoothly, watching Dennis, "her prospects are slight. It's impossible for me to provide the kind of social life a marriageable young lady requires."

Didn't the old man realize that, as his ward, Jeannie would have little difficulty attracting a husband? She was

41

going to be a rich young lady when her cousin died. Heiress to Ransome Island!

A nagging thought rooted itself in his mind. Why *didn't* he marry Jeannie Fleming? Even if Papa turned cantankerous one of these days, cut him off—leaving The Magnolias to Ron—he and Jeannie would eventually own Ransome Island.

Enamored of him the way she was, Jeannie would be a compliant bride. Not one of those strong, dominating women he loathed. *Madeline would eat her heart out if he brought Jeannie home as his bride. Jeannie* would be the mistress of The Magnolias. Mama made no pretense of filling that role.

"Sir," Dennis began with ingratiating deference, "I know it's bold of me to speak on such short acquaintance-ship, but I must leave shortly for Charleston. I find myself completely charmed by Jeannie. I would like your permission to speak to her of marriage. I assure you I'll be tender with her, aware of the shortness of our courtship. I won't rush her, Mr. Ransome." The old man was gloating. Ransome figured the girl had swept him off his feet. Let him believe that. Convince Jeannie it was true. That would be easy. She wanted to believe it.

"You have my permission," Ransome acquiesced with a gracious smile. "But you must remain at least two weeks," he stipulated, his eyes aglow with triumph. "To give Jeannie time to come to know you."

"A week," Dennis substituted. A week with Celeste would suit him fine. Ransome was a practical man. It would not upset him if his ward's suitor enjoyed himself nightly with a slave. "In a week I think I can win her, sir."

"I will leave it in your hands," Ransome agreed with a gesture of capitulation. "You will be married here at Ransome Island, by Mr. King; and then you can begin the trip to Charleston."

Jeannie stood by the window, gazing out into the fog that shrouded the house. Her heart hammered as she remembered the warm glances bestowed on her by Dennis tonight over supper and, later, when they had sat by the fire and listened to Cousin Kevin expound with reverence on Thomas Carlyle.

"Carlyle is a writer—he doesn't demean his talents on frivolous journalism," Kevin had said, with distaste for the newspapers brought weekly from Savannah. "He knows, as we in the South know, that democracy is absurd. A very few people are naturally superior to the rest. The government should be in the hands of one leader. A man capable of ruling." A purple vein had throbbed in his forehead as he talked.

Dennis had not tried to argue with Cousin Kevin, Jeannie remembered tenderly, but she was sure he had been shocked by this attack on democracy.

"Jeannie, I want to talk to you!" Her cousin's voice crashed into her reverie. She spun about with shock. He had not bothered to knock and she had not heard him enter her room.

"What is it?" she asked, her voice uneven. He wouldn't dare come to her that way again, not with Dennis in the house.

"I don't know if it's wise to tell you just yet," he said with an odd air of detachment. "But God tells me that I should prepare you. Dennis Mitchell is quite smitten with you. He came to me tonight, fearful and uneasy, to ask if he might—despite the fact that you two have just met—speak to you of marriage."

She gazed at him in disbelief. *This wasn't happening.* She had known Dennis hardly more than twenty-four hours. Yet she knew she loved him. But then memory flooded her mind and she paled.

"How could I marry Dennis?" she whispered, lowering her eyes. "How can I marry *any* man?"

"Now, you listen to me!" He reached for her wrist and held it in a painful grip. "That young man will ask you to marry him. This is your one chance to save yourself. You will tell him nothing, do you understand?" His harsh voice was ominous, his eyes hypnotic.

"But he'll know," she stammered, her eyes downcast in shame.

"He won't know," her cousin insisted. "He will not expect you to accept him as a husband right away. He will give you time to learn to know him. And when he comes to you, Jeannie, you will pretend that it is the first time you have given yourself to a man. Do you understand what I am saying?" His eyes were mesmerizing as they held hers. "You will pretend that it is the first time. You will know what to do."

"I can't do that to Dennis," she protested. But to be his wife! To escape Ransome Island! This was her deliverance, she thought with a mixture of eagerness and anguish. "I can't do that to him!" she reiterated, reaching for strength to deny herself this gift.

"You *will* do this," Kevin Ransome insisted, his voice ice-cold, "or as God is my witness, I will strip you naked before the black congregation and flog you till you drop to the floor. You will marry Dennis Mitchell and go with him to The Magnolias. You will atone for what you have done to your benefactor by being an exemplary wife for the rest of your days!"

His logic was absurd, Jeannie thought. Cousin Kevin had changed his mind about keeping her a prisoner because he wanted her out of his sight so that he might, deep within his soul, forget his own sin. Yes! Yes, she would marry Dennis, she thought with soaring determination. She would escape from Ransome Island. She would marry the man she loved. A miracle had come to deliver her from her prison.

One week later, with sunlight streaming into the small church, Jeannie and Dennis Mitchell stood up before Mr. King. Though the day was unseasonably warm, Jeannie shivered faintly in her new white silk gown, made by Mama only weeks before her tragic death and never worn until today.

Ninette had supervised the decoration of the altar, with an array of ferns and ivy of varying shades of green. Now Ninette and a cluster of house servants stood, bright-eyed and expectant, at one side of the church while Mr. King read the marriage service. Kevin Ransome listened with an inscrutable smile on his face.

Plainly Mr. King was upset by the briefness of their courtship. He couldn't know, Jeannie thought, that this

44

was her salvation. At intervals, as Mr. King performed the ceremony, Jeannie's eyes stole to Dennis' calm, handsome face. How tender, how understanding he had been when he asked her to marry him! And he had made it so clear that he knew she must have time to grow to know him before he took her as his wife.

Tremulously Jeannie extended her hand for Dennis to slip on the ring that made her his wife. A servant had been sent all the way to Savannah to buy the simple wedding band.

"I now pronounce you man and wife." Mr. King's voice was strangely troubled, but he forced a smile.

"You are the most beautiful bride I have ever seen," Dennis said amorously, and kissed her on her cheek. Tears of happiness filled her eyes. *Her husband.*

"We will go to the house for champagne," Kevin Ransome said with rare high spirits. "I have brought it in from Savannah especially for this occasion."

Jeannie felt gay and carefree as they sat in the family parlor and drank champagne. Mr. King, as usual, was nervous about the time.

"I must leave," Mr. King said finally with an air of apology. "The fog is rolling in already. Jeannie, I hope you will be very happy in Charleston." But his eyes were uneasy when they rested on Dennis.

How absurd for Mr. King to worry! But then, he had no way of knowing that for her this marriage was a deliverance. Again guilt assaulted her. It was wrong to begin any marriage with deceit. But how could she talk to Dennis of her shame? Any man would run from her.

The newlyweds walked with Mr. King to the boat, then returned to the house for the early wedding supper Flora was waiting to serve. And after supper they went separately to their rooms.

In the morning a slave carried their portmanteaus to the schooner that would take them to Savannah. The Island, as was so often the case, was enshrouded in fog. But as they pulled away from shore, Jeannie could see the faint outline of her cousin, kneeling in the sand. She could hear his voice raised in tortured prayer.

Four

The Magnolias swept over four thousand acres, edging the river and moving back over flat gray fields. The house, tall, white, with triple-tiered galleries and a steep slate roof, was shaded by imposing, moss-draped live oaks, long-leaved pines, and exquisite glossy magnolia branches. The gardens, Craig Mitchell's admitted pride, extravagantly cared for by platoons of slaves, featured in season masses of azaleas, vast expanses of violets, roses, jasmine, honey-suckle, and gardenias.

In the rear parlor, with its azure blue window curtains, rich, gilt-ornamented blue wallpaper, and handsomely detailed Persian rug, Craig Mitchell stood by the mantel, straining to be patient as he talked to his wife. He ran one hand nervously through his prematurely white hair, so striking against his perpetual tan. He was still very handsome at forty-four, his body compact and muscular.

"Eleanor, try to understand what I'm telling you." His grip tightened on the sheet of paper in his hand. "By now Dennis is married. He's on his way home with his bride. He married a girl on Ransome Island."

"Craig, why are you so upset? Dennis is twenty-six years old." She smiled with the wistfulness that reminded him of the beautiful young widow he had pursued so amorously. At rare moments he saw the charm, the loveliness that had won him over twenty-three years ago, through features blurred by the years, eyes glazed over in the perpetual wine fog that had been her world for so long. Only the hair was unchanged. Silken, the color of winter moonlight. He remembered the first time he had seen her on the stage in Charleston. There had been something so appealing, so natural about her that he knew he would never be happy until he married her.

Remembering that girl, he felt an unexpected surge of passion. He had not touched his wife in fourteen years. Not since her fifth miscarriage. She had locked her door to him after that.

"Eleanor, don't you give a damn who Dennis married?" he demanded testily. "This is a girl whom Kevin Ransome took in when she was three, along with her mother, because there was nowhere else for them to go." He had hoped desperately that Dennis would marry well. And soon. He was just beginning to see daylight financially, but there was so much equipment in the mill that was faltering, that must be replaced. A bride from the proper family would have brought money with her. "Dennis married a poor relation," Craig said with a contempt he would not have used if he were not so painfully disappointed by this news. What did it matter that in twenty years she might own Ransome Island?

"You married an actress with no dowry," Eleanor reminded with a flicker of humor. But her hands were impatiently fondling the newest romantic novel that had come down to The Magnolias from the New York bookseller who supplied her regularly.

"That was different," Craig objected, faintly brusque. "I had no idea at the time that my father was already in financial troubles." It had been seven years later before he had killed himself in defeat. "I've been candid with Dennis. I'd hoped he would marry Rebecca Burke." Rebecca Burke was a beauty. Dennis had been a carefree bachelor long enough, had sown more than his share of wild oats. He frowned, remembering the scrapes from which he had extricated Dennis. Dennis had a predilection for involvement in bizarre affairs. Why couldn't he be content to marry Rebecca?

"If you had known your father was faced with financial difficulties, you would never have married me." Suddenly Eleanor was entirely lucid. "How you must regret having married me, Craig." Tears welled in her eyes.

"Eleanor, stop being melodramatic," he rebuked guiltily. "I still would have married you," he insisted. Leave it to Eleanor to pick up that slip. How many times had Eleanor put herself through these self-recriminations? He had been hopelessly in love with the twenty-year-old widow who struggled to support herself and her three-year-old son by appearing in small roles in a Charleston theater. His parents had carried on about his marrying an actress, when they had nurtured visions of a fine marriage for him; but he had been adamant. After their marriage he had been devoted to Dennis. Each time Eleanor suffered a miscarriage, he had moved closer to Dennis, until Dennis had become his own child.

When Dennis came home from Europe, just as Rebecca Burke came to visit her great-aunts at Burke Acres, Craig felt that fate was taking a hand. Charlotte Burke had hinted that Rebecca would be receptive to a marriage proposal. Unfortunately, he thought with grim humor, Dennis had that effect on many young ladies. That was why it surprised him to see such hostility between Dennis and Madeline.

"Craig, would you mind if I went up to my room?" Eleanor asked with the oddly deferential voice that infuriated him when he was not in tight control of himself. The voice that had entered their lives when they ceased to live together as man and wife. "I'm going to get a bad headache if I don't just sit down and read awhile. I have this new novel by Currer Bell." She smiled faintly. "It's supposed to be quite sensational."

"All right, Eleanor," he said tiredly. "Go on upstairs to your room and read."

Jeannie sat beside her husband at the long dining table, crowded with strangers, and tried not to show her dismay at dining at a public table. The cacophony of strange voices, the clatter of dishes were jarring to her after the quiet meals on Ransome Island. The dining room was well lighted, overly warm from the coal fire in the grate in the tall fireplace.

The hotel, Dennis had told her, was the finest in Savan-
  Her room, she conceded, was most comfortable, and

48

a maid would draw a warm bath for her when she returned from supper.

"The food here is quite good," Dennis said complacently. He seemed to enjoy the interest they were attracting among the other diners. The eyes of the women kept moving to him, Jeannie thought with pride. She was the envy of every one of them. "Are you enjoying your supper, Jeannie?" he asked with solicitude. Sensing her discomfort, she thought guiltily.

"Yes, it's exciting to be here," she stammered. Not to Dennis, surely, when he had dined in the most famous restaurants of Paris and London!

"We'll have plenty of time for breakfast in the morning," Dennis continued, his eyes moving about the table as he talked, "before we have to board the boat for Charleston. Papa will send a carriage into Charleston to pick us up on our arrival."

Did all these people suspect that they were newly married? Did the hotel manager think it was strange that they were occupying separate rooms? She would have her own room at The Magnolias. Suddenly the palms of her hands were perspiring. How could she have married Dennis under false pretenses? She wished with painful intensity that she could have been honest with him. But she had not dared. If she had not married Dennis, she would never have seen him again. She would have remained a prisoner on Ransome Island, perhaps forever.

"Jeannie, you're not eating," Dennis rebuked lightly. She colored beneath his gaze, believing completely in the sincerity of its ardor.

"I'm not accustomed to eating so heavily," she laughed. "All this food on the table!"

"We'll go up to our rooms soon." At once he was restless, bored with this company of strangers. "Let's get a decent night's rest. I doubt that we'll sleep much the two nights we'll be spending on the boat."

"Two nights?" Her eyes brightened. The journey would be a brief respite before she must come face to face with Dennis' family.

"It won't be a Collins ship," he warned. "Not even seaworthy. We have to follow the inner, slow route along the rivers. But it's better than waiting around in Savannah for another four days." All at once he was impatient to be back at The Magnolias. She saw the look in his eyes.

As soon as they had finished their coffee, Dennis rose from his chair with polite excuses and waited for Jeannie to rise to her feet. She stumbled in her nervousness, knowing that all eyes were upon them. For a moment Dennis' arms were about her, steadying her. Her heart pounded at his closeness. He was her husband. Her tender, understanding husband.

In her hotel bedroom, some of her earlier tension erased by the soothing effects of a warm bath, Jeannie lay against the pillows beneath a comforter that felt too warm at the moment. In a little while, she told herself, the fire in the grate would die out and she would appreciate this warmth.

She was living in a fairy tale, married to Dennis and going to live in the splendor of The Magnolias. But the fairy tale was marred by shadows. Dennis expected his wife to come to him untouched by any other man. So generously he had told her he would not rush her because of the shortness of their acquaintance.

After the horror of that night on Ransome Island, would she be able to receive her husband with wifely ardor? Or would she remember that other night and turn sick with disgust? What should be beautiful had become distasteful because of that brutal attack in the night. A new fear filled her. Was she capable of being a proper wife?

Should she go to Dennis and face him with the truth? Fleetingly she considered this. Her face was hot with confusion as she tried to frame the words in her mind. No! She did not dare take that chance. She must live the lie.

It would be different when Dennis came to take her as his wife. She would not turn sick with revulsion at the touch of his hands. She loved Dennis.

Mama, self-conscious but determined, had told her, when she was sixteen, what she must expect on her wedding night. Mama said that when you loved your husband, it could be beautiful to be submissive. But Cousin Kevin had robbed her of her wedding night. There could be only a pretense.

Tormented by fresh apprehension, Jeannie turned over on one side, away from the dying embers in the grate. Sleep, she willed herself. But sleep was slow in coming.

In midmorning, after a long breakfast—again at the public table which Jeannie found such a trial—they boarded the steamboat that was to carry them to Charleston. The ladies' cabin was so crowded with women and children, so shockingly small for the number it must accommodate, that Jeannie was certain she would not sleep a moment of their two nights aboard.

Her portmanteau stowed away in the ladies' cabin, Jeannie went above, intent on enjoying the view. Dennis was seated on deck, reading the Savannah newspaper he had picked up en route to the boat. He was polite but withdrawn. At his impersonal invitation she settled herself in the empty chair beside him.

The morning sun was rising high and warm, but the view that greeted her as the boat moved over the water was disappointing. The river was displeasingly muddy, the banks presenting a dismal display of yellow swamps and marshes. Here and there Jeannie spied an evergreen oak, the foliage dark and dingy, the leaves tiny and unappealing in form.

The day was monotonously repetitious, a tedious meandering over swollen waters, between low-lying swamps. The hazy afternoon sun soon gave way to fog, which slowed their progress. Dennis was irritated, oddly sullen. Suddenly he had become a stranger.

By the time night fell, the fog gave way to rain. It was necessary to cover the ladies' cabin against the weather. Jeannie was disconcerted to find the cabin too dark for reading. The night would be long and dull. When eventually she retired behind the fawn-colored curtains of her berth, she knew she would sleep little.

The second day and night on board the slow-moving steamboat differed little from the first. Jeannie was conscious of a growing apprehension in Dennis. She guessed that like her he was anxious about the confrontation with his family.

"You'll like Charleston," he said with an effort at throwing aside his somber mood when they sat down to tea. "It's probably the most cultured city in the South." He smiled teasingly, the potent Dennis Mitchell charm on display again. "There is even a large library, where you may borrow books."

He was talking compulsively, Jeannie thought sympathetically, because he was nervous about their arrival in the morning. But though he spoke in rich detail about Charleston, he said nothing about his family.

In the morning Jeannie was on deck early, eager for her first sight of Charleston. The Magnolias, Dennis had told her, was little more than an hour's drive from the city. Dennis said they would remain at the plantation during the hot summer unless he could persuade his father to buy or rent a house in Charleston for those months. Dennis was scornful of this family practice, though Jeannie was accustomed to remaining on Ransome Island the year around.

Most planters, Dennis told her with pent-up reproach, left their plantations for Charleston houses or for country houses for the summer months. Some even went all the way up to Newport or Saratoga. But Dennis was proud of the grandeur of The Magnolias. It was one of the great plantations of the state, he had said with pride.

"We'll be in sight of Charleston any minute now," Dennis said, startling her suddenly.

Her eyes swung to him. Her smile was short-lived, aborted by the anguish etched on his face. His eyes were pained. He was impatient to return to The Magnolias, and simultaneously he dreaded it. Was it because of her? she asked herself with rising panic. Was Dennis already regretting their marriage?

Suddenly the deck was full of passengers. An air of excitement engulfed everyone. Dennis forced himself out of his heavy introspection.

"Charleston lies on a peninsula where the Ashley and Cooper rivers come together to form a harbor. Folks like to joke and say they come together to form the Atlantic

Ocean. Actually the Atlantic is seven and a half miles out, but the harbor channel is thirty-five feet deep at low water."

"Oceangoing steamers come into Charleston, don't they?" Jeannie asked curiously.

"Oh, yes. Charleston is a shorter ocean haul to the main ports of the world than any other Atlantic or Gulf port."

As they approached the harbor, Jeannie avidly inspected the shore around the bay, covered with dark gray cedar woods.

"The seawall there was built after the hurricane of 1804," Dennis told her—as though he were performing a duty, she thought unhappily. "It's made of stone."

But her spirits soared as they slid into the Charleston harbor. From a forest of vessels, flags of many nations floated in the mild breeze. There were German, French, British, and an occasional Spanish or Portuguese flag, in addition to the abundance of American flags. The vigorous, sometimes ribald conversations that ricocheted through the sunlit morning were multilingual. Everywhere cotton and rice were being loaded aboard outgoing ships. A stimulating air of vitality permeated the atmosphere.

"The first cotton that was ever shipped to Europe came from Charleston in 1784," Dennis said with a determined calm that belied the restlessness—no, the anger—in his eyes. Was he angry with her?

Together they went ashore.

"The bay," Dennis said, glancing about as though seeing it for the first time, "is a colorful neighborhood, isn't it?"

"Oh yes, Dennis!" She would have agreed to anything he said.

A carriage with an ornate coat of arms was waiting for them. The coachman, at the sight of Dennis, jumped down with alacrity and moved toward them with a broad, toothless grin.

"Mist' Dennis, sho' good to see yo' home again," he said with an air of genuine affection.

"Thank you, Plato." Dennis smiled faintly at Jeannie's amusement at this high-sounding name. "Drive us through town, please, so that my wife can see a bit of Charleston."

"Yessuh!"

Plato nodded vigorously, but he seemed abashed in her presence, Jeannie thought. Why had Dennis not introduced her to Plato? It would have been the polite thing to do.

As Dennis helped her into the carriage she felt herself aglow with pleasure. And each time Dennis referred to her as "my wife" her feeling was reinforced. How had Dennis' parents received the news that he had taken himself a wife, on such short acquaintanceship? Recurrently this troubled her.

Jeannie glanced avidly out the carriage window while Dennis carried on a running commentary. At the same time she fought to push down the fears that invaded her at the prospect of meeting Dennis' parents.

They were leaving behind them the tumbledown streets of warehouses that were close to the wharves. Here the streets were lined with trees. People swarmed everywhere. Two-thirds of them were Negroes or mulattoes, the women wearing picturesque, bright-colored kerchiefs about their hair. Large flocks of turkey buzzards stalked about in search of food. How brazen they were, Jeannie marveled, forcing people to walk around them. They sat in rows on the roofs and chimneys, stretching their heavy wings in the morning sunlight.

"Why are there so many turkey buzzards?" she asked Dennis in amused protest.

"They're considered city scavengers," he explained. "By law they can't be killed."

The town seemed like an imposing assemblage of elegant country houses, each with magnificent gardens. In addition to many classically beautiful Georgian houses, there were houses of pastel-tinted stucco or brick with iron balconies and tile roofs.

"Charleston reminds me of some of the country towns I saw when I was in England," Dennis said, lighting one of his cigars. Cousin Kevin too had favored cigars, smoking them inside the house, which had delighted his business visitors whose wives forbade such doings within their houses. "Occasionally there were parties at country estates." His face tightened again, strangely. He was shutting her out.

Jeannie, squinting in thought, forced a smile. "I think the houses here follow the lines of the London Sir Christopher Wren reconstructed after the Great Fire of 1666." Dennis turned to her with a look of astonishment. "I read much about architecture at Ransome Island," she explained with sudden shyness. "There was little to do but read."

"Then you'll appreciate old St. Michael's," he said dryly, pointing to the aristocratic white-spired church before them. "It was completed in 1761, I understand," he said with an effort at humor, "and it staggered visiting colonials."

"It reminds me," Jeannie said softly, "of St. Michaels-in-the-Fields in London. I've seen drawings," she said quickly because Dennis was staring at her—again, so oddly. She must talk less of what she had read. This knowledge was displeasing to Dennis. It seemed unwomanly.

"You and Papa will hit it off fine," Dennis guessed with an ironic smile. "Papa always has his nose in a book, when he isn't in the fields or the mill. Mama too," he added, but his eyes were opaque. "Mama favors the romantic novels." His voice showed contempt for this diversion.

They drove beyond the city limits on a dusty, sandy road. The country was flat as far as Jeannie could see, except for occasional plantations of trees and awesome forest tracts. The scent of the sea followed them.

Dennis retreated into a grim silence, his eyes focused unseeingly on the road before them. Jeannie's throat tightened. Her hands lay in her lap, clasped in painful tension. In a little while she would be standing face to face with Dennis' father and mother. She *must* make them like her. She must make them pleased that Dennis had married her.

Each mile seemed to drag endlessly as the horses moved along the sandy road. Jeannie sat motionless, a small set smile on her face. Dennis had spoken so little of his parents, she thought with rising panic. She was not prepared to meet them. She didn't know what to expect of them. And there were his cousin Ron and Ron's wife, Madeline. Would they all be angry that he had chosen to marry without their approval and their attendance at the wedding? Would it be enough to explain that her mother was so briefly dead that a fancy wedding would have been unseemly?

"We'll be turning into the private road to The Magnolias in a few minutes," Dennis interrupted the heavy silence between them.

Jeannie leaned forward, gazing fixedly out the carriage window, waiting with a blend of eagerness and terror for her first view of the house.

"In another month the flowers will be blooming. Everything will be coming alive after the winter months. That's when you can really appreciate The Magnolias," Dennis said, straining to be enthusiastic.

And then the house rose before her. Jeannie's eyes lighted with admiration. The tall, white, triple-galleried mansion was so elegant, so impressive! Far larger than the house on Ransome Island. A pack of beagles pranced about the lawn before the house, barking jubilantly at the approach of the carriage.

"We're overrun with beagles," Dennis warned. "Papa doesn't hunt, but he likes to keep dogs around the place."

As the carriage pulled to a stop before the house, the front door was flung wide. A tall black man garbed in cast-off finery hurried across the gallery with a wide, welcoming smile.

"Jeffrey, yo' lazy boy!" he called to someone out of Jeannie's line of vision. "Git yo'se'f ovuh deah and open dat carriage do'. De Young Mastuh done come home wit' his lady!"

A small boy about ten, grinning broadly, pulled open the carriage door. Dennis stepped down, then reached up to help Jeannie. Her heart was pounding furiously. She knew, at first sight of the house, that she was embarking on a life far different from the austerity of Ransome Island.

"Is my father home, Gilbert?" Dennis asked self-consciously. He was hoping this encounter might be postponed, Jeannie interpreted.

"Yessuh. He settin' wit' yo' Mama in de front pahluh."

Dennis placed his arm reassuringly at Jeannie's waist as he guided her into the front parlor. She was conscious of an assortment of magnificent antiques, Kirman rugs, crystal wall sconces.

Craig Mitchell, scrupulously courteous, came forward to meet his new daughter-in-law. He was making all the perfunctory reproaches about having denied them a wedding at The Magnolias, which Dennis had warned her to expect. What was he thinking behind that handsome, impassive face? Jeannie asked herself unhappily. It was impossible to guess.

"Eleanor!" Craig called sharply over his shoulder. "Eleanor, Dennis and his bride are here." He turned to Jeannie with a smile of apology. "She's gone into the library for a book."

A moment later a small, still-pretty woman emerged from the library door, a book in one hand.

"Dennis! Oh, Dennis, I've missed you so!" Her face lighted with joy at the sight of him.

They embraced, and Dennis reached out to draw Jeannie closer.

"Mama," he said lightly, "let me introduce my bride."

"Dennis, she's lovely," his mother said with a quick, warm smile, but her eyes looked troubled. "Did you have a good trip?"

"Dull as always," Dennis said dryly. "You can't travel well in this country."

"A snob because you've lived in Europe for seven months," Craig Mitchell taunted with an effort at humor. But he was unhappy about this marriage, Jeannie guessed. Could she expect him to feel otherwise? "But why do we stand around this way? Sit down. I'll ring for someone to bring us coffee." He crossed to tug at the bell rope. Eleanor Mitchell seemed faintly disconcerted. Customarily it would be the mistress of the house who would perform this small duty.

"I see you're reading Mr. Currer Bell's book," Jeannie said quickly, turning to Eleanor Mitchell to break the sudden, pained silence that had enveloped the four of them. "Isn't it fascinating?"

Eleanor's eyes lighted.

"I've just begun to read it. I'm sure I'm going to enjoy it."

"I've just finished another wonderful novel." Self-confidence returned to Jeannie in the face of Eleanor Mitchell's wistful nervousness. "It's called *Wuthering Heights*. I understand it's nowhere as popular as *Jane Eyre*, but I'm sure it will be someday."

"Uncle Craig, I have those figures . . ." The young man in the doorway stopped in apology. He was almost as tall as Dennis. Dark-haired, dark-eyed, highly pleasing in appearance. "Excuse me. I didn't know Dennis and his wife had arrived." He smiled with a warmth that Jeannie found endearing. Oh, yes, she liked Dennis' cousin on sight!

"Why are you so damn formal?" Dennis drawled. "Come here and meet my Jeannie." He turned to her with a glint of mockery in his eyes. "Don't mind Ron. He's so involved in raising and milling rice that he forgets the social graces."

"Dennis, you're always teasing Ron," Eleanor protested, but her eyes shone with love for her son. Why was she so ill at ease? Jeannie wondered with a rush of sympathy.

Craig Mitchell insisted that Ron join them for coffee. Ron made conversation less strained, Jeannie thought with relief. She was conscious of the covert scrutiny of Craig Mitchell and Eleanor Mitchell, but talking with Ron she could pretend to be unaware of it. Dennis had slumped into a somber, almost angry silence. His eyes moved constantly toward the double doorway to the parlor. He was waiting for someone. Without knowing why, Jeannie was disturbed.

Suddenly Ron stopped talking in the middle of a sentence. Jeannie followed his gaze to the door. A young woman paused in the entrance to the parlor. She was tall and strikingly beautiful. Her hair was near-black, eyes a shining amber, skin soft ivory. She moved into the room with a provocative awareness. The atmosphere became electric.

"Why didn't someone come to tell me Dennis had arrived with his bride?" she demanded with a brilliant smile, but her eyes were hostile. "Nobody ever tells me anything in this house."

"Madeline," Ron said tersely, "you forget yourself."

"So you're Jeannie." Madeline walked up to Jeannie and inspected her with such thoroughness that Jeannie blushed. How gauche she felt beside Ron's beautiful young wife! "How did a slip of a girl from one of the Sea Islands manage to entrap the most eligible bachelor in Charleston County?" Madeline drawled, her eyes saying she found this slip of a girl blatantly inadequate. "Every girl in the County has tried to marry Dennis since he was twenty. Tell me, Jeannie," she coaxed with deceptive sweetness, "how did you pull this off?"

The air was laced with ugly undertones. Jeannie was conscious of Ron's agonized discomfort, Craig's suppressed indignation, the vague unease of Eleanor.

"Dennis and I were married because we love each other," Jeannie said with quiet conviction, turning her eyes to Dennis for confirmation.

Suddenly Jeannie was encased in ice. Her eyes clung to Dennis' face. He was gazing at Madeline with indecently naked desire.

Why had Dennis married her? Why had he brought her to The Magnolias? He was a captive of the seductive beauty of his cousin's wife. He was bewitched by Madeline Mitchell.

Five

Madeline, her face hot with rage, stalked up the flights of stairs that led to her mother's suite on the third floor. The suite had been provided with true Southern grace by Craig Mitchell out of deference to her mother's "delicate health." Mama, Madeline thought with bitter-edged amusement, would probably live to ninety; but her frequent spells of nerves allowed her "invalid" status. Mama didn't set well with Craig Mitchell, but he was too polite to show it. The private suite kept her out of his sight for what he must consider gratifying intervals.

"Suzette, I don't know why that shop up in New York is taking so long to send those creams I ordered," Mavis was complaining querulously as Madeline flung open the door to the suite and crossed the sitting room, furnished with much of the frippery that had been part of their ultrafeminine Paris flat. She paused in the doorway to the bedroom. Her mother sat before a Louis XVI marquetry *poudreuse*, oblivious—for the moment—of her daughter's presence. Her hair was dyed a harsh, unbecoming black, worn in a fashion slavishly copied from a Parisian magazine and suited to a woman half her age. Her small, pale features were powdered a dead white. She squinted nearsightedly with fading hazel eyes at her reflection in the mirror, unable to see the sagging flesh, the uncompromising lines. "Suzette," she prodded plaintively, "am I beginning to look old?"

"Oh, no, Madame. Yo' ver' prettee. Bee-utiful," young, golden-skinned Suzette emphasized reassuringly, her accent a mixture of Deep South and West Indies. Mavis had taught Suzette to call her Madame.

"Mama, you are so vain!" Madeline reproached with a flicker of impatience.

Mavis started, then turned her head with an awkward movement.

"Madeline, you might at least knock."

"Suzette, get out of here," Madeline ordered imperiously. "Wait in the hall until I call you."

Fleetingly Madeline saw the glint of hostility in Suzette's eyes before the girl decorously lowered them. Arrogant little slut, Madeline thought. But she kept herself in line because she didn't want to be sent out to the fields.

"Madeline, why are you so upset?" Mavis asked petulantly when they were alone. She reached for a bottle of perfume and touched the stopper behind her earlobes.

"Dennis is home. With his bride." Madeline's eyes flashed with fury. "You know why he married her, Mama! To spite me! It kills him that *I'm* a Mitchell now. So he brought home a wife to put me in my place!"

"Madeline, you behave yourself," Mavis warned nervously. "You be nice to that girl."

"I had just about prodded Mr. Mitchell to the point where he was going to let me give some parties. I was going to make The Magnolias come alive again. But now Dennis' wife," Madeline said with contempt, "will be the one to make social decisions. She'll rule it over all of us. Wait and see, Mama."

"I think Craig hoped that Dennis would marry that grandniece of Emmaline and Charlotte Burke," Mavis said with an air of secrecy. "He said she was quite beautiful, and the Burkes are one of the best families around Charleston. Arnold told you, didn't he, that Dennis was there twice before he went down to Ransome Island?"

"And Rebecca was over here once." Madeline frowned with distaste. "So in his mind Mr. Mitchell had Dennis and Rebecca already married. Rebecca's family will inherit Burke Acres when the old ladies die—that's what Mr. Mitchell was thinking about," Madeline guessed maliciously.

"Madeline, you behave yourself," Mavis reiterated,

watching her uneasily. "You did right well, marrying Ron. We've got ourselves a fine home here."

"I am bored to death here, Mama!" Madeline's eyes glowed with restlessness. How could Mama bear living in this deadly dull house after all the years in Paris? Even Charleston, where they had been ignored by the rich families Mama sought to cultivate, had been amusing when they became involved with the theater people as they had in Paris. For a little while, she thought with nostalgia, when they had their tiny town house—before Mama lost it at the gaming rooms—it was almost as though they had their own salon.

"Madeline, you just stop being bored," her mother ordered flatly. "Ron's a fine husband. We're living well."

"Well?" Madeline exploded. "When Mr. Mitchell won't even move the family into Charleston or to the seashore for the hot months the way all civilized planters do?" She sighed impatiently. "I'm going to my room to lie down. I doubt that I'll be downstairs for dinner."

In the hall Madeline ordered Suzette back into her mother's suite, then hurried down the stairs to her own room. Before her door she paused, then crossed to the landing. She heard Arnold in the foyer below, talking to Plato.

"It's all right, Plato," she called down. "Let Arnold come upstairs." It annoyed Plato that Arnold had the run of the house. Plato was afraid of him because he was like a little boy in his mind, though his body was that of a big, burly man. Arnold adored her, she thought complacently, though she suspected Miss Emmaline and Miss Charlotte disapproved of her friendship with their nephew. "Arnold, come on up," she invited with the show of charm she might have presented, before her marriage, to a wealthy prospective suitor.

"I brought over my collection of pressed roses," Arnold said eagerly. His gray eyes were bright with pleasure as he plodded up the stairs. "I want to show them to you."

Arnold hated Rebecca, Madeline remembered with childish satisfaction. In a moment of pique Rebecca had destroyed his honeysuckle collection. Rebecca was going to be furious when she discovered that Dennis was married. He had married a girl named Jeannie Fleming, she thought vindictively, but he desired Madeline Beauchamp Mitchell. Anytime she decided she wanted him, she could take him from Jeannie Fleming.

Jeannie sat in a chair by the window, watching while Aunt Lizzie, the elderly slave who was so plainly delighted with her new young mistress, hung away the contents of the portmanteau that lay across the bed. Jeannie gazed with a recurrent sense of loss at the pretty dresses, so lovingly sewed for her by Mama, who had had such a flair for dressmaking. Mama would be happy, wouldn't she, with this marriage? Dennis was so handsome, so charming.

Unwarily she visualized that painfully revealing moment when Dennis' eyes had rested nakedly on Madeline. Could she have misread what she saw there? Please God, let her be wrong!

She forced herself to inspect the large, square, high-ceilinged, multiwindowed room. How different it was from the barrenness of her room at Ransome Island. The wallpaper was a sunlit yellow with blue flowers. The four-poster bed was delicately canopied in a crisp sheer white that matched the window curtains. The furniture was classically beautiful Hepplewhite. An upholstered easy chair, repeating the blue flowers of the wallpaper, sat invitingly before the low-manteled fireplace.

"Mist' Dennis, he sho' lucky to fin' hisse'f a pow'ful pretty young lady lak yo', Young Missy," Aunt Lizzie crowed. "Ah knowed someday he'd git hisse'f married to somebody mighty fine."

"Do you remember him when he was little, Aunt Lizzie?" Jeannie asked shyly.

"Oh, Young Missy, Ah been heah at de Magnolias since Ah was bo'n," she said solemnly. "Ah 'membuh when Missis come heah wit' her li'l boy to marry de Mastuh. Dat chile, he was so handsome," she clucked admiringly.

Jeannie stared at Aunt Lizzie in astonishment. Then Mr. Mitchell was not Dennis' father. How strange that Dennis had said nothing of this to her. But probably, she told herself guiltily, Dennis felt that Mr. Mitchell *was* his father after all these years. Why should he mention this to her?

Mr. Mitchell was a charming, courteous gentleman, Jeannie conceded; but he was unhappy that Dennis had married her. It would take time to make him believe that this was the right marriage for Dennis; but she would convince him, Jeannie resolved. She must make a friend of Dennis' mother. Instinctively, even then, she sensed how desperately she was going to need a friend in this awesome house.

They had eaten their second breakfast downstairs with the family. She would remain in her room until someone came to summon her to dinner. Mr. Mitchell had said they sat down to the main meal at three. She inspected the Gothic-styled clock that sat atop the mantel. Almost two hours before she would be going downstairs. She wished, wistfully, for the extensive library that had been at her disposal at Ransome Island.

Her thoughts wandered again to Madeline. Dennis was drawn to his cousin's wife against his will. If she were one to harbor superstitions—which she was not—she would believe that Madeline had cast a spell over Dennis. He didn't *want* to feel that way about Madeline. Away from her, he had been so flatteringly attentive. Jeannie trembled with pleasurable recall.

She was Dennis' wife, she told herself firmly. He loved her. She closed her eyes, reliving those moments when they had stood together before Mr. King. Somehow, she must make Dennis forget Madeline.

Jeannie sat with a faint smile on her face, grateful for Aunt Lizzie's good-humored chatter. Outside, a dog barked. She left the chair to go out onto the upstairs gallery and crossed to the railing to look below. A pair of silken-red Irish setters romped beside Madeline as she talked to a man preparing to mount a horse. Something about the man's face captured her attention. Unintentionally she listened to what he was saying to Madeline.

"You're nice. I always tell Aunt Emmaline how nice you are." His face was suddenly stern. "Not like Rebecca.

I don't like her. I hope she goes home soon."

He was what Mama had called one of the "special ones," Jeannie thought tenderly. Gentle and loving, but not quite "right."

"You tell Miss Emmaline that Dennis came home with a bride, do you hear?" Madeline exhorted with a beguiling smile. "And you make sure Rebecca knows about it. I don't think she's going to like that one little bit."

Guiltily Jeannie swung away from the railing and hurried back into the bedroom.

"Young Missy, yo' lay down an' res' befo' dinnuh," Aunt Lizzie ordered. "Ah'll bring up de smoothin' iron to press a dress fo' yo' to weah down to dinnuh."

Obediently Jeannie stretched out on the bed and allowed Aunt Lizzie to cover her with a comforter, knowing she would not sleep. How could she sleep when in a little while she would have to go downstairs to face the family again? She would have to sit at the table and pretend she was unaware of the anger in her father-in-law, of Madeline's seething contempt for her.

"Aunt Lizzie," Jeannie asked compulsively, "how long have Miss Madeline and Mr. Ron been married?"

"Now, lemme figuh dat out." Aunt Lizzie squinted in thought. "Ah guess 'bout fo' months now." Her face was suddenly stern. "He one fine man, Mist' Ron." Obviously Aunt Lizzie disapproved of Madeline.

Dennis could not have known Madeline long, Jeannie realized with astonishment. He said he'd been home from Europe only two weeks when his father had sent him to Ransome Island. Or had Dennis known Madeline *before* she married Ron? The question nagged at her mind.

Jeannie was relieved when a servant came to her room to call her downstairs for dinner. She needed the reassurance of Dennis' presence. Yet here at The Magnolias, she acknowledged somberly, Dennis seemed almost a stranger.

In the comfortably large, heavily beamed family dining room Craig and Eleanor Mitchell sat at opposite ends of the long, linen-covered table, above which hung a Louis XV chandelier, and on which sat four gleaming Queen Anne candlesticks. Lovely Windsor chairs surrounded the table. A gleaming mahogany sideboard graced one wall, and over the fireplace hung a collection of "Queen's Ware" Wedgwood plates.

Dennis stood at a window, seemingly absorbed in some outdoor sight. Eleanor smiled with an uncertain warmth as Jeannie hovered in the doorway.

"Come sit here next to me, Jeannie," she encouraged. "The others will be here in a few moments, I'm sure. Dennis"—her voice was faintly sharp—"do come to the table."

With a small fixed smile on her face, determined not to be intimidated by the family, Jeannie sat in the chair beside Eleanor Mitchell. She was starkly conscious of undercurrents of tension in the room, created by her arrival with Dennis. Dennis took the chair across from her, on his mother's left. His face was defiant, moody.

"You were right about *Jane Eyre*," Eleanor said to Jeannie with determined cordiality, after a defensive glance at her husband. "I find it a fascinating book."

For a few moments Eleanor and Jeannie discussed the novel; and then, almost simultaneously, Ron and Mavis arrived in the dining room. Stiffly Craig introduced Jeannie to Mavis as the new arrivals seated themselves at the table.

"Madeline told me you were pretty," Mavis gushed, but her eyes were cautious. "Oh, she won't be down to dinner." Mavis turned to include Ron in this announcement. "She has another of her migraines." This, Jeannie interpreted, meant that Madeline was suffering one of her temper tantrums.

"She'll be down to tea," Ron prophesied with a forced smile. But his eyes were unhappy, Jeannie thought. That must be a stormy marriage.

"Gilbert," Craig called to the dignified black man in frayed finery who waited at attention at the doorway, "please tell Juno to send in dinner."

Jeannie was intrigued by the superabundance of food served at dinner, as much as would have been served at Ransome Island in two weeks of dinners. Much, she realized, would go back to the kitchen. Two kinds of meat, chicken, sweet potatoes, cranberries, hominy, maize bread, and, of course, rice. Dinner was served by Plato and a tall, slender, golden-skinned young woman whom Mr. Mitchell referred to as Carlotta.

"Who set the table?" Dennis demanded abruptly.

"Ah did, suh," Carlotta said softly.

"This fork is dirty!" he said brusquely. "Can't you at least set a table properly?"

"Ah'm sorry, suh." Pinkness stained Carlotta's golden cheekbones. "Ah'll bring yo' anothuh."

"Next time you won't get off so lightly," Dennis warned as Carlotta turned to leave the room, and his father's face tightened.

"Dennis, don't use that tone when you talk to the servants," Craig reprimanded when Carlotta was beyond hearing.

"Oh, Papa," Dennis said with irritation. "You spoil them all."

"Carlotta is very conscientious," Craig said sternly. "She takes pride in doing things well."

"Papa, don't tell us again about how Carlotta's grandmother was an African princess," Dennis said with an effort at humor.

"It's true enough," Ron shot back. Jeannie sensed the unspoken hostility between Ron and Dennis. "We've got papers to prove it."

"Oh, here comes the abolitionist again," Dennis drawled.

Jeannie lowered her eyes, uncomfortable with this Dennis who was a stranger to her. How could he have humiliated Carlotta that way? For no good reason, she guessed; and instantly she felt guilty. Dennis was her husband; she must respect what he had to say.

"Was it lonely living on Ransome Island?" Mavis asked Jeannie, eager to break the awkward silence that engulfed those at the table. "I believe Mr. Mitchell said there was only one plantation on the whole island." Her eyes rested on Craig with unbecoming coyness for a moment.

"Ransome Island is one plantation," Jeannie confirmed with a flicker of compassion for Madeline's mother. There was such a frightened, insecure expression on her faintly grotesque face. "It was lonely, of course, but I read a lot." She took a deep breath, hating to remember Ransome Island. "My cousin has an excellent library. It's supposed to be one of the finest in the state. He had been a schoolmaster. He tutored me rather extensively."

"What did you study?" Reluctantly, it seemed to Jeannie, Craig was drawn into the discussion.

"Mathematics, Latin, French, German, the classics," Jeannie said seriously. "I read Schiller and Carlyle with Cousin Kevin." Suddenly she was self-conscious. Dennis was frowning in irritation. She had forgotten herself for a moment. Dennis found this learning distasteful. But Mr. Mitchell—and Ron—looked upon her with admiration.

"Did you read Schiller in the German?" Ron asked, his face alight with interest.

"Yes," Jeannie said softly. "I read the plays. I so admired his attacks on tyranny, his pleas for human freedom and dignity."

"Schiller inspired the revolutionary movements that broke out in Germany last year," Ron started somberly, but he was interrupted by Madeline's imperious voice: "I have decided to join you for dinner. My headache seems to have gone." She paused there, her eyes surveying those at the table. Her dress was of ivory silk, showing too much of her bosom and shoulders. It might have been fashionable in Paris. At a plantation in South Carolina, Jeannie thought, it was a shocking display.

"Sit down, Madeline," Mavis said sharply, embarrassed that Madeline showed herself this way. A trace of painful color showed itself along the high cheekbones of Ron's face. His wife's appearance disconcerted him. For a loaded instant Madeline's eyes clashed with Dennis'. They might have been alone at the table.

"Ron . . ." All at once Madeline was exuding a potent charm. "Now that Dennis has brought home a bride, the four of us must do some socializing. There's a fine theater in Charleston, Jeannie." She focused her charm on Jeannie now. "You know, don't you, that Dennis' mother once acted with a Charleston theater company."

"No, I didn't." Jeannie smiled brilliantly, turning to her mother-in-law. But Eleanor's face was white with dismay, her eyes fastened to her plate. "I've never been to the theater," Jeannie acknowledged with candor, "but my mother talked about the marvelous plays she had seen as a girl in New Orleans."

"The racing season in Charleston is exciting," Madeline continued with defiant high spirits. "Then there's the Charleston Carnival, the Dancing Assemblies, the Jockey Ball, and of course, the St. Cecilias. Oh, but we can't go to the St. Cecilias, can we?" Madeline's eyes were deceptively innocent, her smile ingenuously apologetic. "Because of Mrs. Mitchell. The people who organize the St. Cecilias don't allow actors or actresses or their families to attend."

"Was your mother French?" Mavis asked Jeannie nervously, abandoning all pretense of eating. "You said she was from New Orleans."

"Mama, not everybody from New Orleans is French," Madeline said with an air of condescension.

"I had a French grandmother," Jeannie said quietly. "She died before I was born."

"Would you please excuse me?" Dennis said abruptly, pushing back his chair.

"Dennis, we are still at dinner," his mother protested.

"I've lost my appetite." His eyes focused on Madeline for a barely perceptible moment. "And I must go into Charleston. I've just realized I left a package on board the boat. It doesn't leave port again until morning."

Dennis was lying, Jeannie knew unhappily. Why was it so important for him to go into Charleston when they had just arrived from there a few hours ago?

"Will you be back for tea?" Eleanor asked with a troubled smile.

"Don't expect me," Dennis said calmly. "If I find I'm hungry, I'll stop by Eliza Lee's for tea. That's a restaurant in Charleston," he said, turning to Jeannie with a smile. She felt herself grow warm beneath the unexpected ardor in his gaze. "I'll take you there someday."

Jeannie sat in a rocker on the gallery in the deepening dusk. Fog was rolling in from the river, lending an eerie atmosphere to the landscape, isolating the house from the rest of the plantation. The moss-draped live oaks, the pines, and the magnolias towered high into the night sky, seeming to be rootless as the fog moved inexorably toward the gallery.

It would be difficult for the horses tonight, Jeannie thought uneasily, in all this fog. The road from Charleston lay close to the river. She shivered, then reined in her imagination, which could be so vivid. *Nothing was going to happen to Dennis.* The coachman was thoroughly familiar with the road.

Somewhere, behind that ominous fog, a ship's horn sounded plaintively. In the distance dogs howled in response. Inside the house, servants were lighting lamps in the rooms on the lower floor. In a little while one of them would summon her to tea. Mrs. Mitchell had explained that they had their tea in the dining room, rather than on small tables in the parlor, as was the fashion in the big houses in Charleston.

An uneasy stillness engulfed her. Since they had arrived at The Magnolias, a wall had arisen between her and Dennis. He looked at her without seeing her. And yet, she remembered, for a moment before he took off again for Charleston, he had looked at her with the ardor he had shown as they traveled from Ransome Island to Charleston. She must be patient with Dennis.

"Jeannie . . ."

She started at the sound of Craig Mitchell's voice coming to her from the open doorway.

"Good evening, Mr. Mitchell," she said politely.

"Jeannie," he said seriously, "I'd like to talk to you."

"Of course, Mr. Mitchell." Her heart was suddenly thumping. He wanted to talk to her about her marriage to Dennis, she guessed.

She sat upright in the rocker while Dennis' father seated himself beside her. Did Mr. Mitchell think her an opportunist who had snatched at his son to better her station in life? Marriage was an escape from Ransome Island, yes; but she loved Dennis.

"Jeannie," he said gently, "how did you allow yourself to be pushed into marriage so swiftly? I'm sure it was Dennis' doing," he added as she sought for words of protest. "Dennis can be unbelievably persuasive when he

70

wishes to be." His eyes were bitterly reminiscent. "But it wasn't fair to do this to you. You're too fine, too sweet."

"Dennis and I might never have seen each other again," Jeannie stammered. "I wanted to marry him. I wanted that very much."

"I know." His smile was infinitely gentle. "Dennis can be devastatingly charming." He paused, searching for words that would be less than painful to her. "Jeannie, I must be honest," he said finally. "I distrust Dennis' motives in marrying you. Oh, you're a very beautiful young lady," he added quickly with an air of apology. "You're intelligent and well read. But not at all Dennis' sort of girl. I wish you were," he admitted, almost wistfully.

"Mr. Mitchell, how can you say who is Dennis' sort of girl?" she rebuked softly. "We saw each other and something happened between us. Right away it happened." Her eyes glowed as she visualized those first encounters. And then Madeline's face intruded. No, don't think about Dennis and Madeline. She could have been wrong in what she saw. "After all, aren't you making a hasty judgment, Mr. Mitchell?" She strove for a touch of humor. "Dennis and I have been married only a few days—"

"Did Dennis tell you I'm his stepfather?"

"He didn't tell me," Jeannie acknowledged, "but I know."

"Somewhere along the line I must have failed him." He sighed heavily. "I worry about Dennis. Jeannie . . ." He leaned forward urgently, his eyes holding hers. "Leave Dennis before you're hurt. Before this marriage explodes into a catastrophe that will engulf all of us."

Color rose in Jeannie's face. He knew about Madeline. He was terrified of Dennis' feelings for Ron's wife. But how could he ask her to walk out on her marriage? That was not fair to Dennis or to her.

"I can't do that, Mr. Mitchell." Jeannie struggled to keep her voice even.

"I'll help you arrange for a divorce and see that you have enough money on which to live until we can find you a suitable position," he pursued earnestly. "With your education, despite your youngness, you could be a tutor—"

"I won't leave Dennis." Despite her efforts, her voice trembled. "I'm his wife. I love him."

"Dennis doesn't deserve you." Craig's face was anguished. "I love him like my own son, but I know him, Jeannie. He'll make your life miserable!"

"I can't leave," she whispered. She would never leave Dennis, unless Dennis himself asked that of her. "I'm sorry, Mr. Mitchell."

Craig gazed intently at her, sighed, and rose tiredly to his feet.

"God help you, Jeannie. God help all of us."

Six

Slouched on the carriage seat, Dennis stifled a yawn as the horses trotted up the roadway to the house, fog rolling in on all sides. The house was dark except for a lighted room on the third floor. Mavis stayed up till all hours. How did she stand staying here constantly at The Magnolias, never going into Charleston? Like him, the old lady had a yen for the gambling tables. One of these days, he promised himself with amusement, he would take Mavis to André Genet's gaming rooms. Madeline would be mad enough to kill him.

Hell, he had had rotten luck tonight at Joe's. He hated that low-class gaming room, favored by the sailors who came into port; but Joe extended him credit. Genet trusted nobody. He always had bad luck at poker. Why couldn't he learn to stay away?

He had gone through what little cash he had had left over from his trip to Ransome Island. Tomorrow he would go over and visit Emmaline, taking along the perfume he had bought in Paris for Emmaline and Charlotte and had forgotten to give them. When he had returned from Europe and walked into the house to see Madeline set up there, he had forgotten everything. Fresh frustration soared in him. *How had she done it?* But that was why she and Mavis had settled in Charleston—so that Madeline could marry into a rich plantation family.

Madeline had married Ron to become a Mitchell. By now, he thought with bitter humor, Madeline must know that Ron didn't have a cent of his own. Only what he earned as Papa's employee. It must stick in Ron's craw to remember how his father had lost their own plantation, switching from rice to sugar cane, just months before he died. He had been seventeen, Dennis remembered, Ron fourteen, when Papa brought his nephew to live at The Magnolias.

Ron had had no right to marry Madeline. He was a Mitchell. He should have shown more respect for the family name. He would have been welcomed by the best families in South Carolina, even without money.

When the carriage pulled to a stop before the house, Jasper jumped down to open the door for him. Jasper liked being his man. Jasper had a black bitch in Charleston that he managed to see each time they went into the city. Dennis chuckled.

"Good night, Jasper," he said briskly. "I won't need you anymore."

He pulled open the front door, never locked, and walked into the night-dark foyer. He walked up the stairs, past his father's room and Jeannie's room, to his own room just beyond. A hand on his doorknob, he paused at the sound of a door closing on the floor above.

Suzette's tall, slim figure moved into view. He waited, watching the conscious undulation of her provocative body beneath the single garment she wore. She preened as she moved down the carpeted stairs, aware of his presence.

"Evenin'," Suzette said decorously as she approached

him. "Madame wants some coffee. Ah go make it." Her eyes were brightly admiring. Suzette had been brought from the laundry rooms to be Mavis' maid. Dennis had never noticed her until he returned from Europe.

"How long will you be?" Dennis' eyes focused on the high, full breasts beneath her thin cotton dress.

"It'll be a spell fo' she goes to sleep." Suzette's eyes were wise now. Anticipatory.

"Come to my room when you're done," he said brusquely. "I've got something pretty for you."

He let himself into the room. A fire smoldered in the grate. He reached for a log and dropped it into place, enjoying the small business of coaxing it into a blaze. He stripped to the skin, admiring his reflection in the mirror—allowing his eyes to rest with smugness on his broad shoulders, his flat belly. He had everything necessary, he told himself complacently, to make any woman happy.

But all at once anger shone in his eyes. Damn Madeline for flaunting herself before him that way at dinner! She knew he had to fight to keep from grabbing at her in front of everybody at the table.

He swung away from the mirror, reached for a silk dressing gown, pulled it on, and settled himself on the bed. Suzette would make him forget about Madeline. For a little while.

Papa was going to carry on when he asked for money. Maybe he could borrow again from Emmaline. She always helped him out when he was strapped. She never remembered how much she had given him. He always came out ahead when he paid her back. Ever since he could remember, Emmaline had enjoyed spoiling him. He'd tell her vulgar stories about people they both knew, and she'd giggle and pretend to be shocked. "Dennis, you naughty boy!" But she loved it. He smiled with satisfaction. He hadn't met a woman yet whom he couldn't manipulate.

Rebecca had been his one failure, he conceded with a rare honesty. No, he corrected himself; she hadn't been entirely a failure. His mind shot back to those three weeks in Columbia, two years ago, when he had gone to visit

Jake. He had not been particularly friendly with Jake when they were at college together, but he never turned down an invitation to visit in Columbia. Jake had introduced him to Rebecca at a dance assembly. Lord, she was beautiful! Remembering her, he felt aroused.

Right away Rebecca had let him know he could make fast headway with her. Each time they were alone she allowed him more liberties. And then there had been that afternoon—their last afternoon together in Columbia— when they went riding in the carriage and were caught in a spring downpour. He could remember that afternoon as clearly as though it had happened yesterday. . . .

The rain was sloshing right into the carriage. He spied the cottage by the lake—boarded up, but he knew there'd be a way to get inside.

"Pull up before the cottage," he yelled to the coachman. "We'll take refuge in there," he said to Rebecca, his eyes meeting hers with anticipation.

The coachman pulled up as close to the cottage as he could manage. They left the carriage and darted through the rain for the protection of the tiny gallery.

"Dennis, I'm soaking wet!" Rebecca protested, laughing as they hovered breathlessly before the door. Overhead, lightning dashed across the sky. Thunder rumbled. The coachman was heading for the outbuilding behind the cottage.

"Wait," Dennis ordered. He pulled at the plank nailed across the door, pried it loose, and grinned triumphantly. "Enter," he drawled, and urged her into the pretty sitting room that was cold, dank, and musty after months of non-use.

Rebecca stared about her with distaste, shivering in the sudden drop of temperature brought on by the storm.

"Dennis, start a fire," she ordered. "There's wood."

Dennis worked to start up a blaze in the grate. Rebecca threw aside her wet cape and dropped into a chair before the fireplace to remove her shoes. Her eyes followed his every movement. She knew how it would be with them in a few minutes. When the fire was healthily launched, Dennis crossed to each of the windows to close the curtains. He turned around to face Rebecca. She stood before the fire, her clothes in a heap about her feet. Tall and lush in her nakedness. Creamy white skin, huge dark nipples that set his teeth on edge.

"Well?" she drawled. "Are you just going to stand there staring?"

His throat went dry with excitement as he crossed the room to pull her to him. His mouth was rough on hers in his impatience. His hands clutched greedily at her breasts. His hips moved against hers. Here was a woman who was a match for him!

"The sofa," she whispered when they parted for air, her eyes bright with promise. "Pull it closer to the fire."

Together they dragged the sofa before the blaze in the grate. He thrust her upon the sofa, his mouth seeking hers again, his hands moving hotly about her pliant body. And suddenly she was pulling her mouth away from his. Her hands swept meaningfully between them. What the devil?

"Darling, not that," she reproached sweetly. "Not until we're married."

His eyes widened with astonishment. His voice was cold when he spoke.

"Rebecca, we're not getting married," he said bluntly. "I have no intention of marrying anybody."

Her own eyes were reproachful.

"Why not, Dennis?" she asked calmly.

"I enjoy my life the way it is," he said, without moving from her. Could she stop now, heated up the way she was? "Later I'll worry about marrying." There was no percentage in marrying Rebecca. She had two older brothers. The older would inherit the family plantation. The younger would probably inherit Burke Acres. He forced himself into an air of amusement. "But what has that got to do with now?"

"Because, darling," she said, "no man has me until he stands up with me before a minister."

"You're a cheat!" he lashed out at her. "You take off your clothes and you throw yourself at me—and then comes the price tag. But I'm not buying, Rebecca."

She smiled faintly and shrugged.

"Pity," she sighed. "We'd make a brilliant couple. But

I'll give you a consolation prize, darling," she promised with sly sweetness. "There are ways of enjoying ourselves without disturbing the jewels."

Dennis started, then chuckled. He had never heard anyone but a man use that phrase. He'd been taking women since he was fourteen. Rebecca was a new experience.

"Show me how much you know," he jibed. "How good are you, Rebecca Burke?" He might have been talking to a whore in a high-class brothel.

Perspiration glistened on his forehead as he remembered Rebecca. But after that afternoon he had not seen her again until she came to visit her great-aunts. He had not touched her since that night. He knew the price tag she wore.

Rebecca, he thought with brutal candor, he could take or leave. It was Madeline who drove him out of his mind. Why didn't Ron take his wife and leave South Carolina? But if Ron did that, he thought with frustration, he would follow them.

He sat up at the edge of the bed at the staccato knock at the door.

"Come in." He rose to his feet and crossed toward Suzette as she came into the room. "You took long enough!"

"She tak' a long time fallin' asleep," Suzette said hotly.

He reached for her with a low sound of passion. With Suzette he'd forget about Madeline. He pushed her across the bed and went through the motions of satisfying his desire. But even as he lay with Suzette, his mind was tortured by thoughts of Madeline. Was Madeline lying with Ron right this minute? Was Ron doing with her what *he* longed to do? Was Ron enough of a man to take care of Madeline?

Why couldn't he put her out of his mind? *He knew what she was.* Cheap, easy—even worse. But since the day Madeline had walked into his life, he'd found no woman could satisfy him. Even Rebecca, now, would be no more to him than Suzette.

Dennis came awake slowly, conscious that Jasper was

moving about the room. He squinted in reproach as sunlight poured in between the draperies Jasper had pulled wide.

"Ah brung yo' coffee, suh," Jasper said politely, and went to the washstand to pick up the cup and bring it to Dennis. "Thank you, Jasper," Dennis said, yawning broadly.

"It almos' time fo' yo' to be goin' downstaihs to dinnuh," Jasper warned cautiously. Dennis smiled. Jasper was wary of temper outbursts. A year ago he had knocked out two of Jasper's teeth for accidentally stepping on his box of cigars. "Yo' mama down on de gallery waitin' to be called to de table."

Dennis finished his coffee, washed, dressed quickly, and went downstairs. Walking down the hall to the family dining room, he could hear Jeannie talking with his mother. Jeannie knew how to handle herself, he thought with satisfaction. She was a lady. Nobody in the family could deny that. He pushed down uneasy thoughts about the modesty of Jeannie's origins. She was the ward of Kevin Ransome, one of the most important rice planters in Georgia. That was all people had to know.

Jeffrey hovered at the entrance to the dining room, waiting for word that dinner was to be served. Dennis good-humoredly swatted him across the rump. He responded with a broad grin. Dennis sauntered into the dining room.

"How're you feeling, Mama?" he asked with ingratiating charm. "Jeannie, you're looking beautiful today."

Jeannie glowed. "Thank you, Dennis."

"Mama?" Dennis turned inquiringly to his mother.

"Oh, I'm fine, Dennis," she reassured him. Her eyes were familiarly vague. "Papa and Ron are at the mill. They won't be joining us for dinner. Somebody just came to tell us. And Madeline sent down word that she'll be having dinner with her mother in her rooms."

"I'll tell Jeffrey to have dinner sent in," Jeannie said softly, rising to her feet.

Jeannie was taking hold, he thought with pride. Right away she had realized that Mama took no part in running the household. He'd have to figure out a way to have

Jeannie take over the planning of meals, he plotted with an inner defiance. He wasn't going to let Madeline go on playing the lady of the house. That was Jeannie's role.

Jeannie returned to the table with a shy smile for him. Deliberately, as he talked about his last week in London, he allowed his eyes to rest with ardor on Jeannie. He must make Madeline believe he was wildly in love with his bride. She would hate that. Madeline was convinced that no other woman in the world was so desirable as she.

"When you have rested up from our trip, Jeannie," he promised charmingly, "we'll go into Charleston to the theater. Would you like that?" He was pleased with the adoration he saw in Jeannie's eyes. Madeline would see that, too.

"I'd love it," she said without coquetry. "I've never in my whole life been to a theater."

"I was an actress in the Charleston theater when I met Craig." Eleanor's eyes were reminiscently tender. "He was the handsomest man I'd ever known. Except, of course, for Dennis," she added teasingly. "He was three when I married again."

Dennis' gaze swung defensively to Jeannie. He had never told her he had not been born a Mitchell. She didn't seem surprised. Why did Mama have to bring that up regularly? he asked himself with irritation.

He had been thirteen when he learned he had not been born a Mitchell. His face tightened as he remembered the occasion. What an uproar in the house when Mr. Collins had discovered money missing from his room! Later that evening, galvanized with shock, he had stood outside the bedroom assigned to the Collinses and listened to Mrs. Collins accuse *him* of being the thief.

"After all, he's not a Mitchell," she had said with contempt. "His father was quite a bounder. Everybody in Charleston knows that."

He had been less upset by the suspicion that he was guilty of the theft than by the revelation that Craig Mitchell was not his real father. He had gone to his mother and demanded to know the truth.

"I want to know, Mama! I want to know about my father!"

"Craig Mitchell is your father," she said shakily, pale as death.

"You mean, Mama," Dennis insisted ominously, "that he legally adopted me."

"In almost every sense of the word, Dennis, he's your father. My first husband cared little for me and less for you," she said with unaccustomed bluntness. "He was a promoter with an eye for the ladies. He died in a duel with a man who found him dallying with his wife. Craig Mitchell is your father. He feels that. He's been that. Dennis, don't you ever think otherwise!" Her voice rose perilously.

He went into Charleston to search out old newspaper reports about the duel. He went to the cemetery to see his father's grave. And then he determined to be as completely a Mitchell as any man could. He went to Emmaline Burke, who spent much of her time studying genealogy. Emmaline patiently traced the Mitchell family back to colonial days, enjoying his attentions, spoiling him.

"Dennis, you're very quiet," his mother intruded into his reminiscences. "You're not coming down with a headache?"

"Mama, I never have headaches," he responded impatiently. "I was listening to you two talk," he said with an effort at raillery. "You and Jeannie do seem to find plenty to talk about." Mama and Ron, he thought with amusement, were Jeannie's champions in this house. Papa was furious that he had married her. Madeline had hated her on sight. Mavis would dislike anyone who was competition for Madeline.

"We should give a party for the neighbors. So they can meet your wife." Eleanor's eyes were troubled. "But we don't entertain much these days. I just don't seem to be up to it."

"No parties, Mama," Dennis said firmly. "I don't need the neighbors' approval of my wife." He reached for his coffee and drained it. "Now if you two ladies will excuse me, I want to go calling on Emmaline and Miss Charlotte.

I have a small gift I brought back from Paris for each of them and forgot to take over before I left for Ransome Island." He and Emmaline, in private, were on a first-name basis. Her sister, two years her senior, at seventy-four, was always, deferentially, Miss Charlotte.

He left the house and went to the stables for Hannibal, the English thoroughbred his father had brought over for him two years ago. Like Papa, he was partial to everything English. That was a trait of the Mitchell men. His cigars, of course, he thought with ironic humor, came from Cuba.

He rode through the upper fields, gazing beyond them with a sense of proprietorship. In the low rice fields, divided by dikes into monotonous squares, clusters of women were burning the stubble. He enjoyed the sense of power that being astride a fine horse gave him. He was a Mitchell, he reminded himself with recurrent pride. The status might have been acquired, but it was his.

He rode beyond the vast expanse of The Magnolias onto the Burke property, staying clear of the rice fields. The house stood on a slight elevation, a half mile back from the river, commanding a pleasing view of woodland and water. The white stuccoed house, its triple galleries wrought iron-railed in the Spanish manner, faced south to ward off the midday sun and to catch the southwest evening breeze. In front of the house was a wide esplanade of massive oaks. Terraces of evergreens and shrubbery sloped from each side of the house.

Like the Mitchells, the Burkes dated back to the colonial days. Charlotte ruled the plantation with an iron hand, as efficient as any man might have been in the role. She had been running Burke Acres for thirty years. Emmaline, half a head shorter and as slender as an early adolescent, managed the household.

Pulling Hannibal up short before the house, Dennis spied Emmaline, dressed as always in her ruffled black silk with white lace at the collar. Emmaline and Charlotte had worn black since their father's death thirty years ago. Emmaline was leaning over the railing. She and Charlotte received officially every Thursday afternoon. Guests who arrived at other times were met at the door by a regretful servant. But not Dennis. Not any Mitchell. Mitchells were welcome at any time. He hoped, self-consciously, that he would avoid an encounter with Rebecca. She was addicted to long afternoon naps.

"Dennis, I'll be right downstairs," Emmaline called in her high-pitched voice, which today wore an edge of excitement. "Make yourself comfortable on the gallery."

"I've got something pretty for you from Paris," he teased. "Hurry downstairs."

He settled himself in the rocker and reached for one of his inevitable cigars. That was why Emmaline told him to sit on the gallery. Charlotte would have a fit if she detected cigar smoke in the house.

How did Emmaline bear living with Charlotte, who never even allowed her to finish a sentence when they were in the same room? But Charlotte got up at dawn, rode about the fields, ordered supplies, superintended the rice growing and the mill operations. Their plantation was astonishingly productive. In fifty years, he thought dryly, that might be Rebecca.

"Dennis, what is this I hear about a bride?" Emmaline smiled eagerly from the doorway in her old-fashioned puffed-sleeved, wide-skirted, high-necked black, with earrings—diamonds, Dennis knew—at her earlobes, a touch of powder on her face, a hint of pomade on the faded fair hair.

"I'm married, Emmaline," Dennis said with a brilliant smile, bending low to kiss her on the cheek. "To a girl I met on Ransome Island."

"Ransome Island?" She frowned. The unfamiliar coldness in her voice suddenly reminded him of Charlotte. "I don't believe I know that name. It belongs, I assume, to a family named Ransome?"

"Originally it was called Edmunds Island," Dennis said, reaching into his pocket for the two small boxes he had brought along as gifts for the two ladies.

Emmaline's face lighted.

"Yes, I know the Edmunds family. They're on the genealogical chart that hangs on my bedroom wall. But I'm sure there's no Ransome." Her smile faded. Her eyes gazed disapprovingly at Dennis.

"Ransome inherited the island when his wife died," Dennis said uneasily. Leave it to Emmaline to ferret out the fact that this was not a fine old Southern family. "Jeannie is his cousin and ward."

"Is she pretty?" Emmaline asked with an effort at lightness. She was too fond of him to allow him to know she disapproved of his marriage. "I can't imagine you marrying a girl who was not very pretty."

"She's beautiful," Dennis said with unfeigned conviction. Yet misgivings tugged at him. He was a Mitchell. He should have married well, Emmaline was trying to tell him. Because of Madeline he had married in haste. *Was* it a mistake?

"Rebecca left for Montgomery this morning." Emmaline said this with a veiled reproach. She damn well knew, Dennis thought dryly, that Rebecca looked upon him with lechery in her heart and marriage in mind. She didn't know that he and Rebecca had known each other in Columbia two years ago.

"I'm sorry she won't be here to meet Jeannie," he said perfunctorily. That was an encounter he was relieved not to witness.

"Rebecca will probably make a brilliant marriage soon," Emmaline said, eyeing the small boxes that Dennis held casually. "It's time," she added, faintly acerbic. Rebecca was past twenty-three. "Did you know, Dennis, that I have a chart of our family that goes back seven hundred years? Papa used to claim that our family predates the birth of Christ." That was to remind him that he might have joined this illustrious family.

"Now, that's a bit extravagant," he teased, and reached to drop the small boxes into Emmaline's hand. "A little souvenir from Paris for you and Charlotte."

"Which is mine?" she asked with childlike delight.

"The pink-ribboned box," he said.

"Oh, Dennis!" Emmaline glowed as the box lay open before her and she gazed at the charming but inexpensive earrings inside. "They're just beautiful. Dennis, I wish you had been born fifty years ago. I would have snapped you right up." Her smile faded. "Papa never thought any man was good enough for us. We kept looking for royal

83

princes. And then, all at once, it was too late." A rare bitterness showed in her faded blue eyes. "I hope Rebecca won't be that way."

If he had married Rebecca, the marriage would have been viewed with respect by everybody in the Lowlands. But damn it, Rebecca was a willful, dominating bitch. She would have tried to run his life for him.

"While Rebecca was living in Washington, when her father was working for the Government, there was a Senator from an Eastern state who lost his head over her, but Rebecca wouldn't consider marrying any Yankee."

Dennis fabricated an air of interest while Emmaline embarked on a long story about Rebecca's romantic conquests, but his mind was on Madeline. What was he going to do? How long could he go on living in the same house with Madeline without touching her? God, it was rotten to have to lie in his bed and know she was a few rooms away! She deliberately provoked him—wearing her indecently cut dresses; sending him those long, languorous looks when no one else would notice. She wanted him to lose his head over her!

He could go to Ron and tell him the truth about Madeline. All Ron knew about her was that her mother was a Charlestonian and her father had been French, that she had lived in Paris until she was seventeen. Ron didn't know the kind of life Madeline had lived in Charleston. Half the city—including Rebecca—talked about the Beauchamps, mother and daughter. But he knew he would say nothing to Ron.

"Dennis, I declare, you haven't heard a word of what I've been saying," Emmaline protested aggrievedly.

Seven

Jeannie struggled to fit herself unobtrusively into the family life at The Magnolias, always conscious of the strange undercurrents, the hostilities and recriminations that smoldered beneath the surface. Mealtimes, if Dennis and Madeline were both at the table, were tension-laden. Each was prone to bait the other with nasty insinuations. Madeline made no secret of her contempt for Dennis' provincial bride, Jeannie thought with painfully masked humiliation.

Last night at tea Dennis had unnerved her when he complained so boorishly about the menu, knowing that Madeline told Juno what to serve at each meal. He had behaved that way deliberately, hadn't he, to bait Madeline into throwing this task into her lap.

"Have your wife order the meals hereafter!" Madeline had flung at him, her face hot with color, while the others at the table stirred in embarrassment.

Dennis had smiled. That was exactly what he wanted. He wished his wife to appear the mistress of the house, Jeannie recognized, standing in for his mother.

The days moved into weeks, and Jeannie felt a growing frustration at the insurmountable wall between herself and Dennis. Dennis knew she loved him. Why did he make no effort to come to her? Each evening he politely saw her to her door, kissed her on the cheek, and went on to his own room.

Even while she longed for Dennis to claim her as his wife, she was afraid. Would he guess the shocking secret

85

she had kept from him? How would she survive such humiliation?

When Dennis looked upon her with warmth, at intervals, she trembled. Yet would she lie with her husband and remember the horror of that night with Cousin Kevin? Mama had said that it would be beautiful to give herself to her husband, that no pleasure on earth would ever match that. Would she ever have the chance to find out? she asked herself.

Dennis spent so much of his time away from the house, she thought wistfully—riding for hours; going into Charleston, not to return until dawn. So many nights she lay sleepless, waiting to hear his carriage roll up before the house, hoping that he would pause at her door when he came inside. Mr. Mitchell was upset by Dennis' absence from the house. Mrs. Mitchell was too wrapped up in her own private world to realize yet that what had begun as an impetuous marriage was, in truth, no marriage at all.

Jeannie sat on the downstairs gallery, an open book across her lap, aware that spring was fast approaching. Even this early in February the air was fragrant with hyacinths. Double jonquils, snowdrops, and ivory narcissus were blooming. Japonica was aglow with hundreds of flamelike buds, soon to burst into a blaze. Yesterday, striving to walk off her restlessness, she had spied a first pink rose on the sunny side of one of the dikes.

Her eyes followed a pair of cardinals, exquisite in coloring and grace. She ought to bring out her watercolors, she reproved herself. Yet while she tried to lose herself in the beauty around her, Jeannie churned within with anxieties. Last night after tea Ron had awkwardly tried to apologize for Madeline's barely veiled insults. Like her, she thought with compassion, he felt helpless to cope with the situation they faced.

The Magnolias was an open battlefield between Dennis and Madeline. What was this game of torture that Madeline meted out to Dennis? Why did he feel it so urgent to cut her down? *What was between them that nobody else knew?*

Jeannie forced a smile as she saw Arnold approaching

on horseback, a scrapbook tucked carefully in his waist. He was coming to see Madeline again. It astonished her that arrogant, impatient Madeline could be so gentle with Arnold.

"Madeline went into Charleston today," she told Arnold with an air of regret when he dismounted and walked to the gallery. Last night, in Madeline's room she and Ron had argued loudly about the proposed trip into the city. Ron had protested Madeline's extravagance in the shops. "She probably won't be back for hours."

Arnold's eyes were disappointed. He hesitated, inspecting her warily.

"Would you like to see my collection of pressed roses?" he asked eagerly. "I brought one book to show Madeline."

"I'd love to see it," she said enthusiastically, wanting to brush away the wistfulness that Madeline's absence had brought him. "Come up here and sit down beside me."

For a while Arnold was happy to show off his collection, to discuss each flower in detail. He listened absorbedly as she told him how she enjoyed doing watercolors of the birds and flowers. Then he was curiously weighing her.

"Can I call you Jeannie?" he asked cautiously.

"Of course, Arnold," she reassured him, and his face lighted.

"Will you come over and visit with Aunt Emmaline?"

"I'd like that very much someday," she said with a warm smile. Dennis was fond of Miss Emmaline.

"Today," Arnold said firmly, pleased with his decision. "You don't have to wait for her receiving day. Dennis comes over anytime he likes." Jeannie was conscious of the dislike that suddenly edged his voice. He resented Dennis' presence at Burke Acres. "Please, Jeannie. Aunt Emmaline said she was dying to meet you," he parroted. "Send for a carriage and come over right now," he said with rare insistence.

Because she was restless, because it seemed so important to Arnold, she allowed herself to be persuaded. In fifteen minutes the carriage from The Magnolias, with

Arnold riding happily beside it, was pulling up before the impressive Burke mansion.

Arnold sent his horse to the stables with a servant, happily deposited Jeannie in a chair on the gallery, and went off in search of his aunt. All at once Jeannie felt self-conscious about coming here. Would Dennis be angry? Miss Emmaline was his special friend.

"So you're Jeannie." Emmaline moved through the door to Jeannie with a bright smile. "I've been dying to meet Dennis' bride. I knew you'd be beautiful. Dennis has such an eye for pretty young ladies. I told him to bring you over right away. But come on into the house." She rattled on with warmth, yet Jeannie felt she was being evaluated. "We'll have some English biscuits and tea."

Emmaline guided her into the house, into the back parlor elaborately furnished with expensive French pieces, a piano in one corner of the room, a collection of miniatures of Queen Victoria clustered together pretentiously on one wall.

"We're distantly related to Victoria." Emmaline preened with pride. "Papa always wanted to take us to London to be presented at Court, but there just never seemed time. When Papa was alive, we were always entertaining."

Over tea Emmaline seemed to relax. She was being accepted, Jeannie decided with relief. Emmaline was delighted because she was so familiar with all of Mr. Scott's novels.

"Of course, I adore the Waverley novels," Emmaline said earnestly, "but I must confess my favorite author is Charlotte."

"Your sister writes?" Jeannie asked interestedly.

"Oh, nobody knows." All at once Emmaline was uneasy. She should not have made this revelation, Jeannie guessed. "Charlotte writes for a readership of one. Me. I wait for each page," she said gaily.

"Emmaline, I didn't know you were receiving today."

Jeannie turned to face the tall, heavy, imposing woman, ramrod-stiff despite her age, dressed severely in black, who paused in the doorway.

"Charlotte, I'm not receiving." Emmaline strove to be

lightly reproachful, but she was nervous. "This is Jeannie, Dennis' bride."

"I'm so happy to meet you, Miss Charlotte." Jeannie rose to her feet with an ingratiating smile. Miss Charlotte knew Emmaline had told her about her sister's writing. Could she ease this situation for Miss Emmaline? "I have such admiration for anyone who writes," she said impulsively.

"I don't write," Charlotte brushed this aside. Her eyes glowed with an inner fury that belied the calm of her voice. "I amuse myself—and Emmaline—with scribbling." Her eyes said that Emmaline would be harshly upbraided later.

"But you ought to send your books to the publishers up North," Jeannie urged. "There are several ladies who are writing successfully today."

"I have quite enough to do to manage my plantation," Charlotte said austerely, and sat in a small upholstered chair that seemed too fragile to contain her bulk. "Is Eleanor's health at all improved?" she asked with a hint of maliciousness.

"My mother-in-law is quite well," Jeannie said politely, ignoring the veiled implications.

Uncomfortable in Miss Charlotte's presence, Jeannie took her leave as speedily as she could with politeness. Arnold walked with her to the door. Charlotte's voice followed them down the hall.

"I feel so sorry for poor Craig and Eleanor," Charlotte said with an air of specious sympathy. "How different it would have been for them if Dennis had had the good sense to marry Rebecca."

Back at The Magnolias, Jeannie went directly to her room. On the gallery above, Mavis sat talking with Suzette—rambling on about her childhood in Charleston, as she did so often at the dinner table. From the impatient glances Madeline usually bestowed on her mother, Jeannie guessed these reminiscences were fantasies.

"When I was fourteen and my parents were killed in a carriage accident, I went to live in London," Mavis was saying with an air of confidence. "Mama had always wanted me to be reared in London, where my aunt lived."

89

Jeannie leaned forward curiously as a carriage pulled up before the house. Few visitors called at The Magnolias, in contrast to the typical rice plantation. Usually they came to discuss business with Mr. Mitchell and Ron. Why wouldn't Dennis take an active part in running the plantation that someday would belong to him? Several times in the course of their evenings in the parlor Mr. Mitchell had hinted strongly that it was time Dennis became involved.

The carriage pulled to a stop and a portly, middle-aged gentleman approached the gallery. Jeannie heard Plato greeting him. But the guest was not being invited into the house, she realized, perplexed. She saw Plato politely gesture that he have a seat on the gallery.

In a few moments Craig emerged. The voices of the two men did not carry up to Jeannie at first. Then all at once she tensed in her chair. The two men were talking angrily. She heard Dennis' name mentioned. Instinctively she leaned forward to listen.

"Look, Mr. Mitchell, I don't care what Dennis tells you," their caller said brusquely. "He's been at my rooms gambling regularly. He's in to me for five thousand dollars. I've cut off his credit, and I expect him to pay up. We don't take kindly to welshing on gambling debts, sir!" His voice was blatantly menacing.

Her heart pounding, Jeannie fled to the quietness of her room. Dennis was in trouble with the Charleston gamblers. Was that a threat of physical violence? She shivered, hearing the caller's voice in her mind, and alarm spiraled in her.

Where was Dennis? She must warn him of their caller before he encountered his father. She frowned in thought, reconstructing the day. Dennis had left right after the noonday meal. He was going riding, he said. All right, she pushed herself into action, go out to the stables. Wait for Dennis. Tell him about his father's caller.

She hurried out onto the second-floor gallery again and watched the man from the gaming rooms climb back into his carriage. Mr. Mitchell was striding angrily away from the house in the direction of the rice mill. She waited for him to disappear from view, then went downstairs. She gazed involuntarily into the small sitting room off the foyer, where Eleanor stood before a cabinet, unsteadily pouring herself a glass of wine. Jeannie paused in indecision. Should she tell Mrs. Mitchell what she had overheard? No. Mrs. Mitchell could be of no help to Dennis in this situation.

She walked with compulsive swiftness to the stables, her mind in turmoil. Dennis must have told his father that he wasn't going to the gaming rooms. *Look, Mr. Mitchell, I don't care what Dennis tells you.* Had Dennis lied to his father? Instinctively—guiltily—Jeannie guessed that he had. Dennis was so thoroughly charming that people were apt to believe whatever he told them.

"Is Mr. Dennis around here?" she inquired in the blacksmith shop, and the man paused in his work to beam upon her.

"No, Young Missy, he ain' here," he said respectfully. "He still be out wit' Hannibal. But Ah 'spect he be back real soon," he added soothingly.

"Thank you." She forced a smile and moved out into the warm afternoon sunlight.

Show interest in the outbuildings, she exhorted herself nervously. Stall until Dennis returns. The carpentry shop was right next door, and the wagon shed and the carriage house just beyond.

She visited the carpentry shop and talked for a while with the delighted workmen, all the time watching for Dennis. She moved on to the woodshed, and then to the carriage house. *Where was Dennis?* Then, as she was reluctantly deciding she must return to the house, she spied him approaching the stables astride Hannibal. She darted from the carriage house to meet him.

"Sight-seeing?" he asked Jeannie with an air of guarded indulgence as he dismounted.

"Dennis, I have to talk to you," she said urgently, her eyes troubled.

"Wait," he said carefully.

After a brief exchange with the stableman, Dennis joined her. In a tacit agreement, they were silent until they were beyond hearing of the slaves.

"Your father had a visitor," she said breathlessly. "A

man from the gaming rooms in Charleston. . . ."

Dennis whistled softly.

"A middle-aged man? Heavyset, rough voice?"

"Yes."

"What did he say to Papa?"

As calmly as she could contrive, avoiding meeting his eyes, she told Dennis what had passed between the two men. Dennis' eyes darkened with fury.

"Damn Joe!"

"Dennis," she faltered. "He sounded so—so menacing."

"It's all right, Jeannie. Just forget about it," he ordered tersely. "I'll take care of the matter."

Jeannie watched with dismay as Dennis reached out suddenly with one foot and kicked the beagle trotting beside him in the ribs. The dog yelped in protest and darted away. Dennis was upset, she rationalized unhappily. He didn't realize what he was doing.

Dennis pulled the door wide for Jeannie and she walked into the foyer, disturbed by the rage that seethed within Dennis. She had never seen him quite like this. But she was glad she had forewarned him.

Madeline, obviously in a sulky mood, was walking down the stairs with her mother.

"I bought so little," she was complaining vindictively. "Ron refuses to allow me to charge in the shops." She paused when she saw Dennis and Jeannie. Jeannie felt a coldness go through her at the heavy, silent exchange that passed between Dennis and Madeline.

"Jeannie, how pretty you look," Mavis babbled self-consciously. "You should always wear blue. It's such a flattering color for you."

"She looks beautiful in everything," Dennis drawled, putting a hand at her waist. "I must show her off in Charleston." His eyes mocked Madeline. Jeannie stiffened. As he played this small charade, Jeannie realized that he was listening for sounds from the dining room, hoping his father was already at the table, thus delaying the confrontation that must take place. "Jeannie, would you like to go to the opera tonight?"

"I'd love that." Her eyes were aglow with anticipation. Jeannie saw the glint of shock, of hostility, in Madeline's eyes as she prodded her mother down the hall. Mavis was prattling about how the new system of postage stamps started in the United States two years before had been based on the system introduced in England seven years earlier.

"Your father is like me in some ways, Dennis," Mavis said coquettishly. "I too am faithful to everything English."

"I thought it was French," Madeline said dryly.

Sunlight poured into the dining room. A vase of hyacinths, jonquils, and narcissus graced the table with color and fragrance. Craig sat grimly at the head. Eleanor, carrying a glass of wine, was walking to her chair at the foot. Mr. Mitchell wouldn't talk about his visitor at the dinner table, Jeannie soothed herself nervously as she moved to a chair. He would talk to Dennis later. *How had Dennis allowed himself to go five thousand dollars into debt to a gambler?*

When they were all seated, Jeannie signaled to Jeffrey to see that dinner was sent in to the table. Ron's dinner had been sent to him at the mill, she recalled. Mavis, with her need to break the silence that engulfed the table, turned to Eleanor.

"What are you reading now, Eleanor?" she asked with an ingratiating smile.

"A book by Mr. Hugo," Eleanor said uncertainly. "A strange book called *The Hunchback of Notre Dame*. I'm not sure I like it."

"I'm reading a most fascinating book that I brought with me from Ransome Island," Jeannie said. "It's called *Le Comte de Monte Cristo*. There are twelve volumes all together," she said with an apologetic laugh, "but I have only the first two."

"A novel by Monsieur Dumas?" Mavis asked delightedly. "Are you reading it in French?"

"Yes," Jeannie conceded self-consciously.

"Madeline and I knew Dumas in Paris." She smiled archly at her daughter. "He took quite a fancy to Madeline."

"Monsieur Dumas," Madeline said, her eyes focused

on Dennis, "is the grandson of a Negress from Santo Domingo."

"How fortunate for him," Dennis mocked, "that he lives in Paris and not in Charleston."

Jeannie sat silently through the rest of dinner while Dennis and his father argued heatedly about politics. Mr. Mitchell had a sharp, clear mind, Jeannie thought admiringly. Dennis was no match for him in a political discussion.

Before the fruit bowl and coffee were brought to the table, Dennis excused himself. His father looked up with a frown. He was anxious to face Dennis with the five-thousand-dollar gambling debt, Jeannie thought somberly; but Dennis was already striding from the room.

"I'm going out to the rice fields," Craig excused himself politely when he had finished his coffee. "We're plowing for the first seeding."

Moments later Madeline pushed back her chair.

"I'm going upstairs to change into my riding dress," she said abruptly. "Mama, are you coming upstairs?"

"Yes, dear," Mavis said nervously. She was ill at ease with the family, Jeannie thought sympathetically, unless Madeline was with them.

"Would you like to sit with me on the gallery?" Eleanor asked Jeannie with a touching eagerness as they rose from the table.

"That would be pleasant." Jeannie smiled reassuringly, yet she felt an odd discomfort. Was Mrs. Mitchell going to urge her to leave The Magnolias, as her husband had done?

Jeannie walked beside Eleanor down the hall and out onto the gallery. The air was sweet with the coming of spring, and spiced today with the scent of salt from the sea. The peach trees were in magnificent bloom. Close to the house quantities of violets nestled against the grass, and the blue-green leaves of the myrtle were adorned with fragrant white flowers.

"Jeannie, I know it isn't easy for you here," Eleanor said slowly, her expression troubled. Jeannie's eyes reflected her astonishment. She had thought Mrs. Mitchell too introspective to be aware of her daughter-in-law's discomfort at The Magnolias. "I don't know how to cope anymore." She spread her hands in a gesture of futility. "But I'm glad that Dennis married you. Please, Jeannie, be patient with him." Everybody in the house took it for granted that Mrs. Mitchell was totally involved in her own world; but her love for Dennis brought her out of it, Jeannie thought compassionately.

"I love Dennis," Jeannie said softly. "I'll be patient." But did Dennis love her? Beyond his obsession for Madeline, *did* he love her? Was this game he played—at intervals—because Madeline was beyond his reach?

"Craig is furious with him." Eleanor frowned. "I wish I knew why." She lifted her eyes to Jeannie. "Do you know why?"

Jeannie hesitated a moment.

"I think it's because someone came from Charleston today to talk about Dennis' gambling debts," she said candidly, and saw Eleanor pale. "He owes five thousand dollars. I—I went out to the stables to wait for Dennis to warn him. I don't know if that was the right thing to do."

"Craig loathes gambling." Her voice trembled. "He has every reason to. I'll have to try to talk to him." She nervously laced her fingers in her lap. "I'm afraid I haven't been much of a wife to Craig, and he's been so good to Dennis and me. Five times I thought I was going to give Craig the child he wanted so desperately, and five times I miscarried. I failed my husband." Her voice was an agonized whisper. "My fine, deserving husband, but I couldn't give him what he wanted most in the world. He's been a real father to Dennis, but Dennis too disappoints him." She leaned forward urgently. "Jeannie, no matter what happens, promise me you'll stay with Dennis. Things will work out for the two of you. I promise you."

"I'll stay," Jeannie said tremulously.

Eleanor rose awkwardly to her feet with an air of relief.

"I'm really quite tired," she said apologetically. She was concerned, Jeannie guessed, about approaching her husband on Dennis' behalf. "Would you excuse me, Jeannie?"

Eight

Jeannie sat in the library, struggling to concentrate on a novel. Dennis had been away from the house all afternoon. Had he forgotten about his invitation to take her into Charleston to the opera? If they were going into the city, they must leave soon. She ought to tell Gilbert that she and Dennis would not be home for tea.

"Jeannie," Dennis' voice cut peremptorily into her introspection. "You'd better dress. We'll have to leave in twenty minutes if we're to have time for tea in Charleston before the performance."

"I can be ready in ten minutes," she said eagerly, caught up in a surge of anticipation. They were truly going into Charleston! She rose to her feet with a dazzling smile. "I'll tell Gilbert we won't be here for tea; then I'll dress."

She emerged from her room dressed in the blue velvet that Mama had particularly loved. Aunt Lizzie had brushed her hair until it shone. Color becomingly touched her cheekbones. Her eyes glowed. Over her arm was the paisley shawl that would serve to protect her against the night chill.

Dennis waited for her at the foot of the stairs. He gazed up at her with an admiration that set her heart to pounding.

"Jeannie and I are going into Charleston," he said to someone beyond her view, without removing his eyes from her. "To the opera."

"I know," Madeline drawled.

"Jeannie, love, you'll wear this tonight," he said as she approached the bottom of the stairs. Madeline was watching the small tableau with glints of anger in her eyes. He held up a talma mantle of taffeta, outlined with fine needlework and finished with a massive fringe. The mantle was just the proper blue to wear with her dress, Jeannie noted with pleasure. "Mama insists on lending it to you." He closed in amorously about her as he dropped the mantle around her shoulders.

Jeannie lowered her eyes before the heated exchange between Madeline and Dennis, before Madeline swept down the hall toward the dining room.

In the carriage Dennis lapsed into a somber silence. She might not have been with him. Not until the lights of the city appeared did he become animated.

"We'll have tea at the hotel," he announced. "And I'll tell Eliza to be quick about it because we're going to the opera. I don't know what's being performed," he said with charming apology. "I should have noticed."

"It doesn't matter," Jeannie laughed. "I've never been to the opera."

"The new Charleston Theatre is magnificent. It was built back in 1837," he chuckled, "but to Charlestonians it's still the new theater. It's a shame Macready isn't appearing now." She gazed inquiringly at him. "William Charles Macready, the actor. He returned this season for the first time in five years and packed the house with *Macbeth* and *Richelieu*."

"Will we have time for tea?" she asked when he pulled out his watch and gazed at its face with an air of irritation.

"As I said," he told her, unexpectedly testy, "I'll tell Eliza we must be served instantly. While we're eating, Jasper will go to the theater to arrange for our box."

Jasper deposited them before the hotel. Jeannie's eyes widened with respect at the sight of the fine old building, but Dennis regarded it almost with contempt. He hurried her inside, waving impatiently toward a smiling, neatly dressed colored woman who obviously knew Dennis. She inspected Jeannie with covert appraisal.

"Eliza, this is my wife," he said with emphasis, and

Jeannie saw Eliza's start of astonishment. "We want tea immediately."

"Yes, Mr. Mitchell," Eliza said softly, and conducted them to a private table at one side of the room.

"Eliza is a freewoman," Dennis said with amusement, "who runs this place with the slaves she owns."

All through their simple but delicious tea Dennis talked animatedly about past performances at the Charleston Theatre.

"Just last summer," he said with pride as they sipped their coffee, "gas lighting appliances were installed in the theater. And the backstage was rebuilt so as to adapt to 'spectacle pieces.'" Again he consulted his watch. "We'll have to leave in a few minutes."

As they approached the theater, Dennis laughingly pointed out a circus encamped on the vacant lot to the rear. But Jeannie barely heard him. She was leaning forward, entranced by her first view of the resplendent Charleston Theatre.

The theater, two-storied, was Greek Revival in design. Its facade presented a heavy arcade at street level and a portico of four Ionic columns immediately above the vestibule. With anticipation lighting her face, Jeannie allowed Dennis to propel her into the interior of the theater, her eyes enthralled with what met her gaze. There were a horseshoe of three tiers of boxes, a dress circle, and a pit.

"How enormous!" she murmured with awe.

"The theater seats twelve hundred," Dennis said carelessly, his eyes surveying the opulently dressed assemblage. How sweet of Mrs. Mitchell to lend her the mantle, Jeannie thought with gratitude. Her paisley shawl would hardly have been grand enough for the opera.

They settled themselves in their box, Jeannie displaying a lively interest in their surroundings. Four Ionic pilasters, along with an ornamental frieze, framed the proscenium opening. The dome was divided into twelve compartments, each ornamented with arabesques and emblematic figures, richly and exquisitely executed in brilliant colors. A dramatic chandelier hung from the ceiling.

Dennis was nodding to people he knew who sat in a

box on the other side of the theater. Jeannie saw them talking avidly among themselves, then focusing their attention on her. She managed a small, fixed smile.

The lights flickered and dimmed. Jeannie abandoned herself to the stage performance. She was enthralled by the singing, the splendor of the costumes. Not until the last act did she become aware of Dennis' restlessness. He was bored. If it were not for her, she guessed instinctively, Dennis would leave.

After the performance, while the cast was accepting the enthusiastic applause of the audience, Dennis prodded her from their box. He was impatient to get to the carriage before the rush of patrons from the theater, he explained. Or was Dennis nervous about her meeting his acquaintances who had sat across the theater from them?

In the carriage Dennis lapsed again into silence. Jeannie settled back into the opposite corner of the carriage. Why had Dennis bothered to take her to the opera? Because he knew that would infuriate Madeline?

What kind of marriage was she sharing with Dennis? Where was the Dennis she had been so sure she loved?

Jeannie sat pensively on the gallery, watching the dogs cavort about the grounds, chasing after fast-disappearing rabbits and squirrels. Recurrently her mind probed Dennis' withdrawal after their attendance at the opera last night, his abruptness when he had left her at her door. He was disturbed about his gambling debt, she told herself. About his father's anger. He could not avoid a confrontation with his father much longer.

She glanced up with a start as Ron approached. He paused, smiling, to wrestle with the dogs. Wincing with recall, she remembered Dennis' kicking the beagle in the ribs.

"I came up to the house to see if you'd like to sit in on the claying," Ron said cheerfully, walking up the steps of the gallery. "Or have you seen that at Ransome Island?"

"I saw little of what went on with the rice-growing," Jeannie conceded, grateful for this overture of friendship.

"Kevin felt that Mama and I should never go into the fields."

"Won't you come?" he prodded. "It's a pretty sight."

"Yes, I'd like that." She rose eagerly to her feet.

They walked together to the barn. Outside, half a dozen early-teen-age girl slaves played about high-spiritedly. They smiled shyly as Jeannie and Ron approached.

"The men are sending the seed rice down from the loft." Ron pointed to the spout from which the seed rice poured in abundance. "We'll do about sixty bushels," he said. Other slaves were lining up barrels, filling them half full of clay, then adding water and stirring. "When that mixture is like molasses," Ron went on, "we'll pour it over the rice." Again Jeannie was conscious of the mellowness of Ron's voice. How comfortable it was to be with him. "Then comes the action," he said with a chuckle.

Jeannie watched—enjoying Ron's company, knowing that she had a friend at The Magnolias—while the slaves stirred the barrels of clay and water, testing regularly for consistency. The pretty, dark-skinned teen-agers gathered in the doorway with lively interest.

"Pour it now," Ron ordered, finally satisfied that the mixture was ready. "The clay is necessary to hold the seeds," he explained, "because otherwise they would float away when the fields are flooded three inches deep."

Ron grinned and pulled Jeannie back a few feet while the slaves moved forward to pour the clay over the rice. The girls, giggling among themselves, were hoisting their skirts high about their thighs.

"All right," Ron called out, his eyes crinkling with merriment, and the cluster of girls ebulliently leaped upon the rice with their bare feet, singing as they danced about, determined to cover every grain of rice with the clay mixture.

Jeannie watched the effervescent dance with Ron until he declared the rice adequately clayed.

"All right, pile it into pyramids," he ordered briskly. "We let it soak until morning," he explained to Jeannie, "and then it's sacked and taken out to the fields." His eyes were bitterly reminiscent for a moment. "Madeline found this too primitive to be of interest."

"Ron, I truly enjoyed it," Jeannie said with a warm smile. "Thanks for inviting me."

By the time Jeannie left the barn to return to the house, the sun was sinking into a hazy red glow. The rice-field banks were colorful with white and blue violets, wisteria, blue jessamine, and blackberry blossoms. For a few minutes she paused near the bridge, to watch two women fishing. She marveled at the string of bass and perch that lay on the bank.

Jeannie walked back to the house with a transient sense of well-being, watching the turkey buzzards spread their broad black wings and fly over the river. She remembered the turkey buzzards she and Dennis had seen in Charleston. In Charleston she had been giddy with childish dreams of the life she would share with Dennis. All these weeks at The Magnolias, and her husband had not once entered her bedroom!

Approaching the house, she spied the carriage that sat before the gallery. Did this signify more trouble for Dennis? Her heart began to pound. She walked up the steps and across the gallery with a sense of urgency. At the door, hearing the voice inside the foyer, she stopped dead, her face drained of color. Her throat tightened with consternation. *This could not be happening.*

"I had to be in Charleston on business," Kevin Ransome was saying in unfamiliarly gracious tones to Craig as they stood together in the foyer. "And I could not resist the opportunity to call on Jeannie and her new family."

Nine

Jeannie willed herself into calmness as she reached the door. Why had Kevin come here? She didn't believe this story of business in Charleston. What havoc did he mean to bring upon her?

"Mr. Ransome, you don't know how happy I am to see you at The Magnolias," Craig was saying as she walked into the foyer. "This is an honor, sir. Dennis gave me a report on what he had seen at Ransome Island, but he has no head for the problems of running a rice plantation." Craig tried to sound indulgent. "Now I'll be able to talk to you about this face to face. Of course," he said warmly, "you'll remain with us for several days." His face brightened as he spied Jeannie. "Here's Jeannie now." It was the first time since her arrival at The Magnolias, she thought wryly, that Mr. Mitchell had looked upon her with genuine friendliness. Because the great authority on rice-growing was here!

"Jeannie, you're looking well." Kevin's eyes were inscrutable, but his smile was deliberately ingratiating. *Why was he here?*

"Thank you, Cousin Kevin. I am well." Her voice was uneven. She was grateful that he made no move to touch her. The horror of that night when he had invaded her room was upon her again. That night, she thought with pain, of which Dennis knew nothing.

"We must send your coachman into Charleston for your portmanteau," Craig said. "I'll have a room prepared for you immediately. You'll refresh yourself and then we'll all sit down to tea."

In a daze Jeannie found herself marshaled along with Kevin into the exquisitely furnished front parlor, opened only to favored guests. Her father-in-law and her cousin were talking avidly about developing new strains of rice that would be superior to both the Oriental and the Mediterranean rice. Plato had been dispatched to summon Ron from the mill. Jeannie had excused herself briefly to tell Juno that they would have a guest for tea, and to send Eloise from the kitchen to inform the other members of the family about Kevin Ransome's arrival at The Magnolias.

When Jeannie returned to the front parlor, Kevin digressed from business talk to admire the fine French furniture, the exquisite Kirman carpet. Eleanor arrived, smiling stiffly and fighting discomfort. She sat beside Jeannie on one of the pair of Louis XV carved and gilded marquises that flanked the fireplace, seeming, unexpectedly, to find comfort in this closeness to her daughter-in-law.

Madeline entered, imperious and defiant, dressed in ivory velvet that set off her flamboyant beauty. Craig presented her to Kevin, who smiled perfunctorily. Her cousin, Jeannie suspected, disapproved of Madeline on sight. There was an air of royal decadence about Madeline that would, of course, set his teeth on edge.

Dennis and Ron arrived almost simultaneously. Jeannie watched the greeting between Dennis and Kevin with painful questions hurtling through her mind. Was *Dennis* the reason for Kevin's being here? Had he regretted forcing her to deceive Dennis? Had his religious fanaticism brought him here to repair that deceit? No! Please, no! She felt her face grow hot with fear.

Covertly she watched Kevin for some sign, some indication of the reason for his presence at The Magnolias. His eyes were opaque, revealing nothing. This charming, gracious Kevin Ransome was a stranger to her. Only on very rare occasions, when there were important visitors at Ransome Island, had he presented himself in this guise.

Ron, like his uncle, was eager to question Kevin about some of his innovations in raising rice. Ron, Jeannie noted with respect, was well read on the subject.

"It seems to me absurd," Kevin said with a flicker of impatience, "that we must consider that we can plant only from the fifteenth of March to the fifteenth of April, then again from the first to the tenth of May, and the last planting for ten days in June. Why should we waste the valuable planting time in between?"

"It's hard to combat the Maybirds in the spring and the ricebirds in August and September," Craig said with a deferential smile.

"Have you studied a way to fight off the Maybirds?" Ron asked, leaning forward interestedly.

"Why not kill them off?" Madeline asked flippantly. "Heavens knows, enough of the ricebirds are shot in late summer for plantation breakfasts." Jeannie shivered; she could not abide the habit of eating the black-and-yellow bobolinks. Kevin was known to eat a dozen at dinner.

"Someday we'll cope with the ricebirds with chemicals," Kevin predicted, ignoring Madeline's comments. "I've been working on that myself, though I'm not too well versed in chemistry. But whatever has to do with rice," he said with pride, "I make my business."

Gilbert arrived in the parlor to announce that a room had been prepared for their guest. Craig himself conducted Kevin upstairs. After he had refreshed himself, they would sit down to tea.

When the family convened in the dining room, Juno began to send in the sumptuous tea that was protocol when guests were present. Jeannie sat tensely in her usual place, making small talk with Eleanor, who seemed strained in the presence of company. Eleanor's hand trembled as she brought her wineglass to her lips. Without prompting, Gilbert came forward regularly to refill her glass.

Both Craig and Ron were intensely involved in discussion with Kevin about the Dutch system of diking, which Kevin had studied on a trip to Holland years earlier. Madeline spoke in a defiant undertone to her mother about the contents of a Paris fashion magazine that had arrived at The Magnolias after an unconscionably long time. Dennis sulked. But again, Jeannie thought, he was avoiding a confrontation with his father about his gambling debts.

Jeannie was relieved when tea was over. Dennis mumbled a hasty excuse and withdrew. Craig retired to the library with Ron and Kevin. The ladies went into the rear parlor, because this was ritual after tea.

"Mrs. Mitchell, I don't know how you have been able to bear it here the year around, year after year," Madeline said with deceptive sympathy. "I don't know how you've survived," she added dramatically. "Everybody knows that from May till October it's taking your life in your hands to stay in this swamp-infested country." Last night, Jeannie remembered, she had heard Madeline in her room screaming at Ron because he still refused to rent a house in Charleston for the summer. "Only the blacks don't come down with the fever."

"If we spend much of the time resting in our rooms and sipping iced drinks," Eleanor said placatingly, "the months go past." But her mother-in-law was moving away from them, Jeannie thought compassionately. She would talk no more with them this evening. Jeannie had come to recognize that haze that seemed to separate Eleanor Mitchell from the rest of the world.

"I used to love the country when I was a young girl in England," Mavis said sentimentally. "My aunt used to take me to her country house in Suffolk."

"Mama, your aunt lived with her drunken lout of a husband and four brats in the worst section of London," Madeline said with brutality. "The only time she might have seen a country house in Suffolk was scrubbing floors."

Mavis dropped her eyes, flushed.

"Your father used to take us to the country outside Paris every summer while he was alive. You were old enough to remember that," she said defensively.

Where was Dennis? Jeannie wondered unhappily. Had he gone into Charleston again? A storm was beginning to blow up. Had he gone into the city to gamble at another place, hoping to recoup his losses? He must face his father. Couldn't he accept that? And then she felt her face grow hot. How disloyal of her to think this way of Dennis!

Bored with the company of those present, Madeline made an early move to go upstairs to her room. Now that she had humiliated her mother, Madeline was angry with herself.

"I think I'll go upstairs too," Mavis said with an effort at casualness. How many times had Madeline humiliated her mother that way? And yet Jeannie observed the deep affection in Mavis' eyes for her daughter. Affection and guilt, Jeannie assessed uneasily. Why did Mavis feel guilty? Was it because she had not provided Madeline with a kingdom?

In her room Jeannie prepared for the night, listening unhappily to the sounds of the approaching storm. If there was a heavy rain, in this low country as on Ransome Island, the roads might become impassable. Dennis would have difficulty getting home.

In her nightdress, too restless to sleep, Jeannie went to a window that faced toward the river. The wind was blowing roughly through the trees. Somewhere in the distance a dog howled. In a flash of lightning Jeannie saw the water of the river, churning furiously.

Someone was striding away from the house. In this weather? She realized with astonishment that Mr. Mitchell was headed toward the cottage that he kept as a study. She watched his figure moving swiftly in the dampness of the night until he disappeared into the house. Moments later, the faint glow of a lamp showed behind the curtains.

Jeannie was about to forsake the grim night view from her window; but another figure, darting with lithe grace along the same route that Mr. Mitchell had just followed, captured her attention. Suddenly she felt color rush to her cheeks. Carlotta was hurrying toward the cottage.

Hastily Jeannie pulled the draperies shut at her window, as though she might erase from her mind the sudden realization of the rendezvous between her father-in-law and Carlotta. She crossed the room to her bed and slid beneath the comforter. But she knew she would not sleep until she heard Dennis arrive safely at the house.

Craig dropped to his haunches before the fireplace, placing more kindling wood strategically about the fire he had just coaxed into being. The night was raw. He hoped the rain would not be heavy when they were in the midst of plowing.

He went to a window, searching for sight of Carlotta. His face brightened as he saw her approach. Poor Carlotta. So proud, so beautiful, so intelligent. Why did Dennis take such savage pleasure in dressing her down? Did he ever suspect something between them?

He hated the practice of many planters of taking advantage of their slave women. He had never availed himself of any woman among his slaves until that night four years ago when Carlotta had brought the hot rum to his room. His mind shot into the past; his face softened with recall. He had had a devil of a cold and had gone to bed early. At no one's behest she had prepared the hot rum and brought it to him. And then—never expecting it to happen—he had taken her into his bed.

He was a man, with a man's desires. Eleanor, so terrified of yet another miscarriage, another painful hope destroyed, had not let him near her for years. Eleanor, who had been so magnificently passionate, such a joy to him in those early years of their marriage, had locked herself up in that private world of hers. Carlotta had brought him an uneasy happiness. He knew she could not conceive; there was no danger of a child to bring guilt to his soul.

"Come in," he called briskly as she knocked.

The door opened. Carlotta walked in with a shy smile. In her amber eyes was the look of quiet adoration that recurrently disturbed him. What had he done to deserve that from Carlotta? She was a third-generation slave in bondage to the Mitchells, he taunted himself. But in these last four years of their togetherness, he had come to talk to her as he might have talked to Eleanor if she had been well.

"Let's have tea." He dropped into the comfortable easy chair by the fireplace. With Carlotta he felt some of the tensions of the day ebbing away from him.

"Ah'll make it," Carlotta said with an air of quiet pleasure. Even her speech was close to that of the family. The other slaves kept their distance from Carlotta, sensing that she was truly not one of them. A hybrid, he thought tenderly, belonging to neither world. Her father, he suspected, had been a Northern gentleman brought to The Magnolias to supervise the installation of mill equipment.

He watched Carlotta move about the room, brewing the tea in the Staffordshire teapot he had bought in Charleston, knowing it would please her. She brought down the matching cups and saucers, the sugar bowl, the two silver spoons.

Carlotta pulled a small table before his chair and drew up a chair for herself, and they leisurely drank their tea. Craig talked about their guest, for whose innovations in rice-growing he had the greatest respect.

"But Carlotta, there is something about that man," he said slowly, "that makes me uneasy."

"Ah don't like him," Carlotta said with her usual candor. "There is something evil in him. Ah feel it here." She touched her breast.

"He's a cousin of my son's wife," Craig reproached, frowning as he sipped the strong India tea.

"She is afraid of him," Carlotta volunteered. "At dinner she sat so stiff in her chair. Yes," Carlotta said with conviction. "She fears her cousin."

"Perhaps that's why she allowed Dennis to rush her into this marriage. Carlotta, I worry about Dennis."

"You have been a good father to him," Carlotta said sternly. "You cannot make him into what he is not."

Craig flinched before her candor. Had Dennis ever tried to force himself on Carlotta? Now and again he wondered about that. But with Carlotta's formidable pride, he dared not question her. Damn Dennis, for taking advantage the way he did sometimes! He behaved like that breed of planter's offspring that he loathed, who felt themselves immune to criticism, royal in their will.

They finished their tea. Craig watched, with desire welling in him, while Carlotta, with infinite care, washed and dried the dishes and put them away in the cupboard.

Then she came to stand before him, smiling slightly because she knew what he felt. He looked into her eyes and he knew she wanted this union as strongly as he.

With that familiarly inscrutable smile on her mouth, Carlotta reached for the hem of her short homespun dress and drew it over her head. His eyes swept over the length of her. Breasts small and high, the belly flat, hips and thighs narrow.

"Carlotta," he whispered, and reached for her.

She pressed her face to his, her arms wound tightly about him while they swayed together—not rushing, knowing how good it could be for them.

At last they lay on a thick pallet before the comforting warmth of the fire, the weight of him above her.

"Oh, Craig, Craig!" she cried out, and he smiled at her familiarity that came only at moments such as this.

Jeannie left the bed to go to the fireplace. The temperature had dropped sharply and a dank chill pervaded the room. Put more wood on the fire before it goes out, she ordered herself. For a few minutes she was busy with the fire.

The wind howled through the trees. She straightened up before the fireplace as claps of thunder rumbled in the sky. Why didn't Dennis come home before the storm? She crossed to a window, pulled aside the draperies, then retreated before the flash of lightning that darted across the sky, seeming almost to invade the room. She moved away from the window, pulling the draperies closed against the storm.

Despite the warmth of the fire, she was cold. She turned away from the window and walked toward the closet for her dressing gown. As she reached for the gown, she heard a sound at the door and spun around in alarm.

Kevin had opened the door. He was walking into the room. The door was shut behind him.

"What do you want?" she whispered, fighting panic as he moved toward her with a hypnotic smile. Not here! Not in her husband's house! "You'd better go," she warned with shaky defiance, "or I'll scream." Dennis' room, on one side of her, was empty. His father was in the cottage with Carlotta. Would the others, on the other side of the house, hear her?

"You won't scream," Kevin contradicted smugly. "Have you told Dennis about us?"

"No," she admitted painfully.

"Dennis will never know," he soothed. "You have nothing to worry about. But I couldn't stand it back there on Ransome Island, thinking about you with him." He paused, his eyes glowing fanatically. "Has he come to you yet?"

"No," she whispered, shamed by this admission. She saw the glow of triumph in his eyes. "Cousin Kevin, I mean it." She struggled to mask her terror. "You touch me and I'll scream! They'll all come running!"

"You don't dare," he taunted. He clutched her roughly by the shoulders. "Because then you'll lose this fancy life you've won for yourself. You enjoy playing the little princess!"

"Take your hands off me!" she cried out as he struggled to pull the nightdress away from her shoulders. "Let me go! Let me go!" Her voice rose to an outraged scream as they wrestled together in the faint firelight.

"Let her go!" Ron's voice commanded sharply. Neither of them had heard him come into the room. "Take your hands off Jeannie!" Ron lunged forward and pulled Kevin from her.

Kevin swayed with shock. His eyes were those of an animal at bay.

"You Jezebel!" he shrieked at Jeannie. "You harlot!" He darted awkwardly from the room.

"Jeannie, did he hurt you?" Ron asked soothingly.

"I'm all right," she stammered, and reached for her dressing gown with a mixture of relief and shame.

"The fire is almost going out," Ron said gently, turning away to give her a moment to pull on her dressing gown. "Let me stir it up for you."

Suddenly they heard a strangled outcry in the hall, a heavy thud:

"What was that?" Jeannie whispered fearfully, but Ron

was already dashing from the room. She followed swiftly behind him.

Ron hovered at the landing. Jeannie peered over his shoulder. Kevin had tripped on the stairs in his rush for escape. He had fallen and rolled down to the bottom.

White with shock, Jeannie followed Ron down the darkened stairs. Her cousin lay with his head at an odd angle. His eyes were closed. He mumbled incoherently.

Jeannie stood two steps from the bottom, clinging to the balustrade, and watched while Ron bent over Kevin.

"Is he badly hurt?" she asked. He was silent now. Motionless.

"He broke his neck in the fall," Ron said quietly, and rose to his feet. "He's dead, Jeannie."

Ten

In the dim light from one wall sconce, with the gale-force winds outside hammering at the house, Jeannie stared down at the lifeless form of Kevin Ransome, lying twisted at the bottom of the stairs. All at once she was trembling violently.

"Let's go into the library," Ron said softly. "I'll get you a glass of wine."

Wordlessly she allowed Ron to guide her down the darkened hall into the library. He lit a candle on the mantel, coaxed her into a chair, and went to the Hepplewhite cabin that held the wine.

"Jeannie, there's nothing we can do for him," Ron said quietly. "Drink this." He held out a glass of wine to her. "I'll call the servants to take care of the body."

"Ron, don't leave me," she pleaded.

"All right, Jeannie," he soothed, his eyes full of compassion. He hesitated. "Had he— Had he ever tried something like that before?"

Jeannie dropped her eyes, her face hot with shame.

"Once," she whispered. "Just before Dennis came to Ransome Island. There was nothing I could do." She gestured helplessly. She was conscious of the low sound of indignation that escaped him. "We had buried Mama that afternoon, and that night he came to my room. We were alone in the house."

"He deserved to die," Ron said, taut with fury.

"Several weeks later, when Dennis came to Ransome Island, Kevin came to me and told me Dennis had asked his permission to speak to me of marriage. He ordered me to accept." Her voice broke. "He threatened terrible things if I didn't. He said I was to say nothing about— about what had happened." She took a deep breath, her eyes filling with tears. "I know it was awful to deceive Dennis, but he—he was so wonderful to me." Had Dennis truly been as ardent as she believed, or had she wished to believe that? "I married Dennis under false pretenses."

"Your cousin was a monster," Ron said bluntly. "You're to tell Dennis nothing," he admonished.

"What about tonight?" she stammered, and shivered, remembering Kevin's body lying at the bottom of the stairs.

Ron gazed into space, his mind working.

"We'll say," Ron decided firmly, "that Mr. Ransome was going downstairs—perhaps for something to drink. He tripped and fell down the stairs. You heard the sounds and came running out to investigate. I had been downstairs to check on the windows to make sure the water was not coming in. There was nothing we could do. He was dead."

Straining to remain in control, Jeannie sipped at her wine, grateful for Ron's presence. The rain was beating at the house. The winds continued at gale force, wreaking havoc in their path.

"If the rain continues this way, we may be flooded," Ron said seriously—talking, Jeannie suspected, to give her time to regain her composure. "The plows in the fields could be underwater by morning."

"We'd better call the servants," Jeannie said, all at once remembering that her father-in-law was at the cottage. They must not allow him to walk into the foyer and stumble upon Kevin's body.

"I'll go out to the kitchen and send one of the women to the cabin where the men sleep," Ron said, his eyes solicitous. "Will you be all right here alone for a moment?"

Before she could reassure him, he stiffened to attention. In the night stillness they could hear the front door opening. Ron sprinted from the library and down the hall to see who had come into the house. Jeannie followed at his heels.

Drenched from the downpour, Craig stood at the open door, removing his sodden shoes lest they stain the Kirman carpet. In the night-darkened foyer he had not spied the inert form at the foot of the stairs.

"Uncle Craig, there's been a terrible accident," Ron called to him breathlessly as he strode down the hall. "Mr. Ransome must have left his room to come downstairs. He stumbled and fell all the way down." He took a deep breath, his eyes moving somberly to the body. "He's dead."

"Good Lord!" Craig's voice ricocheted with shock. "Ron, are you sure?" He dropped his shoes by the door and walked across the foyer to bend over Ransome. Ron shot a reassuring glance at Jeannie, who stood, trembling, at his side. "He's dead," Craig confirmed, slowly rising to his feet.

Nobody would know, Jeannie told herself with relief, that he had invaded her room and tried to take her. No one would wonder if there had been an earlier relationship that had motivated him. Bless Ron.

"Come out to the library and have a drink, Uncle Craig," Ron urged. "Stay there with Jeannie while I go arouse the servants." He hesitated. "All we can do until morning is have his body moved to his room. I'll have someone stay with him through the night."

The three of them walked in heavy silence to the

library. Ron left them at the door to go beyond to the kitchen wing.

"It's cold and damp," Craig said as Jeannie hunched her shoulders in discomfort. "Sit down, Jeannie. I'll start a fire." His eyes were compassionate as they rested on her for a moment before he reached for a log from the box beside the fireplace. "This must be a terrible shock for you." His eyes were sympathetic. "Were you and your cousin very close?"

"No," she acknowledged with candor. "No one was close to Kevin." She stiffened, listening to the outdoor sounds. A carriage was pulling up before the house. "That must be Dennis," she said with relief. Yet guilt filtered through her as she remembered her confession to Ron. She should not have talked so freely, she chastised herself.

"I'd better go to the door." Craig hurried from the room to meet Dennis in the foyer. Jeannie moved compulsively into the hall to watch as her father-in-law pulled the door wide.

"What a bitch of a night!" Dennis said with annoyance as he charged into the foyer. "But at least the rain is letting up now." Dennis' view of the body at the foot of the darkened stairs was blocked by his father.

"Dennis, take off your shoes," his father ordered sharply. "They're muddied."

"Yes, Papa," Dennis said with strained patience, bending down to remove them.

"There's been a tragic accident, Dennis," Craig said quietly. "Mr. Ransome is dead."

Jeannie saw Dennis straighten up with astonishment as he dropped his shoes beside his father's.

"What happened?"

Tersely his father explained about the accident, moving aside so that Dennis saw the body at the foot of the stairs.

"Does Jeannie know?" Dennis demanded.

"Jeannie and Ron discovered him," Craig explained. "She's in the library."

The two men walked briskly down the hall to where Jeannie waited.

"Jeannie, I'm sorry about your cousin," Dennis said with a show of sympathy, reaching to squeeze her hand.

"It was an awful thing to happen," she whispered. It was not wrong to lie to Dennis about tonight, she soothed herself. What would be gained by telling him the truth?

"Come inside and let's get a fire going," Craig said with an effort at calm. "You're cold, Jeannie."

"Jeannie and I will have to take the body back to Ransome Island," Dennis decided, and Jeannie flinched. She didn't want to go back to Ransome Island, ever! "There'll be a lot of legal matters to take care of while we're there." In the hall Ron strode past with a pair of male servants. They would be taking Kevin's body to his room for the night, Jeannie thought, feeling faintly sick. "Jeannie, do you know the name of your cousin's lawyer?"

"Yes, he came to Ransome Island twice a year. He's Mr. Schackelford, of Savannah. Richard Schackelford."

"For a while at least we'll have to arrange for absentee management of the plantation," Dennis said, crossing to the Hepplewhite cabinet to pour himself something stronger than the wine Ron had brought out. "I'm not prepared to leave The Magnolias just yet," he said, his eyes suddenly opaque.

Jeannie stared bewilderedly at him.

"But Mr. Schackelford will take care of everything, won't he?"

"Jeannie, Mr. Schackelford is only your cousin's attorney," Dennis said with an air of indulgence. "You can't expect him to manage your plantation."

"Dennis, Ransome Island isn't mine," she said shakily. Was *that* what Dennis thought? "On Kevin's death his entire estate is to go to the agricultural college where he lectured occasionally. There's to be a Kevin Ransome Hall erected in his memory."

"He left you nothing?" Dennis burst out furiously. "His ward gets nothing?"

"Dennis," Craig rapped sharply. "You forget yourself."

"I think it's unconscionable!" Dennis' voice rose stridently. "We can take it to court. Jeannie was his ward, Papa," Dennis protested, struggling to rein in his fury.

"How could he treat her this way?"

"I gather Mr. Ransome left a will," Craig said coldly. "It was his privilege to dispose of his property as he saw fit." He hesitated. "I see no point in subjecting Jeannie to the ordeal of a trip to Ransome Island after the shock of tonight, however. Dennis, you accompany the body to Ransome Island, stopping in Savannah to report to Mr. Schackelford. He'll make the arrangements for burial. I suggest you leave in the morning."

"Yes, Papa," Dennis said tightly. "Now if you'll excuse me, I'll go to my room. I'll leave with the body early in the morning, so that I can make tomorrow's boat from Charleston to Savannah. Good night, Jeannie. Good night, Papa."

Ron returned to the library to say that Juno was making coffee and would bring it to them shortly. Jeannie was relieved that he had not heard Dennis' outburst. She felt sick inside at Dennis' anger.

By the time a somber-faced Juno arrived with the coffee tray, they could hear—well removed from the house, but the sounds carried in the stillness of the night— the shrill, raucous sawing of boards. Kevin's coffin must be ready by morning so that Dennis might take his body home to Ransome Island.

Jeannie slept little for the balance of the night, awakening even before Aunt Lizzie cautiously opened the door to bring her morning coffee, not sure that she would be awake this early after last night's happening.

"Come in, Aunt Lizzie." Jeannie forced a smile. The aroma of fresh coffee was particularly appealing this morning.

"It's jes' awful, what happen' to dat po' man," Aunt Lizzie commiserated. "Mist' Dennis be leavin' in a few minutes. De wagon's waitin' out front already," she reported.

"Let me see." Impulsively Jeannie thrust aside the comforter and darted to the window.

The rain was over. All nature seemed to be joyous this morning. Sunlight spilled over the expanse of lawn, over the towering trees. A mockingbird sang ecstatically

116

from the bough of a live oak. Jeannie's attention focused on the figure of Dennis, climbing into the carriage. The wagon behind carried the pine coffin, within which lay Kevin Ransome's body.

Dennis had been so sure that she would inherit Ransome Island. But he *knew* the circumstances of her being there, she thought with towering frustration. She had been explicit with him; Kevin had taken in her and Mama because there had been nowhere else for them to go. He had called her his ward at Mama's death, but that meant nothing.

Had Dennis married her because he believed that someday she would own Ransome Island? He had been so entranced with the idea of one man's owning an entire island. No! No, she would not believe that of him.

"Young Missy," Aunt Lizzie scolded indulgently. "Yo' git yo'se'f back in dis bed and drink yo' coffee. In a little while Ah bring up yo' breakfas'."

"No," Jeannie said with unexpected firmness. "I'll go downstairs for breakfast." She forced a smile, lest Aunt Lizzie be hurt. "It's such a beautiful morning I want to go for a walk."

An hour later she sat over breakfast with Ron and her father-in-law. The other ladies only occasionally came down to breakfast. As usual, the heavy plantation meal of boiled meat and fish, rice, eggs, sweet potatoes, and hominy appeared on the table. Feeling little appetite this morning, Jeannie took only a wedge of corn bread on her plate.

"Try the mullet," Ron coaxed, his eyes gentle. "They were caught less than an hour ago."

"I will," Jeannie promised. Involuntarily she glanced at her father-in-law. He was gazing at her with disturbing intensity. She smiled faintly and lowered her eyes to her plate.

While Jeannie and Ron were praising the mullet, Craig abruptly excused himself from the table.

"I want to go out and see the fields," he explained perfunctorily. "That was a lot of rain last night."

Mr. Mitchell was annoyed with her this morning. *Why?* Was it because of her friendliness with Ron? she asked herself after deliberation. Did he suspect her and Ron of lying about what had happened last night? Shaken, she considered this. No, why would Mr. Mitchell think that? But she ate now without tasting the fish that had been so appetizing moments ago.

"Have you ever seen the inside of a threshing mill?" Ron asked curiously—anxious to divert her from unhappy thoughts, Jeannie decided gratefully.

"Never," she confessed with a smile.

"We have three mills here at The Magnolias," Ron explained with a show of enthusiasm. "One is worked by steam, one by the tide, and one by horses. The mills are a big saving, you know," he added seriously. "It saves us about six percent of our preparation costs."

"Kevin had a large mill at Ransome Island. He used to mill the crops from neighboring islands." But don't think about Kevin, she exhorted herself. Don't think about last night. "The steam engine is quite powerful, isn't it?" Mr. Mitchell had no right to frown upon her friendship with Ron, she thought defiantly. Ron was her only friend here at The Magnolias. He and Mrs. Mitchell, she amended.

"Thirty horsepower," Ron said with pride. "Would you like to see it? This morning?" he coaxed.

"I *would* like to see it." She managed a small laugh. "It's shameful that I've grown up on a rice plantation and I've never been inside a mill."

She and Ron walked together in the morning sunlight to the large building on the bank of the river that housed the steam mill. He guided her inside to inspect the fires, the boilers, the machinery of the powerful steam engine, patiently explaining the operation of each.

"Here comes Andrew McKinley, who superintends the mills," Ron said politely, but for an instant Jeannie saw the glow of distrust in Ron's eyes as he gazed toward the massive, broad-shouldered man with dark, rumpled hair and arrogant eyes who moved toward them. "Andrew, this is Miss Jeannie, Mr. Dennis' wife," he introduced her.

"The mill's a dangerous place for a woman," McKinley said brusquely. "Be careful while you're here." With a terse nod he walked away from them, heading for the door. A bitter, angry man, Jeannie thought. Except for that, he would have been handsome.

Ron's face tightened at McKinley's cavalier behavior. "It's difficult to find a truly efficient superintendent," he apologized. "McKinley's good at his job."

From the mill Ron took her to the cooper's shop next door, where all the rice barrels for the crops were made as well as the tubs and buckets that were used around the plantation.

"What a lovely aroma," Jeannie exclaimed spontaneously, sniffing the scent of the freshly cut cedar.

"I'd rather have one of these tubs in my room than any fancy foot tub that ever came out of Staffordshire," Ron said with appreciation.

Leaving Ron—recoiling from the thought of a return to the house just yet—Jeannie decided to walk to the quarters. Mr. Mitchell had talked with such pride about the neat, comfortable cottages he provided for his slaves—a practice Dennis considered overindulgent. Ron referred to The Magnolias as a model plantation.

"There are many months during the year when the field hands work little more than six or seven hours a day. Uncle Craig permits them to raise and sell chickens and to make and sell cypress tubs and canoes. And they receive more food than they can eat," he had said with pride.

Jeannie walked cautiously over the moist brown soil, not yet dried by the spring sun. The beauties of the season were on display on every side. She paused, her attention captured by a huge blue heron stalking on stilt legs. It spied her, spread its wide, heavy wings, and seemed to throw itself upon the air, its long shanks flying after it in an awkwardly appealing manner. The bird flew, Jeannie thought whimsically, as though it had just learned —but it was impressively beautiful.

Beyond she saw the two long rows of small, neat, whitewashed cottages with glass windows. Once, as a small child, she had curiously sought out the quarters on Ransome Island and had been sickened by the floorless, run-down one-room cabins, each of which must serve as home for two families. Mama had been severe with her for venturing to the quarters, but admitted to her unhappiness that human beings could be forced to live in such conditions. Mr. Mitchell harbored more respect for those human beings entrusted to his care.

She could hear the laughter of the children as she approached the quarters, and saw the small, well-tended vegetable garden behind each cabin. Chickens were fenced in behind a cabin here and there.

In the open avenue between the two rows of cabins children played at youthful games, cavorting with noisy good humor. A cluster of small girls, several of them young "nurses" holding babies of mothers working in the fields, turned to face her with shy smiles as they became aware of her presence. She heard a low, familiar feminine voice singing a French lullaby. The little girls moved apart to reveal Madeline, cradling a young black baby in her arms with a tenderness that astonished Jeannie. She was suddenly silent as she spied Jeannie.

"What are you doing in the quarters?" Madeline demanded, her eyes shooting off sparks of hate. "Go back to the big house, Jeannie! You don't belong here!"

Trembling, Jeannie turned and ran.

Eleven

"Take him, Dorothy," Madeline said brusquely to the little girl at her side, and handed over the blanket-wrapped infant. She rose to her feet, watching Jeannie disappear from sight. Why didn't that girl leave The Magnolias? She didn't belong here! Why hadn't she gone back to Ransome Island with her cousin's body?

"Missy?" A tiny black girl tugged at Madeline's skirt and smiled at her appealingly. "Sing some mo'?"

"No," Madeline said flatly. "Not today."

She strode away from the cluster of children, who watched her departure with disappointment. Had Dennis told Jeannie to visit the quarters to make the slaves realize there was a new mistress here? Dennis hated her for marrying Ron and becoming a Mitchell. He hated to have another man own her. How many nights did he lie in his bed and think about her with Ron?

A bitter smile touched her face. It must have been a horrible disappointment to Dennis last night when he discovered his bride was not the heiress to Ransome Island. This morning, when Rose brought her coffee, she reported on Dennis' indignation. Jasper had heard the goings-on from the kitchen, where he had bundled down for the night with Eloise, who was Juno's helper. Eloise had then told Rose.

Madeline walked away from the quarters, past a field that would be planted with turnips in July, then strolled along a narrow dike, the river on one side of her and on the other a patch of unreclaimed forest. Her eyes skimmed with reluctant admiration the pale green cypresses that rose to enormous heights, along with the gentle yellow-green water oaks, the true green hickories, the magnificent maples, running the gamut of pink from pale salmon to a rich crimson. Magnolias, with lustrous leaves and queenly blossoms, vied for space with the wild myrtle that would, before the summer was past, reach a height of ten feet. Beneath all these the spiked palmetto provided a mysterious coverlet.

Her eyes moved beyond to the low rice fields, now being plowed for planting. She would walk out there, see if Andrew was in the fields. It was his habit to walk about the fields in midmorning. Andrew would see her and come to her, she plotted with a flicker of anticipation. They would go back, together, to his cottage. Since the first month of her marriage she had visited Andrew's cottage at least once a week.

She walked along the dike, her mind returning to

Dennis with simmering rage. Had he ever discussed *her* with Ron? Not likely. Dennis had such contempt for Ron, and Ron considered Dennis a profligate. God, Ron was so sanctimonious, so stupidly loyal to his bastard of an uncle! Ron should share the inheritance of the plantation with Dennis—Mr. Mitchell ought to see that!

Did Dennis ever ask himself how she had managed this marriage to Ron? She smiled with defiant triumph, remembering that afternoon on which she had met Ron. She had been invited to be a guest at Mr. Poinsett's plantation near Georgetown. Old Mr. Poinsett enjoyed the company of beautiful young ladies.

"When he lived in Charleston," the journalist who had arranged for her invitation reminisced, "Mr. Poinsett had his own little court. Why, invitations to his once-a-week breakfasts were as much sought after as invitations to the St. Cecilias." To be invited back, a young lady had to be beautiful, charming, or intelligent.

Ron, who had served under Captain Blanding in the War with Mexico and had been with the company that planted the Palmetto flag—the first American flag— within the city of Mexico, had been invited because the former Ambassador to Mexico enjoyed talking with those who knew that country.

She had sat in the beautiful drawing room of the Poinsetts' rice plantation, set in the midst of wild, sandy forest land, determined to be her most charming, to please not only the delightful older French *gentilhomme* but Ron Mitchell as well. The moment she realized this was Dennis' cousin, who lived at The Magnolias, her mind had begun to plot.

She and Mrs. Poinsett had listened to the earnest conversation between Ron and Mr. Poinsett about the internal politics of the nation. She had found satisfaction in Mr. Poinsett's outspoken dislike for slavery. Her sole interest in politics was the European contempt for slavery. Ron too considered slavery morally wrong. But not Dennis, she thought bitterly. The slaves were his subjects.

She had noticed the shy, interested glances that Ron shot regularly in her direction that first afternoon, and again in the evening when they were summoned to tea.

Ron had gone right from college into the regiment with which he had fought in Mexico. He had associated little with young ladies. She had known that first night that she could marry him. It was just a matter of time.

A dog trotting toward her for a pat brought her back to the moment. She scratched him behind the ears, her eyes searching the rice fields. She was disappointed not to see Andrew's massive figure out there with the workers. Then she spied Craig off in the west field, inspecting a plow. Uneasy, she turned to leave the area, impatiently dismissing the friendly setter.

"Madeline . . ." A familiar rough voice spun her about to face its owner. He stood there with feet spread apart, a smug smile on his face.

"I've been looking all over for you, Andrew," she pouted. He was uncouth, arrogant, and hot-tempered; but in bed he made her forget that. He was like some precariously leashed animal, yet she always felt in command.

"Let's go to the cottage," he ordered, his eyes sweeping over her with the look of heat she never failed to elicit from him. He prodded her with a whack on the rump. His eyes swung over his shoulder for a moment. He was aware of Craig's presence in the field. But Mr. Mitchell was too involved in inspecting the plow to notice them.

They walked together in loaded silence to the small white cottage situated two hundred feet beyond the quarters. Andrew made her nervous, Madeline thought, on those occasions when he was invited to the house for tea. Mr. Mitchell insisted on this socializing with the superintendent at regular intervals. A smile touched her mouth. Mr. Mitchell would not be so anxious to prove himself the democratic gentleman if he knew his nephew's wife was bedding down with his superintendent.

What a huge man Andrew was, she thought with a mixture of excitement and revulsion as they entered the cottage. He towered above any man she had ever known. Sometimes, in the heat of passion, she was afraid he might kill her.

"Pour some wine," Andrew told her, striding from the sparsely furnished sitting room into his bedroom. He would go in there, close the curtains, and turn down the bed.

She walked to the cupboard where he kept the Sauterne he favored and brought out the bottle and two glasses. He had to play his little game of getting her slightly drunk. He didn't know that she could drink a bottle of Sauterne and feel nothing. She had been raised in France.

Andrew came back into the sitting room, crossed to each of the windows, and closed the curtains. He walked to the door and dropped the latch into place. His eyes were dark with excitement when he turned around to her.

"Come have your wine," she coaxed, her eyes provocative.

He crossed to her and accepted the glass of Sauterne. Again she was conscious of his height, his strength. There was not a hand on the plantation who would dare tangle with him.

Standing before her, his eyes never leaving her face, he drained his glass.

"Finish your wine," he said impatiently.

Andrew McKinley was, she thought detachedly, a most conventional lover. One of these days, when she felt in an adventurous mood, she would teach him. But not today.

He took the glass from her hand, set it down on a small table, and pulled her roughly to him.

"Andrew," she protested; but she enjoyed the sense of brutality in him. "You're hurting me."

"*You'd* like to hurt *me*," he guessed, startling her with this observation. She would! She would like to beat him into a mass of broken flesh, and then she would like to take him.

"Andrew, you uncouth ox," she complained when he dropped her unceremoniously onto the bed. "When are you going to learn some finesse?"

But there was many a fine young South Carolinian gentleman, she acknowledged as the room ricocheted with the sounds of their passion, who had never aroused her as Andrew McKinley did.

Madeline walked briskly back to the house, enjoying

the fresh sea air in her face. Rose would bring her second breakfast up to her room. It was enough that she presented herself to the family at dinner and tea.

Walking into the house, she could hear her mother-in-law and Jeannie at the table. Those two were getting so thick, she thought warily. Mrs. Mitchell had somebody she could talk to about those infernal books she read day and night. Did Mrs. Mitchell know what she was reading, Madeline asked herself with amusement, when she was saturated with sherry?

Rose was hanging away the dresses she had ironed earlier. She turned around, her rotund body absurdly fitted, with inserts, into one of Madeline's cast-off gowns.

"Ah go git yo' breakfas'," Rose crooned, her eyes bright with admiration for her lady. "An' Suzette come down to say yo' mama want yo' to come to talk to huh fo' a while." Her eyes softened. "She git lonesome up deah by huhse'f."

"I'll go later," Madeline said, brushing this aside. Mama was always getting lonely. What else, when they were imprisoned in this house? She had thought they would live like other plantation families, spending much of their time in the social life of Charleston.

While Rose went downstairs for her tray, Madeline undressed down to her skin and pulled on only her dressing gown, enjoying the sense of freedom this attire provided. She settled herself in bed, her mind dwelling on the time she had spent with Andrew.

Rose came back into the room with a tray bearing oranges, bananas, fresh-baked bread and butter, and a glass of iced milk. Madeline attacked this second, noonday breakfast with relish.

"Rose, go downstairs and heat water. I want a bath." Rose stared at her.

"In de middle o' de day, Missy Madeline?"

"Whenever I feel like it," Madeline tossed back with irritation. She wanted to wash away the scent of Andrew McKinley's sweaty body. It reminded her that for a little while, that ox of a man had dominated her. She listened to the sounds in the hall. Jeannie was talking to one of the servants. "Rose," she said impulsively, a secretive glint in her eyes, "ask Miss Jeannie to come into my room."

She listened with a faint smile on her mouth while Rose delivered her message. A moment later she heard a light knock on her door.

"Come in," Madeline called out, ostensibly in a placating mood.

The door opened. Jeannie, an air of uncertainty about her, walked into the room.

"Jeannie, close the door," she said indulgently. Jeannie didn't trust her. Dennis' bride was not stupid, she conceded. Beautiful and bright. Joel Poinsett would have adored her. But did Dennis care at all for his bride? Despite his sporadic show of ardor, she suspected that he did not.

Silently Jeannie closed the door and turned to Madeline again with a tentative smile.

"I'm sorry about your cousin," Madeline said with perfunctory sympathy. "Rose told me this morning."

"It was a terrible tragedy," Jeannie said, her voice constrained. She felt uncomfortable in this room, Madeline guessed, pleased with the discovery.

"And the bridegroom took the body back to Ransome Island, I gather?" She allowed a veiled flippancy to coat her voice.

"Yes, Dennis took my cousin's body home." Jeannie's eyes were wary, Madeline's flippancy not lost on her. She was trying to fathom the reason for this catechism.

"I'm sure he welcomed the opportunity to get away from The Magnolias," Madeline drawled.

"It was kind of Dennis to offer to do it." Color touched Jeannie's cheekbones.

"Do you ever wonder why Dennis runs so much to Charleston? Has he ever confided in you?" Madeline challenged.

Jeannie hesitated.

"I know," she said, her eyes defying Madeline to pursue this.

"*What* do you know?" Madeline pushed, enjoying Jeannie's discomfort. "That Dennis runs regularly to the gaming rooms?"

"I know," Jeannie confirmed.

"But do you know about his women?" Madeline leaned forward, upsetting the tray across her knees. The dishes, the glass of milk spilled across the bed, but Madeline ignored them. "Dennis has quite a reputation in Charleston. Shall I tell you about some of his women?"

"No!" Jeannie flashed back, but she seemed frozen in shock.

"There are times," Madeline said with deliberate slowness, "that Dennis seeks his satisfaction in odd fashions. There is, in a bawdy house in Charleston, a woman who weighs four hundred pounds. Dennis adores to bury himself beneath her mountain of a breast—"

"I don't want to hear this!" Jeannie blazed. "You're disgusting!"

"And there's a woman who must be sixty if she's a day that Dennis called on regularly for months, they say, because of what she would do to him. . . ." Madeline laughed with relish as Jeannie ran from the room, slamming the door behind her.

Madeline slid from beneath the milk-dampened comforter, crossed the room, and went out onto the upstairs gallery. She saw Carlotta walking with a bundle of clothes toward the washing rooms. She loathed the pride of that one.

Inside Madeline's bedroom, Rose was clucking to herself about the mess on the bed. Madeline returned to the doorway.

"Forget about that mess until you've filled the tub," she commanded Rose, then sauntered back onto the gallery again.

Everything was so green after last night's rain. How strange that Kevin Ransome had died in the midst of that storm. Had he fallen down the stairs, or had somebody pushed him? For a few moments she allowed her mind to probe into this possibility.

"Madeline!" Smiling up at her, Arnold called from down below. "Madeline, I brought over my pressed-magnolia book."

"Come on up to my room," Madeline invited. "I'd

love to see your magnolias." That strange little boy in a man's body.

Rose came into the room weighed down with two more kettles of water, trailed by Arnold.

"Missy Madeline," Rose protested. "It ain' rat fo' him to come into yo' bedroom. Specially wit' yo' dress' lak dat."

"Rose, it's all right," she said serenely, her eyes in secret communication with Rose's. They both knew he was like a small boy. "Fill up the tub." She sat down on a chair and allowed Arnold to place the book with the pressed magnolias across her lap.

For a little while she and Arnold talked about the splendor of the magnolia blossoms in his collection. Then Rose announced the tub was ready.

"Clean off the bed now, Rose," Madeline instructed, but Rose was already sweeping away the soiled comforter.

Madeline crossed to her dresser to bring out the fine English soap with which The Magnolias was always supplied, unwrapped a bar, and sniffed appreciatively.

"Smell, Arnold." She held the bar out invitingly to him. A provocative glint showed itself in her eyes. "Would you like to stay and help me with my bath? You can scrub my back."

"Missy!" Rose screeched.

"Can I, Madeline?" Arnold asked with wistful pleasure. "I'll scrub it good."

"Go on about your business, Rose," Madeline ordered coolly, and dropped the dressing gown from her body to the floor, ignoring Rose's wail of dismay as she stood nude before Arnold, who gazed raptly upon her. With plotted grace she stepped into the water and settled herself in the marble tub. "Now Arnold," she said with a brilliant smile, "scrub my back."

Twelve

Jeannie sat in a chair by a window in her room, a book across her lap, striving futilely to become involved in the novel Mrs. Mitchell had given to her yesterday. But Madeline's face—Madeline's voice—haunted her.

She knew about Dennis' gambling. She remembered, too, his indignation when he discovered she had not inherited Ransome Island. And now Madeline threw in her face that sordid account of Dennis' escapades with women. *No, I won't believe that. Madeline's trying to discredit Dennis, to break up our marriage.*

Why had Dennis married her? This question kept haunting her. Because he thought that she would some-day inherit Ransome Island? But Dennis, so spectacularly handsome, could have married anyone, she thought with frustration. Why had he chosen her? In all these weeks he had not once come to her room. Her belief in his affection was growing shaky.

Dennis was on board ship now, en route to Savannah. He would be bored already with the dullness of his trip. He had not wanted to perform the duty of accompanying Kevin's body back home, but he had not dared to refuse his father.

All at once the shock of last night assaulted her with searing vividness. She was trembling as she mentally re-lived those terrible moments when Kevin had invaded her room, intent—again—on violating her. If the terrible event that followed had happened to someone else, Cousin

Kevin would have been the first to say that this was God's retribution.

Suddenly she could not bear to remain in this room, where Kevin had come to her last night. Bless Ron! If he had not passed her door, her cries would have been futile. Her cousin would have had his will with her again, and afterward she would have killed herself.

She would walk along the river for a while. The sea air was drifting in from the Atlantic today. It was fresh and invigorating.

Reaching for a light cape against the pleasant chill of the day, she strode impatiently from her room. From behind the closed door of Madeline's room Arnold's voice, strong and loud, drifted to her.

"Aunt Emmaline had a letter from Rebecca," Arnold reported. "She's in Paris."

"God, I wish I were back in Paris!" Madeline said with a startling vehemence that reached Jeannie. "I wish I had never left there!"

"Madeline, don't say that," Arnold protested unhappily. "Then I wouldn't know you."

Poor Arnold, Jeannie thought as she hurried down the stairs, impatient to put the house behind her. How strange that Madeline showed such gentleness toward him. She would not have expected that. And in her mind now she saw Madeline in the quarters, cradling the young black baby in her arms, singing the French lullaby. That too was surprising.

She left the house behind her and walked with compulsive swiftness toward the river. As she walked, her mind began to clear. She knew what she must do, Jeannie told herself. She would confront Dennis when he returned from this trip. She would insist that he be candid with her. If this was a marriage he now regretted, she must know. She could still write her cousin in Virginia and ask if she might come to live with her until she could find herself a position.

Color stained her cheeks as she recalled Mr. Mitchell's offer. But no, if she was not to live at The Magnolias as Dennis' wife, then she wanted nothing from the Mitchell family.

Dennis' father knew how fragile this marriage was, she thought with fresh insight. He knew Dennis' weaknesses. But if Dennis truly loved her, she thought with shaky defiance—wishing to believe that he did—then they could start a whole new life together. *If* he loved her. . . .

Jeannie settled in for a siege of waiting. It would surely be a week before Dennis would return to The Magnolias, his obligations fulfilled. She was touched by the sympathy Eleanor Mitchell showed her for her cousin's death. Mrs. Mitchell was genuinely upset. How much more upset she would be, Jeannie thought, if she knew of the events that had led to Kevin's death.

Eleanor Mitchell talked to her about Dennis' childhood, which seemed to have been an infinitely precious time in her life. And once Eleanor timorously confided that Craig was pleased at the way Jeannie was handling the ordering of their meals.

"It makes me very nervous to deal with the servants," she said with an air of apology. "And Craig says you're cutting down the kitchen expenses tremendously." That, Jeannie thought wryly, was something she had learned at Ransome Island, though frugality was not carried here to the extent demanded by her cousin. It had been simply a matter of eliminating some of the enormous waste.

Two days after Dennis left for Ransome Island, his father went into Charleston. Instinctively Jeannie knew he was going into the city to settle Dennis' gambling debts. She had heard him talking to Ron about delaying the purchase of equipment Ron felt they needed in the mill until he could arrange a loan from Mr. Goldberg, a private financier with whom he had dealt in the past. Current available funds must go to Dennis' creditor.

Recurrently Jeannie felt a tug of guilt as she remembered how she had confided in Ron the night of Kevin's death. Had she been disloyal to Dennis? He should have been told, she tortured herself repeatedly, before they stood up before Mr. King and were married.

At a time when she knew Miss Charlotte was in Charleston on business, Jeannie allowed Arnold to persuade her to go over to Burke Acres. Miss Emmaline was pathetically pleased to see her, and reported avidly on Rebecca's visit to Paris. Emmaline would have adored to visit Paris herself.

Exactly a week after Dennis' departure, at breakfast, Craig announced that Dennis' ship would be docking in Charleston that morning.

"I've sent Plato to the wharf to meet him," Craig said, his face all at once tight. Dennis had thus far avoided the confrontation with him on the gambling debts. Now it must be faced. "Dennis should be home well before dinner."

Dennis did not arrive for dinner, though his imminent appearance at The Magnolias was the main topic of table conversation. Eleanor glowed with eagerness.

"It seems that Dennis has been away so long," she said wistfully. "I'm so impatient to see him." Eleanor failed to notice Madeline's smile of contempt.

"How did you manage the seven months when he was in Europe?" Madeline asked with deceptive sympathy, but Eleanor had slipped into a vague, sherry-induced dream.

Craig and Ron talked earnestly about the recent inauguration of President Taylor.

"I have respect for the man," Craig said. "It was against his conscience to take office on Sunday, and he insisted that the inauguration be put off until Monday."

"Still, he must be welcomed in Washington social circles," Ron said whimsically, "after four years of the Polks. Can you imagine the White House without dancing, alcoholic beverages, or card-playing?"

"Sara Polk even refused to go to the theater or the horse races," Madeline remarked. "What a saint she was!" Her voice was vitriolic.

"The Polks had no children, either," Craig said with a dry smile, and Madeline laughed.

"Why, Mr. Mitchell," she drawled, "I wouldn't have expected such a risque remark from you."

After dinner Jeannie self-consciously took up a position on the downstairs gallery. Tonight, she swore—fighting down apprehension at the prospect—she must go to Dennis and talk to him with candor. If she was convinced there could never be a real marriage between them, then she must leave The Magnolias.

Dennis did not arrive until the family was halfway through tea. He made no excuse for his dalliance in Charleston, but he seemed in a festive mood. He displayed an ardor for his bride, when he paused to kiss her as she sat at the table, that Jeannie found suspect. He kissed his mother warmly and took his place.

Dennis had visited the gaming rooms in Charleston, Jeannie interpreted; and he knew his father had settled his debts. That, of course, must be a tremendous relief. She had never truly doubted that Mr. Mitchell would take care of that. If he had not, the consequences could have been ugly.

With Dennis seated, the conversation again became political.

"Thank God, Polk is out," Dennis said with satisfaction, but Jeannie guessed that he was actually indifferent to affairs of state. "I never did like that man."

"He was one of the very best, the most honest Presidents this country ever had," Craig protested.

"But Taylor is a national hero," Dennis reminded. "He won the Mexican War for us."

"An aggressive war," Ron interjected intensely. "He made it that when he ordered the American army to cross the Rio Grande."

"The Rio Grande was not the true boundary, was it?" Jeannie asked earnestly, and the three men looked at her. Women were not expected to be knowledgeable about such things. "That was a political move when Texas joined the Union, to declare the Rio Grande the boundary when, in reality, it was the Nueces River."

"Exactly." Ron leaned forward, his eyes zealous, talking to Jeannie because he felt her sympathy. "And we won that land expensively. There were ninety-six men in my outfit when we left Charleston. Less than forty were alive when we took Mexico City. I'll never fight a war again!" he swore.

"There'll be war," Dennis predicted with an arrogant smile. "It may take years, but South Carolina won't forever take what the Union tries to push upon us. But

133

don't worry, Ron," he soothed with amusement. "We won't have to fight. The planters will surely be exempt. We'll have to take care of our slaves."

"There'll be no slaves left," Madeline refuted triumphantly, "if ever the Union fights the South. They'll take off for freedom."

Jeannie felt a coldness close in about her as she witnessed the clash between Dennis and Madeline. Again it was as though they were alone at the table, locked in some secret conflict. For the week that Dennis had been away, she had pushed from her mind this strange relationship between them.

After tea the family retired to the parlor. Madeline excused herself early on the pretext that her mother was not feeling well and she had promised to visit in her rooms. Eleanor, as usual, settled herself in a chair by the fire, hardly needed tonight but offering a coziness that Jeannie appreciated. A faint smile on her face, Eleanor pretended to listen to the conversation among the three men; but Jeannie suspected that she was mentally far removed from the parlor as she sipped her ever-present sherry.

Before the evening was over, the temperature plunged sharply downward. The fire was necessary for comfort. Outside, the wind whipped through the trees. The sky was a dark sea of ominous clouds. The river churned furiously.

"We'll have a storm before morning," Ron guessed uneasily.

"That's just what we need," Craig shot back with a frown, "with the first seeds in. A bad storm can drive salt water into the fields," he explained for Jeannie's benefit. "That can cause a lot of damage."

"I'll go out and tell Gilbert to send somebody to fasten all the lower-floor shutters," Ron said, rising to his feet. "I hope the cabins are not hit hard."

With Dennis and his father and mother, Jeannie walked up the stairs, saying good night at her door. Dennis dutifully kissed her on the cheek, but it seemed to Jeannie that Craig watched with a quizzical expression.

She closed her door behind her, heart pounding because she had made her decision. She would wait awhile until the members of the household had settled down—until Ron came upstairs and went to his room—and then she would go to Dennis.

Fighting panic, Jeannie prepared for the night, pulling on a warm dressing gown against the unexpected drop in temperature. Outside she could hear several of the men slaves moving about the outside of the house, closing the shutters against the threatening storm, talking loudly to one another.

Suddenly the heavens unleashed their rain. Lightning darted across the sky. Thunder rumbled. Hurriedly Jeannie moved to the windows of her room that were not on the gallery and reached to draw the shutters tight. She listened attentively to footsteps in the hall. Ron was going to his room.

She waited until she heard Ron's door shut, then left her room. Oddly self-conscious, she walked to Dennis' door and knocked lightly.

"Come in," Dennis called brusquely.

She opened the door and walked inside. Dennis appeared startled to see her. He was still dressed, though he had removed his jacket.

"Dennis, may I talk to you?" Her voice sounded strained despite her efforts to retain her equanimity.

"Of course, Jeannie." His eyes were wary.

She closed the door and turned to him, ordering herself to pursue the mission that had brought her here.

"Dennis, I'm afraid that we have no marriage," she said tremulously. "I think that you married in haste and now you regret it." She had shaken him! "But I don't have to remain at The Magnolias, Dennis. I have a cousin in Virginia—"

"Jeannie!" He moved toward her and reached for her shoulders. "How can you talk of leaving me?" he protested. He touched her face with one hand, his handsome face reproachful. "Jeannie, you *can't* leave me. How could I endure that?" His dark eyes glowed with ardor as he pulled her close.

"But Dennis," she stammered, her mind in turmoil, "there is no marriage between us." All these weeks at

The Magnolias and nothing between them but a discreet kiss on the cheek before the others. "I can understand," she said more forcefully, "that you acted in haste in marrying me."

"Jeannie, my darling," he murmured amorously, "you have become my life. I've been afraid to rush you. We had known each other such a little time when we were married. I've waited for some sign from you," he reproached gently, "but there was none."

"Oh, Dennis." Tears filled her eyes. How wrong she had been! Misreading the feud between him and Madeline, thinking he was in bondage to his cousin's wife.

"I love you, Jeannie." His mouth brushed her earlobe as his hands moved about her back, bringing her in tautly against the length of him. "Let me show you how much I love you."

She closed her eyes, her arms clasped about his neck as he swept her from her feet and carried her to the bed. She had been afraid that she would not be able to accept his love. How wrong she had been! She wanted Dennis to love her. She wanted to be his wife in every way.

Her face grew wet with tears of happiness as her husband taught her how to love. The horror of that night on Ransome Island receded into her memory. She responded with joy, sharing completely in their act of love.

They fell asleep in each other's arms, exhausted by their lovemaking, while the storm raged outside. Jeannie heard, subconsciously, the crash of a tree close by. The rain beat raucously against the windowpanes. She would have been uncomfortable in the unseasonable cold that pervaded the house except for the warmth of Dennis' body close to hers.

Jeannie came awake in the morning with a start, aware that she had slept far later than usual. Simultaneously she was aware that she was in her husband's bed, lately in his arms. In sleep he had flung himself to the other side of the bed, his face burrowed against the pillow.

Her face lighted with fresh beauty this morning. How right she had been in coming to Dennis! How wrong she had been in suspecting him of repenting this marriage. She had known his tenderness on the days of their journey

136

to The Magnolias, where he had made it touchingly clear that he would not rush her into a relationship for which she was not yet prepared. How had she allowed her thinking to become so twisted?

With slow, cautious movements, so as not to awaken Dennis, she moved from her bed, found her slippers, crossed to the door, and walked out into the hall. Madeline, striding toward the stairs, stopped dead at the sight of her emerging from Dennis' room. Jeannie felt suddenly self-conscious as Madeline's eyes grew hostile in comprehension.

"Good morning," Madeline said coldly. "The storm was bad last night. A branch of a tree came down across the second-floor gallery. But you wouldn't know about that, would you?" Her voice was insolent.

"No, I wouldn't," Jeannie said politely. But her eyes said that Madeline's meaning was not lost on her. "Excuse me." She smiled and moved to her door.

Thirteen

Jeannie went to her room, startled to find Aunt Lizzie there, industriously sweeping up broken glass. A pair of hands worked on the gallery, removing the green-leaved bough of the live oak that had split away from the tree.

"Mawnin', Young Missy," Aunt Lizzie said lovingly. "It good yo' didn' sleep in heah las' night." Her eyes twinkled. "Dat was some bad sto'm." She leaned over to sweep the broken particles of glass onto a piece of newspaper. "Ah'll go downstaihs an' git yo' breakfas', honey."

"That's all right, Aunt Lizzie," Jeannie said with a serene smile. "I'll go down to the table as soon as I've dressed."

"Yes'm." Aunt Lizzie walked to the windows and pulled the curtains tight against the view of the hands working on the gallery. "It sho' nice today. We'll be gittin' real summuh soon." The summer, Jeannie thought, that was so enervating, so ominous in this proximity to the marshy rice fields and the swamps.

Jeannie allowed Aunt Lizzie to help her wash and dress, then left her bedroom to go downstairs. She could hear her father-in-law and Ron talking at the breakfast table.

"Damn good thing you bought all that board last week, Ron," Craig was saying as she approached the room. "We'll need every foot of it, the way the water's sweeping over the rice fields."

"Is it very bad?" Jeannie asked anxiously. She had witnessed hurricanes at Ransome Island that brought most of the island underwater.

"Bad enough," Craig said wryly while Ron smiled up at her with a warmth that was disconcerting. "I went out for a look around this morning. Several huge oaks are down. One of them snapped right off in falling. Just missed the house." It must have been a bough from that tree that the hands were removing from the gallery. "I suppose the trees really saved the house from damage, breaking the force of the wind the way they did."

"The plows that were left in the far fields are underwater," Ron reported seriously. "And the headman tells me there are at least five breaks in the riverbank, and several bridges are down." He turned to his uncle. "We won't be able to do anything until the tide recedes, and with the strong east wind blowing that's going to be a while."

"Are the roads out?" Jeannie asked.

Ron smiled.

"Arnold won't be able to make his regular trips over from Burke Acres for the next few days. Those roads are all underwater."

"As soon as the water leaves the fields, we'll begin

to work on the breaks," Craig said briskly.

Carlotta came into the dining room with a plate and silver for Jeannie, then returned in a few moments with a cup and saucer and a fresh pot of coffee. This morning Jeannie ate with relish, washing from her mind the memory of the encounter with Madeline in the hall. Today she was too joyous in the knowledge that she was indeed Dennis' wife to feel ill will toward anyone. Yet guilt brushed her when she remembered that she had followed Kevin's instructions. Dennis believed that no other man had ever touched her.

Jeannie listened while the two men discussed the task that lay ahead of them. Those on rice plantations were familiar with the hazards that were inherent in raising rice. Floods could break levees and dikes. Freshets could inundate hundreds of acres as often as three times a winter. Even alligators and muskrats could start disastrous breaks. Yet beneath their concern, Jeannie thought, Mr. Mitchell and Ron seemed stimulated by the need to pit their wits against nature.

After breakfast Jeannie returned to her room and walked out onto the cleared gallery to gaze into the distance at the swollen river. She could hear, clear in the morning air, the voices of the hands as they worked to do what little could be done at this point.

Late in the afternoon she saw Ron approaching the house, tired, his clothes sodden from long hours in the wet fields. A few minutes later she heard him come up the stairs and go into his room. He ought to have a hot bath, she thought worriedly, and suddenly felt self-conscious at her concern for him.

Jeannie saw nothing of Dennis until tea, where the conversation was serious, focused on the tasks of repairing the breaks in the dikes and restoring the bridges. Madeline sulked, off by herself. Eleanor looked on anxiously while Dennis and Mavis carried on a private conversation about contemporary French painters.

"Madeline's father would have surpassed Delacroix if he had not died in a duel when she was seven," Mavis said with pride.

At a prodding from his father, Dennis reluctantly

agreed to supervise a working crew the following day. Jeannie glowed with pride. Perhaps now he would assume his share of the responsibility of running The Magnolias.

For the next few days the men of the household were engrossed in restoring the plantation to order. They left the house immediately after an early breakfast, returned in time for dinner, then went out again until Jeannie sent young Jeffrey out to the fields to summon them for tea.

Each night Jeannie waited hopefully for Dennis to come to her. She lay sleepless, haunted by the memory of the night when she had lain in Dennis' arms. She was conscious of a new awakening in her that was exquisite, yet disturbing.

Dennis was tired from his days in the fields, she told herself as she lay awake in her bed, listening to the sound of the beagles off in the woods. She felt an aching emptiness.

In a burst of restlessness she left her bed to go to the clock on the mantel and lit a candle to see the time. Perhaps a glass of wine would help, she thought exhaustedly, rebelling at this nightly sleeplessness.

She found her slippers, pulled on a robe, and took the candle to see her way down to the library. She would have a glass of sherry, she promised herself, and then she would sleep. She walked down the stairs, a hand on the balustrade, painfully remembering the night Kevin had fallen down these stairs to his death.

At the bottom, she stiffened to attention. Whom was Dennis talking with in the library at this hour of the night? Compulsively she walked on slipper-silent feet toward the library, and then—a dozen feet from the door —she froze, Dennis' words knifing their way into her brain.

"Why did you marry Ron?" Dennis was demanding in a tortured voice. "How could you do this to me?"

"You ran out on me!" Madeline's voice was deep with remembered rage. "You left me in Charleston and ran to Europe."

"Madeline . . ." His voice was an agonized plea; and

all at once Jeannie visualized his face that day they had arrived at The Magnolias. She knew her husband desperately desired his cousin's wife. How had she convinced herself otherwise? How had she allowed herself to lie in his arms and believe that he loved *her*? "Madeline, please!"

"Don't touch me, Dennis." Madeline's voice was icy with bitterness. "I'm your cousin's wife. You are never to touch me again."

Trembling, Jeannie spun around and ran noiselessly toward the stairs. Dennis and Madeline had once been lovers. How could she have been so blind as not to have realized?

In her room she crept into her bed and lay staring into the darkness. Dennis had married her in retaliation for Madeline's marriage to Ron. And Madeline had married Ron to spite Dennis. Suddenly she felt a closeness to Ron, a strange awareness of him. No, she exhorted herself with shock, how could she think of Ron in that fashion?

How was she going to remain at The Magnolias after tonight? How could she look at Dennis and Madeline without giving away her knowledge? How could she *want* to stay, knowing what she knew?

She ought to despise Dennis for what he had done to her, she rebuked herself. Was her pride such a weak, shoddy thing that she could want him to come to her again?

Yet she knew she would not leave The Magnolias. For one magnificent night Dennis had loved her. She would never be free of him again, she taunted herself.

Finally Jeannie fell into slumber. She awoke at her normal time with an overwhelming sense of tiredness. She lay without moving, her mind assaulted by visions of Dennis and Madeline. She again heard the voices in the library last night, her face growing hot as the conversation between them charged across her mind.

She must go through today and all the days to follow pretending she knew nothing. Could she remain, knowing that Madeline and Dennis had once been lovers, that Dennis still desired Madeline?

And poor Ron knew nothing. She fought down an instinct to dress, to seek out Ron and confide this terrible knowledge. *No.* How could she hurt Ron in that fashion?

Jeannie started at the light knock on her door. Aunt Lizzie, she guessed. Yet she tensed, lest it be Dennis. Hopefully Dennis, to wash away the ugliness that haunted her.

"Come in."

The door opened. Aunt Lizzie, smiling broadly, came into the room with her coffee.

"Mawnin', Missy," Aunt Lizzie crooned. "Plato say Ah tell yo' he git ha'f a dozen wild ducks this mawnin'. He say mebbe yo' wan' Juno fix 'em fo' dinnuh."

"Tell Plato I'm delighted," Jeannie said vigorously. The servants respected her, she thought with a touch of pride. After watching Mama handle the servants at Ransome Island, she had found that this task came easily to her. "I'll ask Juno to prepare duck for dinner," she added diplomatically. Juno was growing less touchy with her, at last.

"Dat beagle done drop huh pups," Aunt Lizzie continued with her small store of gossip. "Yo' won't believe it, honey. She have nine pups!"

"I must go to the stables to see them," Jeannie said with an automatic smile.

After breakfast, Jeannie promised herself, she would go over to Burke Acres for a visit with Miss Emmaline. The roads were passable again. Arnold had been over yesterday. For a little while she would take herself away from The Magnolias.

Craig and Ron were at the breakfast table already when she arrived. Both men glanced up at her in welcome. Both men looked tired, Jeannie thought sympathetically as they exchanged good-mornings. This last week had been hard on them.

"Didn't you sleep well, Jeannie?" Ron asked as she smothered yawn after yawn.

"I stayed up too late reading," she fabricated. "I'll nap later."

"Dennis has already given up on helping with the work," Craig said with an effort at humor, but bitterness showed through. "I thought for a few days we were getting him down to business."

"Dennis is spoiled," Jeannie said, and smiled at his father's look of surprise. Did Mr. Mitchell expect her not to see Dennis' faults? She saw them, her mind taunted; and still she stayed.

"You try to talk to him, Jeannie," Craig said carefully. "Maybe you can make him understand there's something in life besides riding and hunting and chasing down to Charleston."

"I'll try," she promised. Did Mr. Mitchell suspect that Dennis and Madeline had known each other before she married Ron? Sometimes he gazed from one to the other with an expression of such distress.

Immediately after breakfast Jeannie asked Gilbert to have a carriage brought around to the front of the house so that she might go visit with Miss Emmaline. She churned with a need to remove herself from The Magnolias, as though in this fashion she might escape the memory of what she had overheard last night in the library. Miss Emmaline adored Dennis. She too spoiled him.

Riding to the Burke plantation, Jeannie was conscious of the imminence of summer. The flowers blossomed in wild abundance, the air fragrant with the mixture of scents. The trees wore their summer lushness. In a little while—a matter of days—the heaviness of summer would be upon them.

Apprehensively she remembered the discomfort of the hot months, when Kevin's temper had been short and explosive. Dennis hated the summer on the plantation. Already he was complaining about the arrival of the insects. She must tell Plato to have a pair of children at the table with peacock feathers to brush away the bugs.

Miss Emmaline greeted her with delight, brought her into the parlor, and sent for lemonade. She was full of talk about the storm, the damage wrought at Burke Acres.

"You wouldn't believe the way Charlotte has been working," she said with affection. "Out there with the men from sunup to sunset, and everything is just about in order again. But where is Dennis?" she reproached. "Why doesn't he come to see me?"

"He will," Jeannie soothed. "He's been working with Mr. Mitchell and Ron."

"Aunt Emmaline . . ." Arnold hovered eagerly in the doorway. "Can I come in?"

"Good morning, Arnold," Jeannie said as Emmaline indulgently beckoned him into the room. "Have you collected anything new?"

"Yellow jessamine," he said with satisfaction. "I'll have a whole book of them soon. Can I go back to The Magnolias when you go, and show them to Madeline?"

"Of course, Arnold," Jeannie said quickly, but she noticed Miss Emmaline's frown. Arnold's aunt disliked Madeline. But then, Jeannie conceded, Madeline was hardly the type to please Miss Emmaline.

"I've had a letter from Rebecca," Miss Emmaline said with a flurry of pleasure. "She's in Paris, you know."

They talked about Rebecca as Arnold shuffled off to find his book of pressed jessamine.

"I worry about Arnold," Miss Emmaline said abruptly with a new seriousness. "I worry about what's going to happen to him when my sister and I are gone."

"Rebecca's father and mother will take him, surely," she said encouragingly. Rebecca's father was, after all, Arnold's older brother.

"How will they manage?" Miss Emmaline spread her hands futilely. "They'll never have the patience with him that I have." She hesitated. "Arnold is like my own child, you know. He's my whole life." Her eyes were wistful. "Charlotte and I should have married, but nobody ever was good enough in Papa's eyes—and then it was too late."

Earlier than she had planned, and disappointing Miss Emmaline, Jeannie allowed Arnold to coax her to return to The Magnolias. He was eager to show his jessamines to Madeline. Jeannie climbed into the carriage, and Arnold rode beside her through the fields to the other house. Perspiration glistened on Arnold's face. Jeannie too was aware of the humidity of the day as the sun rose high in the sky.

Madeline sat in a rocker on the lower gallery, fanning herself against the sudden heat. She leaned forward, tugging at the low neckline of her frock, as Jeannie and Arnold approached the gallery.

"You've been visiting Miss Emmaline?" she mocked. "You are really becoming one of the family, aren't you?"

"I'm Dennis' wife," Jeannie said, and flushed. Why had she said that? "Miss Emmaline is lonely. She enjoys company." But Miss Emmaline disliked Madeline.

"Arnold," Madeline said with deceptive sweetness, "have you come to see me or are you just bringing Jeannie home?"

"I brought you my jessamines," Arnold said with a broad smile. "Will you look at them?"

Madeline was angry that she was becoming friendly with Arnold, Jeannie realized with a shock. But then, she tried to reason calmly, anything she did would displease Madeline because she had dared to marry Dennis.

Jeannie left Arnold with Madeline and went upstairs to her room. As she arrived at the head of the stairs, the door to Dennis' room swung wide. Suzette hurried out. Without seeing her, Suzette ran up the stairs that led to Mavis' room.

Jeannie paused at the landing, her heart pounding. No, she was overly suspicious, Jeannie rebuked herself. Suzette had been in Dennis' room on an errand. Don't look for an ugly meaning in everything.

In her room Jeannie fell into hot, exhausted sleep. The temperature was unreasonably high, she alibied when she awoke, ignoring the sleepless hours that had haunted her last night. She was so grateful that Aunt Lizzie had taken it upon herself to bring her second breakfast up to her room.

When she dressed to go downstairs for dinner, she remembered that she must seek out Gilbert and tell him to arrange for the fans in the dining room. The storm and the swollen river, together with this heat, were bringing out the insects early.

Leaving her room, she could hear Madeline screaming at Rose because the water in her tub was too hot. Poor Rose, Jeannie thought sympathetically, was kept running constantly by Madeline. All those kettles of water for Madeline's tubs, sometimes twice a day.

Jeannie found Gilbert in the library arguing with Jasper.

"But Ah cain' polish dat chandelier dis aftuhnoon," Jasper was saying indignantly. "Ah gotta take de Young Mastuh into Cha'leston."

"Gilbert," Jeannie interrupted, "I have something for you to take care of before we sit down to dinner." She saw the veiled look in Jasper's eyes. Jasper suspected that the Young Master's wife was not happy about his gallivanting around Charleston so frequently.

Craig turned inquiringly to Jeannie when he settled himself at the table ten minutes later.

"I thought I heard a carriage leaving a little while ago. Did Dennis go off somewhere?"

"I think he went into Charleston," Jeannie said self-consciously, and saw Eleanor's look of unease. "That is, Jasper said something about that," she floundered. Madeline was smiling wisely.

Craig had asked her where Dennis was because it would have been natural for Dennis to tell his wife if he was going into the city. Dennis had not told her anything. He never did. She had told herself this was the way with young plantation gentlemen. It was not. It was Dennis' way.

Carlotta was already serving dinner when Ron showed up, apologizing for his lateness. A piece of equipment had broken down; he had remained to repair it. Again Jeannie was conscious of Craig's annoyance. Because of Dennis' gambling debts, there was no money for new equipment. Her father-in-law had the usual planter's reluctance to sell either land or slaves to relieve a financial squeeze.

"We are probably the only family in the state of South Carolina that will remain on a rice plantation for the hot months," Madeline said with simmering bitterness as Carlotta served the crisp wild duck that Plato had bagged in the morning. "Prey to yellow fever, malaria, and heaven knows what."

"Now, Madeline," Mavis said, her voice shrill with

nervousness, "it won't be like that at all." But her eyes were apprehensive. It was the common belief, Jeannie acknowledged, that any white person remaining near the rice fields during the summer months was flirting with death.

"Contrary to the general opinion," Craig said with strained calmness, "it is possible to remain on a rice plantation for the summer if you take the necessary precautions. We'll have netting for the beds, plenty of ice. We've remained here for the past half-dozen summers and none of us has been the worse for it." He smiled humorously. "When I saw the Misses Emmaline and Charlotte remaining, I knew we could do the same. And even before then," he said reminiscently, "I was back and forth frequently during the summer, with Ron, and neither of us suffered any bad effects."

"We stayed all summer on Ransome Island," Jeannie offered, and stiffened before Madeline's glare. "I'll ask about a supply of netting," she said quietly. "I'll see that all the beds are properly prepared."

"The perfect mistress of The Magnolias," Madeline mocked. "One would never expect it of a bride so young."

Dennis did not arrive home for tea. After tea Jeannie went to sit on the gallery with Eleanor and Craig. Ron left for the mill to confer with Andrew McKinley. Madeline had gone up to her room, insisting she would expire without another tub. Mavis had tea in her rooms.

Without being bidden Carlotta brought out tall, frosted glasses with sherry and soda. Craig smiled his gratitude. Eleanor thanked Carlotta effusively, and Jeannie suspected that Eleanor's glass held more sherry than those offered to her father-in-law and herself.

Ron returned from the mill and settled himself in a rocker beside Jeannie, grateful when Carlotta came out to put a frosted glass into his hand. There was at this moment such a strange sense of peace, Jeannie thought.

She leaned back in her chair, content tonight to listen to the reminiscences of the two men, neither of whom was ever totally free of guilt at their involvement in the institution of slavery.

"We took the Africans away from their native culture," Ron was saying unhappily, "and what have we given them in exchange?"

"I try my best, Ron," Craig said heavily; "as your father tried." But there were too many, Jeannie thought unhappily, who did not share their sense of responsibility.

They sat late on the gallery, knowing the upstairs bedrooms would be hot; but Dennis had not returned by the time they went up to their rooms. Aunt Lizzie had brought up fresh water to Jeannie's bedroom, turned down her bed, and laid out a nightdress. Out of delicacy, the slave had resumed sleeping in the kitchen since the night Jeannie had spent away from her own bedroom. Aunt Lizzie thought her husband might wish, one night, to come to her room, Jeannie taunted herself.

She slowly prepared for bed, wistfully listening for sounds of an approaching carriage. Was Dennis gambling in Charleston? *What was he doing in Charleston?* Restless, she left her room and went out onto the gallery.

Jeannie's eyes fastened on the long strip of road that led up to the house. And then a smile touched her face as she heard the clomp of horses' hooves.

The carriage pulled up before the house to allow Dennis to alight; then Jasper moved on to the stables. Quickly Jeannie went back into her room to light the lamp. If Dennis thought she was asleep, he might not wish to disturb her. The glow from the lamp would shine beneath the door.

Oh, where was her pride? How could she want him to come to her, knowing what she knew? she asked herself in torment. Yet with every fiber of her being she longed to lie in Dennis' arms again.

She sat on the edge of her bed, her heart pounding as she listened to the sound of the front door opening and closing. Dennis was walking up the stairs. Oh, please, God, let him come to her!

Her throat tightened when she heard the light knock on her door. Dennis. It must be Dennis.

"Come in," she called unsteadily, rising to her feet.

Dennis walked into the room, smiling charmingly. How handsome he was!

"I was hoping you were awake," he said amorously, reaching for her hand. He had been drinking in Charleston, she thought, conscious of his whiskey breath as he pulled her into his arms. But he wasn't drunk. "Beautiful little Jeannie. Jeannie, my love."

He didn't mean it, her mind taunted. He was playing a strange game with her.

"We missed you at tea," she said unsteadily.

"I had tea at the Burkes'," he lied. *Why did he lie?* "Jeannie . . ." He brushed his mouth against her hair.

She closed her eyes when his mouth reached for hers, and abandoned herself to feeling. Her arms closed about his neck as he swept her off her feet and carried her to the bed. *Oh, Dennis, I love you. I love you.*

But tonight Dennis' hands were rough. Because he had been drinking, she apologized mentally for him. He didn't realize he was hurting her.

Perhaps with her he would forget about Madeline. Could she make him forget Madeline? She clung to him, moved with him, told herself that nothing in life mattered except being with Dennis this way.

"Tell me how you love me, Jeannie," he ordered hoarsely. "Tell me what you want me to do."

"I love you, Dennis," she whispered. How could she have doubted that, even for a moment? "I love you."

"Tell me what you want me to do," he insisted with an edge of anger in his voice.

"I want you to love me," she said, her face hot.

"How, Jeannie?" he pushed. "How do you want me to love you?"

She could not bring herself to use the words that Dennis demanded of her.

"Dennis, please. Love me. . . ."

Quickly—too quickly—he was leaving her bed. She was aware of a painful disappointment, a feeling of loss. He strode to the door without a word of farewell, without any gesture of tenderness. Last time Dennis made love to her, they had fallen asleep in each other's arms.

Jeannie lay back against the pillows, stricken, unhappy. How different it had been with them that other time! How had she failed Dennis? What had she done wrong?

Fourteen

Dennis yawned, stretched, reluctantly opened his eyes. His head ached. His mouth tasted fuzzy. He had sat up late in the library last night, talking and drinking with Papa. Why didn't the old man stop bothering him about helping in running the plantation? Papa had plenty of years ahead of him.

Papa didn't trust his going into Charleston so much, though he hadn't been in the city for several days now, he realized. Papa was sure he was gambling again. Dennis chuckled. Of course he was gambling, when Emmaline supplied him with cash. One of these nights he would make a killing. He'd give back to Emmaline every dollar she filched from the wall safe in the parlor at Burke Acres.

"I guess the money isn't doing much good just sitting there in the safe where Papa left it all those years ago," Emmaline had said airily last time he had charmed her out of four hundred dollars to take with him to the tables. "I know you'll pay it back, Dennis."

The door opened softly. Jasper peered into the room with his customary caution.

"I'm awake, Jasper," Dennis said with irritation. "Bring me my coffee."

"Ah got it heah, suh," Jasper grinned. "An' a letter for yo'." He approached the bed with coffee and letter.

Dennis accepted the coffee and inspected the letter curiously. From Bob Renfrew! His eyes alight, he set down the cup, ripped open the seal of the letter, and unfolded it. Avidly he read its contents. Bob was in Charleston, visiting with his parents. He had left his wife in Mobile.

> *"Come and stay with the folks and me at the Charleston house. We haven't seen each other for two years. We've some catching up to do, old boy! Remember that last time at André's?"*

Dennis allowed the letter to drop across the counter-pane, reached for his coffee, and stared contemplatively into space. He could take Jeannie and go visit the Renfrews for a few days. Papa couldn't complain about that, he thought with satisfaction. They'd leave tomorrow. Jeannie would be delighted to get away from The Magnolias. And in Charleston he and Bob could go to André's every night while Bob's mother entertained Jeannie.

He told her after dinner, and as he'd expected, Jeannie was enthralled with the prospect of visiting in Charleston for a few days.

"But won't you have to let the Renfrews know we're coming?" she asked with sudden reserve. "We can't just arrive there tomorrow."

"Jasper's taking the note into Charleston right now," he said with relish. "They'll be expecting us."

Jeannie waited on the gallery, her portmanteau and Dennis' beside the rocker in which she sat. Jasper would bring the carriage around in a few minutes. Dennis was in the library talking in high good humor with his father. Mr. Mitchell was not fond of Bob Renfrew, she surmised uneasily. He had looked unhappy when Dennis told him they would be spending a few days at the Renfrew house.

She glanced up with a smile as Dennis walked out onto the gallery. She was going into Charleston for several days; she would not allow herself to probe into Dennis' reasons for taking her along. She would enjoy staying with the Renfrews, she promised herself. Maybe away from The Magnolias, Dennis would be different.

"We'll leave now," Dennis said briskly as he beckoned

to Jeffrey to pick up their portmanteaus. The carriage was rolling into view.

They settled themselves in the carriage while Dennis' father watched from the gallery. Madeline stood at the railing of the upstairs gallery, gazing down upon them with an arrogant smile. She was furious that they were going into Charleston while she remained at The Magnolias.

In the carriage, Dennis focused his attention on the newspaper he had brought along with him. Jeannie concentrated on the splendor of the scenery. Magnolias and dogwood were blooming everywhere!

Her eyes lighted as Ron appeared on horseback at the side of the long private road, pulling his roan to a halt to wave them a smiling farewell. Involuntarily Jeannie gazed backward as the carriage rolled past him. Ron was holding his horse in check, watching as they moved away from him. She would miss Ron these coming days in Charleston, Jeannie thought unwarily; and then she felt color staining her cheeks. What ever was the matter with her? she rebuked herself self-consciously.

Dennis must be reading every word in the *Courier*, Jeannie thought, forcing herself to dismiss Ron from her mind. But what did it matter that Dennis ignored her on the drive into Charleston? She was going to enjoy these few days! She would finally have an opportunity to see the beautiful city.

When the carriage arrived in Charleston, Jeannie leaned forward with lively interest to inspect the avenues of fine houses. Every house had been designed to its owner's taste. One street seemed to be like an old English town. Dennis had remarked on that when they arrived, she recalled. The next street had a delightfully Continental air. The trees were beautifully green, and the time-mellowed mansions seemed to blend with them in their forms and coloring.

Many of the houses were built facing away from the street, fronting on semitropical gardens, facing south to ward off the midday sun and catch the southwest evening breeze. The Renfrew house, Jeannie recalled, faced the seawall.

Dennis folded away the *Courier* and turned to her.

"We'll be at the Renfrew house in a few minutes," he said with an air of anticipation. "It was built back in the 1760s by the first Renfrew to live in Charleston."

They turned into a long shrub-edged driveway. The house, flanked by a magnificent display of azaleas in varying colors, was an imposing, square brick structure rising three stories, with an elegant two-story gallery. As they approached, a man rose from a chair on the downstairs gallery and strode down the wide stairs to greet them. He was tall, broad-shouldered, pleasing of appearance.

"Dennis, you old hound dog!" Bob Renfrew greeted him exuberantly while Jeannie stood by admiring the house. "Too lazy even to write to me! I heard about your being married from my family." He turned admiringly to Jeannie, but she felt his soaring curiosity. "How do you put up with this old coot?"

"I manage," Jeannie laughed.

"Jeannie, this is Bob," Dennis said, seeming to relax with his friend. "We went through college together."

"And the last time I heard from him he was whooping it up in Paris," Bob chuckled. "Dennis sure picked him-self a beautiful bride," he added gallantly. "But leave it to him to do that." Jeannie intercepted the amused, secretive exchange between the two men.

A small, smiling woman appeared in the doorway.

"Bob, where are your manners?" she chided. "Bring Dennis and his wife into the house. Don't keep them standing out there in the sun."

Mrs. Renfrew greeted Jeannie and Dennis with a cordiality that was genuine. Jeannie was whisked upstairs to a large, airy corner room, where a maid would unpack for her while she refreshed herself.

"We'll sit down to dinner in a little while," Mrs. Renfrew promised, obviously delighted with her guests.

In one of the pretty summer dresses that Mama had made for her last year, Jeannie went down the wide, curving staircase, to be met affectionately by Mrs. Renfrew and swept toward the magnificent dining room. Dennis and Bob were already at the table, talking with

Mr. Renfrew, a courtly gentleman who rose to his feet to be introduced to her. Bob's brother and his wife were away from Charleston, but their two winsome young daughters appeared briefly in the dining room to be introduced to the guests.

What a charmingly hospitable family, Jeannie thought with relief. She had been afraid that she would feel ill at ease among all these strangers.

After a sumptuous dinner, Bob and Dennis disappeared. Mrs. Renfrew announced that she was taking Jeannie on a carriage tour of the city. As they rode about Charleston, Jeannie politely answered all of Mrs. Renfrew's friendly questions about her life before she met Dennis.

Bob and Dennis did not return for tea, but Mrs. Renfrew made every effort to keep Jeannie entertained. At teatime Jeannie was escorted into the beautiful drawing room, where the lamps were cheerfully lighted and small tables set up for the evening meal. Mrs. Renfrew invited Jeannie to sit beside her on the mustard-velvet sofa, with a huge tea table set before them, loaded with tempting dishes. Now her hostess beckoned to a smiling, fat young boy she called Sam, and Sam moved about the room, dispensing refreshments.

After tea the two little girls joined them, and from a neighboring house came a cluster of young girls, one of whom sat dutifully at the piano upon Mrs. Renfrew's urging and played with impressive skill a selection of waltzes and quadrilles. When the music was over, everyone went out to the gallery to sit and talk in the fragrant night air. Where was Dennis? Jeannie worried with recurrent anxiety. Did he dare to gamble again after that last confrontation with his father?

As the days moved past, Jeannie tried to tell herself she was enjoying this visit. She liked the walks about the Battery, the charming, broad, well-paved esplanade that was a favorite place for promenades, with one side open to the water and the other overlooking some of the finest mansions in Charleston, including the Renfrew house. But she could not grow accustomed to the ominous tolling of bells and beating of drums at nine each evening, which was the curfew for the colored people of Charleston. To remain on the streets after nine, and to be caught by the patrols, meant a sojourn in the guardhouse, where fifty or sixty persons were incarcerated each night.

When Dennis announced that they must leave in another two days, Bob was reproachful, as were his parents. Secretly Jeannie was relieved. She missed The Magnolias.

"We'll take Jeannie with us to the theater tonight," Dennis decided unexpectedly at dinner. How little she had seen of Dennis these past days, she thought suddenly. Dennis and Bob had been leaving the house every day immediately after dinner, not to return until dawn. And yet, she realized guiltily, she had not missed her husband. She was worried about his gambling—but she had not missed him. "Jeannie, you enjoyed the opera, didn't you?" he pursued with warmth.

"I loved the opera," she confirmed enthusiastically.

"The opera is over now. The season is falling apart," Mr. Renfrew reported gloomily. "I hear the performances this week are little more than sideshows."

"I don't believe that," Mrs. Renfrew rejected reproachfully. "Not at the Charleston Theatre. And there's talk of a fine stock company coming next season," she continued with determined cheerfulness. "Charleston won't allow itself to be without the best of entertainment."

"We'll go to the theater tonight," Dennis promised. He exchanged a pleased glance with Bob.

Jeannie waited with anticipation for evening to arrive. She recalled their attendance at the opera, when she had been so sure Dennis' taking her had been motivated by his vendetta with Madeline. But here he was taking her again, with Madeline unaware of it. Could she make something real of this marriage? *She must.* Dennis was her husband.

Again, as she waited with Dennis and Bob for the carriage to pull up before the house, she wore the beautiful mantle her mother-in-law had lent her for her visit to the opera, and which Eleanor had insisted she take with her to Charleston. Dennis and Bob were in festive spirits. Not until they were in the carriage did they enlighten her as to their real destination.

"Jeannie, you heard what Mr. Renfrew said about the performances at the theater this week," Dennis said casually. "You wouldn't mind if we went somewhere else, would you?"

"No," she agreed quickly. "Where are we going?"

"To André Genet's," Dennis told her. "He runs the finest gaming room in Charleston." He paused at her look of consternation. "You don't have to play, my love," he said with calculated charm. "Watch and bring me luck."

"But Dennis, your father," she protested unhappily.

"My father won't know unless you tell him," Dennis said bluntly, his eyes holding hers.

"I won't tell him," she whispered. But she was troubled.

Jeannie was silent for the short drive to the mansion that housed André Genet's gaming rooms. Forcing a smile, she allowed herself to be helped down from the carriage. Between Dennis and Bob she walked to the stately Georgian house which, unlike many others on the High Battery, faced the street. She tried to mask her distaste when a small opening appeared in the door and they were inspected. Immediately the door was opened for them.

Inside the house, they paused at the entrance to the large, sumptuously draped room to the left, where various forms of gambling were provided. There was an air here of almost hysterical conviviality, Jeannie thought as she inspected the assemblage, the men far outweighing the women in number. The women, Jeannie noted, were young, beautiful, and colorfully gowned.

Dennis' eyes swept about the room. He was searching for someone.

"There's Ashley." Bob pointed toward the man at their right, who was forsaking a cloth-covered table where a card game was in progress.

With a hand at Jeannie's elbow, Dennis waited for Mr. Ashley to approach them. He was an impeccably dressed, distinguished middle-aged man with a wide scar across one cheek. The kind of scar, Jeannie thought, that was acquired in a duel with swords. His eyes were dark, sharp, and searching.

"Jeannie, may I present Mr. Ashley," Dennis said with unfamiliar formality. "Mr. Ashley, my wife."

Ashley's eyes held hers until she stirred with discomfort.

"I do believe you *are* Mrs. Mitchell," he said with a strangely wry expression. "How did your husband persuade you to come to André's?"

"He asked me," she said quietly, her eyes daring him to say this was wrong. "Is there any reason I should not come sight-seeing at André's?" But she was trembling. Of course it was wrong. What South Carolina gentleman would take his wife to a gaming room?

"Jeannie, bring me luck at the roulette wheel," Bob said exuberantly, a hand at her elbow. But before they moved out of range, Jeannie spied the exchange of money between Ashley and Dennis. A coldness enclosed her. *Dennis had bet money he could persuade her to come here. He had never intended to take her to the theater.*

"Bob, who is Mr. Ashley?" Jeannie asked, fighting to retain her composure.

"He's one of the richest planters in Georgia. He comes regularly to Charleston on business."

Bob prodded her determinedly toward the gleaming red, green, and gold of the roulette table. Jeannie pretended to be listening to his detailed explanation of the game as they joined the others about the table, but her eyes covertly sought out Dennis. He and Mr. Ashley had been joined by a short, well-groomed man with a small moustache. Instantly, from his manner, Jeannie realized this was André Genet.

Jeannie saw Dennis display a sheaf of bills to Mr. Genet. She saw Genet's smile of acquiescence, and watched Dennis and Ashley follow him out of the room to another directly across the foyer.

"Stand behind me and bring me luck at the wheel," Bob coaxed ingratiatingly, but his eyes followed hers. Dennis was going to a private game, Jeannie interpreted, the money that he had just won being his admission to that game.

She stood directly behind Bob at the roulette table,

157

shaking her head firmly when he invited her to play with his stake.

"I'll watch," she said, holding her head proudly. She noted the sympathetic—and simultaneously curious—glances that André Genet shot in her direction. Had Dennis brought Madeline here? Was that what André Genet was remembering?

After what seemed an interminable length of time, with Dennis closeted in the private room across the foyer, Jeannie allowed Bob to guide her to the dining room, where gourmet refreshment was provided for the patrons at André Genet's gaming rooms. She felt little interest in food tonight, yet it was a way to help pass the time.

At last, sensing Jeannie's concern for Dennis, Bob piloted her across the foyer to the private room. He slowly—as silently as possible—opened the door to reveal a huge table, around which sat fourteen men, including Dennis. Whiskey and glasses sat within easy reach of the players. At one side of the room stood a cluster of avid observers—privileged guests like herself and Bob, Jeannie recognized.

"This is a special game," Bob whispered. "It was arranged two nights ago." When Dennis made his bet with Ashley that he could bring her here, Jeannie guessed bitterly. "Texan poker. Seven-card stud, winner-take-all."

Jeannie's eyes were fastened to the piles of bills on the table. She had no comprehension of the game, but the glow about the faces of the men who watched told her of the drama being enacted. She was the only woman in the room, she realized. She doubted that Dennis was even aware of her presence.

"What a lot of money!" she whispered, mentally tabulating the bills on the table.

"Fourteen thousand dollars," Bob said with awe. "It took a thousand-dollar stake to sit in there."

Jeannie trembled. Dennis had won a thousand-dollar bet by bringing her here! What would have happened if he had lost? Despite herself, she was drawn into the excitement of the game.

Dennis played with a deadly calm, only a tic in his left eye betraying his tension. The gaslight in the room was garishly bright, lending a circuslike aura to the fourteen men about the table. Jeannie watched as though mesmerized as each hand was played. Bills moved about the table from one player to another. An hour passed and then another, with no one leaving the game. Dennis was losing, the pile of bills before him distressingly meager. Bob frowned anxiously.

"He'll have to go out soon," Bob whispered.

But then another hand was dealt and suddenly the situation was changing. Dennis was winning. One man after another was withdrawing. Soon the players numbered only seven. Jeannie shifted from one foot to the other, exhausted from the hours of standing but held compulsively by the drama that pervaded the room.

"Let's go have a glass of champagne," Bob suggested uneasily as Dennis seemed to go into a losing streak.

"No," Jeannie rejected with a heat that was involuntary. "Thank you, no," she said apologetically.

The group of observers was growing. Word of this game had spread through the rooms. Those at the table seemed unaware that they were being watched. More players lost their stakes and withdrew. By midnight only four men remained in the game: Dennis, Ashley, and two men who—Bob told her in a whisper—were from New Orleans. The two New Orleanians had been playing at André Genet's for the past two weeks. Bob suspected they were professionals.

The silence in the room became almost painful as the men stolidly played their hands. Dennis was winning now. Ashley, with a shrug of defeat, finally withdrew. Now there were the two from New Orleans and Dennis playing. Dennis was tight-lipped, pale.

"There's six thousand dollars in that pile before Dennis," Bob whispered to Jeannie with an air of disbelief.

"Why doesn't he quit?" Jeannie asked, shaken.

"He can't," Bob reminded. "It's winner-take-all."

One of the men from New Orleans left the game on the next round. Now it was Dennis and the other man from New Orleans. On the flop, the seven of hearts came up for Dennis. The six of clubs went to the man from New Orleans. Dennis took a deep breath, debated inwardly, then pushed his entire six thousand into the pot. The other man matched it from his eight thousand.

"Dennis has a pair of nines showing," Bob pointed out, his voice deep with excitement.

Jeannie watched, not really knowing what was happening. But all at once Dennis paled. The other man had flipped over his hole cards. Both jacks.

"The pair of jacks takes it all!" Bob said tightly.

The room rippled with excitement. The man from New Orleans had taken the entire pot of fourteen thousand dollars. Dennis had lost every cent.

"Good night, sir," Dennis said loudly, pushing back his chair. "Now that you have cleaned out Charleston, you can go back to your Mississippi riverboats!"

There was an ominous moment of quiet as Dennis' words took effect. The other man at the table rose to his feet also. His face was flushed an angry red.

"I demand satisfaction!" he said contemptuously. "You have insulted me! Pistols," he decided. "At daybreak."

"The choice of weapons is mine," Dennis reminded. He deliberated a moment. "Yes, pistols," he chose.

Jeannie listened, trembling with disbelief, as the duel was swiftly organized. Dennis had not expected this; he had spoken in the heat of frustration, without thought of consequences. The men had forgotten her presence in the room, so involved were they in setting up arrangements. She caught isolated words. Bob would be Dennis' second. They would meet at daybreak at a place called Dustin Woods, at the outskirts of the city.

"I'll arrange for Dr. Maxwell's presence," Bob said briskly, and suddenly he stared at Jeannie with consternation. Like the others, he had forgotten her presence in the room. "Jeannie, I'm sorry," he stammered. "We'll take you home now."

Jeannie sat back in the carriage between Dennis and Bob while the two men talked as though nothing untoward had happened this evening. They planned a picnic for Sullivan's Island the next afternoon. *Dennis might be dead tomorrow afternoon.*

"Isn't it illegal to engage in a duel?" Jeannie asked desperately.

In the spill of moonlight that infiltrated the carriage, Jeannie saw Dennis' face tighten with anger.

"There are times, Jeannie, when gentlemen are above the law."

"Of course, it's beneath you to duel with that man," Bob reminded cautiously. "A riverboat gambler?"

"I've been challenged!" Dennis shot back. "I'll put a bullet through his head!"

In a few minutes they were inside the Renfrew house, the carriage being ordered to wait because within an hour Dennis and Bob must leave for the spot chosen for the duel. Jeannie went to her room and sat in a chair by the window, knowing she would make no effort to retire tonight.

From the room next door came the low hum of Dennis' and Bob's voices, their exchanges unintelligible to Jeannie. Dennis could refuse to fight the man, she thought, fleetingly hopeful. Men of different social stations rarely dueled, as Bob had reminded him. But Dennis was a hothead—and overconfident to boot.

She rose restlessly and moved to the window. What could she do to stop this duel? Dueling was an act of insanity. How could it be stopped? Suddenly she listened attentively to the sounds in the hall. Dennis and Bob were going downstairs to choose the pistols to be used in the duel. And hearing them, she knew what she must do.

She walked to the door and cracked it slightly so that she would know when Dennis and Bob left the house. She waited with mounting impatience. Why were they taking so long? The moment they left she would awaken Mr. Renfrew. Mr. Renfrew could summon the police to stop this duel. *He must.*

Dennis and Bob emerged from the gun room on the lower floor and walked down the hall to the foyer. Jeannie was already out of her room. There, they were leaving the house. Now!

Her throat tight with tension, Jeannie deliberated on which door to knock. There, the door beyond Bob's. She hurried to the room that she was confident was occupied by Mr. Renfrew. She knocked. She waited anxiously for a response. There was none. Fighting against panic, she knocked again, more loudly.

"What is it?" Mr. Renfrew called groggily, obviously drawn from a deep sleep.

"It's Jeannie," she said urgently. "Please, Mr. Renfrew, I must speak to you."

"I'll be there in a moment," he said reassuringly. "Just let me find my dressing gown."

While she heard the carriage pull away from the house, Mr. Renfrew opened the door, tying his dressing gown about his waist.

"Mr. Renfrew," Jeannie said breathlessly, "Dennis is on his way to Dustin Woods to fight a duel! Will you send for the police to stop it?"

Mr. Renfrew looked grave.

"I can't do that, Jeannie," he said unhappily. "Dennis would never forgive me." He frowned in thought. "With whom is he dueling?"

"A cardplayer he met at André Genet's," Jeannie began, and he stared sharply at her. "I don't know his name—"

"Dennis took you to André Genet's?" Mr. Renfrew demanded indignantly.

Jeannie lowered her eyes. What would Mr. Renfrew say if he knew why Dennis had taken her there?

"It—it was a prank," she apologized for Dennis.

"How did this duel come about?" Mr. Renfrew pursued.

Quietly Jeannie explained what had led up to the challenge.

"Do you think this man is a riverboat gambler?" Mr. Renfrew pressed.

"I have no way of knowing," Jeannie inspected his face anxiously. "Bob suspected that he was—"

"Go back to bed, Jeannie," Mr. Renfrew ordered gently. "I'll take care of this."

"Let me go with you," Jeannie pleaded.

"Jeannie, a dueling field is no place for a young lady," he said with a brusqueness born of anxiety.

"I'm Dennis' wife. Let me go in the carriage with you," she insisted.

"All right," he capitulated after a moment. "Give me a few minutes to dress."

Within five minutes they were in the carriage, en route to André Genet's. Jeannie waited apprehensively in the carriage when they arrived at the Genet mansion, while Mr. Renfrew went inside. It seemed that he had barely been admitted when he was returning.

"Dennis' assumptions were correct," he said tersely as he climbed back into the carriage. "The man is Henry Fitzgerald, a professional gambler from New Orleans. I've heard of him."

"What can we do?" Jeannie asked, her heart pounding.

"We're going to call on my friend Judge Sass," he said with an air of confidence, though his eyes were serious. "Then the three of us will head for Dustin Woods."

At Judge Sass' house Jeannie waited, churning with unease, while Mr. Renfrew banged preemptorily to gain entrance. She gazed anxiously at the sky. Daybreak was close upon them. That first faint lightening of the sky was already visible. Let them hurry! Let them not be too late!

With gratifying swiftness Mr. Renfrew, accompanied by a portly, white-haired gentleman with a commanding air, returned to the carriage. As they headed for Dustin Woods, Mr. Renfrew introduced Jeannie to the Judge, who behaved with a Southern courtliness that might have accompanied an introduction at a St. Cecilia ball.

"Dustin Woods is just ahead," Mr. Renfrew announced in a few minutes, his voice—despite himself—displaying his anxiety. Another carriage was directly ahead of them, traveling at a swift gait. "Brutus," Mr. Renfrew leaned from the window to call to the coachman. "Overtake that carriage!"

But not until the carriage ahead arrived at the clearing in the woods, where Jeannie could see Dennis and Bob standing beside another of the Renfrew carriages, was Brutus able to overtake his quarry.

"Stop there, sir!" Judge Sass called out peremptorily as Henry Fitzgerald jumped down from his carriage."

The gambler from New Orleans turned with a start.

"What do you want?" he demanded impatiently.

"I'm Judge Sass," he said sternly. "It has come to my attention that you're Henry Fitzgerald from New Orleans."

"That's right," Fitzgerald said warily.

"You're a professional gambler with charges of cheating pressed against you, sir. I order you out of Charleston by this morning's boat, or you'll face prosecution."

"That bastard Mitchell?" Fitzgerald blazed.

"Not Mr. Mitchell," Mr. Renfrew intervened dryly. "*I* pressed charges. You cheated me at poker last night at André Genet's. I have two witnesses to back me up." His eyes challenged Fitzgerald to deny this.

"I'll join you in your carriage, Mr. Fitzgerald," Judge Sass said matter-of-factly. "You will remain in my custody until your boat sails."

The Judge and Fitzgerald departed in the gambler's carriage. Dennis strode angrily toward Jeannie.

"Why did you do this?" he demanded.

"Because," she said with high color, "I wanted to spare your parents the agony of your death."

Fifteen

Dennis dressed slowly, impatient with the late-morning heat that pervaded the house. Summer would soon be on them in full force. There would be months without relief, a sickly beauty everywhere in the lowlands. Already some rice-plantation families were running to Newport and Saratoga, to houses at the seashore or deep in the pine woods—or to mansions in Charleston, beside the water.

Get out of the house, go over to see Emmaline, he prodded himself. He had not been in Charleston for a week. Tonight he would have Jasper drive him into the city. He felt lucky.

Damn, he had been so close to real money last week, there at André Genet's. Judge Sass should not have let Fitzgerald off so lightly! He should have made the bastard hand over that fourteen thousand to him. The game must have been rigged. At least, he thought wryly, nobody had told Papa or Mama about the duel. That had been a mistake.

A few good hands at the poker table and he could pay back Emmaline and have a real stake for himself. He didn't need Papa now, he thought defiantly—not since Emmaline had confided in him about the money in the safe.

He strode from his room in high spirits. Tonight he would be lucky. Anybody who gambled regularly could feel when a lucky streak was coming.

"Dennis . . ." Mavis' faintly shrill voice called to him. "Dennis, wait." With quick, small steps, careful not to trip, Mavis came down from the third floor. "Dennis, the next time you're in Charleston, put this on twenty-three red for me on the wheel," she whispered nervously, glancing about to make sure Madeline was not in sight.

"Sure, Mavis," he promised, and casually kissed her cheek.

"Dennis . . ." Mavis hesitated, then forced a coquettish smile. "One of these nights will you take me into Charleston with you? I haven't been in a gaming room for such a long time."

"One of these nights," he promised, his eyes making this a secret between them. "I'll bet you miss it."

"Oh, honey, do I!" she said with poignant intensity.

"Madame," Suzette called reproachfully from upstairs. "Yo' breakfas' gittin' cold."

Dennis' gaze shot up the stairs to rest on Suzette. Passionate wench, he thought complacently. She wasn't above giving Mavis a sleeping potion in her coffee when she figured he might want her to come to his room. Not uppity like Carlotta.

165

He left the house, climbed into the carriage, and ordered Jasper to drive him to Burke Acres. Jasper was pleased they were going into Charleston tonight. He was going to see his black bitch.

Arnold was sitting on the gallery as the carriage pulled up before the house.

"Aunt Emmaline went calling," Arnold told Dennis with malicious delight. "Somebody's sick at the Fletchers', and she took some medicine Aunt Callie made up over to them."

"When's she coming back?" Dennis asked, hiding his irritation. Emmaline never left the house unless someone was very sick. Aunt Callie, the ancient slave in charge of the infirmary, and Emmaline took over when the local doctor was too busy to call. "Did she say?"

"Not till teatime," Arnold reported with relish.

He'd have to wait until tomorrow to go into Charleston.

"Take me back to the house, Jasper," he said sullenly as he climbed into the carriage. Damn that Arnold; he was gloating because Emmaline wasn't here. Arnold hated him; had hated him since that time—when he was no more than eighteen—that he had taken Arnold with him into Charleston. Arnold had never been in the city. He had been wide-eyed with excitement. But after that day, he had never gone into Charleston again.

It had been just a prank to take Arnold with him into that fancy whorehouse. Sitting in the room where they waited for the girls to parade before them, he had told Arnold what he must do when he went upstairs into one of the little rooms with a woman.

Arnold had stared at him with consternation.

"Dennis, I want to go home." Suddenly his eyes were fearful. "Please, Dennis, let's go home."

"Later," Dennis soothed. "After you've had your fun. Caprice," he called imperiously to the madam, who sauntered among her clients in gaudy finery. "Send my friend up to Mama Marie."

Caprice had stared at him uneasily. Mama Marie was a three-hundred-pound Negress who catered to the whims of a few special clients. "Arnold's never been with a woman. Mama Marie will teach him."

Quaking, white with alarm, Arnold had allowed himeslf to be led upstairs to Mama Marie's room. A few minutes later they heard her deep, masculine voice raised in outrage. Arnold was unable to perform. Arnold had never trusted him after that, but both had kept their silence about what had happened. . . .

Jasper turned into the road to The Magnolias. Dennis dismissed Arnold from his mind and ordered Jasper to drive him to the stables. He would ride awhile, get rid of some of that restlessness. In the stables he noticed that the roan was missing.

"Elijah, who took out the roan?" he asked curiously. Papa and Ron were out in the fields checking on that new cotton. They would have gone with the wagon.

"Miss Madeline, she ride him all de time," Elijah told him respectfully.

Dennis took out Hannibal and followed the trail through the woods. A pulse hammered low within him as he contemplated catching up with Madeline in the lushness of the forest. He would take her by force, he sliently promised himself. He'd make her remember how it had been with them!

In a small clearing ahead he spied the roan, tied to a tree.

He pulled Hannibal to a stop, dismounted, and walked over the thick green coverlet under his feet, impatient to surprise Madeline. And then he stopped short. Fury colored his face a dark red.

For a moment he hovered there, his eyes fastened to Madeline and Andrew McKinley, caught up in a passionate embrace, unaware of his presence. Clenching his teeth to keep back the tirade that threatened to spill over from him, he silently retraced his steps and mounted Hannibal again. Did Ron know about this? Did Papa? If Papa knew, he'd fire that bastard!

Later he'd tell Papa, he decided—when it suited his purpose.

He rode hard and far into the west fields, trying futilely to wipe from his mind the memory of Madeline and Andrew. Anybody could have her, he thought with frustration—except him. Was that the way it was? Dennis asked himself with soaring anguish. Would she spend the rest of her life punishing him?

He did not bother to return to the house for dinner but put in an appearance at tea, sullen and silent. Madeline glowed. She was always like that after she made love. Each time was a personal triumph for her.

Jeannie was watching him oddly from across the table. She was wondering why he had not come to her room in all these days. Ron had a strange way of looking at Jeannie sometimes, as though she were fragile and in need of special care. Ron wasn't developing ideas about Jeannie, was he? That would be a tremendous joke on Madeline!

The night was sticky, a grim forewarning of the deadly heat almost upon them. The scent of the flowers was sickeningly sweet. The ladies, except for Jeannie, were fanning themselves steadily. They were just stirring up the hot air, he thought with amusement.

Recurrently his eyes moved to Jeannie. A new determination was taking root in his head. Tonight he would call on his bride. And tomorrow night and the next and the next, he thought with vindictive satisfaction. Let Madeline know he was enjoying an active married life.

They left the dining room to sit in the rockers that were lined up on the gallery, hoping for some relief from the river. Madeline twisted about restlessly in her chair. From an open window upstairs came Mavis' voice, pettish as she complained to Suzette about the heat. A smile touched his mouth. Suzette would be disappointed tonight. He was going to his wife.

His father and Ron were arguing good-humoredly about the possibilities of California and New Mexico's coming into the Union.

"What bothers me about Taylor," Ron was saying seriously, "is his determination to build up the Whig party. He's going in heavily for patronage."

"But he's choosing wisely," Craig conceded.

Dennis listened detachedly while Jeannie joined in the conversation with observations of her own. She was the first woman he had ever encountered who was so knowledgeable about what went on within government. Most of them, thank God, were not like that.

"I'm going to my room," Madeline announced at a heavy lapse in conversation. "The only place to get comfortable is in a tub."

He remembered the flat in which Madeline and Mavis had been living in Charleston when he met them. They had already lost the small town house by then. The furniture that they had dragged from Paris had been incongruous in the drab four rooms to which they had been reduced.

His throat tightened as he remembered Madeline's room, with that ornate bathtub smack in the center. He remembered the first time he had lounged in a chair watching Madeline soaking in a perfumed bath. His thighs tightened as he recalled the night they had made love in that ridiculous bathtub with Mavis entertaining at poker in the next room.

"I'm going upstairs." Dennis rose abruptly to his feet minutes after Madeline had gone to her room. "Jeannie, are you going upstairs?"

Startled, she lifted her eyes to his. Color flooded her face. She understood.

"Yes, I'm going up," she said with charming awkwardness.

Papa and Ron knew he was taking his wife to bed, Dennis thought with amusement. They didn't know the motive that had taken root in his mind.

He held the door open for Jeannie and walked into the house with her. Jeannie was easy to manipulate, he thought with satisfaction. She adored him.

"I'm going to my room to get more comfortable," he said, his eyes deliberately amorous as he paused with Jeannie at her door. "I won't be long." He pressed her hand with promise. She was trembling.

Jasper dozed in a chair in his room. He jumped up to attention as Dennis walked inside.

"Jasper, go downstairs and bring up a bucket of ice and a bottle of Burgundy," he ordered crisply. "And a couple of glasses," he added.

He stripped and pulled on one of the silk dressing

169

gowns he had brought back with him from Paris. Madeline, he thought wryly, would appreciate the splendor of these dressing gowns. He splashed water on his face and brushed perspiration-stained hair away from his forehead. It was an unbearably hot night for April, he thought impatiently, and chuckled. It would be a hotter night for him and Jeannie in a little while.

Jasper returned with a tray bearing ice and glasses, a bottle of choice Burgundy beneath his arm.

"All right, get out of here," Dennis dismissed him. "I won't want you anymore tonight."

Whistling softly, he went to Jeannie's room and knocked.

"Come in." Her voice was slightly strained with anticipation.

He walked inside. The room was in shadows, lighted only by a pair of candles on the mantelpiece. The curtains that faced the gallery were sedately drawn. The others were open to allow the maximum of comfort.

"You look beautiful," he said quietly, walking to put the bottle of Burgundy and the tray with the glasses on the table. "But take off that dressing gown," he reproached with mock sternness.

"All right." She smiled, pulled off the dressing gown, and stood there, small and lovely in her sheer white nightdress.

Dennis dropped a chunk of ice into each glass, poured the Burgundy over the ice, and walked to Jeannie with a glass in each hand. She sipped slowly, her hand unsteady on the glass. He drained his own, set it down, then deliberately pulled away his dressing gown and threw it across a chair.

He heard her gasp of shock as he turned back to face her. Her eyes moved pleadingly toward the candles.

"Leave the candles lit," he insisted, reaching for her.

He took her to the bed and made love to her in the shadows with a frenzy that startled her. Once she cried out. Let her grow accustomed to him this way, he thought with savage determination. He would come to her night after night this way—until he knew he had given her a child.

Ron and Madeline would never inherit The Magnolias, he swore. No child conceived by Madeline and Ron would ever rule over The Magnolias. *His child would inherit on his death.*

"Dennis," Jeannie protested. "You're hurting me. . . ."

Jeannie lay sleepless till dawn. She felt disturbed—shocked—by tonight's union with her husband. He had come to her not with love, but with anger. She felt violated, she thought, tears welling in her eyes. What had happened to the Dennis she had loved? Could it ever be right with them again?

Not until the first streaks of dawn splashed across the sky did she fall asleep. For the first time since her arrival at The Magnolias, she slept until almost dinnertime, when Aunt Lizzie came solicitously into her room to make sure she was not ill.

Again that night Dennis came to her, to take her with the same disturbing brutality. At tea he and Madeline had sparred verbally in a fashion that had brought a sharp reprimand from Mr. Mitchell. Dennis battled with Madeline, Jeannie thought with fresh distaste, and then he came to her. He came to her because he could not go to Madeline. He would try, she warned herself with brutal candor; but Madeline had made it clear she would not allow it.

Night after night, in the heat of early May, Dennis came to her to take her with a cold passion, an anger that made her dread each encounter. Yet, paradoxically, she *wanted* him to come to her, praying that each time would be like the first. Willing him to change, to be the Dennis who had enslaved her. Where was the charming, handsome, tender Dennis who had made her tremble with delight when he looked at her, brushed his hand against hers?

Dennis was moody, quick to anger. At tea, Jeannie remembered as she waited for the familiar, imperious knock on her door, he had been insufferably rude to Ron. She had been afraid for a moment that they would come to ugly words. She had seen Ron's mouth tighten, watched him avoid a confrontation by involving his aunt in conversation.

Jeannie started, though she had expected the knock.

"Come in." She rose from the edge of the bed, steeling herself to smile. What was driving Dennis this way? Such fury seethed within him.

He came into the room, already pulling off his dressing gown. Her eyes fell to the floor. It was as though he came to her to perform a task that was demanded of him. Night after night this strange charade between them.

"Dennis," she said impulsively as he reached to draw the nightdress away from her shoulders, "you shouldn't have attacked Ron the way you did tonight. He gave you no provocation."

"Don't tell me what to do!" His face was dark with rage. Suddenly, without warning, he slapped her hard across the face.

"Dennis!" Afraid, she moved backward.

"Don't tell me what to do, Jeannie!" He grabbed her by the shoulders and threw her with such force that she fell to the floor.

"Jeannie!" Suddenly he was contrite. He dropped to his knees and pulled her to him, his face flushed. "I didn't mean to do that, my love. I didn't mean it!"

With a new gentleness, he lifted her to the bed, pulled the nightdress down her trembling slenderness, and tossed it aside.

"Jeannie," he whispered urgently, "give me a child. It'll be our salvation. A child, Jeannie."

She closed her eyes, willing herself to receive him. And strangely, despite this new distaste in her, she was responding to him. Her arms closed about his neck. Her body moved with his. Dennis wanted their child.

She was upset when she realized she had not conceived this month. She knew Dennis would be disappointed. She waited in her room for him to come to her, knowing she must tell him.

"Why aren't you pregnant?" his voice lashed at her. "After all those nights you should be!"

"I'm sorry, Dennis," she faltered.

"You don't want a child," he accused her. "You're glad you haven't conceived."

"No," she whispered. "No, Dennis." Yet a new guilt surged in her. She *didn't* want Dennis' child—not when he was like this. She wanted to run from him, run from The Magnolias.

"You'll have my child!" Dennis swore in the sickly heat of the night. "He'll be the heir to The Magnolias. My child, Jeannie."

Suddenly she understood. He wanted to have a child so that Ron and Madeline would have no hold on The Magnolias. He wanted her to conceive for revenge on Madeline. She felt dizzy with shock.

"Dennis, please go," she said faintly. "Please leave me alone."

Jeannie moved about The Magnolias with a painful new awareness. She avoided meeting Dennis' eyes, knowing what she would see there. She must leave this house, she told herself—before Dennis came to her again.

Three nights after Dennis had come to her room to discover that she was not pregnant, Jeannie packed the portmanteau she had brought with her from Ransome Island. In the morning she would tell Mr. Mitchell that she was leaving Dennis. He would arrange for her passage to Virginia.

She lay sleepless far into the night, trying to envision the new life she must shape for herself, fearful of what she would encounter. But her cousin would surely welcome her until she could find a position. Mr. Mitchell knew people throughout the South; he would help her in this.

But Mrs. Mitchell wished her to stay, she remembered guiltily. She would miss Dennis' mother. She would miss Ron. In these past months she had come to feel such warmth for them. Her allies in this strange household. Ron had been so solicitous, so eager to make her feel at home here at The Magnolias.

The first grayness of dawn was brushing the sky already when she fell asleep. Still, she awoke early, as usual, to lie against the pillows with a terrible heaviness weighting her down. Her eyes fell on the portmanteau sitting beside the washstand. Suddenly, as though prodded by an unseen force, she thrust aside the counterpane and moved with pounding heart to the portmanteau.

Unpack quickly, she exhorted herself, before Aunt Lizzie arrives with the morning coffee. How had she thought last night that she could leave The Magnolias? Her hands trembled as she hurriedly unpacked and put away her meager wardrobe.

She returned to the bed with a strange sense of guilt, to await Aunt Lizzie's morning appearance. *What* was holding her here? she demanded of herself. Dennis had killed her love. Why did she feel this urgency to remain at The Magnolias?

Sixteen

The May heat bore down relentlessly on The Magnolias. There was an incredible lushness about the grounds and in the swamps and the forests. Life had slowed down within the house. The servants moved languidly about their tasks. The members of the family indulged in long afternoon naps.

The rice and the cotton were planted. The vegetables, watermelon, and figs were coming in heavily. Now was a time of waiting, of hoping for good weather for the crops. In his room Ron lay along the length of his bed in unfamiliar postdinner idleness. He ought to nap, his mind insisted. He knew the importance of not becoming overtired, prey to fever.

"Suzette, fix me something cold again," Mavis' voice filtered from an upstairs window. "I declare, I'm so exhausted from this heat. I stay here," she declaimed dramatically, "only because my daughter needs me."

Madeline had stopped carrying on about money to spend in the Charleston shops. She said it wasn't worth the effort in this heat to ride all the way into the city. Ron knew he had made a terrible mistake when he married Madeline. How could he have been so blind? God knew, she was beautiful; but what man could live with her moods, her tantrums?

He stirred, impatient with this idleness. The house was gripped in silence. No one—not even the servants—stirred for two hours after dinner. The kitchen help sat on the porch behind the kitchen, resting in the shade while they leisurely washed the greens for the big salads Jeannie ordered to accompany their teas.

Too often, he reproached himself, his thoughts turned to Jeannie. But that was because he worried about her, he told himself guiltily. Nothing more. Sometimes she looked at Dennis as though she were afraid of him.

With a low sound of impatience he rose from the bed, stretched, and tugged at his shirt, which clung wetly between his shoulderblades. He would go over to the mill and talk to Andrew about that article in the agricultural journal. He had rested enough.

He left the house, remembering to wear a hat against the heat of the afternoon sun, and walked to the mill.

"Mist' Andrew, he go to his house," a slave told him politely. "Ain' rat, white folks movin' aroun' in dis sun," he reproached Ron affectionately.

"Don't worry about me," Ron chuckled. "I've got a tough hide."

He strolled to the stables, waited for a horse to be saddled for him, and rode along the horse path to McKinley's cottage. Beyond the cottage he could hear the laughter, the good-natured fighting of the children in the quarters.

He dismounted, tied the horse to a live oak before the cottage, and walked briskly to the door. Andrew was an abrasive man, but he had an uncanny knowledge about the soil.

The white cottage was surrounded by a profusion of summer flowers, oleanders and roses predominating. The fiery red blooms of the pomegranate trees vied for attention with white velvet blossoms of the magnolias.

He walked up the path to the tiny gallery. Suddenly his throat tightened. He paused with one foot on the bottom step. It was unmistakably Madeline's laughter that floated out from within the house.

Charged into action, Ron stalked across the gallery, pulled open the door, and walked into the low-ceilinged sitting room. The door to the bedroom was open wide. Across the bed, unaware of his presence, sprawled a half-naked Madeline. Andrew, stripped to the waist, hovered over her.

Madeline's eyes saw his shadow as he approached the threshold. She whitened, then cried out suddenly, "Ron, thank God! He attacked me!"

Andrew spun about furiously; then one huge hand swung out to strike Madeline, missing her face as she fortuitously turned away.

"You bitch!" he yelled. "You came running after me like a whore drunk on Spanish fly! You didn't even give me time to latch the door!"

Madeline screamed as Andrew lunged toward her. Ron charged forward and with superhuman effort pulled him away from Madeline.

"Get your clothes on, Madeline!" Ron bellowed as Andrew tore into him.

Ron knew he was no match for the massive superintendent, but pride demanded that he put up a show. Again and again he sagged to his knees, each time staggering to his feet to try to beat off McKinley.

"Andrew, stop before you kill him!" Madeline screamed. "Stop it!"

"All right. You can have him now," Andrew said with vindictive amusement, hovering over Ron, prostrate on the floor. Get up, Ron's mind ordered; but his body refused to cooperate. "I'm getting the hell out of this place!"

Ron felt himself sinking into oblivion. Everything he had ever suspected about Madeline had just been confirmed. God, he hurt! Everywhere.

Jeannie sat by a window in her bedroom, trying to concentrate on the book across her lap. She sipped exhaustedly at the tall, frosted glass of lemonade that Aunt Lizzie had just brought up to her. Downstairs in the library Mr. Mitchell was playing the piano. He played only when he was upset. Dennis' marriage puzzled him; rightly, Jeannie thought unhappily.

Abruptly Mr. Mitchell stopped playing. Minutes later Jeannie, walking to the window for a breath of air, saw him walking toward his study.

She thought about Dennis' determination that they have a child. She didn't want Dennis' child, knowing his reasons for wishing one, and she dreaded the resumption of his nocturnal visits to her room.

"Dennis . . ." Mavis called thinly in the hallway, from the floor above, and Jeannie instinctively listened.

"What is it, Mavis?" Dennis asked indulgently. He made a fuss over Mavis when she came to the dining table or sat with them on the gallery, as though he were punishing Madeline by being on congenial terms with her mother.

"Are you going into Charleston?" Mavis asked archly.

"Maybe," Dennis teased.

"Dennis, I'm going out of my mind staying up here in my rooms. Be a good boy and take me into Charleston," she wheedled. "I won't be any trouble at all. You can just leave me at André Genet's and go on your way."

Dennis chuckled. "You know damn well that's exactly where I'm going to stay. Come along. I'll even stake you at the roulette wheel. But hurry," he exhorted.

Moments later Jeannie heard Mavis darting down the stairs with unfamiliar swiftness.

"See, I didn't take long, Dennis," she simpered.

Compulsively Jeannie went to her door, opened it, and moved into the hallway to gaze at the pair on the stairs. Madeline would be furious, she thought uneasily, and turned to go back into her room. For a moment she froze. Suzette was poised at the top of the flight above, glaring with rage on her pretty face as Mavis and Dennis crossed the foyer and went out into the hot afternoon.

In her room, Jeannie crossed to the chair by the window again. That momentary view of Suzette, hovering in rage at the top of the stairs, clung to her memory. Too restless to read, she put aside her book and hurried from her room. There might be a slight breeze from the river on the downstairs gallery.

Arriving on the gallery, she saw the carriage carrying Mavis and Dennis disappear from sight. Simultaneously she spied Madeline riding up to the house, flailing the roan with her riding crop. Jeannie leaped to her feet, sensing trouble.

"Jeannie," Madeline gasped, dismounting. "Ron's badly hurt! Andrew McKinley beat him unmercifully. Where's Mr. Mitchell?"

"Out in the fields." *Oh, let Ron be all right!* "There's no time to send for Mr. Mitchell," Jeannie said. "We'll go to the stables and get a wagon to bring Ron to the house." She walked quickly to the door. "Gilbert!" she called with a sharpness she had never used. "Gilbert!"

Gilbert appeared at the far end of the hallway.

"Ah'm heah, Young Missy," he said with quiet reproach.

"Gilbert, send somebody for the doctor. Mr. Ron is hurt." She hurried across the gallery and down the stairs. Madeline at her side. "Where is Ron?" she asked.

"In Andrew McKinley's cottage." Madeline paused. "That beast tried to attack me," she said breathlessly. "Ron saved me."

"Where's McKinley?" Instinctively she mistrusted Madeline's story.

"He ran away." Madeline's eyes were defiant.

Madeline knew she suspected the story was different, Jeannie thought; but for Ron's pride they must be silent. At the stables Jeannie ordered that a wagon be brought out and that two men come with them to lift Ron into the wagon.

Elijah insisted that Jeannie and Madeline go to the cottage in the carriage.

"It ain' rat fo' ladies to ride in de wagon," he protested. "An' it's too hot wit' dat sun beatin' down de way it is."

At the cottage they hurried into the bedroom, where Ron lay semiconscious. Jeannie dropped to her knees beside him with a surge of compassion. With her handkerchief she gently touched the bleeding wound on his forehead.

"Madeline, find a towel and wet it," Jeannie ordered while the two men hovered uneasily beside her.

Ron's eyes were swelling, his face bruised. He must have taken some painful punches about the body. Gentle Ron, who loathed violence. And then she saw the peculiar angle of one arm.

"I'm afraid he's broken his left arm," she said unhappily.

"He lucky to be alive," one of the men said bluntly. "Tanglin' wit' dat Mist' Andrew."

Madeline returned with a wet towel. Jeannie gently washed Ron's face, seeing him wince despite his semiconscious state.

"All right," Jeannie said to the men, who had improvised a stretcher with a blanket. "Be easy with him, now."

At the house, the two men carried Ron from the wagon to his room, the house servants watching wide-eyed with shock. Madeline stood by helplessly in Ron's room, on the edge of hysteria, while Jeannie strove to make him as comfortable as possible till the doctor arrived.

"Go tell someone to bring ice," Jeannie told Madeline crisply, "and a pitcher of fresh washing water."

Ron stirred. His eyes fluttered open. Jeannie bent over him.

"Don't move," she urged gently. "I think your left arm is broken."

Her eyes rested on him with a compassion that elicited an unexpected response from him. All at once her heart was pounding. Words were unnecessary. Their eyes spoke with a shattering eloquence. *Ron was in love with her—and she was in love with him.*

"Made a mess of it," Ron whispered weakly. "McKinley was too much for me."

"Don't talk. Rest. The doctor will be here soon." She reached for his right hand and squeezed it reassuringly. Her eyes were aglow with her new discovery. And he knew.

When the stately, white-haired Dr. Brooks arrived,

Jeannie decorously retired from the room, leaving him with Ron and Madeline. But she waited in her room with the door open so that she might approach Dr. Brooks as he left. She winced when she heard Ron's sharp, startled outcry of pain as Dr. Brooks straightened the break in his arm. She stiffened, then shuddered again at a muffled groan.

Eventually Dr. Brooks emerged from the room. Jeannie hurried to him, her eyes wide with questions.

"He'll be all right," Dr. Brooks soothed, a glint of curiosity in his eyes. "I had to set that arm. He'll be uncomfortable tonight, but he'll be all right in a few days, except he won't be able to use the arm for a while." He hesitated. "I don't think his wife is going to be much use in there," he said bluntly. "I think you'd better see that somebody stays with him during the night."

"I'll take care of it," Jeannie promised. "I'm Jeannie Mitchell, Dennis' wife," she added with a smile.

As Dr. Brooks descended the stairs, she head Madeline sobbing hysterically in Ron's room. She hurried to the door and knocked.

"Come in," Ron called tiredly.

"Madeline, I think you should go to your room and rest," Jeannie said quietly. "Ron should try to sleep."

"That man tried to attack me!" Madeline screamed. "He asked me to come into the cottage to have some lemonade because I was overcome with the heat. I—I know I shouldn't ride in this weather. And then—then Andrew tried to attack me!" Her voice became shrill again.

"Madeline, stop it!" Jeannie ordered as Madeline screamed hysterically. "Stop it!" She slapped Madeline sharply across the face.

Madeline collapsed into a chair by the bed, sobbing brokenly. Inadvertently Jeannie's eyes sought Ron's. She could see that he didn't believe Madeline.

Jeannie went upstairs, ordered that a pitcher of ice water be sent up to Ron's room, and arranged for servants to stay at his bedside in shifts. Then she sought out Eleanor and told her about the incident, knowing that Ron must outwardly accept Madeline's explanation of what had happened. Andrew McKinley had fled. This gave credence to Madeline's story.

"Poor Madeline," Eleanor murmured sympathetically, her eyes aglow with shock. "And Ron, to be hurt that way. Does Craig know?"

"Not yet," Jeannie said. "He's not in the house."

"He'll be so upset," Eleanor whispered. "And Dennis? Is he here?"

"Dennis went into Charleston," Jeannie reported. With Mavis, she remembered. "But don't worry about Ron," she soothed. "Except for the broken arm, he'll be fine in three or four days."

Only Craig, Eleanor, and Jeannie sat down in the dining room for tea. Craig was stern-faced and pale when he was told about the happenings at McKinley's cottage.

"I never liked that man," he said tightly. "He was so efficient, yet I distrusted him." Jeannie suspected, though, that not even he believed Madeline's story. No Southern lady entered a man's cottage unchaperoned.

As they sat at tea, they saw Rose—Madeline's maid—walk down the hall with a tray. Madeline was not too upset to dine well, Jeannie thought dryly.

"I'll go up and look in on Ron later," Craig said somberly.

"Ron's like a son to Craig," Eleanor said to Jeannie. "To both of us. He's lived with us since he was fourteen, you know." Her eyes were troubled. She was thinking of Dennis, who was Craig's son in name while Ron was the son in deed.

Eleanor and Jeannie sat alone on the gallery. The night was overcast, no moon or stars on display. The faintest of breezes stirred among the trees.

"Craig doesn't show it," Eleanor said tenderly, "but he's terribly upset about this business with Ron. Craig's such a gentle, compassionate man. I wish I could have been a better wife to him," she added wistfully.

Sometimes, Jeannie thought, Mr. Mitchell looked at his wife as though he were ripping away the years and seeing her as she had been when they were first married. Yet, regularly, Carlotta made the brief trip from house to study. Did Mrs. Mitchell know?

Jeannie remained on the gallery with her mother-in-law until Eleanor decided it was time to retire. For a little while, dreading the heat inside the house, Jeannie remained alone on the gallery. When she went upstairs to her room, she heard her father-in-law talking with Ron. Madeline was climbing the stairs to her mother's room. Did she know that Mavis had gone into Charleston with Dennis? Jeannie wondered nervously.

Jeannie undressed and prepared for bed, knowing sleep would be hard to woo tonight. Eventually, from exhaustion, despite the humid discomfort of her room, she fell asleep.

She awoke with a sense of falling through space, then was immediately fully awake. The events of the day assailed her as she lay back against the pillows. Poor Ron, to have had to face that ugly scene in Andrew McKinley's cottage! But a sudden exhilaration welled in her as she remembered what she had seen in Ron's eyes when she bent over him as consciousness returned to him. For one moment they had recognized the startling truth. Yet what could there ever be for them, except this covert, precious knowledge of how each felt toward the other?

Methodically Dennis had killed her love. With astonishing clarity she traced the step-by-step disintegration of her marriage. How could she have been so believing?

Restlessly she left the bed and walked to the window to gaze out into the night. Had Dennis returned? There were no sounds from his room; but of course, he might be asleep. Was Ron all right? Did he want anything? Dr. Brooks had said he would be uncomfortable tonight.

Impulsively Jeannie pulled on a dressing gown and left her room to walk around the hall to Ron's. Cautiously she opened the door. A single candle glowed on the mantelpiece. Stretched on a pallet was young Brutus, snoring gently.

Jeannie walked into the room and leaned over Ron. "Why aren't you sleeping?" he rebuked with a smile.

"I thought you might want something." She touched his forehead. How hot he was! "Would you like some lemonade?"

"That would be good," he whispered.

"I'll go down and make it for you," she said.

"Send Brutus," he told her.

"No," she said stubbornly. "I want to make it myself."

While she prepared the lemonade in the kitchen wing, she heard the carriage pull up before the house. A few moments later she heard Dennis and Mavis come into the night-darkened house. They were talking as though it were the middle of the afternoon, Jeannie thought in reproach, as they walked up the stairs.

Carrying the ice-laden pitcher of lemonade, Jeannie left the kitchen and started down the hall.

"What do you mean, taking Mama into Charleston?" Madeline screeched from the top of the stairs. "It might have killed her to travel in this heat!"

"Oh, shut up, Madeline," Dennis drawled. "Mavis enjoyed herself. Didn't you, darling?"

"Madeline, it was wonderful," Mavis effervesced. "I don't know when I've enjoyed myself so much. Do you know, this was the first time I've been to Charleston in three months?"

"It was a ridiculous thing to do!" Madeline's voice rose stridently. "Come along, Mama. I'll take you up to your rooms," she said with melodramatic solicitude. "Don't you ever take Mama into Charleston again without consulting me, Dennis!"

Guiltily Jeannie waited at the foot of the stairs until she heard the slam of Dennis' door. Now she silently climbed the stairs and carried the lemonade into Ron's room.

She poured a glass of deliciously cold lemonade for Ron, then held the glass while he sipped the contents. Afterward she sponged his face, then gave him one of the pills Dr. Brooks had left to relieve the pain, glowingly aware of Ron's feelings toward her.

Jeannie was pleased to see that Ron was growing drowsy.

"You'll sleep now," she said, touching his face gently for a moment. "Good night, Ron."

He reached for her hand and for a poignant instant brought it to his lips.

"Beautiful, sweet Jeannie," he whispered. "Be my friend."

"I am that, Ron," she said shakily.

Jeannie opened the door and walked into the hall, then froze at the tableau illuminated by the spill of light from within Dennis' room. No more than thirty feet from her, but oblivious of her presence, stood Dennis and Suzette in amorous embrace.

"Ah hafta go downstaihs fo' ice fo' Madame," Suzette said nervously.

"Later," Dennis said, pulling her into his room. "Let the old bat wait."

Seventeen

Jeannie stood at her bedroom window, gazing out at the drizzle which had faintly alleviated the heat that had gripped the house during the night. With a sickening, overripe sweetness in the air this morning, she thought— like the sickness within this house.

She saw a servant darting through the drizzle to the washing rooms beyond the house. Suzette. She shut her eyes, trying to wash away the vision of Dennis and Suzette, brazenly embracing in his doorway last night. How could she go on being Dennis' wife, knowing about Suzette? Knowing his obsession for Madeline? Knowing so much about Dennis that revolted her?

Why did she remain at The Magnolias? She sought an explanation in her mind; and when it came, she paled. She stayed here because of this secret love for Ron. That was a shameful reason. She knew there could never be anything for them. Dennis and Madeline formed a wall between them.

How was Ron this morning? she wondered solicitously. An eagerness to see him suffused her. She would go to his room, see if there was something she could do to make him more comfortable. It was hardly likely, she thought with a new bitterness, that Madeline would make that effort.

She moved to the mirror that hung over her dresser and searched her reflection. She must do nothing to betray herself. No words must ever pass between her and Ron. But she could see him. She could take comfort in his nearness.

A soft glow of anticipation lighting her face, she left her room and went to Ron's door. She knocked lightly. Brutus pulled the door wide and grinned warmly at her.

"He up and havin' his breakfas'," Brutus reported with an air of importance. "Come in, Young Missy."

Ron, propped in bed, a tray across his lap, glanced at her in welcome.

"I feel more human this morning," he said encouragingly, though dark circles lurked beneath his eyes and there was an air of strain about his face. "Except for this." He touched his arm with an effort at wry amusement.

"It's good that it's your left arm," she said, and laughed. This casual conversation masked the tumultuous emotions that flashed between them. "If there's anything good about breaking an arm."

That one moment of truth last night, when they had gazed unguardedly into each other's eyes, Jeannie thought, had irretrievably changed their lives. Forever they must guard against allowing anyone else in the house into this agonizingly sweet secret between them. Why could she not have met Ron earlier?

"Brutus, take this away." Ron looked with distaste at the food before him.

"You should eat," Jeannie chided. Such pain in his eyes, she thought with a surge of compassion; but this derived not from his physical injuries, she guessed. He was asking himself, why had Madeline gone into An-

185

drew McKinley's cottage? To go alone into that man's house was inviting him to do as he wished with her. When had Ron stopped loving Madeline?

"Sit down and talk to me," Ron invited eagerly while Brutus jumped forward to remove the tray. "Tell me about Ransome Island." He stopped dead, his eyes apologetic as he remembered her nightmare with Kevin Ransome. But her air of serenity reassured him. "Was it fun growing up on an island? Or was it lonely?"

"Mama kept it from being lonely when she was alive," Jeannie said with recall, tears springing into her eyes.

Forcing herself into a convivial mood for Ron's sake, she launched into a series of stories about childhood occasions on Ransome Island. She told Ron about some of the devastating hurricanes that had swept the island almost entirely underwater. And all the while she talked, she was conscious of the intensity of Ron's gaze on her.

"I'd better go," Jeannie said, lowering her eyes lest they speak too boldly. "Aunt Lizzie will be bringing up my coffee. She'll wonder where I am."

Walking down the hall to her room, she heard her father-in-law in Dennis' room.

"Ron's lucky he wasn't hurt worse," Craig was saying seriously. "McKinley's a brute of a man."

"Why in hell didn't you send the sheriff after him?" Dennis demanded furiously. "We ought to hunt McKinley down and string him up!" Nobody had told Dennis last night about what had happened in Andrew McKinley's cottage. He had not heard, Jeannie realized, until his father had come in to tell him just now.

"McKinley's far gone by now," Craig said with calm. "There's no chance of bringing him in."

Jeannie walked quickly to her room, hearing Dennis' recriminations follow her. He was furious because Madeline had been with Andrew, Jeannie told herself realistically—not because Ron had been injured.

She closed the door of her room and leaned against it. What would become of her and Dennis?

Madeline gazed sulkily into the mirror in her hand as she lay back in her second tub of the day. Rose was at the dresser putting away laundered clothes. Madeline churned with recurrent indignation. Mr. Mitchell was a terrible man to keep them here at The Magnolias in this awful heat. She looked all dragged out already. He could sell a few slaves or some acreage, and send the family into Charleston for the hot months. All he cared to spend money on was machinery.

With a sigh of annoyance she reached to put the mirror on a nearby chair. Where was Andrew now? He'd never show his face here again, not after what he had done to Ron. Why had Ron walked into the cottage that way? He *never* came to Andrew's cottage except in the evening when the day's work was finished. Why did he have to come yesterday?

Ron didn't know anything, she told herself defensively. She had covered up, hadn't she? Yet unease trickled through her. She remembered the way Ron had gazed at her when he told her to put on her clothes—as if he had not believed her at all. *But nobody could ever prove anything.*

"Rose, bring me a towel," she ordered. Oh, she had been furious with Dennis when she discovered he had taken Mama into Charleston! He had done that to get back at her. After all, she thought with momentary amusement, Mr. Mitchell might bail out his son at the gaming tables, but he would not bail out his nephew's mother-in-law.

Rose hovered with the towel as Madeline stepped out of the tub. Her eyes focused with pride on the lush thrust of her breasts, her hands unconsciously cupping them as her mind shot back through the years, to the time she had been sixteen.

That was when Henri had fallen in love with the painting of her on display in the gallery in Paris. He had sought her out. Mama had been furious, though he was already—at only twenty-one—a poet who had had two of his books published.

Madeline had adored Henri. He had been her first love. Unaccustomed tears sprang to her eyes as she remembered the months with Henri, Mama constantly fighting their affair. Half of Paris knew she and Henri were lovers. Some approved. Some disapproved. He was tall and slender and golden-skinned. Mama never allowed her to forget that Henri's mother had been a slave in New Orleans. His father had sent him to Paris to be raised when he was barely eight.

Anguish darkened her eyes. Why had Mama made her give up their baby? Why had Mama dragged her away from Paris, away from Henri? Her son, she thought with suddenly fierce pride. She had almost died in giving birth to him. She closed her eyes and remembered the agony of that night. . . .

"She's too young to have a child!" Mama had screamed at Henri while she writhed on the bed, drenched in sweat.

"Slave girls have babies at fourteen," Henri had flashed back, and Mama had slapped him across the face.

"She'll die!" Mama had beaten at Henri with her fists in futile despair.

When the doctor arrived, he sent Henri out of the room. Then she was conscious only of the pains that swept over her, one after another.

"Mama, Mama!" she cried out, and Mama took her hand in hers.

"It's going to be all right, Madeline," Mama promised, her face tear-stained. "And after it's over, we'll leave Paris. We'll go home, Madeline. You'll be a fine lady, living in Charleston! You'll marry a rich planter."

Pain could not be recalled, people always said. Not true, Madeline thought. She would remember forever the agony of bringing forth her son. The waves of pain that had ripped through her writhing body. She would remember forever Mama's outraged cry when the doctor lifted the baby from her.

"My God, he's black! He's black!"

In four days, when she was still so weak from the torturous delivery, Mama had bundled her up and taken her to London—away from Henri. Mama had given *her* baby to Henri to raise in Paris. She had never seen Henri, nor her son, after that night when Mama had told him he must take his child and go.

How old was her baby now? Four, she thought, tears spilling over onto her cheeks. Sometimes she held one of the slave babies in the quarters and pretended it was her own.

"Missy," Rose chided unhappily, "how come yo' cry?"

"I'm crying for somebody I used to know," Madeline said with a defiant smile. "Bring my clothes, Rose."

But Henri had quickly become a memory as Mama kept telling her about the fancy gentleman she was going to marry. Mama thought she was beautiful enough to marry anyone. But Southern gentlemen, she thought with distaste, took their pleasures where they willed—but their wives from other plantation families.

She had never loved anyone the way she loved Dennis. Not even Henri. She had lost her head completely over Dennis. Mama knew all about the rich plantation the Mitchells owned, and she had been sure he was going to marry her.

Madeline closed her eyes, visualizing the tempestuous love affair that had been broken off one crucial night when she lost her head, ending in Dennis' fleeing to Europe. She laughed bitterly. How like Dennis to have chosen that time to visit Europe! In the Year of the Revolutions!

She would go upstairs and talk to Mama, she decided. Why had Dennis taken Mama into Charleston last night? she asked herself again. He must have known she would be furious. She loathed this show of friendship between them.

Powdered and dressed, she left her room, climbed the stairs to her mother's suite and walked inside—as usual—without knocking. Her mother was still in the bedroom, propped against a mound of pillows, sipping the tea that Mr. Mitchell had shipped regularly from England. Suzette was lining up the array of jars into which Mavis dipped each morning before she considered herself ready to greet the day.

"Get out of here, Suzette," Madeline said, and dropped into a chair close to her mother's bed. She saw the covert glint of anger in Suzette's eyes as she stalked from the room.

"I don't know why I'm up so early," Mavis said

peevishly. "I took one of those pills that are supposed to make me sleep."

"Mama, you're always taking pills," Madeline said with distaste.

"You upset me terribly last night, Madeline," Mavis said aggrievedly. "How could you go to that man's cottage?" She shivered with disgust. "He's so uncouth."

"I found him more amusing than Ron," Madeline shot back. "I'm bored here, Mama."

"Madeline, you're going to spoil everything. You're not getting any younger—remember that. You've married well. We're living well. Don't spoil it!" She flushed as her tone became more intense. "I worked hard to bring you this far. You know how I lived. When I was fourteen and my parents died, I left Charleston to live with my aunt in the most awful section of London. You remind me of that on occasion, Madeline," she said maliciously. "I married a man whose hands were always dirty, who beat me when he was drunk. I left my two children with his parents and I ran, Madeline. I ran for something better." The force of her voice demanded Madeline's attention. "Your father gave us a good life in Paris until he died. Don't you forget that. I've always arranged for you to live well."

"You won't let me forget Papa," Madeline reminded resentfully. "You forever remind me of him."

"You have a good life with Ron. Just don't push him too far." Mavis leaned forward and shook her finger for emphasis. "Don't fool yourself, Madeline. Everybody in this house knows why you were in Andrew McKinley's cottage. You take one more false step and Mr. Mitchell will throw us out."

"Dennis had no right to walk out on me that way. He should have married me. _I_ would have been mistress of The Magnolias!" Madeline's voice soared perilously.

"Eleanor is the mistress of The Magnolias," Mavis reproved.

"Eleanor Mitchell is a shadow," Madeline said with contempt. "Dennis' wife is the mistress of this house. It should have been me." She took a deep, anguished breath.

190

"I love Dennis. Don't you know that, Mama? I'll love him till the day I die. But I won't let him touch me again." A fanatic glow showed in her eyes. "I'll punish him forever for what he did to me."

"Madeline, I'm afraid." Her voice was uneven. "This thing between you and Dennis—it scares me to death."

"Don't worry, Mama," Madeline soothed, but her eyes were bitter. "I'm still Ron's wife. He would die before he admitted he caught me with the mill superintendent." She leaned forward and kissed her mother on the cheek. "Stay in bed in this heat, Mama. I'll tell Rose to bring you a tall iced drink."

At the foot of the stairs Madeline hesitated. She was going to have to face Ron. After all, she thought with sardonic humor, he was a man who had defended his wife. He'd die before he admitted anything else to anyone.

She walked into Ron's room without bothering to knock. Jasper nodded respectfully, then moved toward the door as she waved him away. Ron lay against the pillows, his arm positioned across his chest in a sling. With a faintly defiant smile Madeline walked toward him.

"Does your arm hurt?" She avoided a direct confrontation with his eyes.

Ron smiled dryly.

"It has felt better." His eyes were somber as they regarded her.

"Has anybody done anything about going after Andrew?" she demanded uneasily. Bluff this out. Ron didn't know for sure what had happened in Andrew's cottage. It could have been what she said.

"Nobody is going after Andrew," Ron said bluntly, "because that's the way I want it."

Madeline lowered her eyes quickly, flinching before the reproach she saw in his.

"You're going to be quite a hero, going after Andrew that way." Damn, he was going to make it rough for her.

"Andrew McKinley beat me to a pulp," Ron said with thinly suppressed fury. "I didn't have a chance."

"Shall I bring up the newspaper and read to you?" she

asked with a conciliatory smile, spilling over the charm that once had entranced Ron.

"Have someone bring up the newspapers," he said with unfamiliar brusqueness. "I can read them myself."

Eighteen

Jeannie was delighted to see Ron back on his feet within two days. Though he would not be able to use the broken arm for weeks, he insisted on resuming his duties about the plantation. Jeannie worried that he spent such long hours at the mill, even while she realized he sought this refuge from Madeline's presence.

An ominous atmosphere permeated the house. Outwardly Madeline was astonishingly subdued, yet Jeannie sensed the hostility smoldering within her. Mavis too watched Madeline with a constant air of alarm. At meals Ron was scrupulously polite to his wife, but Jeannie was conscious of the insurmountable wall that the afternoon in Andrew McKinley's cottage had erected between them.

Dennis' fluctuating moods ranged from a desperate morbidity to a defiant gaiety, in which Mavis was his eager but uneasy partner. With a frequency that astonished her, Jeannie found her father-in-law's eyes focused on her with an unhappy intensity. He was concerned for her. How could he not know, with his sensitivity, his perception, about Dennis' obsession for Madeline? Even Eleanor seemed aware of something desperately amiss at The Magnolias.

They were moving into the worst of the summer heat,

a parade of days when the sun beat mercilessly upon the house and not a drop of rain fell in relief. The lushness of the flowers was almost unbearable. The swamps and streams were an ominous sickly green.

At least, Jeannie thought with gratitude, as she lay sleepless in the late evening on her perspiration-drenched bed, Dennis had ceased to come to her with nightly brutality since Ron's physical encounter with Andrew McKinley. Had he abandoned his determination to present his parents with a grandson?

She pulled herself up in bed and pushed her hair away from her face. In the spill of moonlight she saw Aunt Lizzie, who was sleeping these hot nights on a pallet on the gallery outside her room, reach for the door and come inside.

"Yo' not sleepin'," Aunt Lizzie protested indulgently, pulling away the voluminous netting that covered the bed. "Ah git yo' a fresh nightdress, Young Missy. An' while yo' put it on, Ah change dem sheets."

In her nightdress Jeannie walked out onto the upstairs gallery, starting at the sight of a figure at the other end. Her mother-in-law's room, like hers, fronted on the gallery.

"It's so hot," she said gently, and walked toward Eleanor.

"I never sleep well," Eleanor said quietly. "Usually at night I read, but not in this heat." Her eyes were fastened on Craig's study, where the faint glow of a candle indicated his presence.

"Shall I tell Aunt Lizzie to bring us some lemonade?" Jeannie asked, touched by the poignance that shone from Eleanor.

"That would be nice," Eleanor acknowledged with a smile. But her eyes, Jeannie noticed, clung to the cottage below.

Jeannie saw the pain that shone in Eleanor Mitchell's eyes as the candle was extinguished. She knew that within the cottage, her husband lay with Carlotta, Jeannie thought compassionately. Eleanor Mitchell still loved her husband.

"I'll go tell Aunt Lizzie," Jeannie said softly, feeling

an intruder at this moment. "She'll bring the lemonade right up to us."

Jeannie remembered the way Craig looked at Eleanor at intervals, as though he were looking upon the young widow he had married despite his family's opposition. How had that marriage gone so wrong? Three marriages within this house, Jeannie thought unhappily, and each of them a mockery.

Jeannie asked Aunt Lizzie to bring them lemonade and returned to the gallery to sit with her mother-in-law. Later, when the slight figure of Carlotta emerged from the cottage, she sought to hold Eleanor's attention until Carlotta was out of sight, hoping that she was successful.

When Jeannie went downstairs for breakfast, no one else had yet arrived at the table. Moments later Craig joined her in the dining room. As they talked about the unhappy lack of rain, Madeline sauntered into view. It was the first time since Jeannie's arrival that Madeline had come down to breakfast.

"I'm going into Charleston," Madeline announced defiantly, as though anticipating opposition, "later in the day."

"It's going to be a long, hot drive," Craig warned calmly.

"It'll be worth it," she said with deceptive sweetness. "I'll come back at dusk, when the sun won't be so unbearable." She glanced up with an arrogant smile as Dennis—also surprising Jeannie with his presence at breakfast—strolled into the room. "Perhaps I'll invite Arnold to go into the city with me." Her eyes clashed with Dennis'. They were like two gladiators in the arena, Jeannie thought, each hungry for blood.

"Don't take Arnold into Charleston!" Dennis snapped at her, seating himself at the table. "Emmaline would be terribly upset."

"Doesn't Arnold have anything to say?" Color touched Madeline's cheekbones. "Does he have to ask Emmaline's permission every time he takes a drink of water?"

"You know about Arnold," Dennis reproached. They were not fighting over Arnold, Jeannie told herself with distaste as she helped herself from the platter of poached eggs. This was a private battle between Dennis and Madeline, at which she and Mr. Mitchell must be onlookers. "It would be upsetting to Arnold to be exposed to all that activity. He wouldn't know how to handle himself."

"I think you all underestimate Arnold," Madeline reproached. "He's a sweet, thoughtful person."

"He's a scared child," Dennis retorted, "and Emmaline has trouble enough keeping him in line."

"Arnold is the most placid, sweetest human being I have ever encountered. How can you be so bigoted?" And then she smiled brilliantly. "But it's a point of pride with you to be bigoted, isn't it?"

"Jeannie," Craig said with a determined effort to derail the tirade between the other two, "Gilbert tells me there'll be a mess of perch coming into the house within the hour. Perhaps you'll want to tell Juno to prepare some for dinner?"

"That'll be nice, Mr. Mitchell." Jeannie was grateful that he brought a more casual note into the table conversation. "Fish is less heavy than pork or beef on a day like this." Mama used to say that, she remembered nostalgically. Being so close to Mama had made it possible for her to cope with the household details here at The Magnolias. "And the salad greens are coming in beautifully." Why did Dennis sit there scowling like that? Madeline enjoyed tormenting him. And yet, there were moments—like now—when Madeline looked upon Dennis with a longing that was painfully naked.

While the others were still eating, Dennis crisply excused himself.

"I'm driving over to see Emmaline," he explained with a vindictive glance at Madeline. "I promised to go over this morning and help her choose the material for their new parlor draperies."

"Dennis," Jeannie said impulsively, "ask Plato to cut some of those red roses and take them to her. She adores them."

"You're really cultivating the Burkes, Jeannie," Madeline remarked with a hint of irony in her voice. "First Arnold and now his aunt."

"I'm very fond of both of them." She would *not* be

195

intimidated by Madeline. But she sensed that Madeline was jealous of Arnold's increasing fondness for her. When he came to The Magnolias now, it was as much to see her as to see Madeline.

"I'll take the roses to Emmaline," Dennis promised with a sardonic grin as he rose to his feet. "Excuse me."

Madeline concentrated sullenly on her rice and eggs, snapping at Carlotta when she walked quietly about the table refilling coffee cups.

"Carlotta, you might ask!" Madeline's voice was edged with irritation. "I don't want any more coffee. Bring me a glass of iced tea."

Craig flinched at Madeline's sharpness to Carlotta. Jeannie sensed that he wished to reproach her for her attitude toward the servants, but he was wary of an ugly confrontation.

"Will you excuse me?" Madeline said abruptly moments later, after barely more than a sip of the iced tea that Carlotta had brought to her. "I want to rest in this awful heat."

"I feel," Craig said heavily, his eyes somber, "that we're living on the edge of a volcano." Jeannie was startled; he voiced her own feelings. "Why can't Ron control his wife?" A tic flickered in his eyelid. "Why can't he keep her in line?" His face wore an aura of frustration.

"I doubt that any man could do that," Jeannie said with honesty.

"Poor Ron." Suddenly Craig was gentle. "I knew the minute he brought Madeline into this house that we were in for a bad time."

Mr. Mitchell had not wanted *her* to remain at The Magnolias when Dennis brought her home, Jeannie recalled. Even then he had been aware of these strange undercurrents between Dennis and Madeline, and he had been afraid for all of them.

"Mr. Mitchell, what can we do?" Jeannie asked quietly. Yet guilt brushed her, because she knew that deep within her, there was little desire to bring Dennis closer to her. She was grateful that he had ceased to come to her room, to take her nightly with anger, intent only on giving her a child. She didn't want Dennis' child.

"Jeannie, I don't know." All at once Craig seemed exhausted. "There are times in life when we can only sit by helplessly and watch." He was silent as Carlotta came into the room again to place a pitcher of iced milk on the table. When Carlotta left the room, he spoke again. "I've watched Eleanor pull into that shell of hers through these last years, and I've been able to do nothing about it. I should have!" He voice rose in anger. "You can't imagine how beautiful she was when I married her. How brave she was. She was only twenty when I met her, recently widowed and with a three-year-old child to support. I used to go to the theater night after night to watch her. Finally I acquired the courage to go backstage and contrived to meet her. She was so charmingly unaffected, so warm." His eyes glowed with nostalgia. "The miracle was that then she loved me."

His eyes were pained. Didn't he know, Jeannie asked herself, that his wife still loved him? "My mother died only a few months after our marriage. My father was bitter toward Eleanor till the day he died, but she never let on that she was aware of it. She was unfailingly polite and attentive to his wants. It was Eleanor who found my father's body when he put the bullet through his head." He paused, reliving the tragedy. "He could no longer cope with the gambling debts that pressed upon him—he was sure he was going to lose The Magnolias. I remember Eleanor's face when she came to tell me."

He closed his eyes for a moment, swept back in time. "I remember Eleanor in her wedding gown. It was white silk with tiny yellow flowers. I thought she was the most beautiful bride in the world." He smiled faintly. "We went through two ceremonies—one in Charleston and one later here at the house, because my mother wouldn't consider us married otherwise."

But now Craig went to Carlotta instead of to his wife. Had Mrs. Mitchell denied herself to him, Jeannie asked herself with compassion, because she had been so afraid through the years of yet another miscarriage, another disappointment for her husband? Eleanor's words shot across her mind. *I failed my husband. I couldn't give that fine, deserving man what he wanted most in this world.*

They sat for another few moments in the enervating heat, then left the table to go their separate ways.

"Go upstairs to your room and rest," Craig urged gently. "I don't want you coming down with the fever."

"All right," Jeannie promised. At last, she thought gratefully, Mr. Mitchell was her friend. He had been, she thought with fresh awareness, since her arrival at The Magnolias.

"I'll get a hat and go over to the mill," Craig decided. "Ron's over there with the new superintendent. If he's through showing the man around, we can talk about that new article in the agricultural journal that has me all steamed up."

Jeannie went up to her room, intending to nap after her sleepless night; but she found it impossible to remain idle in bed. She splashed cool water on her face, then brushed her hair away from her forehead, and tied it at the nape of her neck with a ribbon.

Outside, a pair of dogs barked in play. Jeannie walked to the door and out onto the gallery to watch the beagles romping on the grass below. At the other end of the gallery Eleanor sat with a tray across her lap, which she was eyeing with distaste.

"Missy Eleanor, yo' eat," Danielle—Eleanor's small, round West Indian maid of many years—coaxed worriedly. "How yo' keep up yo' stren'th lessen yo' eat?"

"Danielle, it's so hot," Eleanor said apologetically. "I'll eat later."

"Ah go downstaihs an' bring up a dish o' col' figs," Danielle said firmly. "Dat an' a glass o' col' milk. Yo' lak dat." She took away the nearly untouched tray before her mistress and walked with the languid gait that was a result of the weather into Eleanor's bedroom.

"It was a dreadful night," Jeannie said sympathetically. "I slept hardly at all."

"Do you know where Dennis went?" Eleanor asked hesitantly. "I saw him leave in the carriage."

"He went over to Burke Acres," Jeannie explained, and saw Eleanor's relief that he had not gone into Charleston.

"Jeannie . . ." Eleanor inspected her face. "You've looked so tired these last two weeks." A pinkness stained her cheeks as she forced herself to continue. "I was wondering—is it the heat—or are you in a family way?" Her eyes clung earnestly to Jeannie's face.

"No," Jeannie said gently, sensing that her mother-in-law would be deeply disappointed. "I'm not pregnant."

Eleanor's face fell.

"I was hoping you were," she acknowledged wistfully. "I know Craig would be so pleased."

Would Mr. Mitchell be pleased? Jeannie wondered. Dennis was not his own son, though he treated Dennis as if he were. Ron was his blood kin. Ron's child would be like his own, she decided with unexpected defiance. For a poignant moment she thought of herself carrying Ron's child. A sweet, self-conscious warmth suffused her.

"I was talking with Mr. Mitchell at breakfast." All at once Jeannie was covertly plotting. "He was telling me what a beautiful bride you were. He even remembered the dress you wore," she went on with determined artlessness. "White silk with little yellow flowers." She watched the astonishment well in Eleanor's eyes. "It must be beautiful to know that your husband still loves you after all these years of marriage."

Eleanor leaned forward with an incandescent glow about her.

"Jeannie," she whispered urgently, "do you truly believe that Craig still loves me?"

"I would swear to that," Jeannie reassured her. "I have only to look into his eyes to know that."

"Thank you, Jeannie." Eleanor's voice trembled. "I had not believed that. I thought I had killed whatever he felt for me." She rose to her feet with a new determination shining from her. "Excuse me, Jeannie. There is something I must do."

Jeannie stood alone on the gallery, leaning over the railing to gaze down again at the pair of beagles romping below. She started at the sound of crashing glass inside the bedroom. In alarm she crossed to the open door to Eleanor Mitchell's bedroom.

With methodical precision Eleanor was smashing bottle

after bottle of fine imported wine into a tub at her feet. Danielle charged into the room from the hallway, an anxious look on her face.

"Missy Eleanor, yo' all rat?" she asked worriedly, and stared as another bottle of wine crashed into the tub, spilling golden liquid.

"Danielle, I'm fine," Eleanor reassured her with exhilaration. You know what I'd like you to do for me? I want you to go up into the attic and dig out that white silk with the little yellow flowers. I want you to see if you can let it out enough so that I can wear it again."

Nineteen

Madeline moved about in her bed, searching for a comfortable position. She had no intention of going into Charleston until well into the afternoon, when the sun was in descent. This morning she had gone into Ron's room, while he slept, and coolly helped herself to money.

Her destination would be André Genet's private, very plush gaming rooms, in his elegant town house high on the Battery. It was at André's that she had met Dennis, a little over a year ago. She gambled for amusement, for the pleasure of being in the midst of glittering luxury, surrounded by rich planters—and of course, André had made it worth her while to keep guests playing at the tables. It excited her to see the careless exchange of huge sums of money. But she never truly forgave Mama, or allowed her to forget, that Papa's estate had been lost at the roulette wheel.

She closed her eyes, remembering that night at André's.

Dennis had not seen her at first. He was sitting at a table, staring moodily at the cards in his hands. He was playing *vingt-et-un* that night. And then, as she watched, he threw his cards on the table.

"Deal me out," he said with irritation, and rose to his feet.

She stared at him with a provocative smile, intrigued by his handsomeness. The brooding quality about him strangely aroused her. She had asked André who he was, and André had told her he was Dennis Mitchell. Everybody in South Carolina knew of the wealthy Mitchell family. This, she told herself, was to be the night for which she and Mama had waited for three years.

"Try roulette," she said to Dennis as he pushed back his chair and rose to his feet. "That's less painful."

"I'm broke," he said with contained rage. "I'm through for the night." But his eyes moved avidly over her tall, audaciously gowned figure.

"I'll stake you to a number," she offered. Her eyes moved across the room. Mama was at the faro table. Until she ran out of money, she would remain there. André adored her and Mama, but that adoration did not extend to allowing them credit. If she left here with Dennis, André would so inform Mama. It was no secret to André that she and Mama were here, mainly, in search of a wealthy suitor for her hand.

Dennis grinned and dropped an arm about her waist as she led him to the table.

"Stay by me and bring me luck," he ordered. Immediately there had been a recognition of each other's potentialities. Even if he had not been rich, Madeline told herself recklessly, she would be in pursuit of Dennis Mitchell.

She reached into her reticule, drew out a silver dollar, and dropped it with a flourish into Dennis' hand.

Dennis played the red. Red won. Dennis' money was doubled. He indicated the money was to remain. Again, red. The croupier started the small ball rolling again. Madeline leaned forward, resting a hand on Dennis' shoulder. Again, red. Cool and enigmatic, Dennis continued to play the red, never removing his winnings.

Excitement embraced the onlookers at the table. Dennis' winnings were piling high. Alerted by the croupier, André himself came over to watch.

Madeline started at the hand on her shoulder. She looked down into André's eyes. A full four inches shorter than she, he nonetheless seemed menacing at this moment. His eyes telegraphed a message. André Genet was alarmed that Dennis would break the bank.

"I have had enough," she said carelessly, and withdrew her hand from Dennis' shoulder. "I would like to go in to supper." André served an elegant buffet in an adjoining room as a courtesy to his guests.

"Wait." Dennis reached for Madeline's arm. "Cash me in," he said briskly to the croupier, and rose to his feet.

Together Madeline and Dennis went into the velvet-draped, crystal-chandeliered dining room and ate generously from André Genet's gourmet offering, each knowing the climax of this evening. Yet Madeline was aware of her obligation to André. She must bring Dennis Mitchell back to the gaming tables. Later.

"Would you like to see André's bathhouse?" she invited. "Its services are offered to choice guests." Her eyes were brazenly inviting.

"Where is this bathhouse?" he asked with alacrity.

"Directly behind the main house. I'll show you." She linked an arm through his. "André had it copied from an old tapestry that belonged to his family in France. Bathhouses were quite popular, he told me, back in the twelfth and thirteenth centuries. They became notorious in the fourteenth and fifteenth centuries. Mixed bathing parties were popular."

"A fascinating pastime," Dennis approved, his eyes fastened to the deep décolletage of her gown.

Together they walked from the house to the white stuccoed single-story building centered in the lush gardens to the rear. Madeline slid one hand behind an ornate piece of statuary that stood beside the door and found the key hidden for such occasions as this.

Madeline threw open the door and strode inside, Dennis at her heels. The moonlight poured into the room through an avenue of high, round windows. Dennis lit the candles in a pair of girandoles that sat atop a long table beneath the windows on one side of the room.

"Do you like it?" Madeline asked with a challenging smile, her eyes moving about the large, white room with a proprietary pride.

"It's magnificent," Dennis conceded. Even he was impressed, Madeline thought with satisfaction.

Everything in the room was white except for the gold girandoles and the gleaming gold faucets that would pour water into the eight-foot-square sunken marble tub. The chairs that were provided for after-bath lounging were upholstered in a shining white damask. A bed, Madeline showed Dennis, lay hidden behind white velvet draperies. Thick white rugs were scattered about the marble floor. The fireplace too—provided for chilly days —was marble-faced.

"The water's cold," Madeline said with a hint of laughter in her voice as she leaned to turn on the faucets at either end of the tub. With surprising force water charged into the tub.

"In this heat, who cares that it's cold?" Dennis shrugged.

For a long moment their eyes clung; then Madeline swung about, turning her back to him.

"Undo me," she ordered.

When Dennis reached to pull the dress away from her shoulders, Madeline firmly pushed him into a chair to watch her slowly, enticingly, disrobe.

She knew the effect of this small performance on any man. She noted with triumph the glow in his eyes as they lingered over her, recognizing his arousal. But when he leaped to his feet to reach for her, she slapped him smartly across one cheek.

"My way," she ordered royally. "Take off your clothes while I prepare the bath."

Making no secret of her familiarity with this ritual, Madeline moved with languid grace to a white lacquered commode and brought forth an ornamental bottle, whose contents she proceeded to pour into the bath. Almost immediately the room was exotically scented.

Dennis stood nude before her. He was tall, broad of shoulders, narrow of hips. She laughed at his flagrant excitement.

"Go into the bath," she ordered. "You'll cool off." She laughed at his first screech of protest as he stepped into the tub. He would cool off, temporarily.

Before she joined him in the tub, she brought forth from another commode a pair of white blankets with which they would dry themselves and two bars of a fine English soap. She laid the blankets across the chair and tossed the soap into the water.

"Come on in," Dennis coaxed. "Scared of the cold water?"

Knowing the effect of her actions on him, she leisurely stepped into the sunken tub and settled herself. They visually sparred as each, with mock seriousness, soaped lavishly. Dennis was impatient for the moment when they would abandon this byplay and take themselves to the bed.

"I've had enough," she announced finally. She felt, she thought with exhilaration, like an actress in a daring French play. She could do anything she wanted with Dennis Mitchell.

Madeline left the tub and reached for one of the blankets to pat herself dry. Dennis stood beside her, rubbing himself briskly. She dropped the blanket to the floor and walked with a provocative swaying motion to the bed.

"Madeline . . ." Dennis' voice was hoarse with desire as he reached for her.

"Wait!" she commanded. "Let me show you how we do these things in Paris."

He shrugged, seemingly amused, and allowed her to caress his length as he lay on the bed. He was like a hound dog after a bitch in heat, she thought. But she would teach this aristocratic son of a very rich planter. After a night with her, he would not want to settle for less.

Later—much later—they returned to the gaming rooms. André had been quite happy with her, Madeline recalled. Dennis lost every cent of his winnings at the roulette table. And for the next ten weeks there was hardly a moment that she and Dennis were apart—were not making love or battling with an equal intensity that both found strangely exhilarating—until that horrendous night of their last bitter battle, when she had told Dennis the one thing about herself that he could not endure to hear.

Madeline started at the knock on her door, annoyed at this shortening of her recall.

"Come in," she ordered querulously.

The door opened. Rose walked in warily.

"Ah brought yo' some fruit," Rose said ingratiatingly. "An' some ice' tea."

"All right," Madeline accepted irritably. "And then let me sleep until four. Oh, I'll want a carriage to take me into Charleston. Tell Gilbert to have it brought in front of the house by half-past four."

She would go to André's gaming rooms and spend the evening, she promised herself defiantly. She would not lose much money—Ron would have no cause for anger. At least on that score, she thought humorously. She would gamble just enough to keep her circulating about that glittering assemblage that André always managed to attract. There would be someone eager to entertain her. For the first time since her marriage she would spend a whole evening with another man. It was just as well that she had not invited Arnold to go into Charleston with her.

Promptly at four Rose came in to wake her. The house was wrapped in the summer-afternoon silence. The others had eaten the heavy meal of the day and retired to their rooms to nap until tea. She dressed with an air of vital expectation. She would order the coachman to drive along the waterfront to enjoy the cooling ocean breeze a bit before she went to André's.

Not a breeze stirred from the river as she left the house to climb into the carriage that was to take her into Charleston. Rose gazed wistfully from the upstairs gallery, hopeful until the last moment that her mistress would relent and take her along. Low laughter built in Madeline. Rose would be excess baggage today.

The drive into the city was miserably uncomfortable.

There had been little rain of late, and the carriage wheels circulated unpleasant swirls of dust into the air. But she felt a delicious exhilaration when they arrived in the city and the coachman deposited her before André's house.

"Be back here by nine," she ordered. "I don't care where you go until then." She swept toward the entrance, remembering she had said at the breakfast table that she would be back at dusk. She would return when she was so inclined. She was sick of Ron's grimness. He would not dare put her and Mama out, she thought, because that would defile the fine Mitchell name.

The familiar peephole slid wide to allow an inspection of her, and then she was admitted. Nothing ever changed at André's, she thought with pleasure as she walked into the main gaming room. Some of the faces were changed, but the mood was the same. Her reception was the same, with André delighted to see her. She moved about the room with André at her side, knowing that someone would quickly ask for an introduction. She smiled charmingly when that happened.

The man who hovered amorously above her now was older, almost forty. André said he was a wealthy planter from Augusta, out for amusement beyond the sight of his family. He would be enchanted to sponsor her at the gambling tables. Half of whatever he spent, André promised cajolingly, would be given to her in appreciation. It was an arrangement familiar to both. Only fleetingly did it surprise Madeline that he would offer this to Ron Mitchell's wife. Everybody knew, she thought bitterly, that she had married the poor Mitchell. Only she had not realized that. Did they laugh at her for that?

When her escort at last balked at further gambling, Madeline allowed herself to be persuaded to go upstairs to one of the private rooms André kept available for special patrons. He knew André's facilities. She heard him ask for the room reserved for those with the most erotic of tastes. He would want her to beat him into a frenzy. Then they would make love. It gave her savage satisfaction to see these men cry out beneath the lash, to know she was inflicting pain. No man ever truly used her. She received more than she gave.

At the head of the stairs, she paused to gaze down into the glittering foyer. Suddenly she was ice-cold. Dennis stood below, staring up at her with rage. Fighting the trembling that overtook her, she turned to her companion and reached with both hands to pull his face to hers. With Dennis watching, she moved into a passionate, abandoned embrace.

In the room designed to please her companion, Madeline went through the actions with a savagery that delighted him. And when he took her, at last, to bed, she responded with an animal passion. Exhausted, they fell asleep together. When she awoke, she was alone.

The candles in the girandole on the mantel were low. How late was it? she wondered with alarm. She dressed quic'ly, left the room, and hurried to the stairs. The gaming room ricocheted with the sounds of laughter and activity. André kept the rooms operating until dawn.

She sought out André, who greeted her effusively, his eyes simultaneously wise and admiring.

"A fine night, Madeline," he said with satisfaction, and took her to the cashier.

"André, what time is it?"

"Barely midnight," he soothed. "You have a carriage waiting?"

"Yes," she said with irritation. Ron would be furious with her. The others would have told him that she was in Charleston. He would guess that she was at André's. But there was nothing he could prove, she thought defiantly. He could only guess.

The carriage was waiting in front of the house. The coachman leaped down with an air of relief. He was anxious about her welfare.

"Let's get home as quickly as we can," she ordered. "It's fearfully late."

Clump of dark clouds hung together in the sky. The moon had gone into hiding. A brisk breeze continued to bring the scent of the sea into the city, but now Madeline hardly noticed. She gazed out of the carriage as they moved through the night-empty streets. If they were lucky, they would arrive at The Magnolias before the storm broke.

Had Dennis followed her into Charleston? Of course he had. Let him suffer, knowing what would happen in that upstairs room in André's fine mansion. Let him suffer, the way he had made her suffer!

The carriage clattered with unfamiliar speed over the dusty road, the horses seeming to be conscious of the imminent bad weather. They were minutes away from the house when lightning began to streak across the sky. Thunder rumbled. All at once the heavens unleashed a relentless downpour. From the stables came the terrified whinny of a horse. The roan, Madeline guessed. The roan was terrified of lightning.

They raced through the night. Madeline clung to the side of the carriage, swearing at the coachman as they moved past dark, empty fields. Not a house was within sight, no place where they could take refuge. Yet, paradoxically, Madeline relished this storm, this race with nature.

The carriage pulled up before the house. The sodden coachman leaped down to help Madeline from the carriage. She ran for the protection of the gallery. The door would be open, she remembered with relief.

Running a hand over her rain-brushed hair, she hurried up the stairs to her room. Rose was dozing on a pallet at one side of the room.

"Rose, wake up!" she commanded. "Go downstairs and fix me a tray. I'm famished."

"Yo' is all wet," Rose clucked sympathetically as she scrambled to her feet.

"Never mind that," Madeline brushed this aside. "Go down and fix me a tray. And bring it up to my mother's rooms," she decided impulsively. Mama loved to hear about the goings-on at André's.

She pulled off her shoes, stripped off her clothes, pulled on her nightdress and dressing gown, and slid her feet into slippers. She would give Mama some of the money she had acquired tonight, she decided in a burst of generosity.

She paused to run a brush over her hair, inspected her face in the mirror, and was pleased with what she saw. She had enjoyed this evening in Charleston. Yet she could not wash away the memory of that moment when she had gazed down into the foyer at André's house to see Dennis staring up at her with such rage. Feeling that rage, she trembled.

Why should she care that Dennis saw her? He could do nothing to hurt her. She reached for her reticule, took a handful of bills, and charged from the room. She hurried up the dark stairs to her mother's room and pulled open the door without knocking, as she always did.

The sitting room was engulfed in blackness, but she walked with familiarity to the bedroom door and pulled it wide. A lighted girandole on the mantel spilled light across the ornate bed where her mother lay against a mound of pillows in her disarrayed black dressing gown, sagging breasts on display before the eyes of the man who hovered over her.

Even before the man swung about, at her mother's shriek of dismay, she knew that her mother's lover of the moment was Dennis.

Twenty

Jeannie awoke with a start, conscious of rain pelting the side of the house. Simultaneously she heard Madeline's voice, screaming in rage in the room above hers.

Jeannie's eyes sought out the clock. It was past one-thirty; but then, Madeline had little respect for time, she thought. Still, it was unusual for Madeline to be in her mother's rooms at this hour of the night. She lifted herself uneasily on one elbow, listening compulsively to the sounds of Madeline's tirade, though the words were lost in the hysterical pitch of her voice.

"Madeline, baby, please!" Mavis pleaded shrilly. "Mady, don't carry on this way!"

"Madeline, shut up!" Dennis ordered, and Jeannie stiffened in astonishment. "You'll wake up the whole house."

"I hope I do!" Madeline shrieked. "You get out of here, Dennis! You drunken lout! Get out of Mama's rooms! You're rotten! Rotten clear through!" And then Madeline was sobbing hysterically.

Suddenly trembling, Jeannie tossed aside the light counterpane and lifted up the netting that covered her bed. She walked to her door, then hovered there without opening it, feeling a need for action without knowing what she should do. She could hear Dennis charging down the stairs. He went into his own room next door and slammed the door shut behind him.

Mrs. Mitchell had been distressed when Dennis had not returned to the plantation for dinner, nor for tea. When Arnold came over in the afternoon, he told them Dennis had been at Burke Acres all morning, but then he had left.

"I don't know where he went, Mrs. Mitchell," Arnold had said politely. "He didn't say anything to Aunt Emmaline."

Mrs. Mitchell suspected that Dennis had gone into Charleston to gamble; but halfway through the evening, while the family was still sitting on the gallery, Dennis had driven up to the house in the carriage and, with a brusque good-night, gone directly upstairs to his room. When had he gone to Mavis' room? Why had he gone there?

Jeannie returned to her bed, knowing it would be hours before she fell asleep again. Had Ron heard Madeline screaming in her mother's room? His own, of course, was on the other side of the house. Poor Ron, she thought with a surge of sympathy. He seemed so troubled, so enmeshed in despair. Too often these past days she had fought to keep her eyes away from Ron, lest she betray herself.

"Missy, dat rain comin' down pow'ful ha'd." Aunt Lizzie, knowing she was awake, came in from her pallet on the gallery. "Lemme see if it's comin' in at yo' side windows."

"Aren't you getting wet out there on the gallery?" Jeannie asked solicitously.

"Ah move close to de doah," Aunt Lizzie said placidly. "It don' touch me."

"Bring your pallet inside and sleep in here," Jeannie ordered gently. Out there on the gallery Aunt Lizzie must have heard every word that was said upstairs. Everybody at the plantation—even the field slaves—knew by this time that her husband and Ron's wife had been lovers. What vengeful marriages both had wrought, Jeannie thought with pain. How long could they endure this way, living—as Mr. Mitchell said—on the edge of a volcano that seemed on the point of eruption at any moment?

Would the situation change if she left The Magnolias? Her heart pounding, her throat tight, she tried to consider this. How could she leave, she asked herself, loving Ron the way she did? Let her, at least, be near enough to see him each day.

In the sudden change of temperature brought on by the storm, Jeannie shivered beneath the cotton counterpane.

"Ah'll git yo' a blanket, Young Missy," Aunt Lizzie crooned.

Aunt Lizzie's eyes, as she draped the blanket about Jeannie's slender form, were warm with compassion. How much did Aunt Lizzie know? Jeannie asked herself. Did she know that her mistress felt only revulsion for her husband, but that she loved her husband's cousin?

The early-morning sun shone brightly on the still-damp grass and dripping foliage that surrounded the house. The mockingbirds chirped ecstatically as they hopped from tree to tree. And sitting on the gallery, Ron thought about the fresh stagnation the rain would build up in the swamps to breed the fever that was the terror of the rice plantations.

He had arisen at sunup to go out into the fields to see the effects of last night's rain. It had been desperately needed for the well-being of both the rice and the cotton. They were too much at the mercy of the elements, he thought tiredly.

He had meant to stay awake last night until Madeline returned from Charleston. He must make her understand that this willful behavior was unacceptable. Without a word to him—not bothering to take Rose with her—she had gone into the city, to return shamelessly late.

He had fallen asleep in a chair in his room while he sought to read. He frowned, remembering how he had been jarred awake by Madeline's temperamental outburst in her mother's rooms. She must have awakened the whole household, he thought ashamedly. Was Mavis fighting with her for tearing off into Charleston that way? God knew, Mavis tried to bring Madeline into line.

His mind shot back to that weekend on Mr. Poinsett's plantation, when he had first met Madeline. He had been delighted to claim her attention. How stupid he had been, he taunted himself, to believe that Mr. Poinsett's gloriously beautiful young guest had been so swiftly enamored of him! How had he allowed himself to be swept into marriage so quickly? But he knew why— Madeline had alarmed him with hints that she might return to Paris. He could not, at that point, bear the prospect of an ocean between them. After the lonely, disillusioning months he had spent in Mexico with his outfit, he had been an easy prey for Madeline Beauchamp.

Almost from the beginning he had realized this marriage was a mistake. Madeline had envisioned herself the wife of a wealthy young planter. She had expected to live the busy social life of other planters' families, not realizing how withdrawn they were at The Magnolias. And increasingly, he was convinced there had been a relationship between Madeline and Dennis before he met her.

He should have sent Madeline away after that revolting business with Andrew McKinley. Damn, he knew what was happening in that room when he walked in, despite

Madeline's preposterous protestations. It was enough that Madeline had gone alone into a strange man's house.

Why couldn't he bring himself to send Madeline away? It wasn't that he loved her; that love was dead. Why was he cursed with this absurd sense of responsibility? She had never truly been his wife. He would never touch her again, he swore to himself.

He loved Jeannie, he thought with torturous candor. Sweet, beautiful, compassionate Jeannie. From the moment that she had walked into the house, he admitted with a sweeping realization, he had loved her.

"Thank God for this break in the heat." His uncle's voice shattered his introspection. Craig walked out onto the gallery and gazed about with an air of satisfaction. "Of course, we may be sweating tomorrow."

"I got up early and went out into the fields," Ron said, pulling himself erect in his rocker. "Everything's fine. The rain was exactly what we needed."

"How's the new man coming along?" Craig lowered himself into a chair beside Ron's.

"I think he's going to work out fine," Ron said seriously. "It'll take a while until he's on to everything, but he's intelligent. We were lucky to find him so quickly."

"Ron . . ." Craig hesitated.

"Yes?" Ron leaned forward slightly, alerted by the tone of his uncle's voice.

"I've been giving some serious thought to these complaints of Madeline's." Craig tried to sound matter-of-fact. "She's not without justification," he conceded. "I believe I can raise enough cash for you to send Madeline and her mother into the mountains or to the shore until early October."

"I won't let you do that, Uncle Craig," Ron rejected. "You'll need every cent you can raise for the new equipment." He knew a loan was presently in negotiation.

"I can borrow enough additional to see this project through, Ron," Craig insisted. "I think it'll be good for you," he said with honesty, "to be separated from your wife for a while. You'll have time to clear the air between you."

"I won't let you do that, sir." Ron's face was hot with

color. "I'm—I'll talk to Madeline," he promised unhappily. "I know she's disrupting the household."

"Dennis isn't helping," Craig acknowledged.

"This is Dennis' home. I brought Madeline here." He sighed. "I'm sorry about that outbreak in her mother's room last night." He hadn't really been able to hear what was happening, but Madeline's screeching had been enough to wake up everybody. "She's lived by crazy hours in both Paris and Charleston. I'll talk to her," he reiterated earnestly. "I'll make her understand that she must learn to fit into this household."

"I'll talk to Dennis," Craig said gravely. "Dennis baits her. I'm not blind to that."

The two men went into the house to breakfast alone. By tacit agreement they concentrated their conversation on plantation business. Carlotta moved about the table, seeming to anticipate their every wish.

"Ron," Craig said quietly, when Carlotta left them, "there's something I want you to do for me. I haven't talked to her about it yet, but I want you to make arrangements to send Carlotta up North with papers granting her freedom. She'll have to be spirited out of the state, because I have no intention of dragging this through the County Court. We have enough business contacts in New York," he added with a calmness that told Ron he had thought much about this action, "to guarantee that a job will be found for Carlotta up there."

"Do you believe Carlotta will want to leave The Magnolias?" Ron asked seriously. He knew Carlotta's devotion to his uncle, a devotion that went far beyond the master-slave relationship.

"Ron, what girl of Carlotta's intelligence will not welcome her freedom?" he asked gently. "Say nothing to her, though, until we're prepared to send her on her way," he warned.

"I'll go into Charleston and make discreet inquiries," Ron promised. "I know a man who will handle it—he was with me in Mexico."

After breakfast Ron ordered himself to go upstairs to Madeline's room to talk with her. He had seen Rose walking past the dining room with Madeline's morning coffee in hand. Madeline should be clearheaded enough for conversation, he told himself.

Walking past his aunt's room, he heard her talking with Danielle.

"Danielle, this was my wedding dress," Eleanor was saying with an unfamiliar lilt in her voice. "My husband liked it so much. Our wedding anniversary is coming very soon. I would adore to wear it down to tea that evening."

What was happening with Aunt Eleanor? Last night, when they sat down to tea, she had waved Gilbert away when he came to fill the wineglass always set at her place.

"No, Gilbert," she had said firmly, and he remembered his uncle's start of astonishment. "I don't believe I care for any wine tonight." In the ten years that he had lived at The Magnolias, this was the first time Aunt Eleanor had refused wine.

At Madeline's door Ron paused, mustering strength to challenge his wife. His mouth set, he knocked on the door and waited for a response.

The door swung open slightly. Rose peered out, respectful but wary.

"Missy sleepin'," she reported in a whisper. "She ain' had coffee yet."

"Thank you, Rose." He smiled ruefully, aware of a sense of reprieve. "I'll talk to her later."

He went back downstairs and out of the house, feeling a need to walk in the pleasant morning air. He walked toward the river, pausing to fondle a pair of beagles that charged forward to demand a show of affection.

He spied Arnold, riding toward the house at an earlier-than-normal hour. Poor Arnold, he thought with compassion, as he waved at him. One of these days Madeline would show her arrogant, contemptuous side to him, and Arnold would be crushed.

Ron strode with a compulsive swiftness toward the river, feeling a need to put distance between himself and the house. There was no decent way to end his marriage with Madeline. He had undertaken a lifetime obligation. But it was wrong to foist his mistakes on the family.

He had only one honorable way out of this ugliness

that festered at The Magnolias. That was to take Madeline and her mother and leave. He must wait until he had the new superintendent trained. It wouldn't be easy for Uncle Craig, but his uncle would manage once this new man was thoroughly acquainted with the job. He would no longer inflict his wife on his family.

How would he endure leaving The Magnolias behind him, knowing he would never see Jeannie again? But he must do this. *He must.*

Twenty-one

Madeline sat up in bed, leaning against a mound of pillows while Rose hovered uneasily above her.

"Rose, you tell Juno her coffee is disgustingly bad!" Madeline said with a look of revulsion on her face. "After all these years in the kitchen she still hasn't learned to make a decent pot of coffee."

"Maybe it set on de stove too long," Rose said cajolingly. "Ah'll go down an' bring up some fresh coffee."

"Make sure it's a new pot," Madeline ordered. "What you just brought must have been sitting around for two hours."

"Yes'm." Rose picked up the rejected cup of coffee and headed for the door.

"Wait, Rose," Madeline called out. "Bring me my mirror and the hairbrush."

With the mirror in hand she gravely inspected her reflection. She smiled with approval. Dennis had always said she looked her most beautiful in the morning. She leaned back against the pillows, caught up in memory.

How many times, and not so long ago, Dennis had awakened her with lovemaking! He knew how she relished being awakened in that fashion.

The mirror was forgotten. Madeline's eyes glowed with recall. She was conscious of a faint stirring of passion. What a wild morning they had shared that last day they had spent together! They had gone to sleep at dawn, too satiated with champagne to indulge in anything else. And she had come awake slowly to the weight of Dennis' body on hers, his mouth at her ear. She had opened her eyes as he moved within her, and suddenly she had gone berserk.

Madeline laughed softly. How had Dennis explained the tooth marks she had left on his face and throat that day? That had been a parting gift from her. And then suddenly her levity dissolved; she remembered last night.

How had Mama let Dennis make such a fool of her last night? Mama knew what Dennis was! Dennis had gone to Mama that way to punish *her*. Mama must know that. But Mama was so weak, she thought bitterly. She still thought she was young and beautiful. In Charleston Mama had indulged in her secret little affairs with those stupid young boys, and she had closed her eyes to them. But how could Mama let Dennis come to her that way?

Madeline frowned at the knock on her door.

"Come in," she called without disguising her irritation.

The door opened. Arnold paused eagerly on the threshold, cuddling a tiny calico kitten in his huge hands. His eyes were wistfully eager.

"I brought Patches over to see you," he said, moving into the room.

"Arnold, close the door," Madeline said, straining for patience. She loathed cats. She never felt comfortable with them.

"All right, Madeline."

He shut the door and came close to the bed. Fighting her distaste, she forced herself to accept the kitten from him, to display interest in the furry, meowing morsel as Arnold proudly described the kitten's endearing ways.

"Sit down on the bed, Arnold," she invited. "I can't bear to see you standing there that way."

Rose came into the room with a fresh cup of coffee and brought it warily to the bed, chiding Madeline simultaneously with her eyes for allowing Arnold this repeated intimacy.

"Juno jes' took a fresh pot off de stove," Rose said placatingly.

Madeline dropped the kitten onto the bed, accepted the cup, and brought it experimentally to her mouth. She was conscious of Arnold's pleasure at being with her this way. Arnold thought she was the most beautiful woman alive, for all his chumminess with Jeannie. He might have the mind of a little boy, she thought while she sipped the strong, black coffee, but that man's body looked at her with desire.

Had Arnold ever taken himself a woman? Not likely, she decided. Emmaline watched him like a hawk. Still, he wandered between the two plantations at will. Curiosity welled in her. What would happen if she reached out to touch Arnold? Would he react like a child or like a man?

"Rose," Madeline said on impulse, "go out and pick me a bowl of fresh figs. I don't want any of those that have been lying around in the heat of the kitchen all morning. Bring up two bowls," she amended her order. "For Arnold and me."

She waited with an odd expectation for Rose to leave the room and close the door.

"Arnold," she said with silken softness, "go over to the door and slide the bolt into place."

"Yes'm," he said with polite surprise. "If you're worried about Patches running away, she can't open the door." He giggled, pleased with his observation, as he followed instructions.

"Arnold, come back and sit beside me," Madeline coaxed with a seductive smile, a potent weapon since she was fifteen.

"All right, Madeline." Happily he returned to sit beside her.

Deliberately she leaned toward him, allowing her breasts to fall forward against the delicate fabric of her nightdress, spilling over above the low neckline. A glint of triumph glowed in her eyes. She was right. In some ways Arnold *was* a man.

"Arnold," she whispered with calculated gentleness, "have you ever loved a lady?"

All at once his eyes seemed disturbed.

"I love you, Madeline."

"Have you ever done things with a lady?" she pursued, and reached for his hand and brought it to her breast. "Nice things?"

He hesitated, his face suddenly stormy.

"Once, a long time ago, Dennis took me to a house in the city. He made me go upstairs with this fat lady. He told me what I was supposed to do with her, but I didn't do it, Madeline. And she hit me. She hit me something awful!" His face was stormy with reproach.

"She was a bad lady, Arnold," Madeline crooned. "Let me tell you what to do, honey. You do what Madeline says and it'll be just wonderful."

She pulled him back upon the bed beside her. Her hands moved to him. She saw the first startled arousal in him. She heard his labored breathing. Beside the bed the kitten meowed plaintively. A few moments later she hopped up onto the bed to demand their attention. With one hand Madeline brushed Patches aside.

Surprisingly fast, it was Arnold who was aggressive. His hands were rough on her, his movements frenzied. They were demonstrating what she had always suspected, she thought with triumph. In some areas Arnold was fully a man.

"Sssh," she ordered. "Arnold, be quiet." But the door was locked. Nobody could disturb them.

Madeline left the bed to dress, conscious of Arnold's eyes following her about the room. They shone with a new awareness. Yet as she dressed, she was conscious of an unfamiliar sensation of guilt. But who would know? Arnold would have sense enough to be silent.

"Arnold," she said tenderly, returning to stand beside the bed, "we'll keep this our secret, won't we? We won't tell anybody else?"

"We won't tell anybody," he agreed, pleased to share

a secret with Madeline. And he was bright enough to know that Emmaline would be outraged. "Madeline . . ." He jumped to his feet and reached for her. "Let's do it again."

"No, Arnold," she rejected firmly, uneasily disengaging herself. "Not for a while." Was she going to have trouble controlling Arnold after this?

"When?" he pushed.

"I'll let you know," she evaded. "Arnold, I'm tired now." She forced a smile. "Why don't you take Patches and go on home?"

"I brought Patches to stay with you." He seemed bewildered. "She's a present."

"Then leave her down about the grounds," Madeline said impatiently. "Arnold, take the kitten and go."

His eyes hurt, Arnold scooped up Patches and headed for the door. Opening it, he paused to turn around to gaze accusingly at Madeline.

"Madeline, you're not nice today."

"Arnold, I was very nice to you." Her eyes reproached him.

Unexpectedly he smiled.

"Can we do it again tomorrow?" he persisted. "Please?"

"No, Arnold!" Her voice was faintly strident. "Maybe in a couple of weeks." She spied Rose in the doorway, bearing a bowl of figs in each hand. "For heaven's sake, Rose, what took you so long?"

Jeannie glanced up with a warm smile as Arnold shuffled through the door onto the gallery with an unfamiliar seriousness.

"Arnold, what a beautiful kitten!"

Arnold's face lighted. He held the kitten out to her.

"Her name is Patches. I brought her as a present for Madeline, but she won't let Patches stay in her room. I'm taking her back home with me—she can stay in my room."

"She's very sweet," Jeannie soothed, fondling the kitten.

"*You're* sweet," Arnold said with unexpected intensity. "You're *beautiful*."

Jeannie started at the glow in Arnold's eyes. She felt

strangely uncomfortable beneath his scrutiny. This was not the wistful child-man with whom she was familiar. Something disturbing was happening to Arnold.

He was around Madeline too much. Aunt Lizzie said that Rose told her Madeline allowed Arnold in her bedroom when she was having her bath. Couldn't Madeline understand what that kind of situation could do to Arnold?

Arnold remained briefly with her on the gallery, unfamiliarly restless this morning. He picked up Patches and walked toward his horse, tied up at a tree on the lawn. Jeannie watched while he paused and turned about to gaze upward toward Madeline's window. Even at this distance she could see the expression on Arnold's face. A coldness swept through her.

While she considered going over to Burke Acres to talk confidentially to Miss Emmaline about Arnold, Craig emerged from the house, dressed for going down into the city.

"I'm going into Charleston on business," he explained. His eyes rested speculatively on her. "Jeannie, would you be happier if you and Dennis were able to spend the rest of the summer in a rented house in Charleston?"

"No," she said quickly, and felt the color rise in her face. "I'd rather stay right here at The Magnolias."

"You're sure," he prodded, but she sensed his relief at her response to what must have been an impulsive inquiry.

"Quite sure."

She sat still in her rocker while Craig walked away from the house toward the stables. How could she bear to think of living away from The Magnolias, away from Ron? She shivered at the prospect of the greater closeness with Dennis that such an arrangement would provide.

Jeannie went into the house to ask Jeffrey to cut a bunch of the red roses that Miss Emmaline liked so much and tried to gear herself for what would be a delicate conversation. She waited on the gallery, nervous but determined, for Jeffrey to bring her the roses and for the carriage to arrive before the gallery.

In the carriage Jeannie rehearsed a small speech that

would convey her message to Miss Emmaline. The two old ladies were unmarried, sheltered from the realities of life; but Miss Emmaline would understand.

At Burke Acres, Miss Emmaline greeted her warmly and guided her to the west gallery, where a breeze from the river alleviated the oppressive heat.

"Bertha, bring us a pitcher of lemonade," she called with girlish conviviality into the house. "Oh, we've heard from Rebecca," she told Jeannie with a delightful smile. "She's met some folks who knew Madeline's father."

Over cookies and lemonade Jeannie stammeringly explained her anxiety over Arnold's friendship with Madeline, abstaining from any mention of the liberties Madeline permitted. Miss Emmaline's eyes were unhappy as they clung to Jeannie's. She made no maidenly pretense of not understanding.

"I have been worried about Arnold's closeness with Madeline," Miss Emmaline acknowledged. "I was pleased when he began to show his admiration for you. You're a lady, Jeannie," she said with admiration. "I'm not afraid for my boy when he's with you. But Madeline has always disturbed me." She took a deep breath. "I'm going to tell you something that only Charlotte knows. Papa and Mama knew, of course, but they're gone.

"Arnold is my child, Jeannie. My son." She lifted her head proudly. "I was forty years old when he was born. His father wanted to marry me, even before we found out about Arnold; but Papa would have none of it. He would never allow his daughter to marry his overseer," she said bitterly. "Somebody who was not a Southern aristocrat," she added with contempt. Jeannie remembered Emmaline's seeming preoccupation with family trees, with the importance of belonging to the right family. She was playing her father's game. "Papa personally flogged Jason—in front of all the slaves." Emmaline closed her eyes, reliving the agony. "I was locked in my room, but I knew. And then Papa sent him away. He left the country. I never heard from him again. I kept hoping I would."

"You've been a wonderful mother, Miss Emmaline."

222

Jeannie was touched by this confidence. "I've always admired your devotion to Arnold."

"It was wrong for Papa to flog Jason and send him away," Miss Emmaline flared. "We should have married and had half a dozen sons and daughters. I was forty years old when Arnold was born," she reiterated with pride, "but I had that boy as though I was no more than twenty." A sadness crept into her eyes. "But maybe it was a blessing. Perhaps all of our children might have been like Arnold. But I'll never know."

Jeannie stayed only briefly at Burke Acres. She knew that after today, Miss Emmaline was forever her friend. She felt almost as though she belonged at The Magnolias, that she was truly a Mitchell.

In the days that followed, Arnold returned regularly to The Magnolias. Jeannie sensed that his trips were furtive, unknown to Miss Emmaline. Madeline was irritable with him, brushing him aside with a new impatience.

Poor Arnold, Jeannie thought compassionately. He was bewildered by Madeline's coldness. She made an effort to be close by whenever he appeared at the house. Between herself and Arnold there was a brother-sister warmth.

Dennis went into Charleston to visit friends for a week, with no effort to invite his wife to share this sojourn in the city. It was a relief, Jeannie thought guiltily, to have Dennis away from The Magnolias for a few days.

He returned late one afternoon while Jeannie sat on the gallery trying to read the new novel her mother-in-law had lent her that morning. Madeline walked out onto the gallery as Dennis stalked up the stairs, Plato at his heels with his portmanteau.

For a taut moment Dennis' eyes clashed with Madeline's, and then he turned to Jeannie, drew her to her feet, and kissed her passionately on the mouth.

"I've missed you, Jeannie," he said with a show of ardor, and swept past Madeline into the house.

Was it going to start all over again? Jeannie asked herself, fighting panic. Would Dennis come again to her

223

room, night after night, to take her without love, with a passion born of rage?

"You adored Dennis when he brought you here," Madeline said, eyeing her speculatively, "but he killed that love, didn't he?"

"I love Dennis," Jeannie protested. Guiltily she dropped her eyes before the cynicism in Madeline's. "He's my husband."

"A few words before a minister don't guarantee love!" Madeline lashed back. All at once her face was contorted with anguish. "Why can't Dennis kill my love? How can I loathe and love him simultaneously?" Jeannie whitened at this admission. "Dennis and I love each other," Madeline said with a strange detachment, "because we're two of a kind. Ron's too good for me. I don't deserve him." She fastened her gaze warily on Jeannie. "But don't misunderstand, Jeannie. I'll never let Ron go. I need him."

Jeannie lay sleepless far into the night, fearful of the opening of her door, of Dennis' coming unannounced into her bed. She strained for sounds from his room next door, but there was only silence. Outside, a pair of cats howled in heat.

The moonlight filtered through the draperies to lay a ribbon of pale gold across Jeannie's bed. She thought about Ron, who moved about the house with a disquieting unhappiness. Sometimes Mr. Mitchell looked at her and then at Ron, and she thought, He knows, he *knows*.

All at once the night quiet was broken by the sound of a door opening and closing. Dennis was returning to his room. Jeannie's heart began to pound. Had he gone to Mavis' rooms again, after that horrible scene with Madeline? *Why did he do that?*

She lay back against the pillows, staring into the darkness. How could she continue this absurd marriage with Dennis? She would die if he came to her room again and tried to touch her.

Yet as she had first been bound to The Magnolias because of Dennis, now she was bound by Ron. What was it Mr. Mitchell had said? *There are times in life when we can only sit by helplessly and watch.*

Finally, too restless to remain in bed, Jeannie arose. She would read awhile. But as she reached for a book, a warning scent reached her. Smoke! She grabbed her dressing gown and darted to the door.

In the night-darkened hall she sniffed anxiously as she pulled the dressing gown about her, her eyes searching the area for some indication of fire. Down below, Suzette was hurrying across the foyer into the night. *Where was Suzette running at this time of night?* But the growingly heavy scent of smoke temporarily erased the thought from her mind. She looked about again, and spied the curl of smoke from beneath the door at the head of the stairs. She wasn't wrong. Something was burning! In Mavis' rooms!

She paused only to knock sharply at Craig's door.

"Mr. Mitchell!" she called. "Mr. Mitchell, there's a fire upstairs!"

Without waiting for a reply, she dashed up the stairs and pulled open the door to walk into Mavis' sitting room. From beneath the closed bedroom door seeped an ominous sheet of smoke.

"Mrs. Beauchamp!" Jeannie pulled open the door, pausing momentarily before clouds of smoke that poured from the bedroom. The draperies at either side of Mavis' bed were burning. Mavis lay asleep—or unconscious—across the bed. "Mrs. Beauchamp!" Jeannie darted to throw open a window, then moved to the bed and leaned over the prone woman. "Mrs. Beauchamp, please!" she pleaded urgently, tugging at her shoulders. The smoke had overcome her, Jeannie guessed, and she desperately struggled to pull Mavis to her feet.

"Ron, help Jeannie get Mavis out of here," Craig's voice ordered briskly from the doorway. "I'll take care of the draperies."

Hampered by the sling on his left arm, Ron managed to lift Mavis by the waist, and with Jeannie's help dragged her from the bedroom, through the sitting room to the stairs.

"Mama!" Madeline cried out hysterically, stumbling up the stairs. "Mama!"

"She's just overcome by the smoke," Jeannie reassured while Ron strode back into the room to help his uncle.

"What is it?" Eleanor's voice came anxiously to them as she arrived at the foot of the stairs. "Oh, my God, a fire!"

"Mr. Mitchell and Ron will have it in control in a few minutes," Jeannie soothed. "Would you help Madeline with Mrs. Beauchamp, please?" Where was Dennis? Sleeping soundly, Jeannie thought dryly. The house would have to burn down before he would be aware of a fire.

Her face pale with shock, Eleanor hurried up the stairs as Mavis stirred into consciousness.

"Danielle!" Eleanor called loudly as Jeannie darted back in the smoke-filled suite. "Go down to the kitchen and summon help. Madeline, let's help your mother to your room," Eleanor said with painful calm.

In the bedroom the windows had been opened wide. The burning draperies had been pulled away from the wall and thrown out the window to the ground below. Craig hovered at a window, gazing below.

"The draperies are burning on the grass. We'll have to douse the fire before it spreads to the trees!"

"Ron, you've burned your hand," Jeannie realized with alarm.

"It's nothing," he insisted, but Jeannie saw him wince.

"Let Jeannie put some grease on your hand, Ron," Craig ordered, striding toward the door. "I'll arouse the servants and get that fire out.

"Mrs. Mitchell sent Danielle to the kitchen," Jeannie remembered, and saw Craig's start of astonishment at her taking hold this way. "She's helping Madeline with Mrs. Beauchamp."

Solicitously Jeannie urged Ron down to the library, then went out to the kitchen for grease to apply to Ron's hand. The servants were running out of the house with tubs of water. She returned to the library and liberally spread grease across Ron's burned right palm, conscious of his closeness, of the emotions he kept so tightly reined.

"How touching." Madeline's voice swung their gaze

to the door. For an instant her eyes flashed dangerously. "Mrs. Mitchell sent me down for a bottle of wine for Mama." She walked to the cabinet that held the bottles of imported wine, took one out, and turned about to face Jeannie. "Thank you for saving Mama's life," she said with an effort. "She would have died up there if you had not found her."

Madeline left them abruptly, disappearing into the hallway. When Ron and Jeannie returned to the second floor and walked to the open door to Madeline's room, they found Mavis sitting in a chair.

"Why wasn't Suzette with you?" Madeline was demanding. "Where was she?"

"She should have been in the sitting room," Mavis said nervously. "Mady, she was there when I went to sleep. I didn't send her away. I swear it!"

Jeannie intercepted the heated exchange between Madeline and Mavis. Mavis was distraught, pleading silently with Madeline to believe her. Jeannie felt impelled to intervene.

"I saw Suzette running from the house when I came out of my room," Jeannie said self-consciously, and Madeline's eyes widened with shock as they turned to her.

"Suzette started the fire in Mama's rooms! It couldn't have been anybody else."

"We don't know that somebody started it," Jeannie objected.

"Both sets of draperies were burning," Ron said quietly from the doorway. "It must have been deliberately set."

Jeannie remembered the night Dennis had brought Suzette into his room. She remembered the covert play between them on other occasions. Suzette had started the fire out of jealousy of Mavis—because Dennis had been in Mavis' rooms tonight.

"I suggest we all try to get some sleep," Ron said gently as they heard Craig coming into the house, talking to the servants who had helped him put out the fire. "Tomorrow we'll arrange for repairs on your mother's rooms, Madeline."

Jeannie awoke early as usual, despite the shortness of

227

her sleep. She lay motionless in bed, remembering the excitement of the predawn hours. Ron's hand must have pained him, she thought sympathetically; but he had given no indication of that except for an occasional wince. She remembered those poignantly sweet moments when she had been alone with Ron in the library, caring for his burned hand.

She smiled as Aunt Lizzie cautiously opened the door, not truly expecting her to be awake.

"Come in, Aunt Lizzie," she called, eager this morning for that first cup of strong, fresh coffee.

While Aunt Lizzie had slept through last night's excitement, she had been well informed. She spoke avidly about the happenings, though discreetly refraining from any suggestion that arson had been involved.

"Danielle say dat crazy Suzette run away," Aunt Lizzie reported. "Nobody see huh anyweah," she said emphatically. "She di'n' even come down to de kitchen." Her eyes were bright with curiosity. "De Mastuh oughta sen' de dogs aftuh huh."

With a sudden need to see Ron, to reassure herself that he was all right, Jeannie decided to dress and go downstairs, though breakfast would not be served for an hour. Dennis still slept, she guessed. Not a sound emerged from his bedroom. He would probably sleep till noon.

Jeannie went down to sit on the gallery, pleasantly shaded at this hour of the morning. Today a comforting breeze came from the river. She felt a specious sense of peace.

"Good morning." Craig's voice was warm as he walked out onto the gallery.

"Good morning, Jeannie." Ron followed him. He smiled, but his eyes were serious.

"How's your hand?" Jeannie asked solicitously, after a quick smile for her father-in-law.

Ron chuckled whimsically.

"I think I'll live."

"Ron, how long do you think it'll take to get Mavis' bedroom into proper shape again?" Craig asked, settling himself beside Jeannie.

"I'll put a crew on it right away," Ron promised. "She

ought to be able to move back into it in three or four days. Meanwhile, I've told Gilbert to have a bed set up in her sitting room."

"Mist' Mitchell! Mist' Mitchell!" One of the stable hands came running breathlessly toward them. "Yo' best come quick, suh!"

"What is it?" Craig leaped to his feet.

"Dat Suzette . . ." The stable hand paused to catch his breath. "She layin' nekkid and dead out deah in de woods. Somebody kill huh!"

Twenty-two

Ron leaped to his feet. His eyes met his uncle's with grave concern.

"Jeannie, don't leave the house," he ordered. "Don't allow any of the ladies to leave. We'll return as soon as we can."

Jeannie sat tensely on the gallery, cold with alarm as she watched the two men charge after the stable slave, their figures disappearing in the live oak grove to the west. Only a few hours ago, poised at the head of the stairs, she had seen Suzette darting across the foyer into the night. She must have been the last—except for the murderer—to see Suzette alive.

Where had Suzette been running at that hour of the night? Jeannie's initial reaction, after the excitement of the fire, had been that Suzette was running away from The Magnolias because she had been responsible for the fire. Now a new thought rose harshly in her mind.

Had Suzette been running away from the fire—or had she been running to meet someone?

A coldness started closing in about her.

Was Suzette running to meet Dennis? Did Dennis kill her in one of his rages? No, I won't believe that! It couldn't be true. Dennis returned to his room at least forty minutes before I discovered the fire.

Was Suzette in the sitting room while Dennis visited with Mavis in her bedroom, and had they arranged to meet later? Dennis had not appeared in the hall—everybody believed him to be asleep. *Was he? No, stop this! How can I suspect Dennis of murder?*

Jeannie sat tensely at the edge of her rocker, her eyes turning repeatedly to the live oak grove. Poor Suzette. How had she died? What an awful thing to happen! Her gaze focused now on the two men, emerging from the grove. Their faces were somber as they talked quietly to each other. Jeannie rose to her feet as they arrived at the house.

"She was violated and strangled," Craig reported, his voice shaking with anger. "She's been dead for several hours." He hesitated. "It was a brutal murder."

"How awful," Jeannie whispered. Her mind shot back to her bedroom at Ransome Island, to the night when Kevin had invaded her room and violated her. But, for Suzette, to this outrage had been added murder.

"The others must be told," Ron reminded his uncle, his eyes flashing a message. They were anxious lest there be another murder, Jeannie realized with shock. "I'll arrange for the burial."

"Jeannie, call Gilbert please," Craig said tersely, and Jeannie silently swept past him and into the house.

Searching the lower floor for Gilbert, she found him in the dining room removing crystal from a cabinet and exhorting Carlotta to be careful about the washing.

"Gilbert, will you please come out to the gallery." Jeannie's voice was not quite steady. She saw anxiety well in Carlotta and Gilbert as they recognized her own agitation.

"Yes, Young Missy." Gilbert politely followed her out onto the gallery.

"Gilbert, I want you to send Danielle and Rose upstairs to wake Mrs. Mitchell, Miss Madeline, and Mrs. Beauchamp. Tell them to have the ladies come down to the rear parlors as soon as possible. There is something I must say to them." He sighed before Gilbert's obvious concern. "Gilbert, you'll have to tell the servants. Suzette has been murdered."

"Oh, suh!" Gilbert gasped.

"Please see to it that none of the women leave the house. The men will go outside the house only in pairs until we've looked into this murder."

"Ah'll sen' Danielle and Rose upstaihs rat away, suh," Gilbert said, his face etched with shock.

"Gilbert"—Jeannie stopped him as he turned to go into the house—"will you please ask Juno to put up a pot of coffee and send it into the rear parlor?"

"Yes, ma'am," he said sorrowfully.

With her father-in-law and Ron, Jeannie went into the rear parlor, struggling to retain her composure. Across her mind darted painful visions of Suzette's rendezvous in the night, which had ended so horrendously.

In minutes Gilbert came to set up small tables with china and silver. Loud wails of grief emerging from the kitchen rent the air. Jeannie shivered.

"Who would do a thing like this?" Ron demanded with frustration. "We'll have to go down to the quarters and question every buck on the plantation!"

"It seems unbelievable." Craig shook his head. "We've never had anything like this at The Magnolias."

The two men talked in subdued tones about violence on other plantations, a problem that had always seemed remote from The Magnolias.

"What the devil's going on down here? What's all the carrying-on about?" Dennis demanded, scowling in the doorway. "A man can't even sleep in his own house!"

"Suzette was murdered," Ron told him, and Jeannie saw him whiten with shock. "We're sorry the servants' grief disturbed your sleep."

"What happened?" Dennis' voice was uneven. It had not been Dennis, Jeannie was sure; he was plainly astonished.

Craig tersely reported on the happenings in the woods.

"Who would do a thing like that?" Dennis gazed from his father to Ron, seeking a response in their eyes. "You don't suppose there's a slave uprising in the making?"

"This has nothing to do with a slave uprising," Ron said impatiently. "That's the first thing anyone thinks in South Carolina at any sign of violence."

"What's happened?" Eleanor hovered nervously in the doorway, her eyes seeking her husband.

"It's Suzette," Craig said gently. He went to her and eased her into a chair, his eyes solicitous. "Eleanor, Suzette is dead."

"How did she die?" Instinctively Eleanor knew this had not been a normal death.

As gently as he could, Craig told her about the murder. "Would you like a glass of wine?" he asked with infinite tenderness.

Eleanor pulled herself erect, a glint of pride in her eyes.

"Thank you, no. Coffee will be fine." Her eyes rested on the china set up on the small tables.

Gilbert walked into the room with the heavy silver coffeepot. His eyes were red from weeping, but he had regained his composure. He moved from table to table, pouring the hot black liquid into delicate porcelain cups.

"What ever is this all about?" Madeline demanded arrogantly from the doorway, Mavis hovering nervously at her side. "I never come down this early in the morning. And after being up half the night—"

"Suzette was murdered," Dennis broke in brutally. "Too bad you had to be disturbed."

"Oh, my God! Why are these terrible things happening in this house? Why are we being punished this way?" Mavis' voice rose into a thin, hysterical wail.

"None of you ladies is to stir from the house," Craig said sternly. "We don't know if the murderer is still lurking in the woods, waiting to strike again." He hesitated. "Suzette was—was molested before she was murdered."

Jeannie felt her face grow hot, remembering Kevin in her room here at The Magnolias, when Ron's intervention had saved her from further violation. Two men had taken her, she thought with pain—and neither with love.

Jeannie leaned forward in her chair, sipping at her coffee while her father-in-law explained what security measures would be taken.

"The grounds will be patrolled night and day," he promised grimly, "by field hands with dogs. Any stranger will be seized. Ron and I will go into the quarters and question every man among the hands, one by one."

"I'd better ride over to Burke Acres to caution Emmaline and Charlotte," Dennis decided.

"Take Jasper with you," his father ordered briskly.

"Papa, I'm not afraid," Dennis protested with amusement.

"Take Jasper with you," his father insisted. "We don't know what we're up against."

"Then you do think there might be an uprising on the way!" Dennis pinpointed.

"No," his father shot back. "But we must be cautious."

Madeline rose to her feet.

"If that's all, I'm going back to bed. Come, Mama, I'll take you upstairs."

"If you'll be more comfortable in your own rooms, Mavis, surrounded by your own things," Craig said gently, "Ron has ordered Gilbert to set up a bed temporarily in your sitting room."

"Thank you," Mavis whispered, and her eyes moved gratefully to Ron. "I would like that."

Later Jeannie sat on the upstairs gallery, still too shaken to read, gazing unseeingly into space. The day, which had begun promisingly, was overcast, humidly uncomfortable now. She gritted her teeth as she heard the hammering of nails in the distance. In the quarters, field hands were building the coffin in which Suzette would be buried tonight.

She frowned as she spied Arnold riding toward the house. Dennis had said he was going over to tell the ladies about what had happened. Surely Miss Emmaline would have ordered Arnold to remain at Burke Acres. But even as Arnold dismounted from his horse, Patches lovingly tucked in one arm, she saw a carriage pull away from the stables with Jasper on the box. Only now was Dennis going to report on Suzette's murder to Miss Emmaline. She would be so upset, Jeannie thought compassionately.

Arnold came into the house. Jeannie left the gallery and went into her room. Arnold was coming to see Madeline with the kitten again. Uneasily she walked to the door, feeling a need for action without being sure what it should be.

"Madeline, I brought Patches to see you," Arnold was calling eagerly from outside her door. "Madeline, can't I come in today?"

"Arnold, go away!" Madeline shrieked. "I don't want to see you. I don't ever want to see you again!"

Swiftly, propelled into action, Jeannie pulled open her door and moved into the hall.

"Arnold, is that Patches you have with you?" she asked cajolingly, and he spun about wistfully to face her.

"Would you like to play with Patches?" he asked, smiling broadly as he walked to her.

"Yes, I adore Patches," she said enthusiastically. "Let's go downstairs and sit on the gallery with her."

Together they walked down the stairs and out into the sticky afternoon. Jeannie listened attentively while Arnold talked to her about the kitten, pleased to have this audience.

"You're nice," Arnold said with satisfaction. "Lots nicer than Madeline. If I give you Patches, will you keep her in your room?"

"But don't you want to keep her?" Jeannie protested. "It wouldn't be kind to keep her in one room."

"Would you keep her in your room till she got to know you?" Arnold stipulated after a moment's consideration. "She's scared of folks she doesn't know." He fondled the kitten with poignant affection.

"Of course I will," Jeannie capitulated, and reached to take the small bundle of fur into her arms. "Thank you, Arnold." She brought the kitten to nuzzle against her face for a moment.

"I don't care if I don't have Madeline for a friend anymore," Arnold said defiantly. "I like you better. Aunt Emmaline likes you better."

"Arnold, I'm afraid there's going to be a storm." She

234

gazed apprehensively at the darkening sky. "I think you ought to get home before it starts."

"I like storms," Arnold confided. "And the night. I like to go riding at night, past the swamps. I hear all the animals in there. They're my friends." Suddenly he was somber. "But Aunt Emmaline hates storms. She says they give her a headache. And she can't sleep unless Annabel is sleeping on the floor by her bed."

"Arnold, Miss Emmaline will be angry with me if I don't send you home with a storm brewing," Jeannie said softly. "And I promise to take good care of Patches."

Reluctantly Arnold left to return to Burke Acres. Dennis would stay there talking with Aunt Emmaline for hours, Jeannie thought. She felt a sense of relief when Dennis was away from The Magnolias.

With Patches meowing reproachfully at this restraint, Jeannie carried her up to her room, then allowed her freedom to inspect her new premises. From the quarters came the plaintive wail of a cluster of slaves raising their voices in a spiritual. They had arrived from the fields to learn that Suzette was dead. Suzette too had once worked in the fields.

Aunt Lizzie came into Jeannie's room to put away the dresses she had laundered and ironed. Her face wore a resigned sadness.

"It's a shame de circuit riduh ain' in de neighbo'hood, but Mist' Mitchell and Ephrim—he de driver heads ouh church and he be sharin' de services—sho' to read a pow'ful good sermon. Suzette kin be rat proud of de funeral she'll git tonight." She squinted solicitously at Jeannie. "Yo' lookin' peaked," she scolded. "Yo' di'n' git 'nough res' las' night. Yo' git into dat bed and sleep."

"All right, Aunt Lizzie," Jeannie agreed tiredly, but she refused to change into a nightdress.

She lay on the bed, conscious of the stickiness of the afternoon. Her dress clung wetly to her body. Perspiration dampened her forehead. Despite her conviction that she would lie here resting but fully awake, she dozed.

Jeannie came awake suddenly, the horror of this morning's discovery assaulting her with staggering force. For a few minutes she lay motionless, reliving it. Then she left the bed and went out onto the gallery to gaze at the sky. The threatening storm had dissipated. The sun blazed hotly on the earth again.

"Mama, you are not to go to the church," Madeline was saying firmly, her voice filtering from her mother's sitting room above. "I won't allow you to go through that. Suzette wasn't worth it," she said with contempt, and Jeannie flinched before this crassness. "She was stupid and arrogant, and I know she was messing around with Dennis."

"Madeline, you're married to Ron," Mavis reminded stridently. "What are you trying to do to us? Madeline, there's no more money. You behave yourself, you hear?"

"Dennis is married too, Mama," Madeline reminded coldly. "Have you been forgetting that?"

Shaking, Jeannie moved quickly back into her room. She reached to close the door, and suddenly Patches leaped from the room, onto the gallery railing, and onto the nearest bough of a magnolia. Arnold would be furious with her if the kitten ran away!

Jeannie darted from her room, down the stairs, and out onto the gallery. She spied Patches scampering over the grass toward the woods. She set out in pursuit of the ball of black-and-orange fur. How fast Patches moved!

"Patches! Patches!" she called breathlessly.

All at once Patches paused in flight, hunched her back, and slapped an experimental paw at an insect. Churning with relief, Jeannie bent down to scoop the kitten into her arms.

"Patches, you little monster," she reproached affectionately.

"Jeannie!" Ron's voice was furious. "What do you mean coming into the woods this way?" He grasped her arm and whirled her about to face him. "Didn't I tell you to stay in the house?"

"Ron, I'm sorry," she gasped, exquisitely conscious of his nearness. "Patches ran away and I had to go after her. Arnold would be terribly upset if she was lost."

"Damn Arnold!" he said impatiently. "I won't have you putting your life in danger this way."

"Ron, I'm sorry," Jeannie stammered, her heart pounding at her realization of his concern for her. "I didn't think."

"You *must* think," he said with unfamiliar brusqueness, but what she saw in his eyes was exhilarating.

"Come, Jeannie. I'll take you back to the house. . . ."

But he wasn't taking her back to the house. He was pulling her into his arms. Patches meowed at being closed in between them.

"Jeannie," he whispered. "Oh, Jeannie, I love you."

Involuntarily, ecstatic at his confession, she lifted her face to his. Her hands loosened on Patches as she abandoned herself to the rapture of this moment, and the kitten leaped delightedly to the ground to chase a grasshopper.

"Jeannie, Jeannie, what can we do?" he asked with anguish, his face against hers. "What can there ever be for us?"

"Ron, I love you," Jeannie whispered recklessly. "More than I ever thought it possible to love anyone. But there can never be anything for us. Dennis and Madeline stand in the way." With anguish she forced herself to pull away from Ron. "But I want you to know that I love you, Ron. I'll love you till the day I die."

Twenty-three

After tea, with night already encroaching, the family—except for Madeline and Mavis—climbed into the large carriage for the short drive to the slave church. As they approached the quarters, they could hear the plaintive wailing of the waiting mourners. Men carrying lighted

torches stood solemnly around the entrance of the sma
stone church, whose interior could accommodate no mor
than a third of those who had come to pay their fina
respects to Suzette.

Jeannie shivered as she spied the two men with shovel
in the adjacent burial ground, just now completing th
digging of Suzette's grave. Her throat tightened as he
eyes rested on a cluster of white-turbaned women, rock
ing and wailing in grief, their faces wet with tears. Suzett
might have been the sister of each.

The mourners waiting outside the church parted wit
deep respect as the Master, his son, and his nephev
escorted Eleanor and Jeannie into the church, where
neatly cushioned pew at the rear had been reserved fo
them. Every inch of seating space was occupied, wit
the side walls lined with somber-faced slaves.

"We'll begin in a few moments," Craig told the mem
bers of the family, leaving them at the rear pew to go t
the pulpit, where Ephrim, the driver who served as th
plantation pastor in the absence of the circuit ride
leaned absorbedly over a copy of the Scripture ope
before him.

Jeannie fought back tears as she listened intently t
the grave, compassionate voice of her father-in-law. H
cared about his slaves, she thought. He was one of th
slave owners who felt ownership a serious obligation
Involuntarily her eyes moved to Ron, to discover his gaz
fastened to her. Fleetingly she allowed her eyes to mee
his with infinite tenderness; then—guiltily—she lowere
them again. Dennis was staring morosely at the floor
plainly impatient for the services to be over.

The sobbing among the mourners within the churc
reached a piercing crescendo as Craig relinquished th
pulpit to Ephrim. A new mood overtook the congre
gation, their grief seeming to rise to fresh heights. Ephrin
spoke with florid eloquence, crying out at intervals, be
seeching the Lord to care for the girl they had come t
bury. And as his cries filled the small church, many o
the congregation joined him in loud shrieks of distress

At last, those in the church solemnly walked out int
the torpid night air to the adjoining burial ground. I

the light of the torches Suzette's body was lowered into the grave. A woman, said to be Suzette's aunt, screamed with earsplitting poignance and tried to throw herself into the grave.

The family returned to the carriage while the mourners remained at the grave site, their voices raised in a mournful hymn. As the horses drew them back to the house, Jeannie spied a solitary figure on horseback, and realized with a start that it was Arnold. He shouldn't be here, she thought worriedly. Not with a murderer on the loose. She must get word to Miss Emmaline to watch him more closely.

The carriage deposited the family before the house, where Gilbert was waiting to serve coffee. Mr. Mitchell seemed exhausted, Jeannie thought as they settled themselves in the rear parlor.

"Papa, you ought to offer a reward," Dennis said restlessly, and Jeannie turned to him in surprise. "If the murderer was a person of means, you might recover your investment."

"Dennis!" Craig's face was thunderous. "We don't talk that way in this house. Suzette was more than a property —she was a human being."

"Excuse *me*," Dennis said sarcastically. "I think I'll go to my room. I had little sleep last night."

Jeannie felt a rush of sympathy as she saw her mother-in-law's eyes painfully follow Dennis from the room.

"Eleanor, you're to make sure that Danielle sleeps in your room tonight," Craig said firmly. "And Jeannie, Aunt Lizzie must remain in yours."

"Yes, sir," Jeannie agreed gently.

With a need to puncture the heaviness that enveloped them, Ron drew them into a discussion on Senator Calhoun's recent political activities that became a lively debate. Still, earlier than usual the four in the parlor left to retire to their respective rooms.

"Ah sleep in heah tonight, Young Missy," Aunt Lizzie solemnly greeted Jeannie as she walked into her bedroom. "Rat by yo' bed," she said, pointing to her pallet laid in readiness.

"Thank you, Aunt Lizzie." Jeannie managed a wisp of a smile.

It was hardly likely that anyone would break into the house, Jeannie told herself, yet she started nervously at the sound of dogs barking vociferously in the distance. For a tense moment Jeannie and Aunt Lizzie froze at attention, listening to the outdoor sounds.

"Dat jes' be de dogs chasin' aftuh some li'l animal," Aunt Lizzie soothed. "Dey plenty o' possums and rabbits in de woods."

"We have nothing to worry about, Aunt Lizzie," Jeannie said with an air of confidence. "Let's both go to bed."

Jeannie told herself, as she dressed to go downstairs to breakfast, that it was normal for her to go downstairs this early. Yet she was guiltily conscious of her eagerness to sit across the breakfast table from Ron, to bask in his presence with only Mr. Mitchell at the table in addition to themselves.

"Aunt Lizzie, don't let Patches out of the room," she exhorted, and remembered—her face hot with recall—the rapturous few moments yesterday when Ron had held her in his arms. Briefly they had recklessly forgotten their obligations and tasted happiness.

"Dat kitten, she de crazies' thing," Aunt Lizzie chortled. "She chase flies lak she was a lion."

Craig and Ron were just settling themselves at the breakfast table as Jeannie walked into the dining room. Both greeted her with warmth. How alike the two men were, Jeannie thought with pleasure.

"Did you sleep well, Jeannie?" her father-in-law asked solicitously.

"Straight through the night," she fabricated. In truth she had awakened at regular intervals, overly conscious of the night sounds. Twice Aunt Lizzie had left her pallet to move fearfully to the window. How long would it be, Jeannie asked herself, before they would go to bed without remembering Suzette's murder?

"Ron has worked something out for me with a friend from his Army days," Craig began, something in his voice bringing Jeannie sharply to attention. "I've decided to

240

free Carlotta." He took a deep breath, then glanced warily toward the open door. He pantomimed for silence because Jeffrey was coming forward with the peacock feathers to brush away the flies. "Not this morning, Jeffrey," he said casually. "You go out into the back and weed the herb garden."

"Yessuh." Jeffrey grinned and bolted.

Jeannie leaned forward earnestly, waiting for Craig to continue.

"For three generations Carlotta's family has served this one," Craig said seriously. "She's learned to read and write. She can handle sums as well as I." He smiled whimsically. "Possibly better than I." He paused again, because they heard Carlotta talking in the hallway, en route to serving breakfast. All at once he appeared tense. "We'll talk more later."

Dennis would be furious, Jeannie thought as Carlotta moved about the table placing platters of meat and fish before them. Of all the slaves he particularly resented Carlotta, because of her pride in her ancestry. And there would be one less slave in his patrimony, she thought with a new young bitterness.

Jeannie waited eagerly for Mr. Mitchell to talk again about his plans for Carlotta's future. Questions darted through her mind. Where would Carlotta go? How would she live? But how morally right to free Carlotta, she thought with soaring respect for her father-in-law.

Deliberately Craig discussed the state of the rice and the cotton with Ron as they ate, including Jeannie with polite glances in her direction; but she was conscious of a sense of waiting in him. And then, as Carlotta finished pouring coffee for them, he spoke to her.

"Carlotta, please close the door," he said.

"Yessuh," Carlotta said softly, but Jeannie saw her astonishment at this request.

"Carlotta, I have something to tell you," he said in even tones belied by the intensity of his gaze. "I've given this matter deep thought, and I feel it's the just thing to do. You must tell no one, understand," he said with mock sternness. "None of the other servants is to know. But I've arranged with the help of Mr. Ron and his

241

friend in Charleston to send you up North to New York." Carlotta's eyes widened in disbelief. "You'll travel with papers verifying your freedom, and money enough to see you through until you begin the job that our factors up in New York have found for you."

"Mist' Mitchell!" Carlotta's eyes shone with visions of freedom. "Oh, Mist' Mitchell!" And then the glow lost some of its intensity as Carlotta realized she would be leaving The Magnolias forever behind her. Jeannie lowered her own eyes as she saw the love that shone from Carlotta's as they rested on her master. "Mist' Mitchell . . ." She hesitated, color staining her golden cheeks. "Yo' sho' yo' wish me to go up No'th?"

"I want you to be free, Carlotta. I want you to be happy. Within forty-eight hours," he continued with determined briskness, "Mr. Ron's friend will send word that your traveling arrangements have been made." Everyone in the room knew about the Underground Railroad that operated in the South. Suddenly there was an atmosphere of tension about the table. "The following night, Mr. Ron will take you by carriage into Charleston. And may God keep you, Carlotta."

"Thank you, suh." Carlotta's voice trembled, but she held her head high with fresh pride, anticipating freedom.

"When you've left, we'll tell the others that you have been sold to a fine family up in Virginia, and that you're going to be a lady's maid up there."

"Yessuh," Carlotta whispered. "Thank yo', suh."

Jeannie felt a strange new bond to Mr. Mitchell and Ron in having shared these moments with them. Mr. Mitchell had deliberately chosen this time, she realized, because he knew she would approve this gift of freedom to Carlotta. And perhaps he had chosen to avoid a private emotional encounter.

After breakfast the men went off to their plantation tasks. Jeannie sat on the gallery, watching half a dozen slaves working among the flowers. She was just about to go upstairs to her room when Eleanor came outside.

"It's a beautiful morning despite the heat," Eleanor said, clear-eyed and confident, sitting in the rocker beside Jeannie's. How she had changed in the past two weeks,

Jeannie thought with delight. Mr. Mitchell was noticing, too. She had seen the hopeful look in his eyes when they rested, at odd moments, on his wife.

"It's a glorious morning," Jeannie agreed exuberantly, and felt a surge of guilt that she should be aware of this when only last night they had watched Suzette's body placed in the ground.

"I'm particularly pleased this morning," Eleanor went on, "though truly I shouldn't be thinking of myself after what's happened." Her eyes were pained as she clutched her hands together in her lap.

"There's nothing we can do for Suzette," Jeannie said earnestly. "What particularly pleased you this morning?" she pursued persuasively.

"Danielle has washed my wedding dress and she's let it out so I can wear it. Our twenty-fourth wedding anniversary is just two days away. I plan to wear it down to tea that night." She paused, aglow with anticipation.

"We must make it a party," Jeannie said impulsively, but Eleanor was all wrapped up in remembrance.

"We were married in Charleston at the minister's house, and afterward Craig took me to dinner at a fine restaurant. He had gone to the owner and ordered a special menu for us. I remember it perfectly."

"Mrs. Mitchell, why don't we have that same dinner on your anniversary?" Jeannie coaxed. "If Juno knows today, she can send into Charleston tomorrow for whatever she doesn't have on hand."

Eleanor smiled brilliantly.

"Jeannie, do you suppose my husband will remember?"

"I'm sure he will," Jeannie said confidently.

"Would you ask Juno to prepare the same menu? I'll write it out for you," Eleanor said, a luminous glow in her eyes.

"Mrs. Mitchell, *you* go into the kitchen and tell Juno what you would like her to prepare," Jeannie ordered gently. "You're the mistress of The Magnolias."

Their eyes clung. Jeannie saw the inner struggle within her mother-in-law. And then Eleanor Mitchell rose to her feet.

"Yes, I think I will go out and talk to Juno." It had

been at least fourteen years, Jeannie guessed, since she had walked into the kitchen. "She'll have to send into Charleston for the oysters."

The remainder of the day dragged interminably for Jeannie. All the ladies were conscious of the exhortation not to leave the house. Even the servants walked around with unease in their eyes, conscious that Suzette's murderer was still unapprehended.

Sitting on the upstairs gallery, waiting to go down to tea, Jeannie could hear Madeline talking in her mother's room.

"I don't know how you all can be so calm!" she shrieked. "We could all be ravished and murdered in our beds!"

"Only the ladies," Mavis reminded her with an effort at humor. "I'm sure the men are perfectly safe."

"Oh, Mama." Madeline's voice was contemptuous. "Don't try to be funny with that murderer running loose around the plantation."

"Madeline, I don't think he's hanging around," Mavis said with rare practicality. "He had his way with Suzette; then he killed her and ran off. He's probably miles away now."

The family gathered in the stifling heat of early evening for tea, then in a tacit pact retired to the parlor rather than to the gallery as usual. Madeline demanded a progress report on the search for Suzette's murderer.

"Good Lord, Madeline, Papa's not Scotland Yard!" Dennis said distastefully. "We'll probably never know who killed Suzette." He squinted in thought. "It was probably some runaway slave who's been hiding in the swamps."

"You don't know that," Madeline challenged. "It could be anybody." She took a deep breath, her eyes slyly amused. "It could even be one of us."

"Madeline, *I* didn't ravish and murder Suzette," Dennis said with a sardonic smile, and Jeannie intercepted the heated, silent exchange between them. Dennis had had his way with Suzette whenever he liked, without the need to murder.

"We'll keep up the precautions for at least two weeks,"

Craig decided calmly. "There'll be twenty armed hands prowling the grounds with dogs every night. No stranger will move about The Magnolias without being apprehended."

Gilbert appeared in the door of the parlor.

"Mist' Mitchell, a man jes' come up f'om Charleston with a message fo' yo'."

"Thank you, Gilbert." Craig rose to his feet, exchanging a loaded glance with Ron. The message from Ron's friend in Charleston, Jeannie thought with a sudden tightening in her throat, with news of Carlotta's secret travel arrangements. "Ron, will you come with me, please?"

"Papa's loan for the equipment coming through?" Dennis asked his mother when his father and Ron had left the room.

"I know nothing about these things, Dennis," his mother reproached. "I have no head for business." But Dennis was inspecting her with curiosity. Like the others in the house, he was aware that Eleanor Mitchell was becoming herself again.

Jeannie spied Carlotta's slender, erect figure moving toward the library. Mr. Mitchell had sent for her to tell her the news, Jeannie guessed. Tomorrow Carlotta might be en route for the North. The following day at the latest.

"I think I'll go into Charleston," Dennis said abruptly, rising to his feet.

"Dennis, you're not to leave The Magnolias," his mother protested. "Not now."

"Mama, nobody's going to ravish me," he said humorously. "I completely forgot I was to meet some friends from Columbia this evening." He was lying, Jeannie thought. He was going into Charleston to gamble.

The ladies sat in the parlor, fanning themselves vigorously, talking impersonally about the newest fashions from Paris, though none of them was seriously interested in fashions tonight. Jeannie was relieved when Mavis, pleading exhaustion from the heat, rose to go up to her rooms. It was the impetus for all of them to retire.

Jeannie's room was oppressively humid, heavily scented by the multitude of flowers in bloom. She was tired from the heat, from the strain of the past two days.

"Ah bring yo' a pitchuh o' ice-col' lemonade," Aunt Lizzie crooned when she came into her room. "Yo' stretch yo'se'f out on de bed and Ah be rat back. Git outta my way, yo' crazy kitten," she chuckled as Patches scampered beneath her feet.

Jeannie changed into her nightdress; splashed cooling water on her face, which offered only fleeting relief; then dropped herself onto the bed. She was sure that the messenger from Charleston had brought news about Carlotta. How exciting for Carlotta, she thought tenderly.

Aunt Lizzie returned with the pitcher of lemonade, poured a glass for Jeannie, and brought it to her.

"It nice an' cold, honey." Now Aunt Lizzie turned down the lamp, settled the netting about Jeannie's bed, and lowered herself to her pallet. In minutes she was snoring.

Jeannie lay awake, uncomfortable in the humidity of the night, her mind too active for sleep. Insects buzzed annoyingly about the room. She stirred, impatient that slumber eluded her. Minutes became an hour, and she still stared, fully awake, into the darkness.

With an impatient sigh Jeannie left the perspiration-soaked bed, lifted her hair from her neck, and walked to the pitcher of lemonade. The ice was melted, the lemonade tepid. She moved to the gallery and opened the door. A faint breeze from the river beckoned her outside.

She walked out onto the gallery into the night silence, broken only by the sounds of the crickets and frogs. She saw a field hand, with rifle and dog, march into the woods. Emboldened by his presence, she moved to the gallery railing.

Jeannie spied the light in the cottage beyond, and a moment later saw Carlotta moving about in the sitting room. Her instinct was to turn away. Carlotta had gone to Mr. Mitchell for one last night, she thought self-consciously; but as she turned, she realized that Carlotta was alone in the cottage. In the room beyond her own, Mr. Mitchell was calling to Jeffrey to bring him a pitcher of ice water.

Now Jeannie's eyes focused on the cottage. Carlotta was at a table, washing a tea service in a tub of water. She had gone there to clean up Mr. Mitchell's study for the last time, Jeannie thought. How like Carlotta to do that!

All at once the light was extinguished in the cottage. Jeannie stared uneasily, her mind strangely alert. She had not seen Carlotta go to the lamp. *Who was in the cottage with her?* Jeannie's throat tightened. What was happening in the study? And as fear welled in her, the silence of the night was punctured by a terrified shriek.

"No! No!" Carlotta screamed in frenzy. "Let me go! Let me go!"

Twenty-four

"Stop it!" Jeannie screamed, straining at the railing. "Stop it, whoever you are in the cottage!" She raced toward Mr. Mitchell's door and knocked urgently. "Mr. Mitchell! Mr. Mitchell!"

Jeffrey opened the door. His face was frightened.

"Mist' Mitchell gittin' into his dressin' gown," he reported, his eyes wide with alarm.

"Tell him to go to the cottage," she said. "Somebody's attacking Carlotta!" She ran back to her room, suddenly aware that she stood on the gallery in her nightdress. Trembling, she pulled on her dressing gown while Aunt Lizzie hovered over her.

"Young Missy, yo' don' go out deah! It's fo' de menfolks to do!"

"Aunt Lizzie, go wake Mr. Ron and Mr. Dennis."

She ignored Aunt Lizzie's exhortations and darted from the room. Emerging into the hall she saw Ron, gun in hand, charged from his room. Her father-in-law was bolting down the stairs.

"Jeannie, stay here!" Ron ordered, dashing past her. "Stay in the house," he reiterated tersely as he rushed down the stairs.

But Jeannie followed right behind him, too distraught to remain in the house. Both men were armed, she rationalized as she followed Ron into the night. She was in no danger in their presence. But let Carlotta be all right! Dear God, let Carlotta be all right!

Jeannie trailed Ron by no more than ten feet, tripping once in her haste and almost falling. The dogs were barking raucously in the distance. Why hadn't some of the patrol remained near the house? Then she remembered that only a few minutes earlier she had seen a member of the patrol leave the area and disappear into the woods. Twenty men must patrol four thousand acres. They could hardly remain in one place for more than a few minutes.

Mr. Mitchell was at the cottage. He was shoving open the door. Jeannie saw him disappear inside.

"Uncle Craig, be careful!" Ron called breathlessly after him.

With a determined, painful burst of speed Jeannie caught up with Ron. She was little more than a yard behind him as he followed his uncle into the house, gun in hand.

"Uncle Craig?" he said warily, momentarily halted by the darkness inside the room. "Jeannie, stay by the door."

"Come inside, Ron," his uncle said tautly. "Find the lamp by the window. . . ."

Trembling, apprehensive, Jeannie waited for Ron to find the lamp. In a moment the room was illuminated as it had been when she watched Carlotta through the window minutes ago. Her father-in-law lifted Carlotta from the floor and carried her to the horsehair sofa that flanked the fireplace.

"Ron, is she . . ." Jeannie could not bring herself to finish the question.

"She's dead, Jeannie," Craig's deep voice was anguished. "Ravished and strangled. Why did it have to happen this way?" He drove one fist into the other with frustration. "Tomorrow she would have been gone from here. *Why?*"

"I saw her through the window," Jeannie whispered. "She was washing the tea service . . ." Tears filled her eyes. "Poor Carlotta. How awful."

"Jeannie, honey . . ." Ron pulled her into his arms to comfort her. "It was over quickly. You frightened him away when you screamed at him."

"But not before he killed her," she said with frustration. "Is that why he killed her? Was it my fault?"

"He would have killed her anyway," Ron soothed. "It's a pattern with him. It was all over in a few minutes."

"I want him found!" Craig's face was taut with rage. "We can't let these murders continue." His eyes dropped again to Carlotta, beautiful in death as she had been in life. "Tomorrow night she would have been gone," he reiterated with frustration. "She was so young, so bright. This never should have happened. Why? *Why?*"

But Carlotta had gone to the study in this last gesture toward her master, and now she was dead.

Craig walked to the table where the elegantly beautiful Staffordshire tea set sat on the table, still wet from washing. With infinite care he dried each piece and put the set away in the cupboard. Jeannie knew it would never be used again.

"There's nothing we can do here, Uncle Craig," Ron said compassionately. "Let's go back to the house."

They walked out into the night again, the men protectively flanking Jeannie. With twenty men with guns and dogs, this had happened. What kind of man prowled about The Magnolias? Jeannie asked herself with anguish.

The foyer of the house glowed with startling brilliance. Someone was meticulously lighting every candle in the chandelier, as though—Jeannie thought—this would drive away menace. The upstairs bedrooms too were lighted, except for Dennis' room. He must still be in Charleston.

The door was opened from the inside. Eleanor hovered in the doorway, pale, lacing her hands nervously. Gilbert was lighting the last of the candles in the chandelier.

"What happened?" Eleanor asked tremulously, her eyes clinging to Craig's face. "We heard the screams . . ."

Madeline and Mavis stood fearfully behind her. At the top of the stairs the maids huddled together in alarm.

"Carlotta is dead," Craig said tiredly, his voice loud enough to carry to the women at the head of the stairs. Aunt Lizzie burst into a wailing outcry. "It was the same as before. She was ravished and choked to death." He shook his head in disbelief. "It all happened in a matter of minutes. I ran as quickly as I could. He was gone—and Carlotta was dead."

"Uncle Craig, nobody could have saved her," Ron said earnestly. "We did what we could."

"What was she doing alone in the cottage?" Madeline demanded. "She had no right to be there in the middle of the night."

Craig gazed at her with quiet disgust.

"She went there, Madeline," he said tersely, "to clean my cottage for the last time. I had told her I was sending her North tomorrow. I was giving Carlotta her freedom."

"Gilbert, would you please ask someone in the kitchen to make coffee," Eleanor asked with painfully achieved serenity, "and serve it in the back parlor."

"Yes, ma'am," Gilbert said respectfully. "Rat away."

"Excuse me," Ron said quietly. "I'll send some of the women to stay with Carlotta."

"Craig . . ." Eleanor took a deep breath. "Carlotta was like family to us. Her mother, her grandmother served us so well. It would be fitting, I think, to bury her in the Mitchell cemetery."

Her eyes met his with a new resolve. Gratitude shone on his face for this gesture, this acceptance of Carlotta's place in his life.

"Let's go into the parlor," Craig said gently, taking his wife's arm.

They talked in low tones as they sat about the parlor waiting for coffee to be served, each conscious of every sound in the night. Ron returned with word that he had summoned a pair of the armed hands and instructed them to remain in the vicinity of the house itself until sunup.

"What does it matter?" Madeline challenged, her voice edged with hysteria. "The men are out there with guns and dogs, and still Carlotta was murdered. It could happen to any of us!"

"Madeline, the house will be patrolled," Ron said tightly. "Unfortunately for the field hands," he added dryly, "the whole four thousand acres can't be patrolled every minute. But the house and the quarters will be patrolled," he emphasized. "There won't be a third murder."

"There would not have been this one," Madeline pointed out, "if Carlotta had not left the house in the middle of the night."

Jeannie leaned forward, listening attentively.

"Darling, a murderer doesn't come calling in a carriage," Madeline mocked, and then her eyes narrowed speculatively. "Or does he?"

"That'll be Dennis." Uneasily Eleanor rose to her feet.

"Eleanor, sit down," Craig ordered tenderly. "Dennis can find his way into the house."

Ron walked to the cabinet that held the bottles of Scotch whisky that his uncle favored. He poured two drinks, took one to his uncle, and gulped his own with an air of need. They could hear Dennis talking to Jasper while he approached the door.

Ron crossed to the hallway and called to Dennis as he came into the house.

"Dennis, will you join the family, please?" he asked with unfamiliar formality.

"What's happened now?" Dennis inquired warily, walking toward Ron.

"There's been another murder," Ron said somberly. "Carlotta."

"The African princess?" Dennis said with an air of condescension, hovering in the doorway.

"Dennis, show your respect!" Eleanor lashed at him with an intensity Jeannie had never heard from her.

"I heard news in Charleston about an uprising at a plantation eighteen miles south of here," Dennis reported. "Four slaves escaped. We must have one of them hiding in the swamps around here."

"I'll alert the patrol," Ron said instantly. "At dawn they'll search the swamps."

Dennis' gaze lingered on Madeline.

"I met an old acquaintance of ours in Charleston," he drawled. "Andrew McKinley. He was drunk and talkative."

"Why didn't you summon the police?" Madeline challenged, her eyes flashing. Again, Jeannie thought, Madeline and Dennis might have been alone in the parlor. They had an odd way of obliterating the presence of others. "He attacked me. He nearly killed Ron. He could be the murderer."

"The only murder Andrew McKinley has in mind is yours," Dennis mocked. "But I don't think you have to worry seriously. He's sailing in the morning for New York. We had a farewell drink. A few drinks," he amended, his eyes telegraphing a message to Madeline. And suddenly, fleetingly, the mockery in Dennis' eyes was replaced with pain. Andrew McKinley, Jeannie guessed, had been verbally graphic with Dennis about his last encounter with Madeline.

"If it's a runaway slave who's been responsible, we'll catch him," Craig promised, his face set. "I'll notify the neighboring plantations, in case they haven't heard about the uprising. We'll catch him."

"Miss Emmaline had better be told to keep Arnold at Burke Acres," Jeannie said seriously. "He has a habit of riding at night." He could be dragged into the swamps and murdered, she considered with alarm.

"I'll tell Emmaline in the morning," Dennis offered. All at once his eyes rested on her with disconcerting amorousness. "Poor little Jeannie," he murmured, moving to sit beside her. "Were you terribly frightened?"

"No," she lied, stiffening as he dropped an arm about her shoulders. *Why didn't he stop this pretense?* Why must he use her as a pawn in his vendetta with Madeline? "I was upset," she corrected. "As we all were." Tears welled in her eyes. Poor Carlotta, so close to freedom. "But I was not afraid."

Gilbert arrived to serve them coffee. In moments of stress, Jeannie understood, Gilbert always took it upon himself to serve the family.

"We'll have our coffee and go on upstairs to bed," Craig decreed firmly. "We'll have little enough sleep tonight." He hesitated, all at once seeming drained of strength. "We'll lay Carlotta to rest tomorrow afternoon. In the family cemetery."

Dennis awoke at what he considered an absurdly early hour. His sleep had been disturbed by the sound of the workers digging in the family graveyard to the west of the house. The slaves would mourn Carlotta, he thought dryly; but they had never considered her one of them. Only the house servants would attend the services to be held at the graveside, conducted by the minister whom Papa was bringing up from Charleston. Such airs, he thought with distaste, to be accorded a slave burial.

Madeline was awake too. He could hear her shrieking at Rose. Damn Andrew McKinley, he thought with recurrent rage, so determined in his drunkenness to be explicit about his relationship with Madeline. How could Madeline stoop to giving herself to their superintendent? Anybody, he thought with a surge of pain, could take Madeline—except himself.

If The Magnolias were already his, he would sell enough land and slaves to buy a fancy house in Charleston. Madeline hated living here. He'd set her up in a Charleston house and they would be together constantly. Madeline loved fine living. If he were not so damned strapped financially, he could take her away from Ron.

He would go over to Burke Acres, he decided. He had promised Jeannie he would tell Emmaline to keep Arnold at home. Emmaline would appreciate his show of concern for Arnold. She would sympathize with his rotten luck at the tables. She might even advance him another few hundred. Charlotte never checked the funds in the safe.

He yelled to Jasper, hanging over the gallery railing talking to one of the laundresses, to have Hannibal saddled and ready for him. He would be back at the house well before Carlotta's burial. Papa would never forgive him if he were not there, he thought cynically. The whole family must pay their respects.

Dennis dressed swiftly and hurried to the downstairs gallery to wait for Jasper to bring Hannibal around to the house. From the cottage came the sound of women's voices raised in a mournful hymn. They were standing watch by Carlotta's body. Jeannie was at the rosebushes, earnestly choosing choice blossoms, unaware of his presence. The red roses would be for Carlotta's grave. Such fuss for a slave!

"Hurry up, Jasper," he called out in irritation as Jasper slowly walked Hannibal toward the gallery. "Get your tail moving." Jeannie became aware of his presence and waved with a polite smile. Damn it, she was acting strangely.

He mounted, prepared to take the shortcut toward Burke Acres, though this route past the swamps was normally avoided during the hot months. But as he turned toward the grove that led to the shortcut, his attention was captured by the arrival of the carriage.

"Whoa, Hannibal," he commanded crisply, waiting to see who would emerge from the carriage.

The caller was the courtly Mr. Goldberg, from whom Papa was borrowing for the new equipment. His eyes rested on the small metal box Mr. Goldberg gripped in one hand. That would be cash he was bringing to Papa. Twenty thousand, he had heard Ron say, was what the equipment would cost. Twenty thousand dollars in that small box!

"Let's go, Hannibal." He whacked the horse sharply on the rump.

Arnold was playing with one of the hounds in front of the house as Dennis moved into view. With a sullen glance at Dennis, he hurried off in the direction of the stables. Dennis chuckled. Arnold had never forgiven him for taking him to that whorehouse in Charleston, but he was bright enough not to tell Emmaline.

Emmaline welcomed him with her usual effusiveness, but today she was upset. Word had already reached Burke

Acres via the slave grapevine that murder had struck at The Magnolias again.

"Dennis, I'm just scared to death to put my head down at night," she confessed, playing nervously with the lace at the neck of her frock. "Charlotte carries a rifle with her."

"You're keeping a patrol about the house?" he asked with a show of solicitude.

"Oh, yes, Charlotte was quick to take precautions," she said with pride.

"It must have been a runaway slave. There was trouble at a plantation down below. But don't worry, love," he consoled. "He'll soon be rounded up. He must be in hiding in the swamps. Most likely he'll be tracked down today," he summed up. "It's been terribly depressing to have two murders committed at The Magnolias, one after the other."

"Poor Dennis," Emmaline sympathized.

"Oh, Jeannie asked me to tell you to keep an eye on Arnold," he recalled. "She says he has a habit of riding at night. It might be dangerous right now."

"Oh, I don't let Arnold ride out at night anymore," Emmaline reassured him quickly. "I put a stop to that as soon as I found out about it."

He must ask Emmaline about another loan. What was another few hundred to her with that cache they had in the safe? But as he leaned forward to reach for Emmaline's hand, Charlotte rode up to the house.

"We've just had another letter from Rebecca," Charlotte announced as she walked up the steps to the gallery. Her eyes were faintly reproachful. She had never forgiven him for not marrying her grandniece, Dennis thought with amusement. Imagine Rebecca and Madeline under one roof! "She's having a fine time in Paris. She's met some folks who knew Jacques Beauchamp." Dennis tensed in shock. "She says he was Madeline's father. She's even bought a painting of his that she's bringing home with her." Charlotte frowned distastefully. "A nude. You know the French."

"Beauchamp was quite well known," Dennis said with forced casualness. *How much did Rebecca know?* "I'd better get back to The Magnolias," he said with a regretful smile. "We have a burial this afternoon."

Rebecca would return to South Carolina, Dennis thought bitterly as he rode back to The Magnolias; and she would take such satisfaction in circulating all over Charleston what Madeline and Mavis had managed to keep secret. The Mitchells would be the laughingstock of the city. And Madeline, he thought with reluctant anguish, would be disgraced.

Twenty-five

The bright afternoon sun bathed the grassy knoll where Carlotta was to be buried beside five generations of Mitchells. Within the white-fenced area, in a semi-circle about Carlotta's coffin, stood the somber-faced family—the women, except for Jeannie, garbed in black, with the weeping house servants huddled behind them. Fighting against tears, Jeannie fastened her gaze upon the pastor as he read the simple service with an air of compassion and humility.

Why was Dennis so blatantly restless? Couldn't he show some respect? Ever since his return from Burke Acres he had been moody, strangely withdrawn. As the pastor spoke about Carlotta, Jeannie's eyes moved compulsively, with affection and sympathy, to her father-in-law, who stood ramrod-stiff, gazing at the simple pine coffin. The young African princess had held her fingertips out to freedom, Jeannie thought with infinite sadness, only to be cheated by death. Tears filled her eyes despite her efforts to stem them and spilled over onto her cheeks.

"It was a beautiful service," Mavis said, striving self-consciously to break the heaviness that engulfed the family as they moved away from the burial ground. The pastor had politely rejected an offer of refreshment, pleading that his presence was urgently required at another plantation. He was already walking toward his waiting carriage.

"I do so admire the pastor's style," Mavis prattled.

"It's terribly hot," Madeline said peevishly. "I want to go up to my room to nap." For a hostile moment her eyes clashed with Dennis'. He seemed on the point of speaking, then scowled and stalked off in the opposite direction.

"I must go out to the kitchen and talk to Juno about tea," Eleanor said quietly. "We'll not be wanting anything heavy tonight."

Mr. Mitchell was regaining his wife, Jeannie thought with a surge of tenderness. He understood, didn't he? This awareness shone from him at unguarded moments.

"We'll all nap until tea," Craig said quietly. "This has been a painful day."

"Has there been any word about those runaway slaves?" Mavis asked, apprehension seeping through again.

"The swamps were searched this morning," Craig reported gravely. "There's no sign of them there. They must have moved farther along the river."

"But you won't stop the patrols?" Mavis persisted.

"Not until the slaves are apprehended," Craig promised. A vein throbbed in his forehead. "They *will* be apprehended."

At the house, Eleanor went out to the kitchen to talk to Juno about tea. Craig lingered in the foyer in discussion with Ron about a need for fresh rain to help in flooding the rice fields properly, while the ladies silently climbed the stairs to their rooms.

Jeannie lay in bed, exhausted from the enervating heat and the strain of these past days; but her mind refused to allow her to sleep. She waited stoically for Aunt Lizzie to summon her to tea.

Tea was a strained, silent meal. Again, it was Mavis

who struggled to lift the pall that settled about the table, talking in her high, faintly strident voice about her years in Paris.

"Mama, nobody wants to hear any more about Paris," Madeline said brutally. "They've heard it all a dozen times."

"No, Madeline," Jeannie reproached her, touched by Mavis' crestfallen expression. "I love hearing about Paris from someone who's lived there. It's so much more exciting than reading about it."

Mavis' face lighted.

"Someday you must make Dennis take you there," she said girlishly, and then her eyes darted nervously from Dennis to Madeline in a private communication.

"Dennis was quite intrigued with Paris," Ron reminded dryly, "though he spoke disapprovingly of the Republic."

"Let's have our tea out on the gallery," Eleanor decided with sudden unease. "It's so terribly humid here in the dining room."

While Eloise served tea on the gallery, Ron spoke with a determined enthusiasm about the modern new equipment ordered for the mill. Again Jeannie was uncomfortably aware of the silent, yet almost obscene communication between Dennis and Madeline. Panic in her eyes, Mavis frowned reprovingly at her daughter.

"I'll have to go into Charleston to deposit the cash in the bank tomorow afternoon," Craig said absently, and then he straightened up as though a pleasing idea had invaded his mind. "Ron, do you suppose you could take the afternoon off to go in to the bank for me?"

"Yes, sir," Ron agreed. "The new man's working out well enough for me to leave him alone for a few hours."

Dennis stared belligerently at Ron. He was annoyed, Jeannie thought unhappily, at the closeness between his father and his cousin.

"Oh, I spoke with Miss Emmaline this morning," Dennis said, now with suspect cheerfulness. "She told me she had just heard from her grandniece, Rebecca." His eyes rested with a provocative challenge on Madeline, then moved on to Mavis. But what he was saying, Jeannie sensed, was meant for Madeline's ears. "She's met some folks in Paris who knew Madeline's father. She's even bought a painting by him, to bring back home with her." An odd triumph shone in his eyes. "A nude."

Jeannie saw Mavis pale and turn supplicatingly to Madeline.

For an instant Madeline seemed shaken, but so fleeting was this reaction that Jeannie told herself she might have misread it.

"Rebecca lives in Montgomery, doesn't she?" Madeline asked with a supercilious smile. "After Paris, Montgomery's going to seem quite dull. She'll never come to Burke Acres again." Madeline was reassuring her mother, Jeannie interpreted. What were these strange undercurrents circulating between Madeline, her mother, and Dennis? What kind of threat was Rebecca to Madeline? *Something to do with Madeline's father*. What was Dennis trying to do? Drive Madeline from The Magnolias? No, she couldn't believe that.

A field hand with a gun and dog stalked back and forth on the expanse of grass before the house, reminding them of the horror that had gripped The Magnolias these past days. Dennis' eyes followed the man with an introspective stare.

"Papa, have you done anything about organizing the neighboring planters?" Dennis asked with an air of challenge.

"Everybody knows. Everybody's on the watch," Craig said quietly. "We've had men in the swamps all day." He smiled faintly. "Dennis, we're not facing an insurrection."

"When two slaves have been murdered?" Dennis countered. "How do we know when it might not be a white person?" He was maliciously playing on Madeline's fears. "Remember Denmark Vesey."

"Dennis, that was a year before you were born," Craig said with a frown of irritation. "We're more civilized these days. There are folks who think that was no more than mass hysteria."

"Abolitionists say that!" Dennis shot back.

"There was hysteria in Charleston then because the whites were far outnumbered by the blacks," Ron said with determined calm. "And in the summer many of the whites went away to the resorts. A rumor went berserk. There's not a shred of real proof that Denmark Vesey plotted an insurrection."

"What about the Nat Turner insurrection up in Virginia?" Dennis pursued. "When sixty whites were murdered!"

"Dennis, we have a different situation on our hands," Craig said, straining for patience. He gazed uneasily at the others. "I don't think we should discuss this further before the ladies."

"Mr. Mitchell, I'd like to have a gun to keep beneath my pillow." Madeline's color was high.

"That would be inadvisable," Craig rejected gently. "A gun is too dangerous a weapon to be placed in the hands of anyone who is not highly trained in its use." He hesitated. "I assure you, Madeline, no member of this household will be molested."

Why was Mavis so upset that Rebecca Burke had bought a painting by Jacques Beauchamp? Jeannie's mind focused obsessively on this. Ever since Dennis had mentioned Rebecca's meeting people who had known Madeline's father, Mavis had sat at the edge of her rocker, clutching tightly at a handkerchief that was now almost shredded. *Was she afraid the painting Rebecca had bought was one of her? A nude?*

Up in her room Jeannie prepared for bed, listening to Aunt Lizzie talk sorrowfully about Carlotta. At any unexpected sound Aunt Lizzie started. Again she settled her pallet beside Jeannie's bed, rather than out on the gallery.

Jeannie stirred restlessly in bed, vainly seeking a position that would invite sleep. Would she ever fall asleep tonight? Finally, she pulled herself into a sitting position, debating about remaining in bed. She would go downstairs, choose a book from the library, and come back upstairs and read.

She pushed aside the netting and crossed to the closet for her dressing gown.

"Young Missy, wheah yo' goin' at dis houh o' de night?" Aunt Lizzie rebuked.

"Just down to the library," she soothed.

"Ah'll go wit' yo'," Aunt Lizzie decreed. "You' mus'n' go wanderin' aroun' de house by yo'se'f."

Together they went down the darkened stairs and into the library, guided by the lamp in Aunt Lizzie's hand. Tonight, perhaps for the first time ever, Jeannie thought, the front door was locked.

In the library Jeannie quickly chose a book, and she and Aunt Lizzie headed down the hall and up the stairs. At the door of Craig's room Eleanor stood in conversation with her husband. She wore a white silk dress with yellow flowers.

Neither Eleanor nor Craig was aware of the pair who moved with deliberate slowness up the darkened stairs. Jeannie smiled brilliantly as she saw Craig's arm move about his wife and watched him draw her within his room. This, Jeannie remembered, was their twenty-fourth wedding anniversary.

Jeannie walked out of the house onto the gallery and gazed at the overcast sky. They would be in for rain before the day was out. She settled herself in a rocker with the latest edition of the Charleston newspaper to arrive at the house. Aunt Lizzie was cleaning her room; she was only in the way up there.

A carriage was coming up the driveway. She leaned forward, curious about the arrival of company. The carriage pulled to a stop before the house, and a short, corpulent man with an air of opulence alighted.

"Good morning," he greeted her politely, but she was conscious of his air of excitement. "You must be Dennis' bride," he said with courtly charm.

"Yes, I am."

"I'm Tim Fletcher from the plantation to the west," he introduced himself. "Is your father-in-law home?"

"Yes, he is." Jeannie rose to her feet. "I believe he's in the house."

"Tim, come in," Craig called out in welcome from the door. He must have heard the carriage, Jeannie thought. "What brings you out in the heat of morning?"

"The four runaways," Tim Fletcher was saying with

satisfaction as he walked into the foyer. "They were caught about eight miles down the road."

It was over, Jeannie told herself with relief. Carlotta's and Suzette's murderer would be brought to justice. They would not have to be fearful anymore. Yet even with the knowledge that the runaway slaves had been caught, she felt herself churning with unease. Again she was conscious of what her father-in-law had said about their living on the edge of a volcano on the point of erupting. Repetitiously his words shuttled through her mind.

How long could they live this way, in a house shaken by unspoken accusations, covert passions? How long could she and Ron deny the love they had acknowledged for a few moments in the midst of tragedy? Yet deny it they must.

Her eyes moved compulsively to the small cottage where Carlotta had died. The murders had brought into sharp relief the horror of her own violation at the hands of her cousin. Impulsively she rose to her feet, feeling a need to express her grief for Carlotta's death. Clusters of roses—pale pink, red, yellow—grew about the steps of the cottage. She would cut some roses from the cottage garden and place them on Carlotta's grave. Let there be a sign that she was remembered.

Jeannie walked down the stairs and across the sweep of lawn toward the cottage. The runaway slaves had been captured; there was no longer a need to move about The Magnolias with caution. Sunlight lent an air of joyousness to the riotously blooming rosebushes. Jeannie concentrated on choosing the choice blossoms, finding pleasure in their beauty. And then, inadvertently, her eyes settled on something on the ground. All at once she was cold. Sick with disbelief.

Jeannie knelt down and lifted from the ground the carefully pressed magnolia. Her heart pounding, she focused on the flower in her hand. It came from Arnold's collection. Why was it lying here by the steps to the cottage? *The cottage where Carlotta had died.* Arnold? Sweet, gentle, shy Arnold?

She drew her handkerchief from the bodice of her dress and, her hands trembling, carefully wrapped the

pressed magnolia. She must not jump to dreadful conclusions. *There must be an explanation for the magnolia's
presence by Mr. Mitchell's cottage.*

She walked quickly, without direction, away from the
cottage. She must have time to think, to consider what
she had discovered. Through her mind darted bits of
gossip from Aunt Lizzie. *It ain' rat fo' Missy Madeline to
let dat Arnold in huh room when she take huh bath.* Why
did Madeline allow him such intimacy? What had happened in the privacy of her bedroom? She remembered
Arnold's face, one day when Madeline had sent him away
and he had stood on the grass gazing up at her window.
A man's face, etched with a man's emotions.

She must talk to Miss Emmaline. She must tell her
what she had discovered by the steps to the cottage.
Miss Emmaline would tell her if Arnold had been riding
the nights when Suzette and Carlotta were killed. Oh,
how could she go to Miss Emmaline with these horrible
suspicions? Yet she knew she must.

Jeannie walked farther into the woods, straining to
steel herself for what must be done. And then suddenly,
distracted by voices close by, she stopped dead. She
heard a low cry of bodily pain.

"Dennis, stop it!" Madeline was pleading frenziedly.
"Stop it! You've flogged him unconscious already!"

"How could you do it, Madeline? To let him touch
you that way?" Dennis demanded with anguish. "How
could you lower yourself to that?"

Compulsively Jeannie walked forward. She flinched at
the sight of the unconscious slave, naked to the waist,
who lay bleeding at Dennis' feet. Neither Dennis nor
Madeline was aware of her presence barely a dozen feet
away.

"I did it to make you know how I felt!" she flung at
him defiantly. "When you ran away from me that way!"

"Madeline, when are we going to stop punishing each
other this way? I would have married you, Madeline, if
you hadn't flung your father in my face that way! Why
did you tell me Jacques Beauchamp was a black man?"

"It was that fine, expensive champagne you fancied,"

she mocked. "You always had to have champagne when we made love!"

"You should not have told me he was black! How could I marry a girl whose father was black? How could I disgrace the Mitchell name?"

"It's not your name!" Madeline flung at him. "Any more than it is mine."

"Madeline, we have to leave," he said urgently. "Rebecca will stop in Charleston before she goes on to Montgomery. She'll talk all over the city about your father. She bought one of his paintings. A nude."

"Papa always painted nudes," Madeline shot back with pride. "Usually of Mama. She was still beautiful in those days."

"Madeline, all of Charleston will know about your father!" he shouted. "How can you live in the South in a situation like that? We'll go to Paris together," he said with a surge of enthusiasm. "It'll be wonderful, Madeline. Even better than before!"

"What'll we live on?" Madeline taunted.

"There's money in the safe. Twenty thousand in cash. Papa plans to send it to the bank this afternoon. Madeline, I'll take the money and we'll go to Paris!"

"How will you get into the safe?" Madeline demanded.

"I've known the combination since I was fourteen," he said with triumph. "Madeline, you love Paris. On that twenty thousand we can live for years! But we can't waste a minute," he warned, drunk with decision. "You go to the stables, tell Elijah that I want the chaise. You bring it around in front of the house and wait. We'll drive up the river and hire a boat. We'll be on our way to New York, Madeline, before anybody knows we've gone!"

"Dennis, I can't leave like that," she protested. "What about my clothes?"

"With twenty thousand in cash, my love, we'll buy all the clothes you want," he chortled. "Mady, it has to be now! This afternoon Papa sends the cash to the bank!"

"Dennis, I'm afraid!"

"Mady, we have to leave now," he pushed. "We can't waste time."

"Dennis, love me," Madeline implored. "First, love me. Show me the way it can be with us."

Sick and shaken, Jeannie spun about as Dennis reached for Madeline. She dashed frantically through the woods toward the house. Mr. Mitchell! She must warn Mr. Mitchell about what Dennis and Madeline planned to do!

Twenty-six

Jeannie charged breathlessly into the house and down the hall to the library in search of her father-in-law. He was not there. She looked in room after room with rising frustration. Where *was* Mr. Mitchell? *He* must be here to stop Dennis. What could she do?

"Gilbert!" She called to him as he emerged from the kitchen wing. "Gilbert, do you know where Mr. Mitchell is?"

"He gone to de fields." Gilbert inspected her anxiously. "Yo' all rat, Young Missy?"

"He went to the fields this time of day?" She frowned, upset at his absence.

"He took de carriage and he wo' a hat," Gilbert said respectfully. His eyes glowed with concern. "Yo' wan' me to sen' somebody to fetch him?"

"Please, Gilbert." She took a deep breath. "And when he arrives, please tell him to come directly up to my room. *Directly*, Gilbert," she urged, trying to blot out of her mind the vision of Dennis reaching for Madeline there in the woods. It would be a while, she realized with distaste, before Dennis would approach the safe.

"Gilbert . . ." She stopped him with an imperiousness

born of urgency. "Do you know where Mr. Ron is?"

"No, ma'am." He hesitated, his eyes questioning.

"All right, Gilbert, just send for Mr. Mitchell right away."

Shaking, impatient for the privacy of her room, Jeannie hurried upstairs. In her room, she crossed to the window to watch for her father-in-law's return. Let him come to the house before Dennis! Where was Ron? she asked herself with frustration. One of them must stop Dennis! That money had been borrowed for badly needed equipment for the mill.

She reached for Patches, who meowed reproachfully at her feet. She cuddled her affectionately, finding consolation in her presence. Clouds were gathering together in foreboding dark clumps, in sharp contrast to the brilliant sunlight that had bathed the earth only a little while ago. A breeze from the river stirred through the trees. They were going to have a storm, she thought uneasily.

Why didn't Mr. Mitchell return to the house? What was taking him so long?

She started at the timid knock.

"Come in," she called eagerly, dropping Patches to the floor and moving toward the door.

The door opened. Arnold walked in, clutching a book in his hand. He smiled shyly.

"I brought over my magnolia collection," he said. His eyes were overbright. "You never saw it, Jeannie."

"Yes, you showed it to me, Arnold," she reminded, straining to hide her alarm at his presence in her bedroom. But she might be wrong about Arnold, she exhorted herself. It was wrong to jump to conclusions the way she had. "The magnolias are beautiful."

"Let me show them to you again," he coaxed eagerly, moving with the book toward the bed. "You haven't seen the new ones," he said with an air of triumph. "I just put them in."

"Let's go downstairs and look at them," she said with a forced air of conviviality, but Arnold was already opening the book.

Suddenly her throat was tight with shock. Her eyes

were galvanized to the second page of the book, where a flower was missing. Only paste stains showed where it had been earlier. *The magnolia she had found outside the cottage.*

"Come look at them, Jeannie," Arnold pleaded, his eyes on her. His breathing was heavy, labored.

"Let's go downstairs with the flowers," she repeated firmly. Why was she suddenly so frightened? Nothing could happen here in the house. "Arnold, let's go downstairs and have some cookies and lemonade. Eloise will bring them to us out on the gallery. I think there's going to be a storm. You like storms, don't you, Arnold?" Why was he moving toward her that way?

"Jeannie, you're pretty," he said softly. "And nice." He reached for her hand to pull her to him.

"Arnold, let's go downstairs," she reiterated unsteadily.

"Jeannie, don't be mean to me. Like those two slave girls. I didn't want to kill them, but they kept hollering and I had to shut them up. All I wanted to do was what Madeline taught me to do with ladies. Jeannie, I want to do it now," he said hoarsely. "Right this minute. With you."

"Arnold, no!" She struggled with him, helpless as his arms closed about her. "Arnold, no! No!" Her voice rose to a scream as she fought to free herself. Again! How could it be happening to her again?"

"Arnold, let her go!" Ron's voice ordered. She had not heard the bedroom door open. "Let her go!"

Though hampered by the injury to his left arm, Ron pulled Arnold away from her, with such force that Jeannie stumbled and fell to the floor. Arnold, his face chalk-white with terror, fled.

"Jeannie!" Ron reached solicitously to help her to her feet. "Are you all right?"

"Oh, Ron, Ron!" She collapsed, sobbing, in his arms. "It was that night on Ransome Island all over again. . . ."

"You're all right," Ron soothed, cradling her against him. His hands caressed her hair. "Nobody'll ever hurt you again. I won't let them."

"Ron . . ." she pulled herself away so that she could

look up into his face. "Arnold killed Suzette and Carlotta. He admitted it to me."

Ron's face was pained as he digested this.

"We'll have to tell Miss Emmaline and Miss Charlotte," he said unhappily. "The police will have to know." He brought her hand to his mouth. "We'll have to go after Arnold."

"Ron, wait, there's more," she said tremulously, and he tensed, waiting for her to continue. "Dennis and Madeline—I saw them in the fields . . ." She flinched, visualizing that moment, before she turned away from them, when Dennis had reached for Madeline.

"Jeannie, what about Dennis and Madeline?" Ron asked gently with hard-earned calm.

"They're planning to run away," she whispered. "Dennis is going to take the twenty thousand from the safe. He said they could live in Paris on that for years."

The color drained from Ron's face as he stared at Jeannie, trying to absorb what she had said.

"Jeannie . . ." His voice was uneven. "Jeannie, you heard Dennis say that?"

"Yes," she reiterated. "I sent Gilbert for Mr. Mitchell—"

"They could be gone by the time he gets here from the fields!" Ron strode toward the door. "I'll have to stop them. They can't do this to Uncle Craig!"

"Ron, wait for me!" She followed at his heels.

Together Jeannie and Ron hurried down the stairs and darted down the lower-floor hallway to the library. As they walked into the room, they froze for a moment before the onslaught of a blinding flash of lightning.

"Ron, look!" Jeannie pointed to the safe, its door swung wide. The metal box that had contained the money was gone.

"Stay here, Jeannie." Ron's face was grim. "I'll catch up with them!"

Ignoring Ron's exhortation, Jeannie followed him out of the library and down the hallway to the gallery. The sky was night-dark as they emerged on the gallery. Thunder ricocheted with such force that Jeannie reached instinctively for Ron's arm. And then all at once a crackle of lightning lent an eerie brilliance to the sky. The view before them was bathed in an unworldly brightness. Jeannie spied the chaise, moving down the roadway.

"Ron, there they are!" Why had they taken the roan? *They knew he was terrified of lightning.*

"Jeannie, you're not to leave the gallery!" Ron ordered tersely. "I'll get a horse and follow them."

"Ron!" Alarm deepened her voice as another white flash of lightning raced across the sky. The roan reared, then took off with frenzied speed.

"Whoa!" They could hear Dennis calling out frantically. "Whoa!"

As Jeannie and Ron darted from the gallery, they saw the chaise overturn with a clattering thud. Madeline and Dennis were thrown to the ground as though they were a pair of rag dolls. The roan charged forward, dragging the overturned chaise behind him.

Despite the nauseating sickness that assaulted her, Jeannie followed Ron down the roadway, disregarding the downpour that was suddenly drenching the earth. She hovered above the two prone bodies, fighting off dizziness as Ron knelt before his wife and his cousin. Madeline had been thrown in such a position that she seemed to be embracing Dennis. Dennis' arms were widespread, as though receiving her. The metal box that contained the money lay beside them.

Ron rose slowly to his feet, seemingly unaware, as was Jeannie, of the pelting rain.

"They're both dead, Jeannie."

"Oh, Ron!" She turned away, overwhelmed by this fresh tragedy.

"Jeannie . . ." Ron reached out to pull her to him. "They're together. I guess that's what they wanted most in this world."

"*Where were they going?*" The words were wrenched from Craig, who stood a few feet beyond them. Only now did Jeannie and Ron realize he had witnessed the bizzare accident that had claimed Dennis' and Madeline's lives. "Where were they going in the chaise in this storm?" He stared in sudden comprehension at the metal box beside the pair on the ground. "Oh, my God."

"We'd better go back to the house," Ron said gently. "I'll send the servants to bring them home."

"How will I tell Eleanor?" Craig's face was etched with grief. "This will destroy her."

"No," Jeannie refuted with sudden strength. "It won't destroy her, because she has you."

"We'll have to go to Miss Emmaline," Ron said tiredly as they turned away from the rain-drenched bodies to walk somberly back to the house. "She'll have to know about Arnold."

Craig stopped dead.

"What about Arnold?"

Haltingly Jeannie told him, seeing fresh anguish well in him. The volcano that he had talked about with such prescient fears had finally erupted.

"Poor Miss Emmaline," Craig said quietly. He turned to Ron. "Will you tell her?"

"Ron and I will go to her," Jeannie promised. She hesitated, her eyes fearful. "What will happen to Arnold?"

"They'll put him away," Ron said unhappily. "He's murdered twice."

Jeannie and Ron sat opposite Miss Emmaline in the Burkes' back parlor. Miss Emmaline cradled Patches in her arms. The magnolia collection lay on the small horsehair sofa beside her.

"Thank you for bringing me Arnold's kitten," she said in a voice that was barely audible. "And his magnolias. He's always been particularly fond of the magnolias." She paused and took a deep breath, straining to retain her composure. "They've been looking for Arnold for almost an hour. Where could he be?"

Before Ron or Jeannie could offer a conjecture, a servant came into the doorway and hovered there with desolation written across his face.

"What is it, Timothy?" Miss Emmaline asked with a fatalistic calm. "Have they found Mr. Arnold?"

"Yes, ma'am," he said in an agonized whisper. "He—he dead in de swamp. Drownded."

"He's not dead," Miss Emmaline rebuked. "He has gone to God. I must send for Charlotte." She sat sternly

270

erect, her eyes staring straight ahead. "I've lost both my boys. Arnold and Dennis. Dennis was always like my own, you know. I adored him."

The ugliness that hung over The Magnolias was gone, leaving a grief that would heal. There would be an heir to The Magnolias, Jeannie promised herself. When their mourning period was over, she and Ron would marry. Ron, much more than Dennis, was truly Craig Mitchell's son, she thought with pride. Their children would be Craig and Eleanor Mitchell's grandchildren.

Life was not over. For those who remained at The Magnolias, it was just beginning.

FAWCETT CREST
BESTSELLERS